WE ARE OMEGA

JUSTIN WOOLLEY

We Are Omega

Print format ISBN: 9780646598185

Cover design by Tania Walker.

www.taniawalker.com

Edited by Vanessa Lanaway.

For Teddy - About time you got a book too.

1 / MOLLY

I PUSH my face into the pillow, trying to muffle the sound of my sobs. I don't want to cry, but it's hard when it feels like someone's ramming a hot fork through my temple. In an angry outburst I kick at the sheet draped over me, sending it sliding off the bed. I don't know whether it's because I can't stand the feeling of it sticking to my sweaty skin or that when I've had these headaches, night after night, sometimes for weeks, I get so neffing sick of them my frustration boils over and I've got to let it out somehow.

I wrap the foam of the pillow up over my ears and groan. If I'm too loud Uncle Art will hear. He'll come in and sit on the edge of my bed. He'll ask me if I want any painkillers. He'll stroke my back and tell me everything will be okay. I don't want that. I'd prefer if he just left me alone.

Even buried in the pillow I hear the rumble of a plane flying over our house. It'll be one of those big grey military planes coming in to land inside the N.E.Z. carrying whoever from the government has secret dealings with the Crabs. The military, scientists, politicians – everyone wants something from the aliens. Humans have become the scrawny little orphans begging please-sir-can-I-have-some-more, as if we've forgotten what they brought with them.

Lifting my head, I shove the alarm clock so I can see the display. The harsh red glow of the numbers reads 2:36 am – still hours until I need to be up for school. I roll onto my back, the pain in my skull stabbing in time with my pulse. My room is full of that middle-of-the-night kind of dark, the kind where everything looks blue. The world is quiet and still, until the silence is broken by the telephone.

Uncle Art will answer it. It'll be for him anyway. They'll be calling him into the Alpha Compound to cover a shift or something. Just his lucky night I guess.

Sure enough, the sound is cut off mid-ring and the muffled bass of Uncle Art's voice floats through the wall. I can't make out what he's saying, but the conversation is short, and a second later there's a knock on my door. Three gentle taps. The door creaks open, just enough to spread hallway light across my face, and Uncle Art pokes his head in.

"Molly," he whispers. "Are you awake?"

"Mmmm," I mumble, as if Uncle Art has woken me and I haven't been lying awake crying with pain for the last hour.

"Sorry, I've got to go in."

"Ok," I say, rolling over, turning my back to him. "Have fun protecting the Crabs."

Uncle Art hovers at the door like maybe he wants to say something else. There's nothing he can say though, nothing he's ever been able to say, and after a moment the door clicks shut.

I lie like that for a while, staring at the wall, running my eyes along the crack that appeared in the plaster during a heatwave we had two summers ago. It stretches from the roof to the floor, zigzagging through the faded pink paint like a tear in the world. I asked Uncle Art to fix it but he said it didn't matter, that it was just cosmetic damage. I suppose that shouldn't surprise me. Uncle Art doesn't try to fix things that are broken.

$$\Omega$$

I step off the bus onto the cracked, uneven sidewalk. The sound of another military plane rolls overhead. I don't look up. My headache has eased slightly, but there's no way I can deal with the bright morning sky. I look down the road. It stretches off into the ass-end-of-the-Earth that is Little Basin, Nevada. Once just a tiny blip on Highway 50 with a faded sign reading "*Gateway to Little Basin National Park*", Little Basin has grown into an actual town now and not because of the national park – this place is famous for something else.

You know when people talk about being in the middle of nowhere? They only say that about other places because they've never been to Little Basin. Houses, shops, schools, supermarkets – a whole town dropped into the desert and surrounded by nothing but miles of dry scrub, sandy earth, and rattlesnakes. I've lived here for more than four years now and I'm still not used to it. It's so empty. Plus, the heat. Man. *The heat*. The way the highway shimmers in the distance and dust just hangs in the air because there's not a breath of wind. It's stupid hot.

Urgh. I really don't want to be here today, and not just because it's hot and my head feels like it was used to make a gravel milkshake. Today is test day.

"Morning, Mol."

Jesse Hill, my best friend – more or less my only friend – is standing on the path, smiling his goofy smile. Jesse has a warmth about him, a genuineness that can disarm even the coldest person. He managed to become *my* friend, after all. We're a neffing strange pair, though. Me with my ginger hair dyed black, wearing my black Doom Sisters t-shirt and black jeans with the pockets torn off, and him with his pastel-colored polo shirts and beaming smile. Everyone thinks Jesse's my boyfriend. He's definitely not.

"Did you remember it's test day?" Jesse asks.

"Yeah, of course."

"And are you going to tie yourself to a tree again?"

"No," I say, as we walk toward the front of the school. "I'm just going to show up and not try."

The Test. Pretty much every teenager on the planet knows what those words mean. One day a year we have to sit through hours of jank testing so we can be graded for possible admission to the Institute for the Betterment of Humanity. Neffing stupid name. Supposedly the world's best and brightest go there to learn about advanced science and technology from the Crusties.

"You're smart, Molly," Jesse says. "You might get in if you try."

"Even if I wanted to go and live with the Crabs, which I don't, what do you think the chances are? They test everyone in the world, and how many people get in? A hundred? Two hundred maybe?"

"Well, I'm going to try. Imagine having aliens as teachers. Don't you think that would be awesome?"

I see Mrs Bowls, our overdressed monster of a principal. She's standing at the front door with her wiry hair pinned back and too much make-up plastered on a face it can't help.

"I think we already do."

Jesse chuckles. "Hey, did you hear last night's announcement about integration?"

I stop. "No. What do you mean, 'integration'?"

"The President and this guy from the Department of Extraterrestrial Affairs made an announcement on TV last night. They're going to let the Crusties live outside the N.E.Z., side-by-side with humans."

"That's a neffing stupid idea."

"Why?"

"Well," I say, trying to think of a reason other than me hating the idea, "it's too dangerous isn't it? What if there's another plague?"

"I'm sure people have thought of that. They're going to have to let them out eventually. They're not going anywhere."

"If they're not going anywhere then I will be."

"Your uncle works for the SECPOL, Molly. He can't just get a job somewhere else."

"He's a glorified security guard," I say. "Of course he can get a job somewhere else. Anyway, what makes you think I mean with him? I'll go on my own. You'll see. I'm going to get as far away from the Crabs as I possibly can."

I walk up the concrete steps and into the front of the school. Jesse hurries to catch up.

"Good morning Molly," Mrs Bowls says as I pass. "Just so you're aware I'm expecting no hijinks today. I'm not sure you've got the brains for the Institute, but I expect you to behave and do the testing regardless, just as is mandated for every student."

I stop and look at Mrs Bowls. A hundred different comments fight their way along my tongue, any one of which would probably get me suspended again. Nasty old cow. She does it on purpose. Tries to bait me. Luckily, Jesse takes my arm and leads me through the doors before I say anything stupid.

"They've been here six years Molly," Jesse says. "I know you don't want to admit it, but the Crusties are doing good for people."

I shoot Jesse a cold look. He should know better than to start this argument with me. "Everyone always talks about the advances the Crusties are making for humanity. Why don't they do something useful and figure out how we can permanently change our hair color? That way people wouldn't have to live with ginger hair their whole neffing lives."

"I'm being serious, Mol. My Nan is getting better because of them. Imagine if no one died from cancer anymore."

"I don't care, Jesse."

Jesse's not smiling anymore. "I'd never say something like that to you."

Oh jank. I'm not good at this.

"You know, most people are excited, happy about what's happening in the world," Jesse continues. "You don't have to be so angry all the time."

"People are stupid."

"You think I'm stupid?"

"About the Crabs? Yes, I do."

We walk in silence until we reach my locker. Our all-too-familiar disagreement hangs in the air. I stop, but Jesse keeps walking. I've annoyed him. Again.

"Jesse," I call, but he doesn't turn around.

THE CARGO RAMP lowers with a mechanical drone and comes to a stop against the tarmac with a controlled thud. Usually I find the sound of machines soothing, but I didn't realize how loud it would be in the back of a military plane – even with the earplugs they gave me. I pluck the small pieces of yellow foam free from my ears and prepare to disembark.

"Watch your step down the ramp," Sergeant Elliot says.

Sergeant Elliot is an officer with the Nevada Exclusion Zone Security Police, apparently just referred to as the SECPOL. They're a force set up by the United Nations to protect the N.E.Z. and the Xenocrustaceans inside. Although her short hair and stiff blue-black uniform makes her look stern, Sergeant Elliot is actually quite friendly. She sat opposite me the whole way from Dallas-Fort Worth, her hands resting casually on an MP5 submachine gun – at least, that's what she told me it was. She was very patient in answering my questions about how long the flight would be, what sort of weapon she was carrying, what being in the SECPOL was like, and what would happen at the compound. I tend to ask a lot of questions when I'm nervous.

"Where do I need to go?" I ask. "Is someone going to meet me?"

"Someone from the Institute will meet you, Wells," Sergeant Elliot says. "Don't worry, and good luck."

I push my glasses up the bridge of my nose, another thing I do when I'm nervous. I'm trying to control my nervous mannerisms. My psychologist says that continuing to perform actions associated with anxiety reinforces the problem. But between trying to recognize anxious thoughts and remembering to control my breathing and ignore every physical twinge and tickle and lump and bump that makes me think I've got cancer or some other deadly disease, it's easy to forget the little things.

The plane's engines are still loud, even as they wind down. The sound reverberates off the buildings, filling the whole area with a resounding buzz. Beside the runway are several aircraft hangers, a control tower and three or four smaller buildings. Behind the hangers, perhaps half a kilometer away, I can see the shining dome of the Xenocrustacean ship and the top of a protective wall built around it.

The sight catches me off guard, and I find myself standing at the bottom of the ramp, staring. That's it. That's the vessel another race used to travel through the stars, technology so advanced that it's capable of faster-than-light interstellar travel, something human physicists had previously thought impossible.

A black jeep approaches, pulling to a stop near the aircraft. The back door opens and a girl climbs out. She's dressed in a grey jumpsuit with a white band around the collar and thick white stripes down the sides. There's a shoulder patch sewn on the top of her right arm – a stylized picture of a human and a Xenocrustacean, each holding one side of a book, the words *Institute for the Betterment of Humanity* arranged in a ring around it. YORKE is embroidered above her left chest pocket – I assume that's her surname. I recognize the uniform. She's a student at the Institute.

"Hi," she says. She's taller than me, and very attractive. Her shoulder-length black hair is pinned back on either side of her head. Her eyes are dark, almost black, and her cheeks rise high on her face as her lips part in a wide smile. I push my glasses up my nose.

"You must be Wells." The girl extends her hand. "I'm Charlotte." She has an English accent, which somehow makes her seem all the more attractive. I wipe my sweaty palm down the side of my thigh before reaching out and taking her hand. Her skin is soft, and I hope I'm not blushing.

"Um, pleased to meet you," I say. "I'm Wells – but you already knew that, you just said so. Sorry."

I let go of her hand, realizing I've been holding it the whole time. I've made a terrible first impression as usual.

But Charlotte smiles again. "I know loads of things about you, Wells."

"Um," I say. "That's...that's good."

"I'm your Buddy," Charlotte says. "Orientation Partner is the official name, but we prefer to call ourselves Buddies because it sounds a little friendlier. I'll be showing you around. Come on," she turns back to the jeep, "we'd better get going."

I try not to look down as Charlotte leads the way. The Institute jumpsuits are significantly tighter than they seemed in the pictures.

We climb into the back of the jeep and another soldier in the dark blue SECPOL uniform comes around to close the door. He's carrying a rifle slung over his shoulder, but it doesn't look anything like Sergeant Elliot's MP5. In fact, it doesn't look like any rifle I've ever seen. Not that I've seen many rifles in real life, but I've played a lot of video games. I know what a gun is supposed to look like.

This rifle is short and stocky, a cold grey instrument. Unlike most guns, it doesn't have a circular barrel – instead, the barrel is a squat square tube protruding out from the body of the weapon. There are slots in the side that pulse with a bright blue, almost white light.

"Is that alien tech?" I ask.

"That's classified," the SECPOL says without changing his expression. He closes the door and makes his way to the front. Apparently not all SECPOL are as friendly as Sergeant Elliot. I look at Charlotte, embarrassed.

"It's alright," Charlotte says. "He's always like that."

The SECPOL driver turns the jeep and drives us back down the runway.

"You must be tired," Charlotte says. "It's a long trip from Australia."

"Twenty-three hours," I say. "I'm pretty exhausted."

"Don't worry, you've just got orientation today and tomorrow. We'll start you off easy."

As the jeep rounds the buildings at the end of the runway the ship comes into view, the sunlight glinting off its metallic silver-blue surface. It's enormous, towering over the high walls and buildings that have been erected around its perimeter. It looks too large to have ever been able to fly. The ship is oval shaped, like a giant metallic almond, with a criss-crossing of organic-looking lattice structure around the middle. The front of the ship is still buried underground from its impact with Earth.

"It sure is something, isn't it?"

I turn to find Charlotte leaning over me, looking out the window. Our faces are close, and she smells sweet, like clean skin and coconut shampoo. I swallow nervously.

"Yeah," I say, turning to look out the window again. "It's amazing."

"Blows me away every time."

"So, what are they like?" I ask. "The aliens?"

"We try not to call them that," Charlotte says, sitting back.

WE ARE OMEGA / 11

"Oh, sorry. I didn't know."

"That's okay, it's not untrue. We just prefer to call them Xenocrustaceans, Xenos for short if you like. Just don't get caught calling them any of those horrible insults like Crabs or Crusties."

"Okay."

"But to answer your question, they're amazing. Very different to humans, though, and not just in their physical appearance. They've evolved on another planet, in a completely different environment, so of course their behavior and culture are very different to ours."

We continue travelling toward the ship. Beside it, within the wall that seems to enclose the central part of the compound, I can see the top of a large cylindrical building made up mostly of silvered windows. Lettering emblazoned around the top says *Institute for the Betterment of Humanity*. We pass through a security checkpoint where two SECPOL officers check the driver's ID and glance over Charlotte and I before allowing us to drive forward to the wall. A pair of remotely operated steel doors begin to retract in front of us, orange lights flash, and there's the whoop of a warning alarm. I have the sense of being before the gates of a castle, like something in *Swords of the Dungeonmaster*, an online game I used to play all the time.

We drive through the gates and continue on toward the Institute. When we reach the building, the road slopes down to travel beneath it, as if we're entering an underground car park. As we descend, yellow lights in the tunnel flick past, casting light, then dark, over the inside of the jeep. I feel the familiar build of anxiety in my chest and wonder, not for the first time, if I really want to be here. But like my father said, being selected for the Institute isn't an offer you can turn down. And besides, I want to make my parents proud. I could really use a +1 to courage, as if this was *Swords of the Dungeonmaster*. Charlotte gives me a reassuring smile, and I take control of my breathing. Long in. Hold. Long out.

Hopefully I'll get a chance to call my parents soon. Our farewell at the airport was brief, but my mother said she was proud of me and it's been a long time since either of them have said that. Dad just told me to keep my head down, but that's not unusual – he never says much. He shook my hand though, which is the equivalent of a hug coming from him.

I don't know how far underground we are, but eventually the ramp ends at a sealed blast door and we turn left into an open space with pillars supporting the roof above. There are other jeeps parked in marked spaces. We continue past them and pull to a stop in front of a large opaque glass wall that stretches from floor to ceiling. Two SECPOL holding the same strange rifles stand either side of a revolving door, watching our approach. I see them shift, moving their weapons in front of their bodies, fingers near the triggers.

"We're here," Charlotte says.

The SECPOL officer who growled at me earlier comes around and opens the door. I try not to look at him as I climb out, or at the two SECPOL by the door. It all seems very tense, but they relax when they see Charlotte. She enters the revolving door first. I push my glasses up my nose and follow.

The room beyond the door is circular, and feels like the enormous lobby of an expensive hotel. The ceiling must be two stories above us. Large columns encircle the room just inside the bright white walls. The floor is mostly white, with a large black emblem inlaid in the tiles, the same human and Xeno logo that Charlotte wears on her arm.

There's another security checkpoint ahead of us, manned by more SECPOL, glass gates, X-ray machines and body scanners. Beyond that are several doors, and a series of glass elevators that rise up and down like clear bubbles against the wall. People move in all directions, students of the Institute in their grey and white jumpsuits, SECPOL in their intimidating blue uniforms, and adults wearing military uniforms or business attire.

Charlotte, noticing I've stopped, turns back to me and smiles. "Congratulations on your selection, by the way. Welcome to the Institute."

INSTEAD OF FIRST PERIOD CLASSES, all of eleventh grade file into the stuffy school gym. Row after row of desks are spaced out over the basketball court like tiny islands of boredom, each one set up with a tablet and headphones.

Mrs Bowls stands in the doorway, watching me. I slip the headphones over my ears and stare back. She thinks I'm going to start trouble like I usually do. Last year I tied myself to a tree out the front of the school, the year before that I set off the fire alarm, and the year before that – well, let's just say it took me two weeks to catch the snake. Today though, I'm not going to do anything. I'm just going to sit here. And that's the best part, because Mrs Bowls is going to be so neffing edgy, doing nothing is basically a prank on its own.

In front of me the tablet screen reads:

PLEASE ENTER YOUR STUDENT ID.

I tap in the numbers.

PLEASE VALIDATE YOUR IDENTITY BY PLACING YOUR THUMB ON THE SCREEN.

I press my thumb against it.

IDENTITY VALID.

"Good morning, Molly McManus," a voice says through my headphones. "Today you will undertake testing for admission to the Institute for the Betterment of Humanity. This will include a series of tests designed to measure your cognitive ability in a range of areas. The total time of this test will be one hundred and thirteen minutes. Today you will be tested in the following areas: visual thinking, quantitative reasoning and logic, recognition and processing speed..."

Same old shit. I feel a dull ache forming behind my eyes. It's not another migraine, but it's enough to be distracting. I tune out, looking around the room. Most students are staring at their screens, listening, or already tapping away. It's moments like these I feel most like an outsider. It's not that I can't do the testing – I already know I could do pretty well – it's that I don't want to. That's what makes me feel alone. All the other students want to get into the Institute, even those who usually couldn't care less about school. It's weird.

People seem to have forgotten the damage the Crabs did. Earth's population is twenty percent smaller than before they arrived. That's how many people died in the plague. Twenty percent. Jank. That's one out of every five people you've ever met, dead. One in five. People hardly even talk about it anymore, and when they do they call it a natural disaster, an unavoidable tragedy, a regrettable side effect. My parents weren't a side effect. They'd still be alive if the neffing Crabs pointed their crappy ship somewhere else. I'm not going to forgive them just because they give humanity a few new toys. Jesse wants to know why I'm angry all the time. I want to know why no one else is.

"The first component of testing is visual thinking," the voice says in my ears. "We will begin now."

A spinning cube appears on the screen, something like a Rubik's cube with green, yellow and blue colored blocks.

"Select the object that would remain after the green and blue pieces were removed."

Four different yellow shapes appear along the bottom. I see the answer straight away. It's easy. But I don't want any part of the Crusties' test, so I pick the wrong answer.

I pick wrong answers for the next one hundred and thirteen minutes.

Ω

After we're done in the gym we get an extended lunch break. I guess that's one positive of test day. I grab an apple and yoghurt from the cafeteria counter and walk to the tables where Jesse and I normally sit. I spot him sitting with Trinity Lee, Chuck Jordan and Zadie King. I like Trin – she goes a little overboard with the kawaii thing but at least she's more into rock music than *Hello Kitty*. Chuck I can handle in small doses, but Zadie, she's on my avoid-as-much-as-neffing-possible list. But that's Jesse for you – friendly with everyone.

"You're so funny Chuck," Zadie is saying as I walk over. She's laughing and smiling, and putting her hand so deliberately on Chuck's arm that you'd have to be blind not to see the giant FLIRT sign flashing in neon lights above her perfect head.

Trin is staring down at her tablet. She's obsessed with that thing – takes it everywhere she goes. She's always playing some game on it, *Swords and Dungeons* or something. She tried to explain it to me once, something about role-playing and levelling up and whatever. I didn't get it.

Jesse waves at me as I approach. Chuck lifts his head in something like a greeting. Trin lifts her hand and says, "Hey Molly," without looking up from her tablet. Zadie, of course, ignores me.

"You *are* joking though right?" Zadie continues. "You're not actually going to do it, are you?"

"Not going to do what?" I ask.

Zadie looks at me. "Chuck's going to do the climb," she says dismissively. My face must show my confusion, because she quickly adds, "tonight," as if that should explain it.

I look to Jesse for a less cryptic explanation.

"There's a party tonight," he says, "out on Dry Springs Road. A bunch of people are going to climb the fence."

"The N.E.Z. fence?"

"Yeah," Chuck says. "It's going to be a rush. Can you imagine getting into the N.E.Z. and then climbing back out without getting busted?"

"I still think it's a jank idea," Trin says. Despite constantly staring at her tablet, she always seems to be following the conversation. "A party at the fence is fine, but climbing into the Exclusion Zone? How many laws does that break?"

"Yeah," Jesse says. "It's stupid. No one's actually going to do it. They'll all chicken out."

"I'll do it," I say.

Jesse, Trinity, Chuck and Zadie look at me without saying anything. I don't know why, but suddenly I'm determined to climb over the N.E.Z. fence. I guess it's my chance to show everyone that I'm not afraid of the Crabs. I don't care about their stupid Exclusion Zone.

Jesse opens his mouth to say something but I cut him off. "I'm doing it. I'm climbing the neffing fence."

I'M SITTING on the edge of a white-sheeted examination table in nothing but my underwear. When I was told about Institute orientation, nobody mentioned this.

"Alright," Dr Plotnikova says, her Russian accent thick enough that it seems to hit you in the face. She taps on her tablet. "Just need to take blood sample and give nanomites and we are done."

I'll be glad to be finished with all this medical testing. I'm not fond of doctors – mostly because every time I go to see one my brain tells me I've got cancer, or Ebola, or some other terrible disease. So far today I've had my height and weight recorded, my blood pressure taken, my reflexes tested, my brain and heart monitored, my body fat measured and my eyesight and hearing assessed, all in my underwear. If I'd known I'd be spending so much time undressed, I wouldn't have worn Sesame Street boxer shorts.

"Do I really need a blood test?" I ask. "I don't particularly like needles."

"Standard procedure, Wells. Two needles. One for nanomites and one for blood screen."

"And what are you screening my blood for?"

"Any conditions you have that might harm the Xenos."

It makes sense they'd be careful about that. We've already seen the devastating effect an alien virus can have on the human population. It's safe to assume exposure to a human virus could be just as deadly for the Xenos. I certainly wouldn't want to be responsible for bringing a virus into the Alpha Compound and wiping out the entire Xenocrustacean population. I don't imagine that would be considered a very good first day.

My family were lucky during the plague, which I'm especially thankful for because my parents have had enough tragedy in their lives already. Initially, Australia's isolation proved beneficial. Once the disease had begun spreading so rampantly through the United States and Europe – and had been recognized for what it was, an alien virus – Australia, like many countries, closed its borders. We remained insulated for a time, but with the plague being able to survive for so long in its airborne state it reached us eventually, just as it reached every corner of the planet.

I read an article in *New Scientist* recently claiming that everyone in the world has been infected with the virus now, and that's why it seems to have completely disappeared. Most people had flu-like symptoms: headaches for a few days and a runny nose. That came to be called EV-A, Extraterrestrial Virus Stage A. That's what my parents had – nothing a little bed rest wouldn't fix. For some reason an unlucky fifth of the population had the virus progress to EV-B, a much nastier stage of infection. At first, people with EV-B had the same flu-like symptoms, but then they started bleeding from the nose, gums, ears and eyes, followed by seizures and then, in most cases, death. Only a small fraction of those showing symptoms of EV-B managed to survive – less than one per cent – and all of those were young people. I was one of those few.

"Ow," I say, reacting to the sting of a needle in my arm. "I wasn't ready."

Dr Plotnikova clicks the test tube into the needle and it begins filling with my dark red blood.

"I was, though," Dr Plotnikova says. "You were daydreaming." She takes the needle out and tapes a piece of cotton wool over the puncture in my arm. "Now, do not move."

Dr Plotnikova reaches for a metallic gun that looks like the kind of thing a farmer would use to inject a cow. She's going to shoot nano-sized robots into me – tiny medical robots that float around in your blood, keeping track of your health and helping your body heal. I stand up.

"Um, I don't think I want that."

Dr Plotnikova looks at me and smiles. "It is for your own good, Wells, and compulsory if you wish to attend the Institute."

I remain standing. Maybe I can just tell them I don't want to attend the Institute, that this has all been some enormous mistake, but then what? I'd just end up back where I started – same old failure. I sit back on the bed.

"Good," Dr Plotnikova says. "Now be still."

She presses the end of the metallic gun against the back of my neck. It's cold. After a click and a sharp jab of pain there's a pressure under my skin as the nanomites rush into me, spreading out from my neck like ice water in my veins, and then, after a moment, nothing.

"Your uniform is in the cupboard behind you," Dr Plotnikova says, putting the gun down and snapping the white rubber gloves off her hands. "You can get dressed. I'll inform Mr Thorn that you're ready for your tour."

"Alright," I say, even though I have no idea who Mr Thorn is.

"Nice to meet you, Wells," Dr Plotnikova says as she leaves the room. "Don't be so nervous, you're going to make a valuable contribution."

"Thanks."

She smiles and closes the door behind her. I climb down and open the cupboard. Inside, just as she'd said, are a folded grey jumpsuit, a grey undershirt and a pair of black boots. I take out the jumpsuit and hold it up by the shoulders. Above the chest pocket I see my surname, sewn on just as Charlotte's had been: MARSDEN.

I slip the undershirt on first and then step into the jumpsuit, pulling it over my shoulders and zipping up the front. I pull the black boots on and lace them up. Everything fits perfectly. I've never really fit in anywhere so I hope this place fits me the way the clothes do.

Ω

"Uneasy lies the head that wears the crown," Mr Thorn says as I follow him down the corridor, away from the infirmary.

"Pardon me, Mr Thorn?"

He stops so suddenly I almost crash into him. He turns to face me, fixing me with his eyes, which are so dark it's difficult to discern where his pupils end and his irises begin.

"Shakespeare, Mr Marsden. *Henry the Fourth*," he says. "You seem nervous wearing that uniform. Does it make you nervous?"

I push my glasses up my nose. "Well, no," I say. "I mean, yes, but I'm trying not to be."

Mr Thorn – that's how he introduced himself, with no first name – runs the Institute for the Betterment of Humanity. I suppose that makes him the Principal or the Headmaster, although he didn't call himself that. He said his title was Director of Operations.

Mr Thorn is a long man. I know that's a strange way to describe someone, but he is strange. He's tall, dark and thin, with limbs that appear longer and thinner than a person's should. The whole combination lends him the appearance of a spider moving with slow purpose along the hallway, and gives a looming sense that at any moment he may scuttle off at high speed to strike at prey.

"You should be nervous," he says.

"I should?"

"Indeed you should." He turns and begins walking again, gesturing broadly to indicate the building around him. "You and the other Institute students are going to lead humanity into a bright new era. The world will be a new place, a better place, one in which we are truly citizens of the cosmos. Thanks to the knowledge of the Xenocrustaceans, our species is primed to take a giant leap forward, and it is the students of the Institute who have been selected as the conduits for this knowledge. That uniform signifies a great responsibility to this planet."

"Why teenagers?" I ask. "I mean, with all the experts in the world, why is it teenagers the Xenocrustaceans want to teach?"

Mr Thorn smiles. "Malleability, Mr Marsden," he says, stretching the words out. "You are at an age where you are not yet fixed with the dogged mindset of the old. The Xenocrustaceans place great emphasis on the ethical use of the gifts they are bestowing on humanity, and they wish to teach the young, not only to enhance your knowledge, but your ethical mindset, too. You will become an adult ready to make great change in the world, but also you will possess the desire for that change to be positive. Now come, on with our tour."

We walk the grey, undecorated halls of the Institute. Mr Thorn shows me the fitness center, complete with gymnasium and swimming pool, the chemistry laboratories – vast white rooms of spectrometers, centrifuges and long benches covered in glassware – hundred-seat lecture theatres and physics laboratories with sealed doors and radiation warnings. All the rooms are filled with students in grey jumpsuits, hurrying around or sitting at desks reading, writing or tapping on keyboards. It's an incredible place.

"But this," Mr Thorn says when we reach a door marked COMPUTER SCIENCE LABORATORY, "is no doubt what you will be most excited to see. You should already be coded for entry."

Mr Thorn indicates the retinal scan security lock. I look into it and a flash of green momentarily fills my vision. With a buzz and a click, the door opens.

Inside are a number of hefty computer workstations. Each has all the familiar components of a computer – monitor, keyboard, touchslate, VR headset, mouse – but there are other odd devices scattered around too, input devices I don't recognize. One student even has electrodes running from his skull to the computer.

"Each student at the Institute has an area of expertise, Mr Marsden," Mr Thorn says. "Along with generalized studies, you will undertake a project of significance in your area. Given your," he pauses, "background, you will be working in the area of interfacing Xenocrustacean and human computer systems."

His heavy pause doesn't escape my notice. I knew the Institute would be aware of my past – they were the ones who negotiated my pardon, after all – I was just hoping that coming here would allow me to leave it behind.

"The computer systems here at the Institute are among the most advanced in the world," Mr Thorn continues, "security included. You will be given complete access to the computers, just like any other student, but you should know that the system is monitored. Unauthorized activities will result in consequences."

"I can assure you all that is behind me."

"Good." Mr Thorn looks over to see another student

approaching, a tall Indian boy with short cropped hair. "Ah, Sunny, perfect timing."

"Good morning, Mr Thorn," Sunny says. He looks at me. "You must be Wells."

I nod, taking the boy's hand as he offers it. "Hello."

"I'm Sunny," he says. "I'm not sure what Mr Thorn has told you yet, but I'm the computer science research lead. You'll be working with me and my project team. There's a lot of exciting work happening, and from what I've heard, your skills will be very helpful. We're basically exploiting SSH protocols and trying to reprogram them to allow remote access to Xeno systems."

"Great," I say.

"Thank you, Sunny," Mr Thorn says. "I'll let you two talk technical details later. For now, if you'll follow me, Wells, I'll show you where your accommodations are located."

I follow Mr Thorn through a maze of corridors. We leave the laboratories and classrooms behind and step onto an elevated glass walkway. Below is a flourishing indoor garden with grass, tables and chairs, flower beds and trees, all underground. Above us, covering the whole thing, is a dome with a simulated blue sky and floating clouds. I try not to look down – heights are another thing I don't handle very well, and though the glass walkway is completely enclosed, I can still see straight through the floor. The grass must be at least ten meters below us.

"We're now heading into the accommodation and recreation areas of the Institute," Mr Thorn says. "As you can see, given the necessity that students be isolated from the outside world, we have spared no expense in maintaining a pleasant environment."

Once it passes through the other side of the dome, the glass walkway once again becomes a corridor that splits off in several directions. Signs point to Accommodation Wings A, B and C. Mr Thorn leads me down the corridor into Accommodation Wing B.

Dormitory-style doors line the walls on either side. There are two names next to each door, one on either side.

"This is your accommodation wing," Mr Thorn says. "Your room should be just up here. B Wing, Room 32. Here we are."

We stop outside a door that looks identical to all the others, except it has the number 32 on it. On one side of the door the name plaque reads MARSDEN, WELLS, and on the other: DUFORT, REMY.

"Remy Dufort," I read out loud.

"Yes," Mr Thorn says. "He'll be your roommate. French. Quite a young expert in applied mathematics. He's indisposed at the moment, deeply involved in some research, but I expect you'll meet him soon."

Beside the door is a retinal scanner. Mr Thorn points to it. "Your room has secure bio-coded entry," he says, "same as the labs. Go ahead and take a quick look inside."

I use the scanner and that same flash of green fills my vision, then the door buzzes. I push it open and stand in the entrance to this strange room, trying to reconcile the fact that this will be my new home. I know this feeling of being displaced. This is exactly how I felt when I was locked in juvenile detention for the first time.

I make my way into the room. It's larger than I thought it would be. A door off to my right is ajar, and I can see it's the bathroom. Ahead of me the room opens out wider. The wall opposite is one big floor-to-ceiling window. It's tinted, but looks out on the underground garden. The rest of the room is designed symmetrically, with a bed against each of the side walls. Beside each bed is a desk with a large curving monitor fixed to the wall, and the sliding door of a closet. One of the desks has mathematics books spread over the surface and two photographs stuck with tape to the wall, one of two women, a mother and daughter I'd guess, and another the view of a beach at sunset. This must be Remy's side

of the room. Inside the closet on my side of are several grey jumpsuits, each with my name on the chest, and the single black suit-
case I brought with me.

Something beeps behind me, and Mr Thorn pulls out his
phone. "Ah, I've just received word that your blood has come
back clear, which means we're able to conclude the tour with
something I'm sure you're keen to do: meet the Xenocrustaceans.
Come along."

If I wasn't nervous before, I certainly am now. I'm actually
going to see a Xenocrustacean, a real-life alien. I hurry after Mr
Thorn, closing the door behind me. He leads me back through
the accommodation building, across the elevated walkway and
into the glass elevators, then presses the button for level S. Here,
away from the lobby and mezzanine levels, the view through the
glass of the elevator is just orange lights, pipes and wiring looms
flashing by. The elevator stops at level S.

"What does the 'S' mean?" I ask.

"Ship," Mr Thorn says as the doors open onto a long corridor
that ends in a sealed double door.

"We need to pass through an airlock and get sprayed down.
Then we'll be inside the Xenocrustacean vessel." Mr Thorn looks
at me, fixing me again with those dark eyes. "But before we go
any further, you need to make a commitment. Being a student of
the Institute is a privilege, but not an easy one. You will be giving
up your life to serve humanity. You understand that, don't you?"

I nod.

"Good. Are you willing to fully commit to this program in
accordance with the regulations of the Institute? There's no
turning back after this point. Only a select few have passed
through these doors."

I push my glasses up my nose.

"Mr Marsden?"

I nod. "Yes."

Mr Thorn watches me for a moment longer, then places his hand on my shoulder. "Excellent. Let's go through."

Thorn scans his retinas at the double doors, and we enter the airlock. Another set of doors ahead of us remain tightly sealed as the doors behind us close, shutting us into the tight space. I feel a rise in my chest, like water filling my lungs. I can't take a deep breath. I try, but my chest is constricted. I feel my heart pounding, my skin prickling with sweat. I can't breathe. I can't breathe.

No. I'm having a panic attack. I need to wait it out. I need to breathe into my belly like my therapist says. It's okay. It's alright to be afraid. I can still breathe. I can breathe. This will pass. I exhale long and slow.

Mr Thorn takes some white plastic shoe covers down off a shelf and hands me a pair.

"Slip these over your shoes," he says, "they'll save your feet getting wet."

If Mr Thorn has noticed my panic he isn't saying anything. As I pull the white covers over my boots, the lights above us drop to a gloomy red. There's the brief sound of a warning siren, then a white spray billows in to fill up the room. I cover my mouth and nose.

"It's alright." Mr Thorn speaks loudly over the sound of the spray. "It's quite harmless. Unless you're a viral or bacterial contaminant, of course."

In a few moments the doors in front of us open, and liquid filled with floating particles and strings of green flows into the airlock until it's ankle deep.

"It's just water," Mr Thorn says when he sees me lifting one of my feet. "It covers the floor of the ship and contains a number of nutrients, algae and bacteria that the Xenocrustaceans absorb through their shells. It's also in the walls, acting as a kind of filter for the air and even offering radiation protection. The symbiotic use of biology and technology is one of the main things we can learn from the Xenocrustaceans."

I look up and swallow the rock that's suddenly appeared in my throat. Ahead is another corridor, but this one is instantly recognizable as being from another world. The structure itself is built from the same metal as the exterior of the ship. The walls are curved with beams that jut out, as if we're walking down the inside of a long rib cage. The ship is a machine, no doubt about that, but there are streaks of green through the walls, clear pipes carrying a flowing green liquid, like veins, as if the ship were alive and pumping blood through its body. The ankle-deep water covers the floor, and where the walls meet the water, a green-blue moss grows upwards in organic paths.

Mr Thorn stops at a circular doorway and touches a panel beside the door. It lights up, and a symbol like a circle with several intersecting lines flashes green and then vanishes. A moment later the door opens, retracting like a spiral into the wall around it. And there, inside the room, sitting in the curve of an egg-shaped chair, is a Xenocrustacean.

As THE SUN drops below the hills, the semicircle of pick-up trucks and busted up old cars parked off the side of Dry Springs Road switch on their headlights, highlighting the high, razor-wire topped fence. A stereo is blasting out some awful auto-tuned crap about dance-floor love, and the thirty or so people here are sitting around drinking, smoking, talking about football or movies or who's hooking up with who.

I'm sitting on the tray of Jesse's dad's pick-up. Jesse's got his driver's permit, so he drove us out here. He's not supposed to drive with passengers, but everyone around here does it anyway. I hear the crack and pop of a can beside me. Trin has opened a beer.

"You want one?"

"No thanks," I say. "So, is anyone going to climb this fence or what?"

Jesse shrugs. "I told you no one would."

"Okay," I say, standing up in the tray, "one of us better do this then."

A few people look over, but most don't seem to notice.

They've forgotten the whole point of coming out here was to actually try and get over the fence.

"Sit down Molly," Zadie calls from the next truck over, where she's still trying to wrap herself around Chuck. "Everyone knows you're not going to do it."

Why is no one willing to stand up to the neffing Crabs? I jump down and walk to the fence. Standing in the beam of the headlights, I slip my fingers through the chain link and start to climb. Behind me the conversations go quiet. Someone turns the music down.

"Molly," Jesse calls. "What are you doing? Get down."

The stiff wire hurts as it digs into my fingers, but I continue to climb.

"Mol-ly, Mol-ly, Mol-ly."

A chant starts. It spurs me on. Not that I take their chanting as genuine encouragement – it's more of a reminder that I've got something to prove. I'm always a joke. The angry goth girl who hates the nice aliens. The girl who always freaks out and does something weird on test day. The girl who acts up in school and does dumb shit that they think is for their entertainment. Just like they think this is.

Eventually my hand reaches the solid bar at the top of the fence. Above me are looping curls of razor wire. It looks neffing sharp. I awkwardly pull myself up between two loops of wire.

"Alright Molly," Jesse calls out again. "You proved your point. Get down now please."

I look back. Everyone is staring. I start maneuvering my foot between the loops of razor wire, sliding it over the top of the fence. I move slowly, twisting my body so that I'm straddling the steel bar. As I turn I feel the wire catch the back of my shirt, cutting through it and dragging lightly across the surface of my skin. Dammit. I like this top. I balance on top of the fence and reach behind me to free the fabric from the barb.

"Molly!" Jesse yells. "Don't!"

There's no chanting anymore. Everyone is silent as they watch. I lift my other leg and strain to get it over the wire. I don't think I've attempted this much flexibility since I took up gymnastics when I first moved to Little Basin – plus I only lasted a few months in those leotards. The edge of one barb slices the inside of my calf right through my jeans. It stings. Crap. I can tell straight away that it's deep. I lift my leg higher, forcing it over the wire. My leg is cut pretty bad, blood soaks into my jeans, but I'm on the other side of the fence now, so I start climbing down. I drop down off the fence and land on the ground, taking my weight on my uninjured leg. Everyone starts cheering. Everyone except Jesse. He walks to the fence.

"Now what are you going to do?" he says. "Shit, Molly, you're in the N.E.Z. for jank sake and look at your leg, are you going to be able climb back over?"

I look at him. He looks as frightened as I should probably be. My leg throbs. He's right, I don't know if I can get back over. I might have gone too far this time.

"I'm going to call your uncle," Jesse says, pulling his phone from his pocket. "He can come and get you."

"No," I say. "Don't do that. He'll hit the roof."

"Well," Jesse says. "What else –"

"There's someone out there!"

I don't know who shouts, but I turn to look. It's getting dark out across the desert. A wide flat plain that meets the base of some distant hills. The Alpha Compound is just over those hills, but still far enough away that I didn't think anyone would be out here. Everyone says the N.E.Z. is much bigger than it needs to be, and this is only the outer fence. There's another, bigger fence further in. But sure enough, there's movement in the dark. Two figures are running toward us in the dying light. They're probably, I don't know, half a mile away.

On the other side of the fence engines turn over, rumble and fire. People are hurrying away, climbing into their friends' cars or up onto the trays of trucks, ready to get the jank out of here. Tires skid on the dirt and gravel as people flee. Everyone except Jesse.

The figures are still running toward us. They're both wearing grey jumpsuits with white stripes down the side. Students from the Institute. I've seen the uniform on TV. The front one, a dark-skinned boy, keeps looking back. The student chasing him looks like a girl with dark hair. I don't think they're running toward us, though. I think he's running away from her.

Without warning the boy flies into the air. He just launches upwards, tumbling head over feet like he's been hit with an enormous baseball bat. It looks like he'll continue his wild flight toward me, but he suddenly crashes to a stop in midair. Blue light that crackles like lightning spreads out in a circle, right from the spot he made impact, like he's hit some kind of force field or something. What the hell?

The boy falls about twenty feet, straight down. His arms and legs are flailing, and he holds them out in front of him as if trying to soften the blow. The weird thing is, he does seem to slow down right before he hits the ground, but he still hits neffing hard, and doesn't move.

The girl chasing him stops. She's still a distance away, but I know she's watching me. Without a word she turns and runs back in the other direction.

I look toward Jesse, who's still at the fence, clutching the wire and staring at me. "Come on Molly," he says, his voice shaky. "Try and climb over. We've got to get out of here."

"He could be hurt," I say, glancing back at the boy from the Institute.

"Just leave him. I'm calling your uncle."

I start walking to where the boy lies on the ground. He might need help. He could have broken bones. Maybe worse.

"Molly, don't."

"I'm just going to see if he's alright." I look back. "And Jesse, don't you *dare* call Uncle Art."

Jesse watches me for a long moment. "Just hurry."

I hobble over to the boy, favoring my left leg. Just before I reach him I come to a crashing stop and fall back on my butt. Crackles of blue light fade away in front of me.

"Jank."

I stand uneasily and approach the force field, holding my hand out. The ends of my fingers touch it first. It's cold, and feels solid. I push my palm against it and electric blue light flickers around my hand like one of those plasma ball things they have in the science room at school.

I kneel down. The boy is just on the other side.

"Hello?"

He doesn't move, but his chest is rising and falling slowly.

"Are you alright?"

'elp me.

I stand quickly, stumbling backwards, startled by the sudden loud voice. I don't really hear it, not with my ears – it's more like sounds rattling around inside my brain.

"What the hell?!" I blurt out.

"Molly, what's wrong?" Jesse calls. "You okay?"

Can you 'elp me? The voice in my head again. It has an accent. French. *Don't be frightened. We are touching minds. Can you 'ear me?*

Seriously, what the neffing hell? I move further back. "Quit it! Get out of my head!"

Don't fight against me. Please. Let me –

The voice stops as suddenly as it started. What the fuck? I mean, seriously. What. The. Fuck? It really sounded like someone, this boy on the ground, was trying to talk to me inside my head. Am I going crazy?

"Um, Molly?" Jesse says from behind me. "Something's coming."

I look up. Something is moving through the air toward us, a wide flat aircraft casting blue light over the ground. I hear a deep, steady *whomp whomp whomp* sound. It moves like a helicopter, hovering over the ground, but there are no blades or wings or anything. It's a fluxer. Uncle Art has talked about them. A human-made aircraft powered by Crustie technology.

The fluxer slows and drops close to the ground, hovering twenty or thirty feet away. The desert grass beneath it bends, and dust is pushed away in swirls.

"Remain still and place your hands on your head," a voice blasts from external speakers. "You are under arrest for trespassing within the Nevada Exclusion Zone. Any attempt to flee will be interpreted as an act of aggression."

Three legs fold out from the fluxer and it settles on the ground. A ramp lowers at the back and two SECPOL officers walk out holding the weirdest looking guns I've ever seen. The ends glow with a bright light. They point them at me and I put my hands in the air.

"Molly!"

I turn to Jesse. "Go!" I say.

"It was just some fun," Jesse calls to the SECPOL officers. "We were just goofing around."

The SECPOL don't react to him, they just keep coming toward me. One of them kneels beside the boy on the ground, checking his pulse. He nods to the other one, who still has his gun raised. He touches a button on his collar and says, "Delta-Four-Five-Niner-One. Incoming with one wounded and one trespasser in custody."

I'm in deep jank now. The SECPOL stands, takes something out of his pocket and presses a button on it. He and the SECPOL next to him move forward. They reach the force field but it doesn't stop them – it glows blue around them but they pass straight through it, coming toward me with their weapons raised.

"Leave her alone," Jesse says.

This time I turn and fix Jesse with my heaviest stare. "Neffing get out of here, Jesse. Go!"

He does, walking backward toward his dad's pickup without taking his eyes off me. I, on the other hand, have no choice but to go with the SECPOL.

Oh boy. Uncle Art is going to straight up murder me for this.

MY LEGS ARE TREMBLING, wobbling like jelly wrapped around bone. I'm probably the most nervous I've ever been in my life – and trust me, that's saying something. I try and steady myself, hoping to stave off another panic attack, but my body has turned into a churning, twitching, hot, sweating mess. Rationally, I know the Xenocrustacean before me isn't dangerous. Even the two other Xenos standing back against the far wall, guards or attendants of some sort, don't seem threatening. But still, if I didn't know any better it would be easy to assume the unfamiliar shapes of the Xenos were monsters stepped straight from a nightmare. My brain just keeps telling me these creatures look like predators.

Mr Thorn's hand on my shoulder steadies me. "It's alright Wells," he says. "No harm will come to you here."

I nod and take a deep breath. The room has an unfamiliar smell, a faint odor of salt water, bleach and something like wet moss. At first I think the smell is in the air, but I soon realize it's coming from the Xenos themselves.

"Are you feeling alright?" Mr Thorn asks.

"Sorry," I say, "sometimes I get these anxiety attacks."

He smiles. "It's understandable. You wouldn't believe the

reactions of some people on their first meeting with the Xenocrustaceans. I won't tell you what the President did." He winks at me – an odd gesture on his sharply cut and serious face.

I turn my attention back to the Xeno. Everyone in the world knows what the Xenos look like. Images of them began appearing in the press only weeks after the crash – they were released at the request of the Xenos themselves to avoid any speculation or shock. Still, seeing a picture of something and seeing the real thing are very different. It's like the difference, I imagine, between seeing photos of the Grand Canyon and standing on the precipice looking down. There is an alien life-form in front of me, and right now I feel as though I'm on the precipice of reality, staring at something my Earth-evolved brain is telling me shouldn't exist.

The seated Xenocrustacean rises from its chair. Its body is covered with overlapping plates of external carapace shell, dark brown spotted with flecks of white, over its head and shoulders. The resemblance to an Earth crustacean is obvious, but a Xenocrustacean is to a crab what humans are to bacteria.

It's the intricacies of movement that really distinguish this Xeno from the pictures I've seen. The way the segments of shell slide over each other as it bends and rises is like a complex dance. I see glimpses of a white membrane expanding and contracting beneath the shell, pulsing with blue blood, only to be covered up again as the segments slide back into place.

When it reaches full height, the Xeno is at least seven feet tall, maybe closer to eight. Its arms and legs, both covered in thick plates of shell, are long, the torso short and stubby by comparison. The Xeno's head is wide and flat, like the body of an Earth crab. Its eyes, two black marbles close together in the front, sit only slightly above its mouth, a set of jaws that open horizontally, rather than vertically. Two short antennae protrude from either side of its mouth, flicking around in short, sharp movements.

These antennae are some sort of chemoreceptors, similar to those used by insects on Earth; the Xenos use them to "smell" each other. I've read about this. Xenos use pheromones to communicate, similar to the way humans use and interpret body language.

I suppose it's accurate to say the Xeno is naked. It isn't wearing clothes, not that I can tell which parts would need to be covered anyway. I don't know what gender the Xeno is, or even how to tell. Its shell is covered with curling blue lines, a deliberate pattern that appears to be painted on, or carved like a tattoo maybe. The other two Xenocrustaceans standing against the back wall have similar etchings in red.

The Xeno moves toward me, extending its hand, three long fingers and a thumb stretching out toward me. Its solid black eyes make it impossible to discern where it's looking, but I know it's examining me. A series of clicks rise from its throat.

"Wells," Mr Thorn says, "this is Number-One."

I swallow and push my glasses up my nose before reaching out. The Xeno's fingers curl around my hand. The surface of its shell is solid, and although it has a gentle grip, I can tell it could crush my hand if it wanted to.

I look at the Xeno towering over me, wearing its own organic suit of armor and seemingly with the strength to snap me in half. It seems unlikely that this is a species that would run from anything, but that's what they've told humanity, that they're refugees from a distant war across the stars.

The Xeno lets go of my hand, and I resist the urge to examine my palm, wondering if there's some residue on my skin. Do I need to wash now?

"Number-One is the leader of the Xenocrustaceans," Mr Thorn says.

"You just call him Number-One?"

"Xenocrustaceans have names," Mr Thorn says, "but not in a way we could replicate with speech. She will introduce herself once your mind has calmed from the initial shock of your meeting."

I look from Mr Thorn to Number-One again. She – Mr Thorn referred to the Xeno as female – is still watching me.

Number-One turns her wide flat head to look at Mr Thorn. Mr Thorn's face goes blank for a moment, expressionless, his eyes distant as if someone's just switched him off. Then, as if reawakening, he smiles at me.

"Number-One says you're ready for your first melding."

"Melding?" I say. "What do you mean?"

"Number-One is going to communicate with you the way Xenocrustaceans communicate with each other. They have no spoken language, they have only the melding, a joining of minds."

"What? What do you mean, a joining of minds?"

"Every student regularly experiences melding. But the initial melding must proceed gently, as humans are not accustomed to direct mind-to-mind contact. Number-One insists on being the conduit for each initial melding."

"Is it going to hurt?" I ask. "What's going to happen? Can she read my mind?"

"Relax, Mr Marsden. The melding is not mind reading, it is just communication within your mind. All you need to do is be open to it. Try not to fight it. Ready?"

"No."

"Outside the ship you made a commitment to the Institute," Mr Thorn says, his voice flat – not cruel, but a threat all the same. "The melding is part of that commitment."

"And if I refuse?"

"Then you will be flown back to Australia and returned to juvenile detention."

"Alright," I say, trying to sound more confident than I am. "What do I need to do?"

"Nothing. Just be ready."

Just being ready would be easier if I knew what I'm meant –

The world rushes away. I don't know how else to describe it. The room in front of me stretches and moves as if my surroundings are a two-dimensional picture being sucked into a distant vacuum cleaner.

Number-One is standing in front of me, just the two of us amidst a dark world of swirling grey mist. Then from somewhere there's a flash of light and I'm submerged in water. I panic. I try to swim to the surface but I can't move. I have to breathe. My lungs are screaming for air. I can't help myself, I take a deep breath, and with relief discover that it's air, not water, that rushes into my lungs. The panic settles as some part of me understands that I'm still in the room on the Xeno ship, but also here, in the water.

Another flash strikes, like a jolt of electricity inside my mind, and then I'm somewhere else, no longer underwater, but there's water around my feet, covering my legs up to my knees. It's soothing. I'm looking up at two Xenos. I'm young, and I know these are my parents, Harvey and Lydia Marsden. I know it like it's a fact, but not in my brain – I know it elsewhere, somewhere deeper within me.

The flashes continue and each time, the images change. Sights, sounds and smells of an alien world fill my mind as if I had experienced them myself. My surroundings are completely alien, a marshy landscape where tall grassy trees protrude from the swampy water. It's nothing like Earth, but at the same time the place feels familiar.

I'm walking through a city of tall towers that are a blend of deliberate and organic construction. Tall, twisting buildings both built and grown. I'm an adult. I've lived my life on this world but now something has gone wrong. There's been an argument. An incident between factions. Two sides are forming.

I see the same city from a distance. It burns. Dark ships hover in the sky, raining down white heat to destroy our great towers.

Smaller craft dart through the air, fighting to save the city, but it's too late. We've lost. We must leave. The smell of fear surrounds me.

I'm with others who are boarding a ship, fleeing from a world being torn apart by war. We're leaving our home, everything we've ever known, but I have my own young to care for now, to keep safe. There's an image of something else I care about, something tall – a rust-colored pillar covered in symbols. The Obelisk. I reach out and touch it. My three fingers caress the symbols carved into its surface. It hums beneath my touch. I take a blade of bright blue plasma and cut a sliver free, taking a piece for contingency. I feel a sense of panic now, confusion at what's happening. It's not mine though. It's coming from Number-One. I'm too deep and she's pushing me away. Another flash and the image is gone.

We are out among the stars, finally escaped from our devastated home world. We've travelled so far, escaped the evils, but now, after everything, there's been a malfunction. We're going to crash into a planet. Part of me recognizes it as Earth, my world, but also not my world as I watch from our ship.

Another flash and I'm me again, Wells Alexander Marsden, but I'm me from years ago. I'm outside our house. Margaret, my younger sister, is with me. Maggie. I feel annoyed at her but also miss her with an intensity that causes me to choke. I know this day. My parents have gone to do some last-minute Christmas shopping and left her at home with me. I'm supposed to look after her. I don't want to be here. I don't want to see this. Not again. I don't want Number-One to see this either. I push against the memory. Maggie and I are arguing. I push her. The sound of the car horn. The screeching of tires. No!

Another flash, another burst of sound and light, and the world of the Xeno ship rushes back. My own mind returns and I'm left panting, sucking in deep breaths.

"That was your first melding," Mr Thorn says. "Take a moment, let your mind recover. Don't worry, it gets easier with time."

I look at Number-One. I see her differently now. Even as it was happening I understood that whole experience was Number-One introducing herself to me. All that feeling and experience that passed into my mind was Number-One, her life, her world, the environment and experiences that make up her essence.

Number-One is not her name, just a label we give this sentient being, just as Wells is only a label for who and what I am – a word to collect all my experiences and consciousness. Xenocrustaceans don't have language like us. When a Xenocrustacean tells you its name you don't learn a label, you learn *who* it is. It's difficult to explain, but I know this Xenocrustacean's name not as a word but as a collection of feelings, emotions and experiences that together make up what we call Number-One. It suddenly seems like the way language should be: not words, but shared meaning.

But all through that experience I could tell there was more. Even though the melding felt intimate, I know Number-One was holding back. There were private things she wouldn't share. I could feel her push me away from that pillar, that *obelisk*. I wasn't supposed to see that, just as I didn't want to share what happened to Maggie.

I'm left feeling empty, drained and alone. I'm amazed at the experience of the melding, but also a little bit concerned. I have this lingering feeling that there's something here, buried somewhere beneath the surface, something they're hiding from us.

I KNEW IT. I knew the Crabs were hiding something. Why else would they be keeping me prisoner?

"I've got rights, you know!" I call out. "You can't just keep me here!"

I'm sitting in a chair with a black bag over my head. My hands are bound at the wrists with sturdy plastic handcuffs. I pull at the handcuffs, but they've been locked to the metal table in front of me, and no matter how hard I thrash my hands from side to side, the cuffs won't come free. They cut the bottom of my jeans off, too – my favorite jeans – and bandaged my leg, but it's still throbbing, and bleeding enough that the bandage is quickly getting soaked.

"Hello? You can't do this to me!"

Seriously, you can't just throw a bag over someone's head and drag them into a cold room without a phone call or water or anything. I don't know how long I've been here – an hour? Two hours? The only thing they've done is scan my fingerprints and jab a needle in my arm to take some blood. Probably so they can identify me. Urgh. This is bad. This is really neffing bad. I should've listened to Jesse. Why don't I ever listen to Jesse?

Can you 'ear me? Please. Let me speak to you.

I jump as the words enter my head. Oh god. Not this again. I try to answer, thinking my reply. *Get the hell out of my head you freak.*

You were there? At the fence? I need 'elp. We all need 'elp.

GET OUT OF MY HEAD!

The voice goes silent.

Great. Am I going nuts? I don't think so. The voice feels too real to be me going nuts. But that's what a nuts person would think right? This is weird. Weird and stupid and why the hell am I such a janking idiot? I thrash at the handcuffs. "Let me out! You can't keep me here!"

I hear the door open.

"You were captured trying to infiltrate the Nevada Exclusion Zone, so we can indeed keep you here. What is your name?" It's a man's voice. Not threatening, as I might have expected, but not gentle either. Just calm and stern.

Someone pulls the bag off my head, and I look around. The room is plain, with grey painted walls. Opposite me is a door with mirrored windows on either side. The only other person in the room is the man speaking. He sits in a chair across the table from me. He's tall, thin and dressed in a black suit. His dark hair is cut short on the sides and styled neatly over the top in a side part. He looks like a neffing Bond villain – he just needs a scar over his eye and a white cat or something.

"About time," I say. "You can't keep me here. This is illegal detention of a minor without charge." I have no idea whether that's an actual thing, but it sounds good to me.

"Sorry to keep you waiting," he says. "I would have been here sooner, but I had some other business to attend to, I'm afraid. Now, I'll repeat my question. What is your name?"

"What's *your* name?" I say.

The man stares at me for a long time. "My name is Mr

Thorn. Now, while I'm still managing to be polite I'll ask you one more time: what is your name?"

"Molly."

"Just Molly?"

"Just Mr Thorn?"

Mr Thorn smiles at me, but it isn't friendly. "Indeed. Now, Molly, are you going to tell me which group you're affiliated with?"

"What do you mean, which group?"

"Which terrorist group do you belong to? The Children of Earth? Terran United Front? Omega?"

"What?! I'm not a neffing terrorist, I was just fooling around. Some kids from school were joking about climbing the fence. My uncle is in the SECPOL. He'll tell you I'm no terrorist."

Mr Thorn watches me, sizing me up. "Are you telling me you crossed the border fence of one of the most secure areas on the planet on a schoolyard dare?"

"Yes," I say, "that's what I'm telling you."

"Well, unfortunately that doesn't change the fact that you've broken the law."

"Can't you just let me off with a warning or something?"

"I'm afraid that's not possible."

"You can't keep me here forever. People were with me. There were witnesses. What are you so afraid of anyway? I've seen too much, right?"

"You must understand there are important secrets inside the Institute for the Betterment of Humanity, secrets that could be dangerous if they fall into the wrong hands."

"And how do we know your hands aren't the wrong hands?"

Mr Thorn smiles. "I assure you, here at the Institute we have the best interests of humanity in mind."

"Sure. Now let me go."

"I'm afraid you're not really in a position to be making demands."

Something beeps. Mr Thorn pulls his phone from his pocket and looks at it. He seems distracted, flicking at the screen with his finger.

"Alright Molly," he says when he eventually looks up again, "perhaps we can see to releasing you with a warning. First we'll get you to the infirmary and have the doctor take a look at your leg. After that we'll discuss the terms of your release."

"You're just going to let me go?" I say, surprised by this sudden change in attitude. "After all that?"

Mr Thorn smiles again, slipping his phone back into his jacket pocket. "I apologize if I came across as heavy-handed, but you must understand the pressure we're under here. Come, I'll have some SECPOL help you to the infirmary."

$$\Omega$$

At least there's no bag over my head this time. I don't know what they were so worried about me seeing anyway. There's nothing but a lot of closed doors, opaque windows and a bunch of students walking around in grey jumpsuits, all of them looking like the cast of a bad teen drama, too handsome or too pretty or too nerdy to be real. The whole thing looks shiny and wonderful, but I still get a jank vibe. I don't understand the sudden flip from threatening me to letting me go. Something's not right. I need to get out of here though, so I'll take the chance when it's offered.

After a short walk with me hobbling along, SECPOL looming over me like prison guards, we get to the infirmary. Inside, a female doctor with a thick Russian accent greets us.

"If you'll just climb up here, Molly," she says, gesturing toward an examination table.

It looks like an ordinary enough doctor's room – white-sheeted examination table, a desk with a computer, a stainless-steel bench on wheels and a bookshelf. The doctor unwraps the blood-soaked bandage, looking at the deep cut in my calf.

"What are you going to do?" I ask.

"I'm going to treat your injury, of course."

I pull my leg back, slipping it out of her grip. It stings as the flesh pulls apart. "I've got my own doctor at home. I'll just go and see him."

"You are losing blood and at risk of infection. This injury requires prompt treatment," the Russian says. "I can have the SECPOL hold you or you can let me do my job."

I hesitate, but in the end I give in. The doctor looks at my leg and reaches for a silver spray bottle sitting on the stainless-steel bench. She sprays something blue and cold on my leg.

"What's that?"

"Nanomite-infused antibacterial accelerated healing agent."

I jump down off the table. "I didn't say you could spray Crab juice on my leg. You should have asked me first."

The doctor looks down. I follow her gaze and realize I've landed on both legs. My injured leg feels better already. It still suffers a little under my weight, but when I twist my leg to look, I see the wound closing. It seals itself, and the angry red begins to fade until there's a just thin pink line, like it was a cut that happened weeks ago. That's great and whatever, but I still didn't want them giving me any Crustie stuff.

The door opens and Mr Thorn comes back in. He looks at my miraculously healed leg.

"Good," he says. "Thank you, Doctor." He holds the door open for me. "This way, Molly."

As we leave the doctor's office the two SECPOL swing out behind me again, following along like a bad stink. I glance in a passing window and stop. The boy from the fence, the boy who was running away, the one who seemed to talk straight into my neffing head is lying on a hospital bed on the other side of the glass.

"That's the boy from the fence," I say, more of a statement than a question. "The one who hit the force field."

Mr Thorn looks in the window and then turns to me. "That's right," he says. "An unfortunate accident. He was participating in some tests with another student and the equipment they were using suffered a malfunction. It's fortunate that he collided with the force field, actually, it helped absorb some of the energy, and likely saved his life."

There's no neffing way that's true. He's trying to cover up whatever's going on.

"His name is Remy Dufort."

Remy is lying on a hospital bed wired up to monitoring machines with tubes snaking out of his face. While I stand there watching him, wondering what he's involved in and why he was running away, he starts shaking. The whole bed begins vibrating underneath him, rattling from side to side. Alarms ring and nurses hurry over. Crap. He's having a seizure or something.

I'm about to call out and ask what's happening when everything rushes away. I feel dizzy. I think I'm going to vomit, but then there's nothing around me but darkness and grey mist, and through the mist there's Remy. He's not in his bed anymore, he's standing, watching me. There's nothing between us, no force field, no glass, no anything.

There's a bright flash and I'm somewhere else, standing on grass in bare feet with the sun shining down. It's a park. There's a woman selling balloons, the colorful spheres bumping into each other in an enormous bunch. A clown stands on an upside-down wooden crate juggling balls. A carousel with lights and music spins in the distance, its horses bobbing up and down. I know I haven't been here before, but it's somehow familiar. The people around me speak French, but it doesn't sound foreign. I can understand them. I'm holding an ice cream in one hand and my mother's hand in the other, but it's not my hand, and I'm only a child.

You're 'ere again. 'ave you come to 'elp?

What's going on?

What is your name?

WHAT IS GOING ON?

Please, tell me your name.

My name is Molly. Now will you tell me what the hell is going on?

Oui. I will show you.

There's a flash again. I'm on a bed. Someone's injecting something into my arm, but again, it's not my arm. I'm sick, sweating and hot. I cough something up – I think it's blood. My mother and sister are sick too, but maybe it's too late for them. I want to ask if they're alright but I don't have the strength. It's the plague. EV-B. I cough again, lurching with the force of it and unable to stop the fountain of blood erupting from my mouth. This isn't happening now. It's like I'm in a memory.

You see what 'appens 'ere Molly. What they do to us. This place is not what it seems.

Flash. I'm in a cold room lit by blue lights. Goose pimples ripple over my bare skin. I'm lying flat, reclining in a chair. My legs and arms are strapped down and there's something wrapped around my head, pinning me. People in white coats and masks are hovering around and I sense an object being lowered toward me. My head is numb, but I can feel the end of something cold pressing into my skin, right in the middle of my forehead. I try to move, squirming on the bed, but I can't. Not just because of the restraints, but because it's not me in the chair – it's Remy. I call out for them to stop, or at least Remy does – or he did whenever this happened. I'm scared. I don't want to be here. What the jank is going on?

"Alright Remy," I hear a voice from one of the white coats say. Russian accent. The same Russian doctor who fixed my leg. "Just relax and we will begin."

I scream. I'm Remy and I'm screaming in pain. My head. Holy shit it hurts. It feels like my brain is being shredded.

"Subject A37 responding to cerebral cortex stimulation with pain response."

I scream again, or maybe I'm still screaming.

They make us forget. Remy's voice echoes in my mind. I can hear him clearly, even over the sound of his screaming. *They are changing us but they make us forget.*

There's a flash again. The world comes rushing back and nearly knocks me off my feet. I'm back in front of the infirmary window, panting, trying to catch my breath. What was that? I was in Remy's head, or he was in mine, showing me his memories. How is that possible? And how do I make sure it doesn't happen again?

Remy's family, his mother and sister, were killed in the plague, the same way I lost my mom and dad. He was sick too, one of the few people who caught EV-B and survived. I've never told anyone that happened to me. Not even Jesse knows that. Before I came to Little Basin I was sick with EV-B. Real sick. But I survived. By the time I got sick my mom and dad were already in the makeshift hospital that had been set up in the football stadium. I visited them every day until one morning I felt so sick I couldn't get out of bed. I got worse and worse until I started to cough up blood and my nose started to bleed. I thought I was going to die. But I survived through the night, and the next morning I managed to get myself some water. Late the next day my fever broke. I slept for days, but when I woke I was better. When I got back to the hospital I was too late, my parents were already dead.

Remy showed me images from here at the Institute too.

What's going on in this place? They were doing experiments on him. He said they were changing him. What does that mean?

I turn to see Mr Thorn looking at me. His eyes are thin. "Is everything alright Molly?"

I look back at Remy behind the glass. He's stopped shaking. Doctors and nurses are standing around, injecting something into his arm, checking him over. Seriously, something weird is going on here. Maybe Remy does need help, but I don't know what he thinks I can do. I just want to get myself out of here.

"No," I say, "sorry. I'm fine. That just scared me."

Mr Thorn stares at me for a long time. "As you can see, Remy is receiving the best treatment we can give him, as do all our students."

"Yeah," I say. "I can see that."

"Tell me Molly, how have you scored on the entry test for the Institute?"

I look at Mr Thorn, wondering why he would ask that. "Just average," I say.

"Well, that's a shame."

When he doesn't say any more I ask, "Can I call my uncle?" I try not to think about how insane his anger is going to be when he gets here.

"Yes, Arthur Mussington, SECPOL officer. That is your uncle, is it not?"

"I didn't tell you that," I say, then suddenly I understand. "You knew who I was all along."

"Molly McManus, seventeen, student at the local high school and someone, it seems, who has purposely failed the Institute Entrance Test every time they've taken it. Did you really think I would have entered that room without knowing who you were? I am not, Miss McManus, a man who likes to be on the back foot. Your blood also shows that you suffered from EV-B." I stare at Mr Thorn, not knowing what to say. He gives me a creepy little smile. "Not many people know this, but the testing is only one aspect of selection to the Institute. One of the other criteria is the need to have been exposed to EV-B."

I don't say anything.

"We would like you to join the Institute, Miss McManus."

"I don't think so. You just had me sitting in a room with a bag over my head. Why would I join your little school?"

Mr Thorn smiles his creepy smile again. "I'm afraid you misunderstand me Molly," he says. "You don't actually have a choice."

"Code Blue in the infirmary," a speaker in the corner of the room announces into the dining hall. "Code Blue in the infirmary."

I adjust my glasses. That sounds ominous. "What's a Code Blue?" I ask Charlotte.

"A medical alert," she says, and smiles reassuringly. "Nothing to worry about. The medical staff will handle it."

Charlotte is sitting across the table from me. We're in the Institute's large student dining room, a broad open space filled with six long tables that could easily seat several hundred people. The room reminds me of a Viking hall, like the Hall of Valhalla in *Swords of the Dungeonmaster*, albeit one with security cameras and soldiers standing around idly, their arms resting on alien space rifles. At the moment the room is about half full. Students sit around the tables in groups, talking and laughing while they eat, the room abuzz with the noise of chatter. Tonight's meal is spaghetti, one of my favorite foods, and yet I'm finding it difficult to enjoy.

"So, how was your day? Settling in alright?" Charlotte asks

before lifting a forkful of spaghetti to her mouth. She somehow manages to suck in the errant strands of pasta without flicking red sauce everywhere like I do. I nonchalantly wipe my mouth, suddenly feeling self-conscious. Charlotte takes a sip of tea from the mug in front of her. Tea and spaghetti doesn't seem like a good pairing to me – it must be a British thing.

"Yeah," I say, trying to stifle a yawn. "I think the jet lag is catching up with me though."

"The nanomites will help with that. They should start regulating your melatonin levels soon."

I'm about to ask Charlotte about the melding, and whether she's ever felt like the Xenos have dug too deep, but I don't get a chance because Sunny, the student I met in the computer lab, approaches the table.

"Good evening, Charlotte," he says.

"Sunny," Charlotte replies.

He turns to me. "I don't think we've met."

I stare at Sunny for a moment. Is this a joke? But Sunny just stands there, his hand outstretched, waiting for me to shake it. He's starting to look at me oddly, so I push my glasses up my nose and reach out to take his hand.

"We've met," I say. "We met this morning."

Sunny's face twists in confusion. "Really?" he says, looking like someone who's walked into a room and forgotten what they came in there for. "You're sure?"

I nod. "In the computer lab."

"I wouldn't worry about it Sunny," Charlotte says. "You've been so busy lately."

"Yeah," Sunny says, though he seems unconvinced. "Sorry then. What was your name?"

"It's Wells. Wells Marsden."

I see recognition dawn. "Oh," he says. "Oh no, I'd remember

if we'd met." Sunny leans in toward me, whispering as if he's sharing a secret. "Word around here is that you're some kind of criminal."

"I don't believe that's any concern of yours, Sunny," Charlotte says.

"I just think," Sunny continues, "seeing as we're supposed to be the best the planet has to offer, it's strange they let him in."

"Alright Sunny," Charlotte says. "Just leave it."

"I heard you were charged with federal computer crime," Sunny says. "Is it true you breached security at a bunch of government departments in Australia, the US and Europe? I heard you called yourself Daksec or something – one of those stupid hacker names."

I should say something, but my throat is suddenly dry.

"Sunny," Charlotte says. "The Institute is a new start for humanity and it's a new start for Wells, too. A place he can start forgiving himself for past mistakes."

"Right," Sunny says, obviously unconvinced.

"I don't do that anymore," I say.

"You say that, but if you hadn't been caught you'd still be doing it, wouldn't you?"

I don't respond. The truth is, I don't really know the answer. Hacking was my hobby, but it was more than that. It gave me a rush, the same as some people get from car racing, or sports, or jumping out of perfectly good airplanes. After Maggie died, computers were the only thing I found any pleasure in, and the best part was beating them. I wanted to break through their security, find whatever people wanted to keep hidden. It was a game, a puzzle to solve. I never meant any harm.

"I'm the senior student in Computer Sciences here," Sunny continues. "I know all about you reckless hacker types, and I don't want you here."

"I said I don't do that anymore."

"I don't want you here," Sunny says again, more aggressive now.

Why is he doing this? Is he just trying to mess with me? Sweat breaks out on my forehead and my breath comes fast. It can't be like this here, too. In juvie they attacked me for being a nerd, now here they're going to do the opposite.

"I never hurt anybody."

"You stole half a million credit card numbers."

"I never used them. I just wanted to see if I could do it."

"You just wanted to be a big shot hacker."

"Sunny!" Charlotte says.

"Then when the authorities started to track you down you hacked them too, and changed the information they had on you. Some people might be impressed by that, but not me."

"Alright," I say, standing up, my eyes hot. "I got in trouble but I was pardoned. I just want to move on."

"Move on from here then," Sunny says.

My glasses are fogging. I don't want Charlotte to see this. She'll think I'm a coward as well as a criminal. I turn from the table.

"You're just going to run away?"

"Leave me alone," I say as I walk away. I know it sounds lame. The students around me are watching. I feel drops of sweat running down my back. I need to get out of here. I hurry toward the exit before I lose my thinly held composure.

"Wells!" Charlotte calls, but I'm not going to turn around. I don't care if I look stupid. I don't stop until I reach the elevator, where I press the button repeatedly, willing the doors to open.

"Wells, wait!" I hear Charlotte as she rounds the corner.

The door opens and I hurry in, pressing the button for level 5, where my room is.

"Wells!"

I press the "door close" button. I see Charlotte approaching the lift just as the doors slide shut. Her concerned face is the last thing I see before the door seals. I lean back against the wall, take my glasses off and wipe my eyes with the back of my hand. I didn't want Charlotte to see me like this, but I'm sure she saw me crying.

$$\Omega$$

I open my eyes. My head is fuzzy. After I returned to my room, where my roommate was thankfully still absent, I lay on the bed and must have drifted off. It takes me a moment to realize what's woken me: there's noise coming from the corridor outside, someone knocking on a door. I look at the clock at the top of the glass wall opposite my bed. The numbers seem to hang suspended in space: 01:26.

The knocking is repeated, an insistent thumping.

"Sunny," a voice says. I recognize it immediately – Charlotte. "Mr Thorn needs to see you."

I climb off the bed as quietly as I can and creep toward the door, pressing myself against it to listen.

"Sunny," Charlotte calls again.

I hear Sunny's muffled voice. "What? What's going on?"

"Mr Thorn wants to see you."

"I didn't do anything," Sunny calls out. "Is this because of what I said to that new kid?"

"Please dress and come out. Mr Thorn will discuss it with you."

Sunny doesn't respond.

"Open it," Charlotte says, her voice stern.

"Yes, Miss Yorke." It's a man's voice this time.

I look at the control panel beside the door. I know there's an external viewing camera. I saw it positioned in the center of the door, an electronic peephole. I activate it and a vision of the hallway appears projected as a holographic display on the door.

Charlotte is standing with two SECPOL officers outside the door directly across the hall – that must be Sunny's room. One of them is holding a card in front of the lock, some kind of override. In the quiet of the corridor I hear the click of the lock, and the door opens. Is Sunny really getting into trouble for what he said to me in the dining hall? Part of me hopes so, but at the same time I wonder why they're dragging him out of his room in the middle of the night. And why is Charlotte doing it?

"Go and get him," Charlotte says. Her voice sounds harsh, angry at this inconvenience. Both of the SECPOL enter the room.

"Alright," I hear Sunny say. "I'm coming. You don't have to – Ow! Get off me!"

Sunny soon appears in the doorway, only half dressed in a white undershirt and white underwear, a SECPOL officer holding him under each arm.

"Charlotte, what's going on?" Sunny says, struggling against the grip of the SECPOL. "Why are you with the SECPOL?"

"You're being rather loud for this time of night," Charlotte says. "No more talking."

"You can't –ghurgh..."

Sunny's voice stops in a strained sound, as if his throat is being squeezed shut. No one is touching him but he's thrashing and gasping like he's being choked. Sunny increases his panicked flailing.

"Will you please be still?" Charlotte says.

Sunny's violent fighting stops. He stands completely still. It's eerily quiet.

"Better," Charlotte says. "Pick him up and carry him. We'll take him to Mr Thorn."

Sunny maintains his stiff, standing posture even as the SECPOL lift him, one under each arm, and carry him away like department store workers moving a mannequin. They walk out of view of the camera. I stay at the door for several minutes, listening for any other sounds, but there's nothing.

I walk to my desk and collapse into the chair. What was that? I mean, really, what the bloody hell was that? Charlotte and the SECPOL dragging students off in the middle of the night? I thought the SECPOL were meant to be protecting us. What's even weirder was the way he just started choking and then froze solid.

I stare at the curved monitor fixed to the wall in front of me. I can't see a mouse or a VR headset or even a keyboard. There's a tablet in a dock at the back left corner of the desk, but that's all. It's only as I look down that I realize the whole surface of the desk is a glass touch interface. At the back right of the desk there's a shape engraved on the surface, the power symbol. I press it.

The surface of the desk lights up with the white outline of a keyboard. A grey grid flashes up on the monitor, and then I see the Institute symbol spinning in three dimensions front of me. It's a holo-screen, a curved monitor that projects its image out as a hologram at the apex of curvature. I've never actually used one before. When the screen changes I'm looking at the graphical display of an operating system, icons arranged on the surface of a sphere that floats in the air.

I reach out into the hologram and turn my hand to spin the sphere. There's a web browser, but when I open it I see that external internet access is blocked. They don't want us going on the internet, they don't want us communicating with the outside world. That feels like another red flag.

Sure I was nervous about coming here, but I always thought –

always hoped – this might finally be the place I fit in. Now I can't help but think something nefarious is going on, something that wasn't in the shiny brochure for this place. I stare at the computer. If I can access the server I might be able to find out some information, work out if my feelings are just my crazy anxiety or if they're warranted.

A voice in the back of my mind chastises me for even thinking these things. This is what got me arrested, what got me locked up and what I promised I would never do again. I promised my parents. I promised the Institute. I promised myself. I move to switch off the computer.

But I don't.

The truth is, the Institute feels more than just a little weird. It feels *dangerous*. I can't ignore that. I need to examine this gnawing feeling of unease. Maybe Sunny is right, maybe this is just who I am.

I open a command line and trawl through the network to find the central server. It's password and firewall protected. My primary tools for cracking this type of security were on a USB flash drive but that, along with all my computer equipment, was confiscated by the police. It's not a problem, it's just going to take a little longer.

I start coding a new crack program, studying the system as I go. I just need to get onto the main server, have a little look around. The part of me that knows this is wrong becomes quieter and quieter as I tap the keys. I'm flooded with the joy of the game again, the challenge of the puzzle. I never really understand people. People are complicated. They always do and say things they don't mean. They react in unpredictable ways. Computers, on the other hand, all they do is react logically to the inputs given. I understand them. Soon I sink fully into my familiar place and I feel nothing but the satisfaction of a hack.

Ω

I'm still typing when an alarm begins beeping. I glance at the clock and see that it's 06:30 am, the prescribed wake-up time for all Institute students.

I've spent the last few hours looking for a way through the security firewall to the server – which I found. Then it was a simple matter of using SQL injection to get the server to dump the usernames and hashed passwords. The tricky bit is actually using those encrypted passwords to get secure shell access. That's what I'm working on now, coding an algorithm to fake a legitimate login. Despite being up most of the night I feel surprisingly good. That must be the nanomites. As the alarm ceases I float my fingers just above the touch display keyboard, debating whether I should stop and get ready for the day, but the sound of the door breaks my thoughts.

A dark-skinned boy in an Institute jumpsuit walks into the room. He's tall and skinny, his hair clipped short.

"Bonjour," the boy says. "You must be Wells. I am Remy."

"Hi," I say, trying to act calm.

He walks toward me and I stand. We shake hands.

"A pleasure to meet you," he says. "You are from Australia, no?"

"That's right," I say. "Melbourne. You're French?"

"Oui," Remy says. "Paris, Toulouse, a bit of everywhere between."

We stand awkwardly for a moment. "So, how long have you been here?" I ask. "At the Institute, I mean?"

"Some time now," Remy says. "Since almost two years. Breakfast will be in the dining 'all soon. You would like to walk down together?"

I see Remy glance at the monitor behind me. I try to move slightly, just enough to obscure his view.

"Wells?"

"Huh?"

"Will you be 'aving breakfast? Do you want to go down?"

"Yeah, I was just about to get ready. We can walk down together."

Remy tilts his head, trying to see the computer screen. My palms grow sweaty and I push my glasses up my nose. I shouldn't have done it. Guilt hits me like a freight train. Why did I let myself be tempted into hacking again?

"What are you doing on the computer?"

"Nothing." I hastily move to switch it off, but as I reach to press the button my finger won't move. It just hovers in the air. But it's not just my finger that won't move – it's all of me. I feel a tingle, a cold shiver like icy water running down my spine. I can't move my hands, arms or legs. I can't even turn my head. I try to scream, but my mouth won't open. I can't make any noise at all. My breath comes fast as panic floods my body. I don't even try to calm myself. Why should I try to calm myself? I'm suddenly paralyzed, and that seems like a perfectly acceptable reason to be panicking.

"I am doing that to you," I hear Remy say from behind me. "I will allow you to speak, but only if you do not cry out. Nod if you agree."

I feel my neck release. I can turn my head, but the remainder of my body remains paralyzed. No matter how much I will my muscles to move, there's no response – it's like I'm submerged in concrete from the neck down. I turn my head as far as I can, enough that I can see Remy in my peripheral vision. He moves to stand beside me.

"Do you agree not to call out?" he says. "I will do more than paralyze you if you do."

I nod. Remy looks into my eyes as if examining them for truth. I feel my throat relax. I swallow and try to control my breathing, at least enough that I can speak. My first instinct is to scream for help, but I don't. I have no idea what Remy is capable of. If he can paralyze my body, who knows what else he could do?

"How are you doing this?" I ask between breaths, only just managing to keep my voice steady. "Why can't I move?"

"First," Remy says, "what is this?" He points to the computer screen. "I 'ave 'eard about you. Are you trying to 'ack the computer?"

"No," I say.

My hand rises from where it's resting on the desk, completely against my will. I try to stop it, try to move it back down, but it won't listen. It's as if it doesn't even belong to my body.

"What are you doing?" I say.

Before I can blink, my hand flies up and slaps me across the face, sending my glasses crooked and whipping my head sideways.

"Ow!"

My arm pulls back, and my hand curls into a fist this time.

"Okay," I say. "Okay, okay. Yes. I'm trying to hack into the server."

"Why?"

"Because," I say, wishing I could straighten my glasses and rub my burning cheek, "because something strange is going on and I want to know what."

"Good."

My arm drops back onto the desk and my body relaxes as I regain control of my muscles. I move quickly across the room, knocking the chair over in my haste to put as much space between Remy and myself as I can. I shake my hands, flex my fingers, bend my knees, reassuring myself that I still know how to control my own body. I breathe deeply, trying to calm the incessant thumping of my heart.

"I apologize for making you 'it yourself," Remy says, "but I 'ad to be sure you were lucid."

"Lucid?"

"Oui, that you 'ave a clear mind, not brainwashed like the others."

"Brainwashed?" I ask, realizing how stupid I must sound repeating everything Remy says.

"They do it to all of us. They make us forget. Tell me what you did yesterday. Your first day and you cannot remember where you were, no?"

"I was doing orientation," I say, "with Mr Thorn."

"Were you?"

I know I was doing orientation with Mr Thorn. I know it just like I know what I had for dinner last night, but when I do think about it, when I really concentrate, I can't remember what that orientation was actually about. I had medical testing, a tour, met Number-One and then, before I knew it, it was dinnertime and I was here. There does seem to be something of a gap.

"I can't...I can't remember what I did after the tour."

"They were doing it to you sometime around then, the brain-washing. I 'ave 'ad whole days go missing."

I sit on the side of my bed, the realization making my legs weak. "No," I say, but it's a weak objection. I can't really remember it at all. Just like...just like Sunny couldn't remember meeting me.

"No," I say again, but only because I don't want to believe it's possible that someone could erase things from my brain. "How do you know this?" I look up at Remy. "Why haven't they made you forget?"

"They 'ave," Remy says. "I was the same, brainwashed like everyone else. I think I 'ave forgotten most, but a little while ago I started 'aving flashes, memories that do not fit, experiments. I started to remember what they are turning us into. I am telling you this because you are new 'ere, you are not yet controlled. You see that something is wrong. I think we all see it at first, then we forget."

"Alright," I say, taking a deep breath. "And what about before? How did you do that to me?"

"I had EV-B," Remy says. "Something 'appens after EV-B, something they try to, 'ow you say, 'arness. They made me able to control things with my mind."

Remy points at my desk chair, still toppled over on the ground. Slowly it rises into the air, rights itself, and then settles back on its wheels.

"Oh my god," I say. "That's telekinesis. That's impossible."

"Oui," Remy says. "As you say, telekinesis. But it is possible. They are giving us this power and they are training us. I think they are training us to fight."

"To fight what?" I say. "Do you think it's an invasion? Are they trying to take over?"

"I don't know," Remy says. "But we need to escape this place. We need to warn people. I need 'elp. Will you 'elp me?"

"Right, we're just going to escape the most secure compound on the planet and tell the world that the benevolent aliens who are curing cancer and feeding the poor and giving us the technology to fix humanity's problems are turning the Institute for the Betterment of Humanity students into an army of telekinetic freaks," I say. "No offence."

"Oui."

"Okay. Don't you think that's a long shot?"

"Until now I 'aven't been able to prove anything." Remy points at the computer. "But if you can do this 'acking, maybe you can find the proof we need."

This is exactly what I was arrested for in the first place. But if what Remy is saying is true, then this really is something the world needs to be warned about. I don't want to believe him, but I know something weird is happening. Even before he walked into the room, paralyzed me and started making chairs float, I already knew. I'd already started hunting for the truth. My stomach flutters. I didn't come here for this. I didn't ask to become the whistleblower on an alien conspiracy.

"I don't know, Remy."

"Feel behind your right ear," Remy says.

I press my finger behind my ear and wince in pain. There's a fresh wound there, like a puncture in my skin.

"That is where they go in with the probe," Remy says, "when they are brainwashing you."

I remember being injected with nanomites, and having blood taken, but I'm sure they never put anything in behind my ear. I look at Remy. The idea that someone is doing secret medical procedures to me makes my mind up. "Okay, what are we looking for?"

$$\Omega$$

I type as fast as I can think, stopping intermittently to run the code through my head. I have a sense this will be my only chance. If they suspect I'm digging around in the computer system I'm certain it won't be long before I'm dragged away like Sunny. Charlotte will already be wondering why I'm not at breakfast.

Remy is standing behind me, looking over my shoulder. He's making me anxious. Not that I wouldn't be anxious anyway – I'm hacking into a computer server in one of the most secure places on the planet with someone I met less than an hour ago.

"Could you stand somewhere else?"

"Sorry."

He sits on the corner of his bed, still watching me. I try to ignore him as I tap at the glowing keys until I think I'm done, then I save the file and open a command prompt. I type the name of my program, "Daksec.bat" and then stop, looking at the cursor blinking at the end of the line. It's a self-compiling code that will run as soon as I hit enter, worming out across the network, locating the server and loading a back door that should fool it into thinking my remote access is actually a local administrator using one of the hashed passwords I uncovered.

"Alright," I say.

Remy almost leaps off the bed. "Did you find something?"

"No, but I'm ready to try and get onto the server."

Remy comes and stands behind me. "Will this work?"

I shrug. "It's the best I could do without more time."

"Well, go on then, 'it the button."

I hover my index finger over the enter key. It's shaking. There's a chance this won't work. There's also the nagging voice that always crops up when I'm attempting to breach a system's security, the voice that tells me I'm going to get caught. I just need to be quick. The quicker I am, the less likely someone monitoring the system will notice anything odd.

I take a moment, push my glasses up the bridge of my nose, and then, before I completely lose my nerve, I hit enter. The floating holographic screen fills with running lines of code.

"What's 'appening?" Remy asks.

"Shhh," I say, trying to concentrate on the code as it streams past. I see what I'm looking for, a ping back from the server, although I still don't know whether I've managed to forge administrator access.

The program sits there, frozen on the words "Administrator Login", seemingly doing nothing. The system hangs and hangs until I feel a nervous warmth rising up my neck.

"Did it work?"

I'm about to say no and admit my defeat when the words on the screen change to "Administrator Login Granted".

"It worked," I say, wishing I sounded less surprised.

The screen changes back to a simple command prompt and a blinking cursor. It doesn't look like much but I'm in the back door – all the files on the server are accessible. I sit for a moment, not sure exactly how to proceed.

I turn in my chair to look at Remy. "What now?"

"You are the 'acker, you don't know what to do?"

"I mean what should I look for? I can run a global file search, but I need to know what we want to find."

"Try looking for information about brainwashing. Maybe they 'ave records."

I type the commands to search for any files containing the word "brainwash" or "brainwashing". The computer sits for a while running the search – the server must contain an enormous amount of data. After a few moments the computer returns the results of the search: "o files found." I stare at the screen, then I change the search criteria to my own name, "Marsden", and search again. A number of files appear on the screen: a student record, emails sent about my arrival, medical reports, results of my testing, but the file that grabs my attention is one called "Indoctrination Session A183/22/001 – Marsden, Wells." I open it.

The file is a report dated yesterday, outlining what the author refers to as "Subject A183's initial indoctrination". I scroll down, looking for the author of the report and see in the footer of the first page that it was written by Dr A. Plotnikova, the Russian doctor.

The report goes on to discuss the "administration of sevoflurane," "injection with bio-nanomite-encoded serum," "recoding of dendritic spines" and a number of other medical statements I don't understand. The conclusion of the report is clear, though: "the first stage of Subject A183's indoctrination completed satisfactorily but with need for further treatments in cognitive realignment before attempts at resonance with the Obelisk. Subject deemed suitable for Operation Vassal."

I turn to Remy. "When I melded with Number-One I saw something, a kind of pillar thing. I immediately thought of it as an obelisk, as though somehow I knew that's what it was called. What about Operation Vassal, have you heard of that?"

Remy shakes his head.

I search again, this time looking for any files containing the phrase "Operation Vassal". The list that returns is hundreds of files long.

"Whatever they're doing here," I say, "it's part of this Operation Vassal."

I scan through the search results, choosing a file at random, but when I try to open it I find that it's encrypted. Even with administrator access to the server, I'm being blocked. Some of the files even have encrypted filenames. I don't have time to even think about cracking the encryption now, but I start the process of copying the files across to the tablet sitting on the desk. A progress bar appears on screen and the percentage complete begins moving steadily upwards. 1%. 2%. 3%. I hope this transfers quickly. I need to get off the system before –

There's a thumping on the door. Remy and I both spin in that direction and then lock eyes. Neither of us speaks. Neither of us moves. The knocking comes again.

"Yes?" I call out.

Remy shoots me a look, as if to ask what I'm doing. I shrug. I think it's better to answer and seem less guilty than to try and pretend we're not here. We don't even know that it's the SECPOL.

"Remy Dufort, Wells Marsden," a hoarse voice calls from the other side of the door, "this is the SECPOL. Open the door please."

I feel a sinking in my stomach. Sweat breaks out across my

forehead. I look at the screen. The files are still copying. 63%. 64%. 65%.

"What do we do?" I whisper to Remy.

"I think I 'ave 'ad enough time at the Institute," Remy says. "We take this information and we make, 'ow you say, a break of it."

"A break for it?"

"Oui. A break for it."

"This is your final chance to come voluntarily."

The numbers on the screen tick up. 98%. 99%. 100%. Transfer complete.

"And how exactly are we supposed to escape?" I say.

"They are not expecting me to 'ave control of my abilities," Remy says. "I think I can get us out."

I shake my head. "No way. You're crazy. You're not going to be able to fight your way out. Anyway, just because the SECPOL are here doesn't mean they're here because of the hacking."

"We know you were messing around with the computer," the voice of the SECPOL calls through the door.

I grimace. "Alright, so maybe they *do* know about the hacking."

"They will not go easy on you," Remy says. He points at the tablet. "They know you 'ave taken those files. They are not going to forgive you."

I swallow. What the heck was I thinking? I know he's right. Mr Thorn was incredibly clear that there would be consequences if I fell back to my old ways, and based on what I've seen here, I'm sure the consequences are going to be a lot worse than a sternly worded letter home. I'm stuck with Remy now, dragged into whatever he's planning to do. I grab the tablet, snap the cover closed and slip it in my jumpsuit's large inside pocket, zipping my jumpsuit back up to hide it as best I can. I feel it resting against my chest as if it's burning a hole right through me.

There's the sound of a high-pitched beep and then the sliding of the electronic lock on the door. The SECPOL are overriding the retinal scanner. Remy and I both turn to face the door as it swings inward. Sergeant Elliot, the SECPOL officer I met on my flight to the compound, is first in the room, with two more soldiers parading in behind her. The three of them block our exit. Their rifles, pulsing with blue light, are aimed directly at us.

I STARE across the table at the two SECPOL standing either side of the door. They've got their rifles lowered, but I can tell they're ready to shoot me if I try anything. Idiots. What do they think I'm going to do? I'm back in the interrogation cell, handcuffed to that stainless-steel table again. I'm not exactly a threat.

I've been in here all neffing night. I slept for a little while, my forehead resting on the table, but it wasn't comfortable enough for anything more than a drifting doze. Now my head has started pounding again. The pain's grown over the last hour, and it's turning into a full blown rip-my-hair-out migraine. I lower my head onto the cool table and clamp my handcuffed hands over my temples, trying to squeeze the pain out.

I look up through watering eyes as the cell door opens. It's Thorn. Just what I need when I'm hitting peak migraine. I lower my head again.

"Molly?" Mr Thorn says. "Are you feeling alright?"

"I'm fine, leave me alone."

"You've got a headache, don't you?"

I look up at him again as he sits opposite me.

"Just leave me alone," I repeat.

"Turn the light off," Mr Thorn says to the SECPOL. "Quickly now."

The room drops into darkness. That relieves some of the pain, or the irritation from the fluorescent lights, at least.

"Better?"

"Not really. You're still here."

He laughs. "I do admire your spark," he says. "Even in the throes of severe pain you still manage a witty retort."

"Glad I'm able to entertain."

"You've been having these headaches since you recovered from EV-B, haven't you?" Mr Thorn asks.

I shrug.

"It's common in EV-B survivors," he continues. "Many of the students at the Institute have been through it. You'll find that none of them have to go through it anymore, though. We're able to cure the headaches. Would you like that?"

The Bond Villain is right. I started getting headaches not long after EV-B. The doctors Uncle Art sent me to, even as far away as a neurologist in Houston, all said they couldn't find anything wrong. They just said they were migraines, and there was nothing they could do but give me drugs. I knew they were linked to EV-B, though. The Crustie plague messed something up in my brain. I've tried all sorts of medication, but nothing works. At best, drugs take the edge off, but usually they don't do anything at all.

"Would you like us to help you Molly?" Mr Thorn says. "You'll never have to suffer these headaches again."

I feel the tears run down my cheeks. I want to tell myself it's the pain making me cry but I know that's not true. It's knowing the Crabs could fix it. I'm crying because I want to let them. Even after they released a virus that killed more than a billion people, including my parents. I'm just like everyone else after all, willing to take whatever the aliens can give me.

"This is the final time I'm going to offer, Molly," Mr Thorn says. "Would you like us to treat your headaches?"

I look up at him through my tears and pain. I look up at him and then flick my gaze down. He follows the line of my eyes. I can't raise my hand because of the handcuffs, but I can still raise my middle finger.

$$\Omega$$

"We have been patient with you," Mr Thorn says as two of his SECPOL goons grab me by the arms and lead me out of the interrogation room. "We had Doctor Plotnikova attend to your injuries. We even offered to heal your headaches. We have tried to make this as easy on you as we can."

"Yes," I say. "You've done so much for me. How could I forget that time you stuck a bag over my head or that time you kept me locked in a room all night? And let's not forget the most important thing – you're a dick."

"You don't seem to understand, Miss McManus. You are not leaving this place. You will be joining us here at the Institute, voluntarily or not."

The SECPOL drag me to a room that looks like an operating theatre. Medical machines are scattered all around, with loops of tubing and wires hanging out like electronic tentacles. It's cold and sterile and gives me the neffing creeps.

They take me to a chair in the center of the room. It's like a dentist's chair, but my wrists and ankles are held in place with buckled straps. The SECPOL force my head back and wrap a strap around my forehead to hold it in place. The chair hums and starts lowering until I'm angled back, half lying down. The blue-tinted lights in the roof are bright. My head throbs.

"Back again," the Russian doctor says, appearing beside me. "Mr Thorn says you've been experiencing headaches. This is common after EV-B. I give you painkiller first, and then treatment with nanomites programmed to fix the problem in brain structure."

"Don't touch me," I say, squirming against my restraints.

"No." I hear Mr Thorn's voice from the corner of the room. "Don't treat her headaches yet. Indoctrination first. Once she comes around to joining the Institute, then she can receive the benefits of being a student here."

The doctor looks like she's going to argue, but she doesn't. She turns to a waist-high stainless-steel table and picks up what looks like one of those guns they use to pierce ears. She moves behind me and I feel the gun pressed against my skull behind my right ear. There's a click, then a sudden stabbing pain. The taste of vomit rises in my throat and a wild dizziness floods through me. I feel like I'm spinning in circles. I try to focus on the lights above me. Those blue lights. This chair. Jank. This is the room Remy showed me. This is where they do their experiments.

"What are you doing?" I say, but it comes out as little more than a mumble. My mouth is filling with pre-barf saliva.

Mr Thorn laughs a little, and I half expect him to reveal his evil plan before leaving me being slowly lowered into a tank of robot sharks or something. "As I said before, you have a place here now. This is where you join us."

"Um, no," I say. "I've got to wash my hair."

"You are amusing Miss McManus. I'm going to enjoy your company. Don't worry, you'll be happy here soon enough."

Coldness fills my chest. What happened to Remy is going to happen to me. They're going to brainwash me into wanting to stay here. They're going to experiment on me like a rat in a lab. Remembering Remy gives me an idea. An idea that's probably stupid.

Remy, I call out inside my mind. *Can you hear me? I need help.*

There's no response. Of course there isn't.

"It's alright Molly," Mr Thorn says. "This is for the best. Soon you'll be an integral part of the Institute for the Betterment of Humanity."

The doctor is doing something behind me, I feel a tugging sensation behind my right ear. I can't turn my head, but in my peripheral vision I see her grabbing some sort of wire. I squirm against my restraints but don't accomplish anything. The doctor starts powering up machines around the room. They're actually going to do this. Shit. How in the neffing hell am I going to get out of this?

REMY! I scream inside my own head. I concentrate, trying to remember what it felt like when he connected his mind with mine. I can feel the doctor pushing that cold metal wire in behind my ear. *REMY!*

Molly. Remy's voice hits my mind as loud as if he were standing behind me. This time I'm almost relieved to have someone speaking directly into my brain. *I 'ear you. We will 'elp you.*

Whatever he does, I hope he does it quickly.

Remy and I raise our hands above our heads as the SECPOL move into the room, their rifles pointed at us.

"Sergeant Elliot," I say. "Please, let me explain."

"Sorry Wells," Sergeant Elliot says. "You need to come with us."

"No," Remy says. "We're not letting you brainwash us again."

A look of surprise crosses the soldiers' faces. Either they don't know what Remy is talking about or they didn't expect him to know about it.

"I don't know anything about that," Sergeant Elliot says. "Our orders are to take you to Mr Thorn for a breach of security." She speaks calmly, trying to keep the situation under control.

"You know what they do to us?" Remy says, both a question and a statement. "They torture us."

"Sergeant Elliot," I say. "Please. You know what's happening here is wrong."

"You know what they do, non?" Remy continues. "And what, you tell yourself you only follow orders?"

"That's enough," the gruff-voiced SECPOL officer says, stepping toward Remy with his rifle aimed at his face. "Shut it."

Remy's voice drops into a snarl. "Stop pointing that thing at me."

The SECPOL's eyes grow wide as he turns ninety degrees until he's no longer pointing his rifle at Remy – he's pointing it at Sergeant Elliot. He pushes it forward onto Sergeant Elliot's temple. She turns her head against the pressure of the barrel, trying to look at the soldier, confusion and anger in her eyes.

"Reynolds," she says. "What the hell do you think you're doing?"

"I...I can't help it. I can't move."

"Remy," I say quietly. "What are you doing?"

The soldier on the other side of Sergeant Elliot – Jackson, according to the embroidered name on his uniform – starts moving, taking a step forward and raising his rifle at Reynolds.

"Jackson!" Sergeant Elliot barks. "Stand down!"

"I can't help it either Sergeant," Jackson says, his voice filled with barely controlled panic.

Sergeant Elliot raises her own rifle, moving it hastily between Remy and myself, uncertain where she should be pointing it. "Whatever you're doing," she says, "stop it."

Sergeant Elliot's rifle turns away from us, pointing toward Jackson so that the three SECPOL soldiers are all pointing their weapons at each other. Remy has them trapped in a triangle of rifles. A thin trickle of blood has started snaking out of Remy's right nostril and is slowly creeping down his face.

"Come on," I say. "Come on Remy, let's go."

"I can't 'old them when we leave."

"You've given us a head start at least. Please, let's just go."

"No," Remy says. "They'll follow. I need to stop them from following us."

"No," I say, feeling a burst of panic when I realize what he means. "Don't."

"They deserve it."

"No, they don't," I say.

I look at the SECPOL. They understand what Remy is planning just as well as I do. Each of their faces wears a mask of stern defiance, but I can see the fear in their eyes. Despite their military training and their hard exteriors, they're terrified.

I catch Sergeant Elliot's eye. She can't move, but she looks at me with a sort of pleading desperation. She's the only SECPOL I've met who's actually been nice to me. Even now she was the calm one, trying to make everything seem less frightening.

"Remy," I say. "Listen, you don't need to do this."

He looks at me with ferocious eyes. "You don't know what they've done to us!"

I move toward Remy. "You can't "

There's a flash of white-hot blue, three flashes all occurring at once. The sound of the rifles going off isn't like a normal gunshot. It's like an electrical discharge, the sound of electricity set free from a capacitor, or a lightning spell from *Swords of the Dungeonmaster*. The smell is worse than the sound though – the room is filled with the thick odor of burning.

Sergeant Elliot lands on her side, facing us. I wish she hadn't, because I don't want to see her face. She's lying like a fallen rag doll, her limbs all splayed out and her eyes open, looking at me as if asking why I didn't help. The side of her head is blackened and burned and not entirely there, and thin tendrils of smoke curl up from it. I force myself to look away. I've never seen a dead body before, and seeing this one, Sergeant Elliot, who was nice to me and answered all my nervous questions, makes me feel sick right from the pit of my stomach to my throat. I have to swallow rising vomit.

Remy is breathing heavily beside me.

"What have you done?" I say. Eventually I manage to look at him. "Remy, what have you done?"

"I needed to," Remy says, but his voice is shaking. "We have to escape. Get one of their rifles."

Remy bends over and takes the rifle from Reynolds' hand, stepping over his body as he moves toward the door.

"Remy..."

He turns back to me. "Pick up a rifle Wells," he says, his voice edged with a sudden hardness. I'm not sure Remy is someone I should be following out this door, but I don't really have much of a choice. I'm getting in deeper with every passing moment. I'm in so far over my head I can't even see the surface now.

I bend down, trying not to look at Sergeant Elliot, and grab Jackson's rifle. I have to pry his fingers away from the grip before I can take it. My eyes blur and I feel hot, bitter vomit in my throat again as I pull the dead man's fingers apart one by one.

I stand and move toward Remy, trying not to think. The rifle is awkward in my arms, heavier than I thought and oddly balanced. Remy opens the door, looking out into the corridor, and doesn't hesitate before moving forward. I follow.

"Stop!"

The voice comes from one end of the corridor. We turn to see two more SECPOL hurrying toward us.

"Run," Remy says.

And we do.

$$\Omega$$

My feet pound against the floor and my breath comes in deep, wheezing gasps as I follow Remy through the corridors of the accommodation wing. I've never been into exercise or played any sport on account of the asthma I had as a child. Maybe I should have taken some time to try and get fit, but I never expected I'd need to run through a joint alien-human training facility while being pursued by soldiers.

We turn a corner and run out onto the enclosed glass walkway that extends over the artificial parkland. The park no one ever seems to be enjoying – probably because they're too busy being turned into telekinetic mutants.

"Stop where you are!"

The voice comes from ahead of us. Three SECPOL have appeared, seemingly from nowhere, to block the end of the walkway. I glance behind us. The two officers who were chasing us are still there. We're trapped.

Remy lifts his rifle, aiming it at the officers ahead of us.

"I'm leaving," he calls to them.

"Drop your weapons or we *will* open fire."

Remy doesn't drop his rifle. He doesn't even lower it. He just stands in the middle of the walkway, the grey rifle raised to his shoulder. The glow from the vents lights the side of his face blue – a face that looks determined and angry and also a little afraid, but in a way that makes me think he'll keep doing whatever it takes to get out of here.

"Drop your weapons!" one of the SECPOL shouts again. "Do it now!"

It's only then that I remember I'm holding a rifle too. I bend slowly, not wanting to alarm the SECPOL, who seem jittery and ready to shoot at the smallest provocation. I place the heavy grey rifle on the glass floor. When I look up, Remy is still unmoved. My face fills with nervous heat. I want him to put his rifle down. We need to give up – there's no way we can make it out of this compound alive.

"Remy," I whisper, "I think you should do what they say."

"Do it!" the SECPOL shout. "Weapon on the floor!"

"Remy," I repeat, but he still doesn't flinch, he just stares them down like this is a stand-off in one of the old western movies my dad used to watch.

I see the front most soldier set himself, looking down the

sights of his weapon. I don't want to get shot. I'm only seventeen, and that doesn't seem like a very fair age to get shot. I see the flash of blue light and hear the sound of electrical discharge as the officer fires. He misses, whether deliberately or not I'm unsure, and the bolt of plasma hits just in front of our feet, burning into the glass and causing a pattern of spiderweb cracks to spread outward.

"That is your last warning!"

The SECPOL are doing everything they can to avoid shooting us. They must have been told to take us alive. Remy lifts his heavy black boot and slams it down on the cracked glass. There's the sound of splintering as the cracks grow and the glass weakens.

"Stop that!"

Remy turns to me. "Grab on."

"What?" I say.

Remy reaches out with his left hand, wrapping his fist tightly around the loose-fitting cloth in the arm of my jumpsuit. With his right arm he lowers his rifle until it's pointing toward the glass at his feet, then fires. The glass beneath us gives way with a final shattering burst.

We fall, plummeting toward the ground amid shards of glass. Just before we hit the ground, the jumpsuit around my arm pulls tight as Remy slows himself and tries to slow me too. I scramble to try and get a grip on his arm but I'm too late, and the fabric of my jumpsuit slips free of his grip. I hit the grass flat on my back and air bursts from my lungs in a gasping rush. I cough and try to breathe, but I can barely manage shallow breaths without pain.

"Wells," Remy says as he grabs me and pulls at my arm, "we must move."

I roll onto my side and let Remy drag me up to sitting. Small shards of glass fall from my arms and legs as I climb hesitantly to my feet. I double over, still winded and coughing. Sharp pains stab into my back with every breath, but I can move, and nothing seems to be broken. Remy must have slowed me enough before his grip slipped free.

Bolts of plasma start slamming into the ground around us, leaving smoke curling upwards from spots of burned grass. Remy turns and starts firing back, his own plasma bolts slamming into the walkway above.

"Get your gun and come on," Remy yells between bursts from his rifle.

I hesitate as more bolts of plasma slam into the ground around us.

"Wells!" Remy all but screams at me.

I grab the rifle from where it's fallen nearby and follow Remy across the grass toward what looks like a door in the wall of the dome. Remy struggles to open it. Each time he leans forward and tries to scan his retina the display lights up red and blinks with the words "Access Denied".

"What now?" I ask.

He turns to look at me. "We are getting Molly," he says, "then we are leaving this place."

Remy turns back to the door and furrows his brow. There is a creak of metal. At first I can't see any movement but then, as the slow, low groan builds into a wrenching, twisting sound, the top of the door begins to curl downward like a dog-eared page in a book. Remy begins to grunt. When the door has peeled open enough we squeeze through and continue along the corridors of the Institute. The place will be crawling with SECPOL hunting for us, but instead of getting out as fast as we can, Remy turns and heads for the Infirmary.

"Wait, what?" I say as we run. "Who's Molly?"

Doctor Russia hovers over me like a dark cloud. Cold electrodes are attached to my forehead. She's telling me this won't be so bad. I call bullshit on that. I remember what Remy showed me. I remember the screaming.

"I don't want any part of what you're doing here."

"We exist for the betterment of humanity," Mr Thorn says, "just as our name implies."

"Bullshit," I say. "You're evil. I know you're doing experiments on the students."

"Evil is a point of view, Miss McManus," Mr Thorn says. "The church considered Galileo heretical for his scientific explorations. If you lived during his conquest you might have considered Alexander the Great evil, yet today he is recognized for spreading a culture that shaped the modern world. Genghis Khan's conquest was bloody, and yet now we see the value in his linking the East and the West."

"None of them tortured teenagers to help aliens invade the planet though, did they?"

"Is that what you think is happening here?"

"I'm not going to be part of your neffing alien invasion plans, no matter what you do to me."

Mr Thorn doesn't say anything, he just smiles. An infuriating, I-know-something-you-don't-know smile that I wish I could wipe off his smug face.

Something beeps. Mr Thorn answers his phone. "Yes, Charlotte?" he says, then pauses to listen. "I see. I'll meet you at security." He turns back to me as he hangs up. "You'll have to excuse me, Molly," he says. "I have something pressing to attend to. I'll leave you in Doctor Plotnikova's capable hands. I look forward to seeing you after the procedure is complete. I'm sure you'll be much more receptive to joining us then."

Thorn leaves the room. That guy is such an asshole. Doctor Plotnikova steps back, apparently finished sticking the metal electrodes on my head.

"You'll feel a slight tingle on your skin," she says.

The doctor nods to one of the two other white lab coats in the room. He presses some buttons on the machine I'm hooked up to and I do feel a tingle on the skin of my head, which soon becomes an uncomfortable burning sensation – a sensation that quickly becomes painful. I grit my teeth and suck in a sharp breath.

"What the –"

I lose the rest of what I was going to say to a painful scream. I try to speak, but I can't seem to remember how to say anything. I feel. My. Strange. Muddled. Can't. Think.

What's happening? Everything I try slips away.

Remy. I squeeze my concentrate. *Help. Please.*

Fight it. We are coming.

"Increase the voltage."

The burning pain increases. All I can hear is the buzzing inside my head. I can feel my thoughts slipping away again. Like bobbing for apples. County fair. Mom and Dad. Miss them.

"Prepare the sevoflurane and the beta serum. Administer both once her neural pathways are clear and ready for recoding."

Almost there Molly.

Sleepy now.

I can feel you leaving, Molly. Keep fighting it.

MoM DAd. OCEAN BeacH. Kitty CATTY. Flying PAPER AirPlaNES. MRS BoWls and VOODOO Dolls. JesSE BessiE bo BESSIE.

"Alright, begin recording. Molly McManus. Subject A184. Subject entering oscillating delta-theta brainwave state in preparation for initial indoctrination. Subject showing strong resistance but beginning to stabilize. Preparing to administer sevoflurane."

Get ready. I'm opening the door.

Loud noise. Bending metal.

"What's happening?"

"Call security!"

"Wells! Shoot her!"

"We can't shoot the doctor!"

"Remy, please. I'm just doing my job. I saved your life when you were injured."

"No! You ruined my life."

Strange zapping sounds. Again and again.

"Remy, stop!"

"Turn that machine off, Wells!"

The pain stops. Thoughts start to come back. Everything gets a bit clearer. Someone is near me, releasing me from the chair. It's Remy.

"Let's get you out of 'ere."

The room comes back into focus. The door has been forced open, buckled inward like it was punched by a neffing giant. One of the doctors must have been standing too close when that happened because he's splayed across the floor, unconscious. The other is face down with a hole shot through the middle of his back. Dead, I think. Doctor Plotnikova is slumped against one of the white benches. The cabinet doors are stained black and red behind her. She's got the same sort of hole punched right through her chest.

Remy releases the strap from around my head and holds out his hand to help me down from the chair. I place my hand in his and he wraps his fingers around it. The touch of his hand is new and yet it feels familiar. I look into his dark eyes; take in his dark skin, the angular lines of his face. He's so different from any of the boys in Little Basin and, if I'm going to have a voice communicating directly into my brain it might as well be one with an accent like his.

"Are you quite finished shooting people, do you think?"

Pulled, thankfully, from my overly doe-eyed thoughts of attraction to this boy in front of me, I turn to the other boy in the room – he's dressed in an Institute jumpsuit too and must be with Remy. His hair is shaggy and he's wearing Harry Potter glasses, which he keeps pushing up his nose. He looks like an absolute geek. No doubt some mega-nerd who got into the Institute during testing. Once I would have thought of him as a Crustie sympathizer. I feel a little sorry for him now, though, like I do for all the Institute students. They must have been through what I nearly went through. Maybe worse. Duped by the Crabs like the rest of mankind.

"We are not free of 'ere yet Wells," Remy says. "If I 'ave to shoot more I will."

"No."

"No?"

"You need to stop."

"When we are out of 'ere, when these people are not a threat, then I will stop." Remy turns to me. "Are you alright?"

"Yeah, thanks." I look at Doctor Plotnikova slumped back against the bench. Maybe it's because I'm still spaced out from whatever they were doing to my brain, but this doesn't seem real. It's like I'm watching a movie play out in front of me – I feel completely disconnected from reality. "Did you really kill her?"

"You've seen what she did to me, what she was going to do to you. Why should I 'ave mercy? Mercy will not get us out of 'ere. It will not 'elp all the others."

I've never spent a lot of time wondering how I'd react to someone getting shot, but I thought I'd feel more than this. I feel nothing. No, that's not true, it's more like I feel empty – as if there should be a feeling there, but there's just not. I don't want to condone murder, but I do agree with Remy – at least, I think I do. What these people have done is wrong, and we need to get out of here. I mean, what would I do if I had the chance to kill the Crusties? Six years of built-up hate is a lot to try and contain.

"Remy and, um, Molly, is it?" I look at the other boy. He pushes his glasses up his nose again. "Hello, hi, I'm Wells." He pats the chest of his jumpsuit. "I'm the one with the top-secret alien conspiracy files burning a hole in my chest, so if it's alright with you, do you think we can go?"

Wow. This guy really is a neffing nerd. He's got a goofy accent too. Australian maybe? I don't know. He looks exactly how I pictured all Institute students would look. Pretty much the exact opposite of Remy.

"Okay," I say. "How do we get the hell out of here?"

THE FIRST THING I notice about Molly is that she's not wearing an Institute uniform. She's dressed in a black t-shirt with a picture of two skulls and the words "Doom Sisters" emblazoned beneath. She's also wearing a pair of black jeans that have been torn on the legs so badly that I can't tell if it's a deliberate fashion statement or if she was attacked by a sentient lawnmower. Her hair is dyed black, bits of what I assume is the natural red showing through, and she's got a nose ring. All in all, she doesn't appear to be a very big fan of color.

"Hello, hi, I'm Wells." I say. "I'm the one with the top-secret alien conspiracy files burning a hole in my chest, so if it's alright with you, do you think we can go?"

Molly just sort of stares at me. I can tell she's evaluating me – either that or she's trying to cast a spell on me. I push my glasses up my nose. I feel a building anxiety. I can't work out why we're risking being captured and causing the deaths of more people to help this girl who looks like she should be causing trouble at a heavy metal concert.

"Okay, how do we get the hell out of here?" Molly says.

I look at Remy. "Alright, you've got her. Now how *do* we get out of here?"

"We 'ead for the surface."

"Yes, that's a promising start," I say, "but what do we do when we're actually up there? How do we get out of the compound? And then how do we get out of the N.E.Z.?"

"We will 'ave to figure it out."

"Figure it out?" I say, exasperated. "I thought you had an escape plan?"

"I never said that, Wells. My plan was to escape. I 'ave not got further than that."

"Oh good," I say. "Good, good, good, terrific."

"Look," Molly says, "whether you've got a plan or not, we can't stay here. We need to get to the surface. Maybe don't stand around arguing like idiots. Come on."

She heads for the door.

"I see why you thought you had to rescue her," I say. "She's really nice."

She ignores me, and Remy and I follow. If I was leading a raid like this in *Swords of the Dungeonmaster* I wouldn't be attempting an escape without some sort of plan. When my guild team escaped from the underground lair of Shaggaroth the Beastly I had each level clearance timed down to a thirty-second window. But now, when it's real life and real soldiers with real alien space rifles, we're just going to wing it. This isn't good for my anxiety.

$$\Omega$$

Luckily the elevator to the surface is just down the hall from the infirmary. I follow Molly and Remy as they run toward the doors. Molly begins bashing the up button. It seems to take an eternity, but finally the metal doors slide open, revealing the glass-walled elevator inside. We get in, and I stare down the corridor, expecting to see SECPOL soldiers appear around the corner like Stormtroopers, but the doors slide closed.

Molly is standing at the panel inside the door, waving her finger indecisively over the numbered buttons. "Which level?"

Remy moves to press the button for the main lobby, but I grab his wrist before he does. He looks at me, a little startled.

"No," I say. "There's no chance we're getting out through the front. There's security everywhere and the tunnel to the surface is sealed by blast doors."

"There's no other way out," Remy says.

I scan the buttons and see "S" for ship. When Mr Thorn took me up to the Xeno ship we walked down that long tunnel with the sealed doorway at the end. I'm sure the metallic hull of the ship was connected to the buildings around it by a tunnel running along the surface of the desert. Maybe there's a way out through there. I press the button and the elevator begins rising. The concrete shaft, metal pipes, and orange lighting flash past us.

"The ship?" Remy asks. "What do you think Wells, we are going to take off and fly away?"

I shake my head. "Not the ship, the tunnel to the ship. It runs along the surface – perhaps there's a way out."

Remy looks at me for a moment, as if evaluating the plausibility of my theory, and then nods.

"The ship?" Molly says in disbelief. "You two are taking me up to the neffing Crustie ship?"

"Yes," I say, "but we won't be going in."

"I hope not," Molly says, "because jank that for a joke. I'm not stepping foot inside that flying Crab tank. You think for –"

She doesn't get to finish her sentence, because the elevator comes to a sudden, jolting stop, midway between floors. The lights on the roof go out and the interior of the elevator is lit only by the orange glow from the lights in the shaft outside. The digital display above the door, which was showing the numbers of the passing floors, has gone dark as well.

"Shit," Molly says.

"Yes," I say. "At least that's something we can agree on."

We stand in silence for a long moment. A single bead of sweat rolls down the middle of my back. Remy tries pressing all the buttons, but they're dead. The SECPOL must have remotely overridden the elevator.

"We're trapped, aren't we?" I say. "Are we trapped? How far from the surface are we?"

"We passed level B12 before we stopped," Remy says. "That would make us fourteen floors below the ship. Maybe we climb?"

Molly is already standing on the silver handrail around the wall and is reaching up, pushing at a panel in the roof. "No good," she says. "I think it's locked."

"I think I can move the elevator," Remy says.

He looks pale, already worn out from using his telekinetic abilities so much. I'm not sure lifting a steel and structural glass box with three people inside is something he's going to be capable of.

"Remy," I say. "Are you sure?"

But his eyes have already gone distant, squinted in concentration and staring ahead at the doors of the elevator as if they were a thousand kilometers away. A straining, creaking sound echoes around us as the elevator is forced upward. I can see ripples pass through the glass itself, waves of undulation as the walls wobble under the power of Remy's mind. The elevator floats up the shaft in eerie silence, occasionally scraping against the side.

"What the jank?" Molly says, gripping the handrail with white-knuckled fingers. "What's happening?"

I realize she hasn't seen him use his abilities. She was completely out of it when we first entered the infirmary.

"Shhh," I say, holding my finger to my lips. "He needs to concentrate. I don't particularly want him to drop us."

It's not lost on me that I'm talking about someone using telekinetic powers like I'm a seasoned veteran, when I was just as freaked out by it only a few hours ago. Of course, it's significantly more terrifying when it's your own body being controlled, but then again, I am in a glass box and the only thing holding me up is Remy's mind.

Two trickles of blood are running down over Remy's lips, one from each nostril. His eyes are drooping closed. As his eyelids begin to flutter and his eyeballs roll back, the elevator drops, a sudden, stomach-lurching fall that stops abruptly as Remy snaps his eyes open again.

"Remy," I say loudly, trying to keep him awake. I don't want him to pass out and drop us. I don't know if the elevator cable could take that sudden application of tensile force.

"What level?" Remy mutters. "What level are we?"

Molly looks out at the black-stenciled numbers that have been passing on the gray concrete walls.

"B2," she says, and then, as the next one appears, "B1."

And before I can say that means we'll reach the lobby next, the dark concrete walls, pipes, and orange lights are replaced by illuminating white as we rush up into the open space of the lobby. I see the human and Xenocrustacean logo on the floor, each holding one side of a book, but it doesn't seem like such an inspiring symbol anymore. I want to know what the fine print in that book says – I don't think humanity is fully across the terms and conditions. Students and staff wander across the white tiled floor, unaware of our escape attempt. The SECPOL at the security checkpoints are all facing the clear elevator shafts though, and as soon as we appear they begin firing bullets and ultra-heated plasma at our glass box.

The bullets ping or make dull thudding sounds as they hit the thick glass, but they don't puncture it – at worst they leave tiny patterns of cracks. The plasma does more damage, hitting with a sound like scorching metal dunked in cold water. It blooms outward in blue bursts, leaving blackened and burned holes in the elevator shaft. Superheated liquid glass leaves dripping runs as it cools. Remy keeps us moving upward fast enough that none of the SECPOL manage to land shots in quick enough succession to burn through both the shaft and the elevator walls, and soon we're safely surrounded by concrete and pipes once more.

"Holy shit," Molly says. "That was neffing intense."

"This is it," I say after a moment, seeing level S coming down the wall beside us.

Remy slows our ascent, stopping the elevator and forcing the doors open. He drops to his knees, his head falling forward. Molly and I grab him and hurry out, pulling him with us. As soon as we've stepped out, the elevator drops. A cacophony of bashing and scraping echoes up the shaft, then there's the almighty twang of steel cable snapping and whipping free. The Institute continues deep underground, but the horrendous sound of the glass elevator hitting the bottom of the shaft and exploding into fragments is loud even from up here. I suppose that answers the question of whether we would have survived the drop.

Remy pushes himself to his hands and knees.

Molly kneels beside him. "You okay?"

He nods, but it's not convincing. He wipes the back of his hand beneath his nose, spreading blood across his cheek rather than clearing it away.

Molly looks down the long corridor toward the doors that lead to the ship. I follow her gaze. There isn't any way out. I was hoping there'd be a door to outside, or a service hatch, or something, but it seems to be completely sealed. She looks at me. "What now, genius?"

"Well," I say, pushing my glasses up and wiping my damp

palms on my jumpsuit. I don't like that she's blaming me for this situation. What were we supposed to do, try escaping through the lobby where an army of SECPOL were waiting? I don't say anything though. Now is not the time to argue. "We need to find a way out. There might be something we can't see, a door or a hatch maybe?"

"I don't see anything."

"Look, this isn't my fault."

"You chose to come up here."

"What would you know? I don't even know who you are!"

Remy begins to stand. "Out the wall," he says. "I can get us a 'ole in the wall."

"You can barely stand," Molly says, "and there's neffing blood coming out of your nose."

"I agree," I say. "There's no telling what could happen if you push yourself too hard. You could kill yourself."

"'Ow is that different to staying 'ere?" Remy says, turning to face the wall. "Let me try."

Remy's face twists and he lets out a primal grunt, exerting all the energy he has left. The trickle of blood becomes a stream, but the wall of the tunnel bulges away from him and then cracks open. It's not the explosive power he used to burst into the Infirmary, but the gap is wide enough for us to get through. Remy begins to move forward – at least, that's what it looks like until I realize he's simply falling. Molly grabs for him but can't catch him in time, and he lands limp on the floor with a heavy thud.

"Shit!" Molly says, dropping to his side.

"Is he breathing?" I ask. "Is he alive?"

"I don't know!"

"Well, can you check? Roll him over."

"Maybe you could neffing help me," Molly snaps, glaring up at me.

"Right. Yeah, okay."

I crouch beside Molly and help her turn Remy onto his back. His legs twist and his arms flop limply as we move him. Panic surges through me. He's dead. I'm sure of it. He talked me into stealing this information and escaping from the Institute, made me an accessory to murder and now he's dead and soon I will be too.

"He's alive!" Molly lifts her head from his chest. "He's breathing."

Relief rushes through me, but it's temporary, quickly disappearing and leaving anxiety in its wake. Remy might be alive, but he's not very useful as an unconscious pile on the floor.

"How do we get him out of here?" I ask. "How are we going to get ourselves out of here, for that matter?"

Molly grabs Remy's arms and starts dragging him around, pulling him toward the hole he opened in the tunnel wall. "Get his legs."

"We're going to carry him?"

"We can't stay here, can we?"

I bend down and pick up Remy's legs. It's amazing how unwieldy an unconscious body is – it's like a collection of sandbags all held together by floppy rubber joints. Molly and I manage to maneuver him through the opening in the tunnel, Molly backing out onto the dry desert ground first, being careful not to hit Remy's head on the jagged, torn metal. I'm about to ask what our next step is when the answer is provided for me. Four black jeeps speed along a nearby road, kicking up sprays of dirt as they tear toward us. Molly and I simultaneously lower Remy onto the ground. It's clear that the next step in our escape plan is, in fact, not to escape.

"Goddammit," Molly mutters.

The black vehicles stop and the doors open. SECPOL officers step out, raising their rifles as they come toward us – all except one. She's wearing the uniform of an Institute student, her dark hair pulled into a tight ponytail. Charlotte.

"Wells," Charlotte says as she walks toward us, "that was all very dramatic, wasn't it? I've got to say, I was surprised when I heard you were involved in all this. Disappointed, too. I thought we were friends. Maybe we could have been more than friends."

I don't answer, but I know I'm blushing.

"Why don't you come with me?" Charlotte says. "We can sort this out."

I know what she means by "sort this out." She means "sort this out" the same way they "sorted out" Sunny, by taking me back and re-indoctrinating me, probably removing all memory of this. That makes me wonder if others have tried to escape before, and they've just been made to forget. Remy said people have misgivings when they first get here, but they're brainwashed away. If Remy hadn't dragged me into this madness, what would have happened? Would I have been indoctrinated again forgetting what I'd seen with Sunny, forgetting my attempt at hacking, forgetting it all?

"Charlotte," I say, "if you really thought we could be more than friends then please, let me explain what happened. *Please.*"

Charlotte chuckles. "Oh, Wells, I'm sorry, I just can't keep this up. Do you honestly think someone like me would be interested in someone like you? I mean please, look at me," she holds her arms out, gesturing for me to take in the view, "then look in the mirror. You are just another nobody lucky enough to be touched by the gift given to us by the Xenos."

My face is hot and I have to swallow down the twisting feeling that rises into my throat. This feels like that time Veronica Winters agreed to go on a date with me. We organized to meet at the cinema at 1 pm on a Saturday, but she never came. Or so I thought. It turned out she did come, and was hiding across the street with her friends, laughing and giggling and taking photos of me waiting. When they finally revealed themselves they told me I should have figured it out ages ago and just gone home. "As if she would be interested in you," Veronica's friend had said. I should have known, but I had such a crush on her I wanted to believe it was true. Now this, even with the danger I'm in, feels exactly the same.

"Gift?" Molly says. "You call this a gift? You call a virus that kills so many people a gift? You call neffing experiments on people a gift?"

"Molly McManus," Charlotte says. "Mr Thorn sent me the report on you. You're a rebellious one, aren't you? Not really Institute material, I wouldn't have thought, but your levels are off the charts. Maybe they can examine your brain under a microscope. I'm sure you'd be useful that way."

"Levels?" Molly says. "What are you talking about?"

"Take them into custody please," Charlotte says.

A pulsing sound fills the air. The SECPOL turn to see an aircraft swing out from behind the cover of a building. I recognize it immediately, having watched videos and read all about them online. It's a fluxer. A human air-vehicle using anti-gravity flux engines developed from Xeno technology. It's insanely maneuverable, completely ignoring the laws of flight, because it doesn't rely on aerodynamics at all. It flies toward us, low and fast, swooping over the top of the SECPOL and their vehicles, then turning sharply and floating down over us. I thought it must be cover for the SECPOL, but oddly, it's facing them and descending down into the space between us, almost protectively. The look on Charlotte's face suggests that she doesn't understand this turn of events either.

Without warning, the fluxer begins firing at the SECPOL. Large bolts of plasma slam into the ground, throwing them backward. A burst of plasma hits one of the jeeps. Then another. They explode in concussive fireballs, popping up into the air and slamming back down, wheels ejecting out sideways like champagne corks. Charlotte starts shouting, but her words are lost in the chaos as she's thrown to the side. I lift my arms over my face protectively – even from here I can feel the intense heat of the explosion. Those SECPOL not already dead or knocked off their feet by the blasts begin firing. Their plasma bolts hit the fluxer, but I can't see how much damage they do.

Even as it floats in front of us, continuing to fire on the SECPOL, a ramp drops down at the rear.

"Hurry up!" The voice from inside is barely audible over the fluxer's engines, its plasma fire, and the answering fire and shouts of the SECPOL. "Get in!"

I look at Molly to see if she heard the voice too, trying to work out whether doing what it says is a terrible idea or our only hope. She seems to be struggling with the same thing.

"Go," she says, grabbing Remy's arms again.

I lift Remy's legs and we carry him up onto the fluxer's ramp. The ramp starts closing when we're only halfway up. We manage to slide Remy onto the floor as the ramp seals shut. It's a small space, four seats on each side, set back against the walls. In front of us, in clear view, is the cockpit of the fluxer. There are two seats in the cockpit but only one of them is occupied. The pilot, his hands still on the controls, turns to looks over his shoulder at us. He's wearing a helmet, the mirrored visor pulled down, obscuring his face.

"Hold on to something," he says.

The suggestion is moot – he doesn't give us any time at all before pulling hard on the controls. The fluxer lurches violently to the side and pitches up. Remy slides across the floor and Molly and I fall in a heap against the seats on one side. I grab the harness hanging down over one of the seats and manage to pull myself into an almost sitting position. As the fluxer levels out, I manage to slip into the seat. Molly, two seats down from me, has done the same.

"Buckle in," the pilot says. "I'mma get you out of here."

"Who the neffing hell are you?" Molly asks.

The pilot turns to look back at us.

"We are Omega," is all he says before turning away.

SHIT. I exhale heavily and drop back against the seat. I can't believe we managed to escape. This whole thing is neffing crazy. As soon as it's over I'm getting the jank away from Little Basin forever – whether Uncle Art wants me to or not.

"Who are you?" I ask the pilot. "Why did you save us?"

"We are Omega," he says again, but this time he doesn't bother turning around.

"Yes, right, I heard that, but I have no idea what you're talking about."

The pilot doesn't respond.

"Where are we going?"

"You'll find out soon enough," he says, and it's obvious that's the end of the conversation.

Remy is still lying unconscious on the floor. Wells is sitting two chairs down from me, staring straight ahead. His eyes are red, his glasses fogging, and his lips squeezed into a just-managing-to-hold-back-the-tears face. I know I wouldn't have escaped if it wasn't for Remy, but Wells had a part in my rescue too, however disagreeable he may have been.

"Thanks for helping get me out of there, Wells."

"No worries," he says, but he doesn't look at me.

"That Charlotte girl," I say, "I saw her when I first climbed the fence. Remy was trying to escape from her, I'm sure of it."

Wells doesn't reply. He turns his head away trying to hide the emotion on his face.

"You know what I think about Charlotte?" I say.

"What?" Wells says.

"I think she's a bitch."

He laughs. It's just a short chuckle, but it's something. "Yeah, I guess she is."

"That whole place is designed to screw with your head, Wells. Her included. But you're out of there now."

As if to call me a liar, a low whooping alarm starts hooting at us from the cockpit.

"Are you strapped in?" the pilot calls. "I'm gonna need to pull some evasive maneuvers."

"Why?" Wells asks. "What's happening?"

"We've got three other fluxers in pursuit," the pilot replies. The warning alarm changes from low whoops to a high-pitched squeal. "Shit, they've got us locked. Strap in."

I slip my arms through the harness on the seat but don't manage to do it up before the fluxer rolls over. Remy slides across the floor, slamming into the base of the seats opposite.

"Missiles away," the pilot calls from the cockpit. "Hang on!"

The pilot wrenches the controls in the other direction, and Remy slides back across the floor as I'm slammed into the seat. Out the corner of my eye, through the front window, I see a trail of white smoke whiz past us and away into the open sky. A missile? They're actually shooting neffing missiles at us? My weight lifts off the seat and my stomach lurches as the front window fills with sandy desert. We're diving straight down.

Whoop whoop. "Pull up. Pull up." *Whoop whoop.* "Pull up.

Pull up." An electronic voice starts over the whining of the missile alert alarms.

"Holy heck!" Wells says. "Holy heck! Holy heck!"

"If you're going to swear," I yell at him, "*fucking* do it properly!"

The pilot finally listens to the computer's warnings and pulls the fluxer out of its dive. I drop back into my seat with a lung-emptying slam. Next to me Wells lands heavily, half out of his harness. But Remy gets it the worst. He lands on the floor, his head flicking back and hitting the checker-plate with a crack. If he wasn't already unconscious that surely would've been enough to knock his lights out.

The sound of an explosion roars over everything.

"What was that?!" Wells yells to the pilot.

"It's okay," the pilot says. "The missile hit the ground. We're okay." But then he lets out a groan of frustration, maybe even anger. "Two more missiles – no, three more. I just need to get us a little further. They won't engage outside the N.E.Z."

The fluxer rolls again and I grab the harness with both hands. Remy's body rolls over on the floor. Wells lets out a moan. Another missile flies past. The pilot levels us out, but we only stay that way for a second before rolling sharply the other way.

Remy's body flops over. There's blood on the back of his head. I take the chance while the fluxer is level to slip out of my harness and grab him. I try to lift him onto the seat opposite me.

"What are you doing?" Wells says. "Strap yourself in."

"Help me!" I yell. "He's taking a beating."

I slip my hands under Remy's armpits and manage to get him into a sort of sitting position, but I'm never going to get him onto the seat by myself. The fluxer jags to the side again, causing me to stumble. I grab hold of the seat frame to stop myself from falling.

"Shit, Wells, help me."

Wells lets out a huff, but slips out of his harness to help.

"Grab his other arm," I say. "Okay, ready, on three. One. Two. *Three*."

We both heave at the same time and somehow manage to get Remy onto the seat. We work quickly, slipping his arms through the harness and snapping it closed.

"Get strapped in!" the pilot calls.

We scramble back to our seats and get harnessed in.

"Oh god," the pilot says, which isn't what I want to hear from the cockpit. "Brace for impact."

We roll over to the right again and pull up hard. Suddenly I weigh so much I can't lift my arms. We turn the other way. Then back. Dive. Pull up in a loop. It's like being on the world's most intense rollercoaster.

An explosion engulfs everything. There's an enormous jolt, and a sudden roar of sound so intense that my hearing becomes nothing but a loud ring. My head, arms, and legs are thrown around, slamming against the seat and bouncing uncontrollably. I hear Wells shouting something, but I don't know what.

The fluxer flips upside down and right way up and upside down again. There's daylight out the front. Sky. Ground. Sky. Ground. We land on the roof, roll all the way over and onto the roof again. The chaos seems to continue long after we hit the ground. It's like being inside a Doom Sisters drum kit, or, I suppose, like being in *a neffing aircraft crash*.

When everything stops I'm hanging from the harness in the seat. I open my eyes – I don't even know when I closed them. The inside of the fluxer is filled with dust and smoke. I flex my fingers and toes, feeling for pain. I mean, I'm covered in pain, but it all seems minor. Nothing bad. Nothing broken. Remy is hanging from his harness across from me, his arms and legs angled motionless toward the roof. He looks like a puppet tangled in its strings. Blood is dripping from his short hair. Wells is hanging in his seat too. He suddenly lurches. Tilting his head back, he vomits, just upside-down pukes, coughing and sputtering as he tries to stop it running into his nostrils. Gross.

Worst. Rollercoaster. Ever.

"You okay?" I ask.

He nods.

"Can you get down?"

He nods again.

I twist the clip on the front of my harness. It's jammed. I jiggle it. Neffing thing. Just as I start to swear, it comes away with a click and I drop, hitting the roof with a slam, landing on my shoulders and hitting the back of my head.

"Shit. Neffing crap."

I rub my head as I stand on what used to be the roof. I'm looking straight out at the Nevada desert. The front of the fluxer is gone. Pilot and all. I wonder if he's alright, but then realize of course he's not. If that's where the missile hit us, he would've been blown to pieces.

There's a thump as Wells manages to release himself from his harness.

"Ow!"

I turn and see him noticing the front of the fluxer too.

"Oh man," he says. One lens in his glasses is smashed. A cut above his eye is bleeding, and he's blackened with dust and smoke, but he doesn't look too badly hurt either. "Oh man. Oh man. Oh man. We're screwed now, aren't we? They're going to catch us again."

"Just...just relax," I say. "Let's get Remy down and keep moving. Look," I point out through the hole in the front of the fluxer, "there's the fence. We're nearly out of the N.E.Z. We just need to make it there."

He nods. "Okay."

"You support his body and I'll release the harness."

Wells puts his arm awkwardly around Remy's shoulders, but

when I unclip the harness he still drops heavily to the ground. I shoot Wells a look.

"What?" he says. "He's heavy."

"Grab his legs."

I pick up Remy's arms and we start carrying him out of the fluxer, stepping carefully over shards of metal, smoking pipes, and frayed electrical wires that spark in bursts of yellow, white, and blue. Small fires have started among the wiring and metal, and some of the low grass around the crash site has started to burn, too. My ears are still ringing. Everything smells of smoke and fire and burning plastic.

As we move away, Wells turns to look back at the crash site. "I think," he says, stopping to cough. "I think it's lucky we were so close to the ground."

"Yeah," I say.

We keep hauling Remy along through the dusty dirt and dry grass before I see Wells' eyes go wide.

"There's someone at the fence," he says.

He's right. There's a pick-up parked off the side of the gravel road that runs around the fence. Not just any pick-up – a faded red pick-up with a strip of chrome down the side. It's Jesse's dad's pick-up. The truck door opens and even from here I recognize him stepping out, unmistakable in his blue polo shirt with the collar popped up. Jesse. How many times have I told him to put his collar down? Idiot. But what a wonderful idiot.

"Molly!" he calls as he runs to the fence. "Molly!"

"Jesse!" I shout back.

"You know him?" Wells says.

"Yeah," I say. "Yeah, I do. He'll get us out of here."

The thought of Jesse out there is enough to make Remy suddenly seem lighter. Maybe we'll get out of this after all. My excitement is ripped away in a moment of shock though, as I feel myself walk backward into something solid.

"What is that?" Wells says, his eyes wide behind his smashed glasses.

I lower Remy to the ground. My stomach sinks even before I reach my hand out – I know what this is. Sure enough, when my fingers touch the invisible wall they're surrounded by crackles of blue.

"Jank. It's the force field."

"Force field?" Wells says.

"Yeah, there's some sort of force field around this place and we're on the wrong side of it."

"Molly," Jesse calls from the fence.

"I'm stuck!"

"Hold on," Jesse says as he climbs back into the truck. "I'm coming to get you."

The truck splutters, turns over two or three times, then comes to life with a roar and a burst of smoke from the exhaust. Jesse reverses the truck back onto the road and stops with it facing the fence. Through the windshield I see him pull his seatbelt down, clipping it in place.

"Oh shit Jesse," I say. "You're neffing not."

But he is. He grips the steering wheel and revs the engine of the pick-up once, twice, three times. The engine roars and the rear wheels spin on the gravel before gripping, sending the pick-up lurching forward. The truck bounces off the road, across the dry grass, and spears into the fence. There's the sound of twisting, rending metal as the truck bursts through – it sounds like Mrs Bowls' fingernails on a chalkboard as the wire scrapes along the cab of the vehicle.

"Slow down!" I yell, but there's no way he can hear me. I thrust my hand out in front of me again, planting my palm on the force field so that it lights up and Jesse can see the invisible barrier. The wheels of the pick-up lock as Jesse slams on the brakes and turns the wheel. The vehicle slides to a stop a short distance from the force field and Jesse jumps from the cab, running toward me.

"Molly," he says, reaching out and tentatively touching the force field, then pulling his hand back as it crackles, as if it might shock him. "Are you alright? I saw the fluxer crash."

"I'm okay. What are you even doing here Jesse?"

"No one would do anything. I told the police about what happened last night but they said they don't have jurisdiction inside the N.E.Z."

"Did you tell Uncle Art?"

"Of course," Jesse says. "You were taken by the SECPOL, what was I supposed to do? Plus, he works for them, so I thought he might be able to do something, get them to let you out."

"Did he lose his shit?"

"Not really. He looked worried, but he just said he'd handle it and went off to call someone."

"Well," I say, "he didn't do a very good job of handling it."

"I didn't know what to do so I came out here. I've been driving up and down the fence all night trying to see something."

"You've been out here all night?"

"Of course. I wasn't going to leave you."

The air fills with the sound of fluxers.

"Um, here they come," Wells says.

Two fluxers drop to hover a short distance away. The ramp from the first fluxer lowers and SECPOL soldiers come stomping out, clutching rifles. They move slowly, clearly not in a rush. They know they've got us trapped. We're cornered against the stupid force field.

"Jesse," I say, turning back to him. "Get out of here okay."

"No," he says, putting his hand flat against the force field. "No way. I left you last time, I'm not going to do it again."

I know I'm not going to be able to convince him this time, so instead I put my hand on the other side of the force field. Our

WE ARE OMEGA / 109

palms are together, surrounded by crackling blue lightning. Stupid loyal Jesse.

I turn back to see the SECPOL standing in a semicircle, facing us. The ramp has lowered from the other fluxer and more SECPOL are coming out, along with that bitch Charlotte and the villainous Mr Thorn. Thorn walks out beyond the circle of SECPOL, Charlotte trotting beside him like an obedient dog. Thorn raises his hands, palms facing us, as if somehow that's going to convince us he's not a threat. His beady eyes take in the four of us – me, Wells, Remy on the ground, and Jesse on the other side of the force field.

"Mr Marsden, Miss McManus," he says. "And who is this?"

"Jesse Hill," Jesse says. "You let my friend out of there."

"Jesse," I say. "Don't."

"Ah, Jesse Hill," Mr Thorn says. "Yes, of course, I did some research on you when Miss McManus came to join us here at the Institute."

"I didn't join anything," I say, but he ignores me.

"Jesse Hill. Age seventeen. Student at Little Basin High School. Average scores on testing. No record of anything exemplary anywhere, it seems. Jesse Hill, a nobody."

Jesse slams a closed fist against the force field, sending a wave of crackling blue out from the point of impact. "I'm not a nobody! If you weren't hiding behind that force field I'd show you that."

"Miss Yorke," Mr Thorn says, "would you mind?"

"I'd come in there an –" Jesse voice is cut off mid-sentence in a choking click. He grabs at his throat.

"What are you doing to him?!" I shout.

"He can breathe," Charlotte says. "I've just silenced his rather annoying chatter."

"I'll silence your annoying chatter, you bitch," I say.

"Alright, alright, please," Mr Thorn says, raising his hands again. "There seems to have been a misunderstanding here."

"No misunderstanding," I say. "We know what you're doing in there. We know about the experiments and the weird powers. You're turning teenagers into super-soldiers to help with the Crustie invasion and we've got proof, right Wells?"

"Yes," he says, pushing his fractured glasses up his nose. "Though perhaps we shouldn't have shared that piece of information, Molly."

I look at him sideways. Geez. At least try to act like we've got our neffing shit together.

"It's alright," Mr Thorn says. "We know about the data you stole. I have to say, I'm impressed. That security is not easy to breach. I see we were right in selecting you for the Institute, Wells. Your computing talents will not be wasted with us. I am disappointed, though. You promised you would never do something like that again."

"I needed to know the truth," Wells says.

"Yes, yes," Mr Thorn says, "don't we all want the truth? Aren't we all truth-seekers in one way or another? Well, let me share some truth with you. Your assertions are wrong. There is no invasion. We are working toward mutual habitation – the betterment of humanity is the goal, just as we have always claimed."

"How many people have died because of those things in there?" I say. "What makes you think anyone wants them living among us?"

"No one is denying the tragedy of the plague, Miss McManus, but the Xenocrustaceans are unable to leave our planet, so we are working toward a better world together."

"Yeah, I've heard the advertising."

"Consider the gifts you have. You have seen what Remy can do with his mind. Wells, you have an innate understanding of computers far beyond other humans. And Molly, I have seen your potential. Don't you wish to unlock it?"

"Nope," I say.

"I'm not going back in there," Wells says. "I'm sorry Mr Thorn, but I'm just not. I'm..." He adjusts his glasses again. "I'm dropping out of the Institute."

Mr Thorn laughs. "There is no *dropping out*, Mr Marsden. If you do not wish to return with us then that is a shame, but we haven't invested extensively in you yet. Charlotte?"

Charlotte turns to one of the SECPOL. "Give Wells your pistol."

The soldier pulls a pistol from the holster on his hip and steps forward. He holds it out, grip first, to Wells. Wells looks from the soldier to me, and then to Charlotte.

"Take it, Wells," Charlotte says.

He shakes his head.

"I said take it," Charlotte almost growls.

Wells reaches out and grabs hold of the pistol.

"Wells, what are you doing?" I ask.

"I...I can't help it."

"Now, put it to your head," Charlotte instructs.

Wells holds the gun to his head, pressing the barrel against his temple. Sweat is dripping from his forehead. His eyes are wide and glistening with tears. He's neffing terrified.

"Stop it," I say. "Just stop it!"

"You must understand you are now at a critical decision point in your life, Mr Marsden. You can decide to return to the Institute, or you can decide to *drop out,* as you say. The consequences should be fairly self-explanatory."

"Just let us go," I say.

"No," Mr Thorn says, the cold abruptness of the answer more terrifying than anything he's said yet.

"I'll give you the tablet," Wells says. "That's got all the data I downloaded. You can have it."

"None of you are leaving."

"I'm not going back," I say. "None of us are."

"Please," Wells says, his voice shuddering. "Don't kill me."

"Grab them," Mr Thorn says.

The SECPOL begin moving forward with their guns raised.

"Molly!" Jesse yells from behind me. He bangs on the force field with his fist, blue light crackling with each strike.

I'm not going back. I'm not going back in there so they can mess with my mind again. The SECPOL are almost on us. Wells, still under Charlotte's control, pulls back the hammer of the gun.

"No!" I yell.

A thudding grows inside my head. It's like a building pressure, anger and pressure and fear all inside me. Something's about to burst.

"You're not taking us!"

And as I yell, the pressure in my mind is unleashed, and something explodes out from me. I can't explain the sound. It's like being in a storm of silence. Like a booming, roaring, exploding sound all wrapped up in quiet. For a moment I can't see. Everything is a blur, like heat haze over a desert highway but travelling away from me. And it's taking everything with it.

The wave flattens the grass. It blows dust away in chaotic swirls. It smashes into the SECPOL and they're thrown backward, rolling and sliding along the ground. Charlotte and Mr Thorn are tossed like fabric dolls, flying up into the air and then hitting the ground and rolling over and over. Even the SECPOL's fluxers are driven backward, leaving deep grooves in the ground. The force field lights up with a blue that suddenly bursts in shards of vanishing light, like it's being torn open. Despite the carnage, Wells stands beside me and Remy is lying there, both of them untouched by whatever I just did. Because it was me, I know it was. I just have no neffing idea what happened.

I DROP the pistol with a sudden jerk and it falls to the ground. The thought of how powerless I was, how close I came to squeezing the trigger and ending my life makes my stomach churn. I examine my hands, turning them over. I don't know what I'm looking for exactly – perhaps checking that my skin hasn't been blown off, or that I haven't been liquefied. I watched the shimmering wave, like a blast of energy, emanate from Molly as she shouted. I felt it pass over me, the pressure buffeting my ears, like driving down the highway with the windows open. The blast of power tossed the SECPOL into the air and yet Molly, Remy and I are untouched.

I turn to look at her. "How did you do that?"

She's wide-eyed and shaking. "I don't know. What the hell?" She spins to face me. "Seriously, what the hell?"

"You have powers," I say, "like Remy. That's why they're so keen on keeping you here."

"Molly!"

The boy Molly knows, Jesse, is walking toward us, right through where, just moments ago, there was an impenetrable force field. Whatever Molly did has destroyed the force field, or at least temporarily disrupted it.

"Jesse!" Molly turns to her friend and the two of them embrace.

"What's going on?" Jesse asks as they pull apart. "Are you okay?"

Molly nods.

"Molly," Jesse says, "did you see what you just did? You've got superpowers!"

"This is not a good thing," Molly says.

"Okay, sure," Jesse says, but he doesn't look convinced. "And who's this?"

"Wells," I say. "Wells Marsden."

"You're an Institute student?"

I nod, then add, "Probably not anymore."

"And this?" Jesse says, looking down at Remy, still unconscious on the ground in front of us.

"This is Remy," Molly says. "He's the boy we saw hit the force field."

"We should get moving," I say.

"Right," Jesse says. "Sure, let's get out of here. But you're okay?" he asks Molly again. "You're really okay? Your leg?"

"I'm fine," she says. She holds up her leg, twisting it for Jesse to see. Below the cut-off remnants of her jeans a pink line runs from a few inches below her knee to just above her ankle, right down the inside of her calf muscle. It looks like a freshly healed scar.

"Oh my god, look at it, it's completely healed," Jesse says. "Is that superpowers too?"

"No," Molly says sternly. "They used some crab stuff."

Jesse looks up from Molly's leg to meet her eyes. "I was really worried about you, you know. I'm not sure what I'd do if something happened to you."

"It's okay, Jesse," Molly says. "I'm really okay."

Remy stirs.

"Remy," Molly says. "Can you get up? Can you walk?"

Remy's eyes seem glazed and distant, but he manages a weak nod and sits up. "I'll be alright."

Molly and I reach down and help him to his feet.

"Let's get him to the truck," Molly says.

Jesse nods. "Okay, come on."

Molly and I put Remy's arms around our shoulders, supporting him as we head for the pick-up. We help him into the back seat, then Molly shuts the door and hurries around and climbs into the seat beside him. "Come on you two, get in," she says.

I open the door to climb in the passenger seat. "I'm driving, pal," Jesse says. I see the steering wheel and realize my mistake. It's on the opposite side in America. I push up my glasses. "Sorry," I say, feeling stupid, and hurry to the other side.

Jesse starts the engine, tilts the rear-view mirror so he can see Molly sitting in the back, then hits the accelerator hard, turning the wheel sharply. We spin around on the loose soil then bump up onto the road, sliding in the gravel. Jesse fights to keep us straight as we fishtail along the road. Eventually he manages to get control, and we speed away from the N.E.Z.

I unzip my jumpsuit and pull out the tablet, staring down at it. I know the world doesn't want to think ill of the Xenos, but we need to spread the truth about what's really happening inside the Institute. The information on this tablet might be key to our safety, too. If we can make it public, the SECPOL won't be able to come after us. I flip open the cover and my heart sinks. The screen is shattered. I close it and I slip it back inside my jumpsuit before anyone else can see.

"You know this sounds crazy, right?" Jesse says after Wells and I explain everything that's happened.

"Yes, I know it sounds crazy Jesse, but you know what else is crazy? Neffing aliens landing on Earth."

"So what does all this actually mean?"

"It means I'm going to get as far away from this place as I can."

"It's an invasion," Wells says. "The Xenocrustaceans can't take over the planet on their own, so they've started recruiting teenagers under the guise of accepting them into an elite school, but instead they're turning them into telekinetic super-soldiers."

"But they never did anything to me," I say. "Why am I a freak?"

"EV-B," Remy says. "That's what gives you powers."

"Why don't I have powers then?" Wells asks, twisting around in the front seat to look at us. He actually sounds disappointed. Jank. He can have my powers. I don't neffing want them.

"You do, Wells," Remy answers. "Normally they don't become active until you 'ave been at the Institute for some time.

They 'ave to bring them out. I 'ave never known them to just 'appen, like with you Molly."

"You had EV-B?" Jesse says from the front, looking back at me in the rear-view mirror. "You never told me you had EV-B!"

"It was before I came to Little Basin."

"Still, that seems like the sort of thing you tell your best friend."

"I don't like talking about it."

"Yeah, okay, but this is me."

"Can we not argue, Jesse?"

"What?" he says. "I'm not arguing I'm just...I think I've got the right to be a little freaked out by all this." He glances up into the mirror again before returning his gaze to the windscreen. "So what, you think the aliens crashed, accidentally released a virus, realized what the virus was doing to kids, decided they wanted to take over the world, and started the Institute? They've been here for six years. It's not an invasion. If it was an invasion they wouldn't have crashed in the middle of the Nevada desert, and they probably would've started actually *invading* by now."

"I don't know, Jesse. How am I supposed to know what's going on? I just want to forget all this shit and drive to Canada or something."

"You can't," Wells says.

"I can't what?"

"You can't just run away. We need to get this information out there. We need to warn everyone."

"No," I say. "*I* don't have to do anything. If you want to do that, you go for it. But me, as soon as we get far enough away, I'm going off on my own."

"I didn't want this either," Wells says, "but now I'm carrying what might be the only evidence of what's happening. We should stick together. We should at least try and warn people."

"Look, Wells," I say. "I don't even know you. I mean, I'm glad we all got out of there and everything, but all this warning the world stuff, I'm not down for that."

Molly. I agree with Wells. I hear Remy's voice in my mind. *We are free of that place now, but there are others who are not. We 'ave to warn people what might be coming.*

I spin to look at Remy. "Nope. It's not happening. And don't try and get all inside my head as if that will help."

The inside of the truck is quiet. The long silence is punctuated by the rumble of the old engine under the hood and the rattle of pretty much everything inside. It's Wells who eventually speaks.

"Maybe they just *wanted* it to look like a crash?"

Jesse looks at him. "Don't you think world leaders would have thought of that?"

"I don't know." Wells snaps back. Then calms himself and pushes his glasses up his nose. "Whatever's happening inside the N.E.Z. is not what the rest of the world thinks. That's enough reason to be concerned."

"I agree with Molly," Jesse says. "I don't think you should get involved."

"'Ave you ever 'eard the saying the only thing necessary for the triumph of evil is for good men to do nothing?" Remy asks.

"Yes, but going up against them is stupid," Jesse says.

"No one 'as asked you to do anything," Remy says. "You are not part of this."

"This is my neffing truck!"

"Look," Wells says, inserting the word delicately to break the tension. "First, let's just decide where we're going, okay?"

"Molly's house I guess," Jesse says.

"Nope," I say. "Hell no."

"What? Why not?" Jesse says.

"Uncle Art works for the SECPOL. Who knows which side

he's on? Jank, he might even be part of it, taking kids to get experimented on or something. We can't trust him."

Jesse plants his foot on the brake. The truck slows and he guides it to a stop on the gravel at the side of the road. He jams the column shift into park and turns in his seat. "So if you don't want to go home, where do you want to go?"

Wells turns to look nervously out the back window. "I don't think we should be stopping."

"Well, I need to know where we're going," Jesse says.

I look at him. "I don't know where to go Jesse, but I don't think we can trust Uncle Art."

"He's your uncle. He's worried about you."

"Worried about me finding out the truth maybe."

"No," Jesse says. "I spoke to him. He really didn't seem like he's in on this."

"We don't know that," I say. "He said he needed to go and talk to someone, right? So, he probably talked to Thorn. I bet that's what he did. He's probably the one who told him everything about me, and you too."

"I don't think so," Jesse says, "but let's say you're right, where do we go then?"

"I don't have anywhere else to go," I admit. "But you do. You always say you should visit your nan in Phoenix."

"What?" Jesse says. "No way. We're not bringing my family into this."

"Whatever we do," Remy says, "can we 'urry? I do not like sitting around like rabbits."

"What?" Jesse says. "Why are you talking about rabbits?"

"We'll just use it as a stop, Jesse," I say. "We'll get to Arizona, drop these two somewhere before we even get to your nan's. They won't even know where it is."

"You're just going to abandon us?" Wells says.

"Yes," I say. "I told you, I'm not getting involved in this jank. We'll get far enough away and then you and Remy can go off and warn the world or whatever. I'm going to join the circus or something."

"Molly..." Jesse starts, but I fix him with a pleading stare.

"Please, Jesse," I say. "I can't stay here."

He sighs. "Alright, we'll head for Phoenix, but I just want to make it clear I think this is a bad idea."

"I knew you wouldn't let me down."

Ω

Little Basin is a small place and the N.E.Z. fence is only ten minutes' drive past the outskirts of town. It isn't long before we're heading onto main street, crossing the train tracks and rounding the corner past the shops and the supermarket. It's early on a Saturday morning and the streets are quiet. A few people are out in their oversized pick-up trucks or riding bikes to weekend jobs. No one gives us a second look. Even so, I keep thinking that any second I'll hear the whoop of a siren and see the flash of red and blue behind us. It doesn't happen though.

We blow through town and start down the long road north, following the signs for Route 50. But before we're even halfway to the interstate, Jesse notices something in the rear-view mirror.

"Someone's following us."

I turn to look out the back window. "Jank." A black SUV has appeared behind us. Its windows are tinted almost as dark as its paint. It grows rapidly in size as it roars toward us.

"Jesse, you need to go faster."

"Do you know how old this truck is?"

"Step on it, Jesse!"

The engine of the pick-up whines as Jesse pushes his foot flat to the floor.

"They're gaining on us," I say.

"Holy heck! Holy heck!"

"Wells! Shut up!"

The SUV, much more powerful than our rusting clunker, reaches us and swings out to pass. It gets in front of us, then swerves across into our lane. Its taillights light up red as it brakes hard. Jesse has no choice but to do the same. He swerves back toward the other lane, but the SUV anticipates this and turns, coming to a stop and blocking the road. Jesse slams his palms down on the steering wheel as we come to a stop a short distance from the dark vehicle.

"Just back up!" I shout.

Jesse puts the truck in reverse, but the window of the SUV is already down and a rifle has extended out. A blast of blue hits our front left wheel just as Jesse starts reversing. There's a loud burst as the tire explodes. The whole front of the truck drops and we stop with a horrendous squeal of metal on tarmac. Now we're neffed.

The SUV's door opens and the blue fatigues of a SECPOL officer appear. The SECPOL wears a cap that matches his uniform, and dark sunglasses. He's also got a black balaclava on, so his face is completely hidden. He looks like a walking shadow. He stands with his bulky alien rifle held casually in front of him. I wait for the rest of the squad to unload from the vehicle like a group of military clowns, but no one does. It's just him.

"Everyone alright in there?" he calls. "Sorry about that. I need you to exit the vehicle and come with me. It's safe. We are Omega."

We are Omega. It's the same thing the pilot in the fluxer said, but this time I know who it is. I recognize the voice.

"Molly," Jesse says in warning as I open the door and climb out.

The SECPOL lowers his rifle, pulls off his hat and sunglasses, and lifts the balaclava. It's Uncle Art. I hear the other doors of the truck squeal open behind me. Jesse, Wells, and Remy all climb out.

I look at Uncle Art with a lump in my throat, unwanted emotion welling inside me. I feel happy to see him, terrified of him, furious at him. Uncle Art's face is still. He doesn't speak.

"Well," I say, unable to take the tension any longer, "are you going to say anything?"

"What do you want me to say, Molly? You really screwed up this time. Climbing the N.E.Z. fence, what the hell were you thinking?"

"I don't know. We were just climbing a stupid fence. I didn't expect any of this to happen."

"You never expect consequences though, do you? You never take responsibility for your actions. You have no idea what you might have jeopardized."

"Of course." I lean my head back and shout at the sky. "Did you hear that, everyone? Uncle Art's job with the SECPOL is more important than me!"

"You don't understand."

"You're right," I say, the anger pulsing through my veins, "I don't understand!" We've argued about his job with the SECPOL more times than I can remember, but this feels like another level. It's all pouring out – this is the argument we've been building up to all this time. "I don't understand how you can work for the *fucking* Crabs when it was the *fucking* Crabs that killed Mom and Dad. You don't even care!"

"Your Mom was my sister, Molly. Of course I care. Don't you *dare* say I don't care. I took you in and tried to raise you the best I could, and it hasn't been easy." He points a finger at me. "*You* haven't made it easy Molly. You're too stubborn and you're just a fucking kid, you don't get what's going on here. Nothing's as black and white as you would goddamn like it to be!"

Uncle Art has been mad at me before. He's yelled before. But

I've never heard him like this. We're both quiet for a moment. My face is hot and my eyes are wet. I can sense Remy, Wells, and Jesse behind me, watching in silence, trying not to breathe. They're probably wishing they weren't here right now. Jank, I wish *I* wasn't here.

"I could have sent you to a boarding school, you know that don't you?" Uncle Art says. "I had the application forms and everything, but I thought it would be better if you had at least some family. I thought I could raise you like my own daughter, but maybe I was wrong."

"Yeah," I say. "Maybe you were. Maybe you should've sent me away, then at least I wouldn't have to live with a traitor who works for my parents' killers."

Even as I spout as much vitriol as I can muster, I can't help but think about what he's saying, that he wanted to treat me like his daughter. I've wanted that too. I just don't get how he can work for them.

"Things are happening Molly," Uncle Art says, suddenly calmer. "Things you don't understand."

"Oh, I understand," I say, my voice as icy as I can make it. "I understand what's going on. You've chosen the Crusties over your own family. I wish it was you who died."

Uncle Art is quiet for a long time. "So do I," he says. "I wish for that all the time, but I didn't." He raises his head to look at me again. "So instead I'm with Omega."

"What the neffing shit is Omega?" I yell. "What is everyone talking about?"

"You need to come with me. All of you."

"No," I say. "We're not going back to be brainwashed or whatever."

"Molly, I'm trying to protect you."

"Like you protect all the students at the Institute? I don't want that sort of protection."

"What is it that you think you know, Molly?"

"I know there's weird shit going on in that place and I know the SECPOL are involved. I know what you people do to the students there."

"Molly, whatever you think my involvement is, I can assure you that's not the case. Come with me and we'll talk about this."

I shake my head. "No way."

I'm not going to do what he wants. Who knows what might happen? Next thing I know I'll wake up back inside the neffing compound, or in Guantanamo Bay or something.

"Alright," he says, exhaling. He glances around, checking our surroundings like he's worried about being watched, even though we're in the middle of nowhere. "You can trust Omega. It's a group of people who also believe something sinister is happening. I've been working with them since we moved here. My job as SECPOL is cover, always has been, a chance to get inside the enemy's lair, though I suspect I'm compromised now. You know how close I was to your mom, Molly. Do you think I'd just let that go?"

I don't answer. I don't know what to believe.

"As soon as Jesse told me what happened I contacted other Omega agents inside the SECPOL and begged them to get you out."

"The pilot," I say.

"Yes. Anthony," Uncle Art says. "He was a good man, and a damn good pilot. He must have given them a run for their money."

"He did," Wells says from behind me. I turn to look at him. He looks at the ground. "Sorry."

"Molly, please come with me," Uncle Art says. "Omega is your only chance at safety. These people won't stop chasing you, and it's not just the SECPOL you need to worry about."

"I just want to get away from all this," I say.

"Where are you going to go? Jesse's family? His nan?" Uncle Art must notice my surprise because he adds, "It won't take them much longer to figure it out than it took me. "

I turn and look at the others. They don't say anything. They're waiting for me to decide. I look back at Uncle Art.

"I just want to keep you safe," he says. "I promise you that."

My eyes grow hot and my vision swims with tears. "So what?" I say, fighting the lump in my throat. "You've been lying to me? The whole time?"

"I was trying to keep you away from it," Uncle Art says. "Believe me, I've wanted to tell you. Do you know how many times it would have been easier to tell you? How many fights it could have stopped? How many times I thought if I just told you, maybe I could get you to stop hating me?"

I bite my lip to force the emotion back down, fighting an urge to throw my arms around his neck and hug him. There's relief and confusion and anger all swirling around inside me, but I need to keep my emotions in check. "Alright," I say. "I'll come." I turn to look at the others. "But what about them?"

"They're coming too," Uncle Art says. "I'm sorry Molly. I know you don't want to be involved in this, and I didn't want you to be either, but you're in it now."

I sit in the front of the black SUV while Molly's uncle drives. Molly is behind me. Remy has fallen asleep beside her, his head on her shoulder, and behind them Jesse is sitting alone, staring out the window.

"So, your name's Wells?" Molly's uncle asks without taking his eyes off the road.

"That's right."

"Arthur Mussington," he says. "You can call me Art."

We pass a large sign showing a picturesque mineral blue lake set within red, rocky mountains. WELCOME TO UTAH, the sign reads. I'm certainly no expert on American geography, but I know we're headed in the opposite direction to what Molly and Jesse had planned.

"So, Mr. Mussington –"

"Art, please."

"Art," I say. "It's like Alpha and Omega isn't it? The name of your group. When the Xenos first arrived they were designated Extraterrestrial Biological Entity Alpha. Alpha and Omega – the beginning and the end."

"Something like that."

"Do you really think they're planning an invasion?"

"We don't know, Wells. All we really know is that something is happening inside the Institute, and we have strong reason to believe the arrival of the Xenos was no accident. We're trying to gather evidence of what's really going on, although who knows if anyone will listen."

"This is why you are bringing us, no?" Remy asks, now awake. "We are the evidence."

Art looks at him in the rear-view mirror. "We want to keep you safe, Remy, but I'm not going to lie to you. We've been trying to get some students from the Institute to join our cause for a while. We'd planned on having them on the inside, sharing intelligence with us and maybe, if the opportunity ever arose, helping us take down the Institute. But we're certainly not going to turn down the opportunity to have you with us. With everything you've seen, you three could be the best chance we have at revealing the truth."

"What did you mean when you said no one will listen?" I ask.

"Twenty percent of the world's population was killed within the first year of the Xenos arriving on this planet. Society is still disrupted. Families were destroyed. Cities, hell even whole countries, started rioting. There were anti-alien protests, bombings – it looked like the world was tearing itself apart. But even before the plague was over, while there were still burning cars in front of the White House, it all just stopped. By midway through the second year of the Xenos' presence on Earth, even as we still mourned the deaths of so many people, all that anger toward the aliens, it was just *gone*. Doesn't that strike you as odd?"

"That's what I've been saying this whole time," Molly says. "Everyone loves the neffing Crabs, and it's freakin' weird."

"We believe the Xenos have somehow manipulated the

public consciousness," Art says. "As Molly puts it, they made the world love them."

"That's stupid," Jesse says, jumping into the conversation. "We like them because of all the good things they've done for humanity, like curing diseases and feeding the poor and whatever."

"That's the common answer Jesse, but the thing is, none of that had happened yet. The advances humanity gained from the Xenos didn't start until more than two or three years after they arrived, once everything had already calmed down."

"So how did they do it?" I say. "We've seen the type of brain-washing going on in the Institute, but there's no way they could be doing that to everyone on the planet. I know what it feels like to experience the type of mind control Remy and Charlotte are capable of – it's obvious it's happening to you. Unless..." The answer hits me. "The plague."

Art nods. "Exactly. We know the virus changes the brains of young people who survive EV-B, but perhaps that's not the extent of it. Perhaps the virus has affected the brains of everyone on the planet."

"Makes sense," Remy says. "I always wondered 'ow everybody just, 'ow you say, got over it."

"Goddamn Crusties," Molly mutters. "So, it's like they released a love potion, but what about you Uncle Art? And what about Omega? Why don't you love them the way everyone else does? Heck, what about us?"

"I don't know, but our best guess is that it's something to do with how severe an individual's reaction to EV was. It's almost like the sicker someone was, the less affected they are by their...*love potion,* if you want to call it that. Maybe that's why the Institute needs such severe mind control for students. You were all EV-B survivors after all – you survived being the sickest out of everyone."

"Why would they go to all the trouble of curing cancer and giving us all the stuff they have, then, if they're just planning an invasion?" Jesse says. "Doesn't make sense."

"Buttering us up to make it easier? We really don't know, Jesse," Art says. "We just know there are questions nobody seems to be asking."

We continue down the road. All around us is nothing but grassy brown desert broken by scattered outcroppings of rock and distant hills. Only a few vehicles pass us, going the other way, some cars, some trucks. There really isn't anything out here, until we come to a dilapidated roadhouse off the side of the highway. Art slows down and pulls in, the SUV's tires crunching over the gravel of the driveway.

The white sign standing tall above the desert reads GAS AND EAT in sun-faded red. Each of the letters is filled with light globes, which are switched off in the morning light. A curving red arrow points to the only buildings anywhere in sight, as if it's not immediately obvious that's the place for your gas and eats. The cream building and the awning over the petrol pumps are both covered in flaking paint. The windows along the front are dirty and there's a large puddle of liquid under the freezer box labelled ICE.

Art doesn't stop at any of the old, round-topped petrol bowsers or pull into the car park in front of the windows. Instead, he continues driving slowly around the side. Out the back is a separate building, the word GARAGE stenciled in fading black paint above a roller door. Art brings us to a stop in front of the corrugated door, but leaves the engine running. A few seconds pass, ten at the most, before the door starts moving upward in stops and starts. Once it's risen enough, I see someone inside pulling it open with a hanging chain. Art drives through and stops between two vehicle stands, the kind that elevates so mechanics can work underneath cars. They're both empty, and although the garage looks fully operational – tool chests, low stools and greasy rags are spread around the concrete floor – it doesn't look as though it gets a lot of business. Art switches off the truck, and with a rattle and a squeal the roller door closes behind us.

"Alright," Art says. "This is an Omega safe house, but it's exposed and even though I know we weren't followed, I can't say they didn't have us on satellite or drone surveillance. Not that it really matters. Remy and Wells will have tracking nanos we need to get flushed before we'll have any chance of disappearing."

"Tracking nanos?" I say. "What do you mean?"

"You and Remy, like all students at the Institute, will have been injected with a strain of nanomites that operate as a tracking array. They'll be transmitting exactly where we are until we can filter them out of your blood."

"And how do you do that?" I ask.

"By using a fluctuating electromagnetic pulse to temporarily disable them, and then a modified kidney dialysis machine to clean the nanos out of your blood as if they were waste products. It was designed and built here."

"Great," I say, "sounds very safe."

"It is Wells, don't worry. The only downside is that we can't be selective in nanomite removal. It's all or nothing, I'm afraid. You'll lose the health and regenerative effects that come with having nanomites."

"Okay, so no one's had any side-effects or anything from doing this?"

"We haven't actually tried it yet, but think of it this way: if we don't do it, the SECPOL will know where you are every second for the rest of your life."

"Right," I say.

"Come on," Art says, opening his door. "Every minute counts."

We all climb out of the vehicle. The man who opened the roller door has walked over. He's an older man, but still muscular beneath his weathered skin. Tattoos that have greened with age are visible extending from beneath the sleeves of his dirty white t-shirt. His greying hair sits in long waves tucked in behind his ears, and his ashen goatee is neatly trimmed.

"Camp," Art says, reaching out and shaking the man's hand.

"Art," he replies. "All go alright?"

"Yeah," Art says, turning to look at us. "This is my niece, Molly. Remy and Wells are the two Institute students, and this is Jesse, he's Molly's friend."

"You sure 'n' hell got a few of 'em," the man called Camp says. His accent is thick, barely understandable Scottish.

"Yes, well, I'm sure they'll all be useful."

"Aye, well, we only got a wee bit of time, bring them through to the back."

Camp leads us through a doorway at the rear of the garage into a small, plain office with a single desk and an old computer that hums noisily with what sounds like a damaged cooling fan. There's a calendar hanging on the faux wood wall, but it's from August 2018 – seven years out of date.

Camp opens another door in the back of the office and we move through to another small room. In the center of the space is a chair, an IV drip stand, and a medical machine with a pumping mechanism on the front and clear tubing running out from two stainless-steel ports. The whole thing is enclosed within a cage of metal mesh. Beside the professionally manufactured dialysis machine is a much less polished add-on. A small frame houses what looks to be a collection of forty or fifty old mobile phone batteries wired together. On top is a huge coil of copper wire and a metallic cone aimed toward the chair. This must be the EMP generator.

"A Faraday cage?" I say, referring to the metal cage around the dialysis machine.

"Aye, that protects the dialysis machine from the EMP," Camp says. "We don't want that stopping halfway through." He looks at me. "Now, let's see if we can't get these nanos cleared out then."

"*You're* the one who's going to do it?" I ask.

"Aye," Camp says. "Problem with that?"

"Um, no," I say, pushing my glasses up my nose. "No problem."

"You going first then lad?"

"I'll go first," Remy says, "if you don't want to, Wells."

"It's alright," I say, not wanting to seem afraid, even though the muscles in my legs are twitching hysterically as my fight or flight response kicks in. I breathe, trying to control my sympathetic nervous system. It's a natural response, but I control my body. Breathe. I control my body.

I sit in the chair and Camp starts work. He has me roll up the sleeves of my jumpsuit, wipes the crook of my left elbow with an alcohol swab, taps my vein and jabs a needle in, hooking me up to the IV bag and taping the needle in.

"This is just saline," he says. "Bein' we don't want you getting dehydrated."

On my other arm he does the same thing, cleaning and sterilizing the site with a gently burning alcohol, then he jabs two needles in just above my wrist.

"One for blood out, one for blood back in," he says.

"Are you a doctor?"

"Nay lad. I'm a mechanic, but it's all the same isn't it? Just an oil change. As long as the fluids are all going back in the right pipes and you don't go springing a leak on me you'll be fine. Now just sit back and relax – this'll take a few hours."

I sit back, but I don't relax. He starts up the machine next to me, and it soon falls into a steady rhythmic chunk-chunk-chunk sound as the pump begins working. Camp watches as the red trace of my blood begins filling one of the tubes out of my wrist.

"Aye," he says, "that looks good. Now for the EMP."

"Wait!" I say. I unzip the front of my jumpsuit and pull out the tablet, making sure I keep the cover closed so the others don't see the shattered screen. "Put this in the Faraday cage."

Camp nods. He takes the tablet from me and puts it inside the safety of the Faraday cage. If it isn't already damaged, then sitting this close to an EMP will certainly fry the memory.

Camp flicks a series of switches wired onto the much less professional looking machine. It starts up with an electric hum that slowly grows in volume until it begins pulsing. The lights in the room dim with each pulse.

"Art, you want to cut those lights for me?"

Art switches off the lights and the room is dropped into semi-darkness. I can see only by the glow of the LED display on the dialysis machine and whatever light is creeping in beneath the door. The EMP pulses faster and faster until it's oscillating at what I guess must be about 10 Hertz – ten times a second. I sit in the gloom listening to the sound of the EMP and the dialysis machine as they work on filtering the nanomites out of my system. I close my eyes and try my best not to see Sergeant Elliot's face. But there she is on the ground, the side of her head all black, smoke curling up into the air. I push the thoughts aside. Not only because I hope to never see something like that again, but also because right now, I don't want to think too much about what the people I'm with might be capable of.

Ω

It takes just over four hours for Remy and myself to have our blood cleaned of nanomites, or at least that's the hope. Camp doesn't have sensitive enough equipment to verify we're clear. They'll be able to check when we reach Omega headquarters, though that seems a little late – if it hasn't worked we'll have led the enemy straight there.

Even though the EMP will have disrupted the tracking signal during treatment, and we should have dropped off the map, Art has still spent the whole time pacing the room and repeatedly wandering outside to check that the garage isn't being approached by a convoy of black vehicles or swooped on by a flock of helicopters. Our temporary disappearance won't last long, though – the nanomites will eventually use their inbuilt self-replication and repair protocols to recover even though they're outside our bodies now. They're being stored in sealed containers full of clear gel that's designed to keep them operational long enough to act as a diversion.

The black SUV we arrived in was driven away a few hours ago by another Omega agent, Camp's son Henry, hoping to deceive any satellite or drone tracking. Now we're loading into a white van, one of three hidden behind the garage. Our van will head for Omega headquarters while the other two – one carrying the nanomites and the other empty – will act as further decoys. It's an elaborate cover, and hopefully it's enough to throw the SECPOL off our trail.

"Alright," Art says. "Let's go."

All three vans drive out of the garage and back onto the highway. One of them, I think the empty one, turns back toward Little Basin while we follow the van with the nanomites in the other direction. Remy, Molly, myself, and Jesse all sit in the back. The windows have been replaced with white paneling. I can't see anything around us other than what I can make out through the windshield. Eventually the van containing the nanomites turns off, while we continue on.

We drive for close to two hours until we reach a small town set in a valley between dry, desolate hills. A green sign on the side of the road declares the town to be Silver Hollow, population 406. Art slows as he drives past the old, dilapidated shops on the main street. It seems as though every second shop is empty, and even those that are still open are worn and neglected, with flaking paint and render falling from the bricks.

Art pulls off the road down a bumpy concrete alley beside a large warehouse. The painted sign along the top of the brick exterior reads *Morgan's Dry Goods*. He turns into an open door on the side of the warehouse, stops the van, and shuts off the engine.

"This is it," Art says. "Omega's operations center."

"Nice neighborhood," Molly says.

"Silver Hollow. It was a booming mining town once, but the last of the mines closed down years ago. Now it's mostly just a name on a map, and a decent place for us to hide, not too far from the Alpha Compound. Come on, there are some people I want to introduce you to, and we need to make sure Remy and Wells are clear of those tracking nanos."

The four of us follow Art into the warehouse. It's filled with metal shelving loaded with decaying barrels and cardboard boxes that don't appear to have been touched in at least fifty years.

"Arthur." A woman approaches. She's short with long curling hair that seems to move even more than she does. "Welcome back." The woman looks at us. "We weren't expecting four."

"Hi Sally," Art says. "And no, I wasn't expecting four either, but the situation was a little dynamic."

"Are they all Institute?"

"No, two are, Wells and Remy here. This is my niece Molly, the one I told you about, and her friend Jesse."

Sally looks at each of us, her gaze fixing on Remy and myself in particular. She stares at us as though we're covered in text she's trying to read, or an equation she's trying to solve.

"Can they be trusted?"

"I believe so," Art says.

"Camp called ahead, said they were cleaned of their nanomites. His contraption worked then?"

Art nods.

"We better check that. You two," she points at Remy and myself, "follow me please. You can take the others through, Art. Everyone is waiting in the briefing room."

Art nods and leads Molly and Jesse away. Sally indicates for us to follow her.

"So," I say, a little hesitant to speak because this woman seems almost as intimidating as Mr Thorn, despite Art's assurances that these are the good guys, "are you in charge of Omega?"

Sally shakes her head. "No," she says. "Omega is in charge of Omega."

"I don't understand."

"I am in command of this cell," Sally says. "Granted, we're the cell closest to the Alpha Compound, the biggest and most active, so I have a large responsibility, but Omega is ultimately in charge. You see, Omega is a collective, but it's also a person."

"So who is Omega?" Remy asks.

"I don't know."

"You don't know who's running things?"

"No," Sally says, "it's better that way. If we get targeted by the SECPOL, or worse, then we can't give up Omega no matter what they do to us. They can't cut off the head of the snake if they don't know who or where the head is."

"Who's worse than the SECPOL?" I ask.

"Sorry?"

"You said you could get targeted by something worse than the

SECPOL. Art said something about having other people to worry about too. Are there others after us?"

"The SECPOL are the security force within the Nevada Exclusion Zone," Sally says, "but they don't reach much beyond that – certainly not here, across state lines. Outside of the N.E.Z. we've more sinister foes to contend with. We don't know much about them, but there are rumors about government agents. Some Omegas have had run-ins with them. Some have been killed by them. They are, for want of a better word, the Men in Black."

Sally opens the door and leads us into a room lit only by the electronic glow of a multitude of screens. Wires hang in thick looms draped on the walls, and a liquid cooled rack of computers hums against one wall. A chair in front of the screens swivels to face us. Backlit by the light of the screens is a young woman, probably not much older than me, perhaps twenty. She's wearing large, ear-covering headphones over dyed blue hair cut short and shaved up one side. Her t-shirt has the words "I want to believe" written in green on the front. She pulls her headphones off.

"Hi," she says.

"Wells, Remy," Sally says, "this is Mackenzie Hooper, Omega's tech lead."

"Stunning," I say.

"Thanks," Mackenzie says. "My hair could probably do with a wash though."

"What?" I say. "Oh no, sorry, I..." I feel heat rise up my neck and into my face. "I meant your set-up. It's stunning."

"Yeah," Mackenzie says. "Pretty rad, right? Moonshot HPC cluster with 64 cores. Mega speed for crunching numbers on crypto, plus *Swords of the Dungeonmaster* runs wicked good."

"You play *Swords of the Dungeonmaster*?" I ask.

"Sure, doesn't everyone?"

"This is, 'ow you say, like a mirror," Remy says. "There are two of them."

"You two will have plenty of time to get acquainted later," Sally says. "Right now I need you to scan them, Mackenzie. We need to make sure Camp's machine did its job."

"Okay then," Mackenzie says. "Step over here you two, and hold still while I scan for a transmitting array."

Mackenzie walks to one side of the small room where precariously stacked shelving sits against the wall. The room is suddenly lit with harsh white light as the fluorescent overhead blinks on. Sally has flicked the light switch near the door.

"You're not a vampire, Mackenzie," she says. "Why don't you have the lights on occasionally?"

"How do you know I'm not a vampire? There are aliens, who's to say there aren't vampires too?" Mackenzie lifts a black plastic case down from the shelf, knocking over a stack of DVD cases in the process and sending them tumbling to the floor.

"The Xenos are explainable through science," I say, "and it's a long-held theory that, given the size of the universe, the probability of extraterrestrial life is a near certainty. Vampires are just folklore."

Mackenzie looks at me. "I was just joking, kiddo," she says, "and I know about the Drake equation. Not that any of that matters now, does it? The probability that aliens exist is 100% and the Fermi Paradox is shot."

Remy looks at me with a crooked little smile on his face. I turn back and watch as Mackenzie bends over and flicks open the latches on the plastic case, lifting off the lid. The loose neck of her t-shirt droops down as she leans over the case, low enough that I can see the tops of her breasts and the edge of her pink bra. I swallow, and flick my eyes away as she looks up, embarrassed that she might have caught me looking down her top. My face blooms hot again.

"Okay," Mackenzie says as she pulls out a handheld scanner.

She switches it on, adjusts a few settings and then moves toward us. "Stand like the cops are patting you down."

We both stand with our arms out and our legs slightly apart. Mackenzie waves the scanner over Remy first. The base station is beeping in a steady rhythmic tone about once every second. As she moves the scanner over Remy's arms, body and legs, the sound doesn't change. "You're all clear," she says, then turns to face me. I push my glasses up, feeling my chest tighten with anxiety. I hope being flushed of the nanomites worked for me too. I don't want to be the one who inadvertently leads the SECPOL or these mysterious Men in Black straight to the Omega hideout.

My heart quickens as Mackenzie stands and begins waving the scanner over my outstretched arms. I don't know where to look. I don't want to stare into her eyes, but as I drop my gaze I find myself looking at her mouth, which still makes heat rush up my neck. When I look further down I'm just staring at her chest again, so I settle on looking straight up at the ceiling, which seems completely unnatural but is the best I can do right now.

My already racing heart feels like it stops suddenly as the scanner in Mackenzie's hand starts increasing its chirping. Images of fluxers descending on the warehouse and mysterious men in black suits fill my mind. Mackenzie stops and runs the scanner back over my chest where the beeping had intensified, but this time there's no change. She continues running the scanner along my arms and down my legs before looking at the small screen.

"You're all clear too," she says. "Looks like Camp managed to pull it off."

"Excellent," Sally says. "Follow me, I'll take you to the briefing room."

I turn to follow Sally and Remy out of the room but Mackenzie catches up to me, reaching out and touching my arm. I stop and turn to face her.

"What have you got in there," she asks, indicating my chest. "A phone, a tablet?"

Of course. The scanner wasn't reacting to any nanomites in my blood. It was reacting to the tablet. I have a sudden sinking feeling. "Is it transmitting?"

"No," Mackenzie says, "but it's from the Institute, isn't it? They said you'd have some data from inside. What's on it?"

"I don't know," I say, "it's encrypted."

"Well, I guess you and I have some work to do then."

Uncle Art leads us into the briefing room and the first thing I notice is that for the headquarters of the supposed resistance against the Crabs, there aren't many people here – maybe twenty sitting or standing around a long table. I don't know what I was expecting - something like soldiers discussing battle plans, but this looks like a business meeting in an accounting firm.

There are men and women of different ages and ethnicities, but apart from Uncle Art there's only one other person wearing a SECPOL uniform, a tall woman with broad shoulders. I can't imagine any of the others getting into a fight, let alone winning one. I guess Omega's plan doesn't involve a full-frontal attack. Maybe they're going to tax return the Crabs to death.

Everyone looks to Uncle Art as he walks toward the end of the table. There's a whiteboard behind him, and a flat-screen hangs on the wall. The room gets quiet.

"Alright," he says, "I'm sure Sally has briefed you on the recent developments at the Institute. The young person captured by the SECPOL was Molly McManus." He gestures to where I'm standing near the door. Everyone looks at me. "She's my niece. Next to her is Jesse Hill, her best friend and someone we can thank for helping get her out of the N.E.Z. She escaped along with two Institute students, Wells Marsden, seventeen, Australian, and Remy Dufort, eighteen, French. Both, but particularly Remy, seem to be resistant to the Xenos' mind control. They are with Sal and Mackenzie right now, confirming that the removal of their nanomites was successful."

There's unhappy murmuring from around the table. Uncle Art holds up his hand. "Look, I know many of you don't agree with bringing them here before we had confirmation, but we had a situation and needed to respond."

As if to answer these concerns, the door opens and Sally, Remy, Wells and a woman who I suppose is Mackenzie walk into the room. Mackenzie is tall, dressed in jeans and a t-shirt, with the kind of long, slim legs I wish I had. Her hair is short and shaved up one side, and she gives off this kind of grunge-geek vibe.

"Perfect timing," Uncle Art says. "Here they are now."

All eyes fall on Remy and Wells. They're being evaluated, even more than I was. Sally looks at Uncle Art and gives him a thumbs-up. "They're all clear," she says.

Sighs of relief echo around the table.

"Remy and Wells have confirmed our suspicion that students within the Institute are unwilling participants in some sort of experimental program," Uncle Art continues. "While Wells is new, Remy has been a student there for several years. Along with their knowledge of the inside of the compound, Wells, who had previously been incarcerated because of computer crimes committed under the hacker alias Daksec, used his skills to secure a significant amount of classified data."

"I'm sure your minds are racing with the ramifications of all this," Sally says, joining Uncle Art at the front of the room. "I want to stress that we still don't know what this means. Specifically, we still have no proof of an invasion plan. Hopefully Wells can work with Mackenzie to decrypt the data from the Institute and find something. We already know direct action against the Xenos and their human support is not an option. Omega has always held the view that the truth will be our most valuable weapon. Hopefully, very soon, we'll be armed to the teeth."

"Um, we need some assurances first," Wells says. Everyone turns to look at him. Including me. Sure, he sounds hesitant, but it still surprises me that he's spoken at all. He's not the most outgoing person but every now and then, like when he made the decision to go up to level "S", he stands his ground. He does this despite constantly seeming like a neffing nervous wreck. There's something gutsy about that.

"Oh," Sally says, "what assurances are those?"

"Well, we haven't really discussed it," Wells says, looking to me, Jesse, and Remy, "but obviously we need as much protection as possible from the SECPOL and whoever these Men in Black are."

"Of course."

"Also, I don't know whether Omega has a presence in Australia, but I want my parents protected, and I'm sure the others will want the same for their families."

"We only have so many resources," Sally says, "but we'll do what we can."

"And we'd probably like to talk to them."

"Mackenzie can arrange a secure phone call."

"And whatever happens," I say, deciding to jump in, "we get final say on whether we want to participate. No one is going to use us against our will again."

Sally gives me a long look. Eventually, she says, "Of course."

It seems like Sally is going to wrap up the meeting, but Uncle Art holds up his hand.

"There's one other thing," he says, "in the interest of truth." He looks at Remy. "Remy, would you mind providing a small demonstration of what you're capable of, what the Xenos have done to you?"

Remy nods and steps forward. He looks to me, holds me in his gaze for a moment, and then looks at the table in the center of the room. He extends his hands and concentrates, and the table rises until it's hovering three feet off the ground. The realization of what the Xenos have done comes with a whole lot of swearing and stumbling backward in fright.

"This," Uncle Art says, "is what we're up against."

Ω

"No, Wells, I'm not saying I want to leave," I say. "That would be stupid. I'm just saying I'm not convinced."

Me, Remy, Jesse, and Wells stand together between rows of old storage shelves, tucked away in a corner of the warehouse. It's evening now, but after the events of the day we decided to have a little meeting of our own.

"You told us you trust your uncle," Remy says. "'Ave you changed your mind?"

"I do trust him, but that doesn't mean I'm suddenly on board with this Omega thing. I mean, they don't even know who Omega is. Jank, let's not forget, apart from Jesse, I don't really know you guys either, and now you're trying to talk me into joining what the government classifies as a terrorist organization."

"You know me," Remy says.

"Molly and I have been friends for years," Jesse says, a little defensively. "You've just turned up."

Jesse's right, technically. I've known him for years and Remy hardly any time at all, but I know what Remy's saying. When our minds melded inside the compound it was like I saw his whole life. Don't get me wrong, that still freaks me out, but I know there's truth to what he says. I feel a connection to

Remy that I can't quite describe. I was *inside* his memories. I felt his happiness, his loss, his pain, and it was so similar to my own.

"I understand why you're tentative about joining Omega, Molly," Wells says. "Perhaps it's wise to be suspicious. But I don't have to have melded with you to know you hate the Xenos. I thought you'd want to fight them."

"She does," Jesse says.

I shoot him a look.

"Well, you *do* hate them," he says, "and you *do* want to fight them."

"Yes, but I don't need you agreeing with them as they try and drag me into this against my will," I say.

"If anyone gets to feel dragged into this against their neffing will, it's me," Jesse says. "Stop thinking about yourself for a second. Mind-melding or not, I know you, Mol. I know the only reason you're resistant to being here is because you hate not having a choice. You hate being told what to do."

"Alright, Jesse," I say, my tone annoyed. I know he's calling me out on the truth, but that just makes it worse.

"You know what's 'appening in the compound, Molly," Remy says. "You 'ave power. 'Elp us."

I look from Remy, to Wells, to Jesse.

"Fine," I say. "I do hate the Crabs and I want to stop them, but I think we should keep our guard up. And listen – no one tells anyone here about me having powers, okay?"

"I think it would be good for Omega to know," Wells says.

"What did I just say? I'm not convinced yet."

"These powers won't go away just because you ignore them," Wells says.

"You mean like how I could ignore you but you'd still be here?"

Wells doesn't answer.

"Look," I say, "if you want my help, ever, then you're not telling anyone about my powers. Got it?"

"Alright," he says.

"And you two?" I say, looking at Remy and Jesse.

They nod their agreement.

"We should get back," Wells says. "We don't want them thinking we're scheming behind their backs or something."

The four of us turn to leave, but Remy doesn't move. "Molly," he says, "can I speak with you?"

I stop. Jesse stops too, a look of concern on his face. "It's okay," I say to him, "go ahead. I'll catch up." He hesitates, shifting his gaze from me to Remy, but after a moment he turns and follows Wells.

When they're gone I look back at Remy. "What is it?"

He comes closer, fixing me with his dark eyes. "We are the same in a lot of ways, you and I. We both lost our families, we 'ave both been changed in ways we do not understand, and we both do not like feeling vulnerable."

I nod without saying anything.

"I just..." Remy says. "I feel like I can talk to you and maybe you will understand."

"Okay," I say, "what is it?"

"I cannot stop seeing what I did inside the Institute," Remy says. He looks away from me, his eyes going distant. "I just wanted to get out of there so badly I, 'ow you say, lost control. I know Wells is scared of me."

"It's alright," I say.

He shakes his head. "No, I 'ave killed people."

"People who tortured you," I say. "I understand. I'm sure the others understand too."

"But they were SECPOL," he says. "Your uncle is SECPOL."

I don't answer. I don't really know what to say.

"They were scared of me."

"It's okay," I say, because I have to say something.

He looks at the floor, his eyes glazing over as he fights to hold back his emotion. "Please," he says, "I think what they 'ave done to me, it 'as made me lose control in there. What I want to ask," he looks up at me, "I 'ave felt your anger too, maybe we can 'elp each other fight but not lose control?"

I look into his eyes. Does he think I could lose control of myself too? My instinct is to immediately dismiss the idea, insist that I'm perfectly capable of controlling my anger. But I think back to how I let my hatred of the Crusties convince me I should climb over the N.E.Z. fence, and then how my fear and anger caused that wave of power. "You're on," I say. I hold my hand out to him. "We help each other through this. Deal?"

He takes my hand and shakes it. "Oui. We 'elp each other."

MACKENZIE KICKS her foot against the floor and spins on her computer chair, letting it turn slowly through three hundred and sixty degrees. "So, you're really Daksec?"

I look at her. "I'm surprised it's taken you this long to ask. My mistakes are usually something people want to discuss at length."

We're sitting in her den of technology again, just the two of us, lit by the glow of the monitors. We've been tasked with decrypting the data on my tablet and recovering whatever information we can, and we've been at it for two days now.

Mackenzie picks up a cold piece of pizza and bites into it. "You know," she says around a mouthful, "Molly wasn't wrong when she said Art could make a good pizza." She holds the plate out, offering me the final piece. "We should've been making him do this the whole time."

"Thanks," I say, reaching out and taking it.

"So," Mackenzie says, swallowing, "you were Daksec?"

"I gave up that name when I gave up hacking."

Mackenzie spins in her chair again like a child let loose in her parent's office. "It's not something you give up though, is it?" she says. "You thought you gave it up, but you didn't really. You just had it taken away. Banned from using computers while in prison and then, *wham*, as soon as you get out you're back into it. That's not really giving it up."

Mackenzie makes me nervous, although by now I suppose that goes without saying. Doctors, danger, girls, even those tiny stickers they put on apples make me nervous. Sometimes I feel like my moment-to-moment existence is completely ruled by the push and pull of anxiety. It's an overwhelming thing that takes a significant amount of energy to manage – constantly employing coping strategies is almost as exhausting as the anxiety itself. But despite those feelings of trepidation, I like Mackenzie, or perhaps it's more accurate to say I have those feelings *because* I like her. I never really know which way around that goes. But even so, Mackenzie's comments still manage to generate a flare of annoyance inside me.

"I really did try and give it up," I say. "It's not as easy as that. You don't know what it's like."

As Mackenzie's chair spins around to face me again she stops the rotation with her foot, and holds out her hand to me. "Let me introduce myself again then, because I've given you two days and it doesn't seem like you're going to figure it out. My name is Mackenzie Hooper, known across the interwebs as Aunt M."

If this was a cartoon I'm sure the bottom of my jaw would hit the floor and my tongue would unroll across the cold concrete. "You're Aunt M?"

Mackenzie nods. "Yep. So I do know what you're talking about, don't I?"

"No," I say. "You're not Aunt M."

"Why? I don't seem old enough to be the internet's wise aunt?"

"No, it's just, I never expected to actually meet you in person. I've never met anyone from online. I suppose I'm not sure whether we actually know each other already or not."

"We know each other in the way of chat rooms and hacker channels, Wells," Mackenzie says. "Which is to say, not really at all. I followed your progress closely – most decent hackers did. I remember spending a few solid hours trying to convince you to stop hacking for the lolz and start with some actual hactivism. Now look at you, stealing classified information to bring down a possible alien threat. A+, Daksec. A+. It'll make old XenoLeaks look like a school newsletter if we can drop this bomb."

"You know about XenoLeaks?" I say, and immediately regret it. Mackenzie cocks her eyebrow at me. Of course she knows about XenoLeaks.

XenoLeaks, another of the world's most famous hackers, has been providing information about the Xenos across the dark net for the last few years. XenoLeaks is known in deep web circles as one of the only reputable sources out there. Supposedly, they're a government employee, though that's never been confirmed.

"Who do you think gave him that nickname?" Mackenzie says, smirking.

I smile. "I always thought you were the best, but when you disappeared everyone said you'd been arrested, or that one of those doxing claims was actually right and you'd gone dark."

"Puh-lease, I was never arrested and none of those doxing noobs can touch me. I was found by Omega, or at least, we found each other, and they recruited me. That's when I went dark. I'd always suspected something wasn't on the level with the Crabs so I went underground to investigate them. Real hactivism, right? Saving the planet. Exciting isn't it?"

"Right," I say. "I don't precisely know how saving the planet became part of my life. I haven't really had a chance to consider this as anything but utterly terrifying."

"We'll be alright," Mackenzie says. "You're clear of nanos. Omega knows how to keep itself hidden. We work together to keep each other safe. We are Omega, right?"

"We are Omega," I say, not really convinced I'm actually part of this group yet.

"Now, we've spent two days finalizing decryption algorithms, maybe we should actually have a look at this tablet now?"

I swallow, and a cold dread creeps within me. I still haven't come clean about the tablet being smashed. I knew it would come to this eventually, of course, but it feels like the tablet is my only bargaining chip. It's alright for Remy and Molly, they've got their abilities to fall back on. The only thing I bring to Omega is what's on this tablet – what I hope is *still* on this tablet.

"I think I should work on it myself," I say.

Mackenzie gives me a look and I see the playfulness fade from her eyes. "No offense, Wells – you did a great job getting this data off the Institute servers – but I've been working on breaking government and Crustie encryption for the last year. I'm the best positioned to crack this egg, and we haven't been trawling code together for two days for you to go lone wolf on me now."

I don't reply, trying, unsuccessfully, to think up some excuse that will let me hold on to the tablet a little longer.

"Wells, what's going on? You do actually have this data, don't you?"

"Yes. I've got it."

"Sooooooo," Mackenzie says, dragging the "o" sound out for at least a few seconds. "What's the problem?"

"Nothing," I say. "There's no problem. Why would there be a problem?"

"Because you're sitting there like the kid who stole the last cookie."

I give up, knowing I have absolutely no chance of keeping up this increasingly flimsy charade. I unzip the front of my jumpsuit, pull out the tablet and place it on the desk next to Mackenzie's keyboard. She flips the cover open and the screen, shattered into spiderwebs, stares up at both of us.

"That's why you didn't want to show me? Because it's broken?"

I nod.

"You're worried you've lost the data?"

I nod again.

"What?" Mackenzie says. "Did you think we'd toss you back to the SECPOL?"

"I don't know."

Mackenzie plugs the tablet into her system and hits the space bar to wake the monitor. "It's not like you're paying the mob, Wells. It will be a loss to the cause if the data's gone, but you're not going to get sunk to the bottom of a river or something."

"Sorry," I say.

"It's okay," Mackenzie says, "but listen, if we're going to work together there's got to be trust both ways. I know when you're hacking it's easy to hide behind your keyboard. But here, in the flesh, you've got to be all in. You trust me. I trust you. You think you can manage that?"

I nod.

"Good. Now, let's take a look before you panic. It might be fine."

Relief floods through me. Maybe I was being paranoid – Mackenzie seems unfazed by the possibility. I suppose, after Charlotte and the Institute, I'm growing less and less willing to trust people, but maybe I've finally found someone I can trust.

Mackenzie works fast, her fingers flying. "There's some corrupted segments," she says as she runs an analysis of the tablet's memory, "and the operating system looks to be toast, but the data should be okay as long as we haven't lost too many fragments."

Mackenzie boots up a data recovery program and sets it to

work. In ten minutes she's copied the data onto her computer and we're looking at the reconstructed folder I hastily named "Operation Vassal WTF." She looks at me when she sees the name, and I push my glasses up my nose. "What? I didn't know what it was."

Mackenzie just snickers as she sets about examining the reconstructed folder. Just as they were during my cursory examination back at the Institute, the files are encrypted, but at least they're still there. I feel a weight lift from my shoulders. I didn't realize how much the fear of having lost the data was suffocating me. I haven't doomed my species. Still, we have to break the encryption.

"Alright," Mackenzie says. "Let's get started."

We work until the early afternoon stretches into evening and, as with the last few days, once I settle into it, I start to feel at ease. My shock at Mackenzie being Aunt M, legendary hacker and mentor to so many in the dark corners of the internet, fades away as we work. Our relationship has become almost symbiotic. We're brilliant together.

After hours of work Mackenzie stands, sipping a cup of cold coffee and staring at the three screens on the wall. She looks like a general examining a battlefield. Except, of course, her battlefield – *our* battlefield – is lines of code. Unfortunately, I can tell, just as I know she can, that this is a battle we're losing.

"I don't know," I say to her reluctantly, not wanting to give voice to the reality of the situation. "I don't think we can crack it. Not without a brute force attack, and how long would that take? Three years?"

Mackenzie sighs. "I really thought we could do it."

"I know," I say. "So, what now?"

Mackenzie looks at the tablet on the desk. "I've been working on something. It's completely experimental, but it's worth a shot. Do you know whether your tablet uses the same encryption technique as the main servers?"

"I believe it does, but the tablet won't decrypt the files for us – it won't have the right key."

"No," Mackenzie says, "but all we need to fix our algorithm is one encryption key to extrapolate from."

"Right, but we don't have one."

"Once again no, but that's where my experiment comes in. I've been working on this theory that was thrown around a few years ago. Theoretically, if you can record the sounds made by a processor as it decrypts data you can reverse engineer the encryption key. So, we get the tablet to decrypt some of its onboard data, record the processor as it does so, use my experimental frequency analysis tool to reproduce the encryption key, rework our algorithm to use that encryption key as the base, and then brute force crack the Operation Vassal files in hours instead of years. What do you think?"

"Sounds...far-fetched," I say. "But also amazing."

"See," Mackenzie says. " I'm not just a pretty face."

"Yeah," I say.

Mackenzie looks at me with her head tilted to the side and one eyebrow cocked. "Oh, so you think I'm pretty?"

"No," I say, "I mean no, no, yes, I –"

Mackenzie laughs. My face is burning. I don't think there's any possible way I could be worse at talking to girls. Mackenzie just leaves me to stew as she walks toward the door.

"It's almost dinner time," she says. "Let's eat, rest, and we'll try again in the morning. Seems like you need some water."

"I do?"

"Something to put those flames out."

I blush. Again.

STAYING HERE, in this neffing dark and dusty warehouse has left my feet itchy. It's not just being stuck inside for days, it's the idea of not running. It just doesn't feel right parking our butts in one place like this. I know Thorn and his goons will be after us – we're sitting ducks, and I can feel them getting closer. Still, Uncle Art assures me we're safe. It seems counterintuitive, he says, but constantly moving is actually more dangerous. The world is filled with surveillance – satellites, drones, CCTV – and if we run, sooner or later we'll be picked up on something.

I feel useless, too. That's part of the problem. It's alright for Wells, he's been working with Mackenzie, trying to hack the mainframe or whatever jank they're doing. Remy's been with Uncle Art and Sally most of the time, answering questions about the goings-on inside the Institute. Hell, even Jesse's been busy, volunteering to help take inventory of the weapons and supplies Omega has stashed here. I think he's trying to prove he's just as valuable as someone who can float a table. So far they've all kept their mouths shut about my powers like I asked. I don't think anyone suspects. They certainly haven't been interrogating me about what I'm capable of like they have been with Remy. Still, it wouldn't kill them to ask what skills I might have, other than my winged eyeliner game being on point.

I've been dragged into a questioning session now, though. Me, Remy, and Wells are all in a closed room with Uncle Art and Sally. I can feel a tightening around my right temple, a gentle throbbing that acts like a warning, a shadow of the migraine to come. I try to ignore it, but I know that won't help. The head-monster comes whether you ignore it or not.

"To be honest," I say, "I don't know what you'll get from me being here. I'm sure Remy can cover everything. If there's one thing he can do, it's talk."

"Are you still annoyed about last night?" Remy asks. "I told you I would need to ask questions. Sometimes it is 'ard for me to keep up."

"I didn't know that meant I'd have to pause the movie every twelve seconds."

"It was not that bad."

"Alright, every fourteen seconds."

There's not a whole lot to do in an empty warehouse, so Remy and I have watched a bunch of movies. I've been showing him all the American classics he's never seen: *The Godfather*, *Scarface* – you know, the light stuff.

"I told you to put the subtitles on," Remy says. "It is easier for me."

"And I told you it's too distracting."

"If you don't mind," Sally says, "I did say we were ready to begin."

"Sorry," I say. "I just don't know what I can tell you about the Institute that Remy hasn't already."

"We don't expect you to know the Institute like he does," Sally says. "We've brought the three of you in here together because we want to know how you escaped. It shouldn't be possible. Besides, from what he's told us, Remy was incapacitated for a large portion of the escape."

"Well, yes, but it was because of him that we got out," I say.

"You were the one who carried me," Remy says.

"With Wells' help," I say.

"Oui, but –"

"Ahem." Sally interrupts with an obviously fake clearing of her throat.

"Sorry," I say.

"Look, all three of you were involved in the escape and it's important we understand what happened."

"One of my duties as a SECPOL officer," Uncle Art says, "was regular patrol of the N.E.Z. fence, so I'm fully aware of the force field surrounding the area. It's projected out as a large dome that defends the compound from penetration by land or air. It's supposed to be impenetrable by any vehicle, and unable to be damaged by any weapon – the perfect protection system. SECPOL officers with sufficient clearance have transponders that allow them to phase through small sections of the force field. That's how we'd hoped Anthony would get you out – he had the necessary clearance, and all the fluxers have a transponder. We just had to hope the system hadn't been completely locked down. Of course, he didn't make it, but you still managed to get through. How?"

Remy and Wells look sideways at me.

"Someone else must have lowered the force field," I say. "Maybe Anthony brought it down before the crash?"

"No," Uncle Art says. "That's not how it works. It doesn't get lowered, it just allows someone transmitting the correct transponder codes to pass through. Unless you had a transponder and knew the daily code, you couldn't pass the force field."

"Don't know then," I say.

"Remy?" Uncle Art says. "Can you shed any light on this?"

He waits a long beat. "I was unconscious."

"Right then. Wells?"

Wells looks at me, guilty as sin. Jank. Don't make it half obvious or anything. "I don't know either," he eventually says.

I look at Sally sitting opposite me. I don't think she's stopped watching me the whole time.

"I'm getting a migraine," I say. "Can we do this another time?"

I know it seems like I'm making an excuse to get out of here. Jank, maybe I am. But I really do have a neffing migraine coming. A hardcore one, too.

Sally is still watching me like bacteria under a microscope. "Alright Molly," she says. "That's fine. Please, go and rest. We do have to go over this though. Everything we know helps us get stronger. If there's some way of defeating that force field or of gaining any kind of advantage, Omega needs to know. We're really on the back foot here."

I nod as I stand. Wells and Remy start to stand as well.

"No, please," Sally says, holding a hand out to them. "If you two wouldn't mind staying, there are some other things I'd like to go over."

They both look at me. Remy in particular holds me with what might be a concerned look. I break eye contact and head for the door.

Omega have the warehouse pretty well set up. One section has been partitioned off into small rooms where everyone sleeps. There are bathrooms and showers, and a kitchen for communal meals. I head for my little room, a plywood box with a hanging sheet for a door, to lie on the bed and get ready for the neffing pain to hit. Well, I call it a bed, but it's just an old mattress on the floor. Apparently being part of the resistance against an alien invasion isn't glamorous.

I'm almost there when Jesse calls to me. "Molly."

I turn and see him following me. "Hey Jesse."

"I was waiting for you to finish with your Uncle Art and Sally, but Eric said he saw you leave already."

"Yeah, I'm just going to lie down."

"Can I talk to you?"

"Can it wait, Jess? I'm getting a migraine."

"It's never a good time though, is it?"

"What?" I say, confused at his snarky tone. "I've got nothing but time."

"I tried to talk to you last night, but you were with Remy."

"I asked you if you wanted to come watch movies," I say.

"I wanted to talk to you," Jesse says, "not watch movies."

"Well, you should have said something then," I say, "I'm not a mind-reader."

"Not like him, you mean."

"What?" I say. "Are you jealous of Remy?"

"I just don't think you should be getting so close to him. He's killed people."

"Only to escape from the Institute, and I'm not getting close to him."

"Yes you are. You're together all the time."

I sigh. "Look, fine, I like him. Is that so bad?"

"What about me?" Jesse asks.

"Jesse," I say, trying to soften my voice, "you're still my best friend."

"That's the problem," he says. "I'm *just* your best friend."

"What are you talking about?" I say, suddenly afraid of where this conversation is headed.

"I've tried to tell you how I feel so many times, but when you got caught in the N.E.Z. I thought I might have lost you. I couldn't stand that." He pauses, gathering himself. "Because I love you Molly. I love you."

"What? No you don't."

"I do," he says. "I always have."

"Jesse," I say, trying to keep the frustration out of my voice. I can't believe this. I don't want him to love me. He's my friend, and it was perfect like that. And honestly, I don't really want to talk about this right now. Jank, I don't *ever* want to talk about this, but especially not now. I take a moment, staring up at the dark warehouse roof.

"Well," Jesse says, and I can hear the irritation in his voice, "the least you could do is tell me how you feel."

I look at him. He's upset and agitated. I can't tell whether he's about to cry or yell at me. "I don't know what you want me to say, Jesse. I don't want to talk about this."

"Why not? Because of Remy?"

"Jank, Jesse. I have a migraine. I just want to lie down. You're my best friend, that's what you've always been and that's what I want you to be. I don't want our relationship to get all complicated and stupid with any of that stuff."

"I don't think the way I feel is stupid."

"No, I didn't..." I let my voice trail off and pinch the bridge of my nose. It's not worth it. I'm not good at this stuff. Whatever I say, I'm just going to make it worse.

"It's fine," Jesse says as he turns and walks away, "I shouldn't have said anything."

I don't say it out loud but all I can think is that he's right. I wish he'd never said anything. Jesse is the only real friend I have, and now it's neffing ruined.

"IT'S A SECURE CONNECTION, encrypted and routed through VPNs from here to Hong Kong," Mackenzie says. "But I'm sure I don't need to tell you to keep your conversation quick, and don't mention Omega."

I nod. "Of course."

"Okay then." Mackenzie smiles at me. "I'll leave you to it." She turns and exits the room, closing the door behind her. The tech room drops into the constant semi-darkness Mackenzie keeps it in, lit almost entirely by the glow of monitors and holo displays.

I spin my chair to face the monitor in the center of the wall, and hover the cursor over the green dial icon. My palms are tingling and sweaty. I shouldn't be this nervous about calling my parents. I'd like to say it's because I'm anxious about accidentally revealing something about Omega, or because I don't know what I'm going to tell them about not being at the Institute anymore. Perhaps it *is* partly those things, but to be honest, every time I spoke to them while I was in juvie, either on the phone or for their very rare in-person visits, I felt this same sense of dread. My psychologist and I spoke about it a lot – the stereotype of psychologists being obsessed with talking about people's parents is true, by the way. She said it's because I feel responsible for my parents' happiness, or lack thereof.

My psychologist told me to make positive changes in my life, like giving up hacking and pursuing a more constructive path of education, but she said that anything else is beyond my control and I shouldn't feel responsible for it. That's all well and good, but she doesn't know, just as my parents don't know, the truth about what happened to Maggie.

Suddenly, even though I haven't pressed anything, I hear a rhythmic chiming as the call goes through. I try to move the cursor over to the red "end call" button but I can't control it. I'm halfway out of my chair when a small dialog box appears at the bottom right of the screen.

Aunt M: You can do this. Just be honest with them.
    Aunt M: But not TOO honest. ;)

Mackenzie has taken remote control of the computer. I told her about my strained relationship with my parents – most of the story, anyway – and that I don't feel like they'll ever forgive me for my hacking arrest. Her advice was to talk to them openly and explain how I feel. I don't know about that – my family have never been very forthcoming with our emotions.

"Hello."

My mother's face appears on the screen. She's answered on the home computer, a laptop currently sitting on the kitchen bench. It's early morning there – the wooden bench is lit with yellow light streaming in through the window that looks out over the garden. Mum is wearing her fluffy pink robe, pulled tight around her; the kettle is boiling in the corner.

"Hello?" she repeats, looking at the screen in confusion. "Who's this?"

"Hi Mum, it's me."

"Wells?" she says. "You haven't got video on."

"No," I say. "I'm not allowed."

"Oh, I suppose there's a lot of security there."

"Yeah, you could say that."

"I was starting to wonder if you were going to call at all. I didn't know if they weren't letting you make any calls, or if you'd just got caught up in what you're doing. You do that, you know."

"I know."

"Tell me about it then. What's it like at the Institute? What have you been doing?"

"Well, that's the thing –"

"Hold on," Mum says, interrupting me as I start to formulate an answer to her question, "let me go and get your father. He's getting ready for work."

She vanishes off the screen.

"Harvey," I hear her calling out. "Harvey, Wells is on the computer!"

"What?" I hear my father's faint voice from down the hall. "What's he done now?"

"Nothing," Mum says. "He's calling us on the computer. Come and talk to him."

Mum comes back into view and then moments later my father, still in the process of knotting his tie, appears as well.

"Wells?"

"Hi Dad," I say.

"There's no picture."

"He's not allowed," Mum says. "It's very secret at the Institute."

"How is it then?" Dad asks. "Are you doing the right thing?"

I consider the irony of the question. I think standing up to the Xenos and sharing the truth of what they're doing is the right thing, but if I try to explain that I'm no longer at the Institute I know he won't agree. "Yes Dad," I say. "I'm doing the right thing."

"What have they got you learning then?" he asks.

"Well, I can't really say too much but I'm working on computers."

"Alien ones?"

"Yeah," I lie. "I'm working on getting alien computers to talk to human computers."

"And have you met some of the aliens?" Mum asks.

I nod, and then remember I'm not on video link. "Yes, I've met some of them."

"How exciting," Mum says. "And how are the other students? Have you made some friends there?"

The first person who comes to mind is Charlotte, but I'm pretty sure the fact that she made me hold a gun to my head is fairly compelling evidence that we weren't friends. Then I think of Remy, Molly, Jesse, Mackenzie, and the rest of Omega. "Yeah, I've made some friends."

"Good," Mum says. "That's good."

"Alright then," Dad says, flipping his collar down over his tie and flattening it out, "I'd better get to work. You keep your head down and don't go getting into any trouble." He leans over and kisses Mum before turning to leave.

"What?" I say. "That's it?"

I see the look of surprise on my father's face as he stops and turns back to the computer. "That's what?"

"This is the first time I've spoken to you since going to the most exclusive school on the planet, a school run by aliens, and all you can do is tell me to stay out of trouble?" Okay, so I'm not actually at a school run by aliens, but the sentiment is still the same. He's not interested in what I'm doing, just concerned that I don't get into any more trouble.

"Well," Dad says, "you haven't exactly shown great judgment in recent years, Wells. I'm just trying to remind you not to ruin this opportunity."

"Aren't you ever going to forgive me for that?" I say, a little surprised that I'm taking Mackenzie's advice.

"We have forgiven you, Wells," Mum says. "We're very proud of what you're doing now. We really are. Your father just wants you to keep doing well."

"That's the thing though, isn't it?" I say. "If you'd forgiven me, like *really* forgiven me, you wouldn't feel the need to constantly remind me of it. You'd just trust that I can make better choices now."

"Wells," Mum says in her family mediator tone, "your father is just –"

"Lydia," Dad says, holding up his hand to cut her off, "I can speak for myself."

I brace myself, thankful I'm not on video link as I prepare for the dressing down my father is about to give me.

"You're right, Wells," he says, taking a deep breath to prepare himself. "My father was hard on me and it's the only way I know. I just want you to stay out of trouble because I love you and I want what's best for you." He moves to stand next to my mother again. "Work can wait a little while. Why don't you tell us some more about the Institute?"

"Um, there's only so much I'm allowed to say. Why don't you tell me about what's been happening at home instead?" I say.

"Well, you know Nancy and Max from down the road?" Mum says, "They sold their house because they're going to travel around Europe for five years. I'd like to go back to Europe, but I can't imagine going for *that* long." And so Mum launches into the breaking news from friends and family. Dad even jumps in every now and then. It's probably the most we've talked since before my arrest. I drop occasional pieces of information about the Institute, feeling guilty for lying, but it's nice to talk to them. It feels like the first genuine connection we've had in years. In the end we talk about nothing much at all, and it's perfect.

HERE WE GO AGAIN. Same old headaches trying to melt my brain into mush. I grip my skull and roll around on the lumpy mattress, groaning quietly. I catch myself wishing I'd taken Thorn up on his offer, then quickly toss the thought aside, angry that it even snuck in there.

"Molly?"

I roll over to face the hanging sheet door of my little box room. It's Remy.

"What is it?"

"Can I come in?"

"I'm not feeling well, Remy."

Why does everyone want to talk to me when I clearly want to be left alone?

"Sorry," he says. "I just wanted you to know that I remember what it's like. I 'ad 'eadaches too, before I went to the Institute. We said we would 'elp each other through this. I can 'elp you now."

I don't say anything. The truth is, I want Remy to come in. I normally want to be left alone when I have migraines, but I think I'd enjoy having Remy sit with me. Problem is, I can't help thinking about how that would make Jesse feel. Still, I didn't ask Jesse to tell me that he loves me. I shouldn't have to deny my own feelings because of it.

"Molly," Remy repeats, "can I come in?"

"Yeah," I say. "Come in."

He pushes the sheet aside and enters the room. "I think I can 'elp you with the pain," Remy says. "Can I try?"

I nod and Remy sits on the edge of the mattress. I sag toward him as he weighs the old springs down. We don't touch but I let my body move closer as if drawn to him like a magnet.

"I remember an experiment from back at the Institute," he says. "There was a student, Melissa or Melinda, I don't remember. She was in a chair across from me. They were making 'er share 'er experiences, 'er feelings. They would torture 'er, and she would 'ave to send it to me, make me feel the pain she was feeling. And she could do it – I could feel 'er pain. They made it worse and worse, but in the end they pushed too far. She died." He pauses. "I felt that too."

"Jank, Remy. Jesus."

Every time Remy tells me something he remembers from the Institute I think that must be the worst thing, but those bastards always manage to top it.

"I want you to try that," Remy says. "I want you to try to send me your pain."

"I can't."

"Molly," he says, "sometimes you need other people. You are not alone. You are not alone in your 'atred and fear of the Crabs. You are not alone in wanting to fight them. And you don't 'ave to be alone in this. Share your pain with me."

"I don't know how," I say. "And even if I could, it's not fair to make you suffer."

Remy reaches out and gently pushes the hair back from my eyes. His touch is comforting. His fingers trace onto my temple and settle on the spot right where the pain is. I let my muscles relax – I hadn't realized how tense I was. I've never had someone comfort me through this pain. Uncle Art used to try, but that was when I thought he was a traitor to the memory of my parents. It might be different now. I wish he'd told me about Omega. Our relationship might have been so much better. Still, Remy is here now, and he knows what this icepick-wielding devil pain is like. "We take 'alf of this each and we get through this together."

I sob, crying with relief, or pain, or happiness, I don't know – maybe all of the above.

"Please, Molly. Try."

"How do I do it?"

"Everything is connected. Can you feel that? That is 'ow melding works. You are joined to everything around you. Feel for the connection we 'ave. Find the connection with me, and will your pain along it."

He's right. I can feel the threads linking me to everyone else in the warehouse, and, though they're much weaker, I can feel them spreading out to everyone in the world. Weirdly, it doesn't feel overwhelming. It feels like something that's been there my whole life.

I can sense the link between me and Remy. It's there, but it's like a rope made of smoke – I can't grab it. No matter how much I focus on Remy at the other end, I can't send my pain to him.

"Try not to force it," Remy says. "This is less about my mind and more about yours. It is like a dam – you open it and the water will come. You do not push it to me, you just let it go."

I try to stop forcing. I try to concentrate on myself and slowly, like I'm using a muscle I never knew I had, I manage to put pain on the misty link between us. This telepathic connection I have with Remy isn't a physical thing, I realize. I was trying to grab hold of it, trying to force it to do what I want, but this needs a subtle, gentle touch. I've never been a subtle person. Maybe I've never been very good at focusing on what's actually going on inside my head. But Remy's right, this power is more about controlling my own thoughts and feelings.

It's not instant, total relief, but I don't want to burden Remy with all my pain anyway. It goes in a drip, a steady, slow reduction. I pull away from Remy and look him. He nods. His smile has been replaced by a grimace, and his right eye is squinted shut.

"No," he says as I ease the flow of pain. "Keep going."

So I do. I keep letting the pain flow from me into him. My guilt in doing so is only overshadowed by how wonderful it feels to have relief.

"Don't feel bad." It's like he knows what I'm thinking. Maybe he does.

"Thank you," I say.

He smiles back. "I like you Molly."

A warm hollow opens in my stomach. I swallow. "I like you too," I say.

"I do not want you to think bad of me."

"What?" I say. "I don't."

"About what I 'ave done."

"I know. I don't. And besides, you being so worried about it is enough to tell me you're not a bad person."

"I killed people. Wells was telling me not to, but I still did it. I 'ardly even thought about it."

"You had to," I say. "You had to do it to escape."

Remy drops his head, shaking it gently. "No. I did not 'ave to. There is always a choice. I could 'ave found another way. I think 'ow my mother and sister would feel if they knew. We said we would 'elp each other." He sits up and I see his eyes shining with tears. "I don't want you to do anything you'll regret. I don't want you to feel like I do."

I sit myself up and wrap my arms around him, pulling him in close to me. I feel him nestle his face in between my neck and shoulder. I don't really know what to say. Remy wraps his arms around me. His face feels warm against the skin of my neck. His arms are gentle, but I can sense the strength there. I try to relax my body, even though my veins are filled with lightning. My body crupts with excitement and a sudden longing. We stay just like that though, embracing, half a headache each.

THE NEXT MORNING Mackenzie drags me into her computer den straight after breakfast, eager to try her experimental method of cracking the encryption. I tackle the tablet, using Mackenzie's data recovery program to recover enough of the operating system that we can boot it up and get it to open an encrypted file. I know the Institute regulations handbook is on there and, like every-thing to do with the Institute, that's at least base-level encrypted – something the tablet will open.

While I'm doing that, Mackenzie drags out the equipment she needs, setting up an array of extremely sophisticated-looking microphones arranged in a semicircle around the tablet.

"Got it," I say. The tablet boots up and the screen is displayed on one of Mackenzie's wall-mounted monitors.

"Nice work."

She grabs a small screwdriver and starts opening the external plastic shell of the tablet, revealing the processor. This will make it easier to detect the almost imperceptible sounds that emanate from within.

"Now," she continues, "log in and open an encrypted file. And then try to remain perfectly still."

I click the icon for the Institute regulations manual, and a fraction of a second later it pops up on the screen. After another heartbeat, a frequency spectrum appears on Mackenzie's screen, a time history of the tiny sounds made by the tablet's processor as it decrypted the file.

"Okay," Mackenzie says, "now I'll run an analysis and try to match the frequency signature. Then, if my completely untested genius works, it will punch out the encryption key."

Mackenzie starts the analysis and we wait with bated breath as her computer begins cycling through various sounds, the buzzes and chirps of electronic hardware. Tones rise and fall, sounding almost musical. After thirty seconds the words "FRE-QUENCY SIGNATURE MATCH" appear on the screen and a series of numbers begin cycling, eventually settling on 1801-4398-2410-46527. We both stare.

"That's it," Mackenzie says. "That's the encryption key format."

"A seventeen-digit number," I say, "and I think a prime."

Mackenzie nods.

I laugh. "You did it."

Mackenzie claps her hand on my shoulder and smiles back at me. "We did it."

Now that we've found an encryption key we can feed it into our algorithm. In a couple of hours – maybe less – we'll have access to the Operation Vassal files and we can hopefully start working out what the Xenocrustaceans are actually trying to do inside the Institute.

Ω

"Tell me," Mackenzie says as we sit and wait for our code-cracking algorithm to break the encryption. "How did you really escape the N.E.Z.?"

I look at her. "What do you mean?"

"It's pretty clear," Mackenzie says, "to me at least, that the story of you three escaping the Institute is lacking a key step. How did you get through the force field?

"I...um...I don't know," I say, knowing I don't sound very convincing. Did Sally and Art put her up to this?

"Wells," Mackenzie says, "you've got to understand, the ability to get through that force field – to be able to penetrate the compound – if you guys know how to do that then that's even more important than the data we've got here. That's the real secret we need to know. Remember what I said about trust going both ways? Omega needs to know how you got through."

I push my glasses up my nose and swallow. "Are you asking me to tell you?" I say. "Or are you telling me to tell you?"

"I can't tell you what to do," Mackenzie says.

"I promised I wouldn't say anything."

Mackenzie sighs. "Okay."

She sounds disappointed in me, hurt even. I don't want her to feel like that. I want her to trust me. "I just can't tell you," I say. "I'm sorry."

She nods. "That's okay, Wells. I understand." She spins on her chair to tap at some keys and check the progress of our algorithm. "It's still iterating," she says.

She doesn't turn back to look at me.

"You say trust needs to go both ways," I say, the desire to break the silence too much for me, "but if I tell you this then I'd be breaking someone else's trust."

Mackenzie turns to me. "I know," she says. "All I can say is that Omega will appreciate it, and don't worry about Molly. She'll understand eventually."

"You knew it was Molly already?" I ask, shocked.

Mackenzie smiles. "I had my suspicions," she says. "I'm proud of you, by the way."

"What?"

"Yeah," she says. "The fact that you wouldn't tell me it was Molly, that shows me you're the trustworthy person I thought you were."

"Thanks," I say.

"So, she has powers like Remy? Telekinesis?"

I nod.

"But, more powerful?"

"I think so, but she can't control it."

Mackenzie nods. "She might need to learn how to sooner than she wants."

"You won't tell her I told you?"

"You didn't."

Ω

One hour and thirty-eight minutes, that's how long it takes us to crack the encryption – orders of magnitude better than the years it would have taken without Mackenzie's genius. She hovers the cursor over the folder I named *Operation Vassal WTF*.

"Ready?"

I nod. "Ready."

It's a bit of an anti-climax after the amount of time it's taken us to get to this point – all it takes is for Mackenzie to double click and the folder pops open. There's no fireworks or music or dancing cheerleaders. Still, to us, it's the culmination of not only two days' work, but all of our accumulated knowledge, too. We solved the puzzle. We picked the lock. Inside the folder there are hundreds of files. An idea strikes me. "Can you run a global search?"

"Yep. You got an idea what to look for?"

"I think so," I say. "Why don't you search for files with references to something called the Obelisk?"

Mackenzie does this and, just as I suspected, the word is mentioned many times throughout the files. One in particular stands out: "Operation Vassal CONOPS (Concept of Operations)."

"There," I say to Mackenzie, "open that document. The CONOPS. I've seen those types of files before when I've...um... acquired information from the US DoD. It's a military document, outlining the plan for an operation. It should tell us what Operation Vassal is all about."

Mackenzie opens the CONOPS file. It's in a similar format to the others I've read. It starts with a discussion of Operation Vassal, describing it as a joint endeavor between the Xenocrustaceans and a government group called Majestic-12. I almost start laughing. Majestic-12 is real – all the conspiracy nuts online would absolutely lose their minds if they knew this. There have been theories about Majestic-12, a group of twelve people within the US government, since the 1950s. The story is that Majestic-12 exists to either recover alien technology, make first contact with aliens, or cover up the existence of aliens, but the FBI claimed the whole thing was a hoax. Even now, with the existence of extraterrestrials undeniable, no government has ever revealed how much it knew about aliens. The events of Roswell, alien abductions and unexplained lights hovering over country roads don't seem like such ludicrous ideas anymore. Maybe those tinfoil hat wearers weren't quite as crazy as everyone thought.

The more I read, the less it sounds like Operation Vassal is the invasion plan we thought it might have been – at least not in the traditional sense. Mackenzie and I finish reading the first page at about the same time and we turn to look at each other.

"Holy crap," Mackenzie says. "We've got to tell the others about this."

REMY CLOSES THE DOOR. We've appropriated one of the small rooms on the upper level of the warehouse, an office that must once have been for someone more important than those hauling bags of grain around the warehouse floor – the office of a foreman or bean-counter or whoever. The space is small, just two dusty old chairs, one either side of a desk. Whatever had once been on the desk or in the half open filing cabinets has long since been taken away.

I watch Remy as he moves and sits against the edge of the desk. He leans back and crosses his arms. I feel like I'm more aware of his body now, more aware of the shape of it and the way it moves under his clothes. I don't know if it's because of the connection we shared or whether it's just because I *want* to be more aware of his body but neffing hell I fell like I want to be aware of that body.

Nothing happened between us last night, nothing physical anyway. We just lay there together, all night in the end, but things sure feel different this morning. We went down to breakfast and ate and I wonder how many people suspected we'd spent the night in the same room. I didn't see Jesse and I'm not sure whether that's a good thing or a bad thing.

"Are you ready to try then?" Remy says.

Despite what people might think if they found the two of us here we didn't sneak away to make out in a secret warehouse room. It was Remy's suggestion we find somewhere no one could see us so he could try and teach me to use my powers. Last night showed I can control them if I put my mind to it, and if we're going to help each other through whatever's coming then I need to understand my powers as well as Remy does.

"Sure," I say. "What do I do?"

"Lift the desk."

"But you're sitting on it."

"Do not worry about me," Remy says. "Try and find the link between you and the desk. Same as between you and me. It will feel different though. It is easier to find the living things. This is more like, 'ow you say, like a very thin string you can pull."

I stare at the table. I can feel Remy, that smoky link between us is even more prominent than last night. I hardly even have to try to notice it now. What I can't feel is the table. I have no idea how to reach out and lift it up. Powers or no powers I'm staring at the wooden desk with as much success in Jedi force-ing it into the air as anyone would have. I give up, unfurrowing my brow as I look to Remy.

"No good," I say. "I can't do it."

"Do not give up after only one try," Remy says. "It takes practice. Come over here. If you are closer to the object you might find it easier."

I move closer to the desk, standing only a few feet away now. I look at the old, faded wood, chipped and scratched along the edges where it looks like it's been bumped and damaged as it's been moved between rooms over the years. I try to find some link between myself and it, some string like Remy said, but it's just an inanimate object, just a thing that's there.

I stare at it. I try closing my eyes. I will the stupid desk to float into the air with everything I can muster, but when I open my eyes it's still on the floor, Remy still sitting on top of it. I sigh, letting my lips billow out.

"Here," Remy reaches out and takes my hand. Just this touch, an almost casual connection of his fingers to mine sends a flutter starting in my chest. He guides my palm onto the surface on the desk. "Can you feel it?"

"Yes," I say. "I can feel it because you've put my hand on the desk, Remy."

Remy rolls his eyes at me. "You know what it is I mean. You touch it like that but you touch it with your mind."

I look down at my hand. Remy has not lifted his away. It's like we both notice this long contact for the first time, but neither of us make to move. I spread my fingers winder and he slips his fingers down to intertwine with mine. "Maybe we can have a break," I say, "try and lift tables again in a minute."

Remy smiles. He lifts my hand from the desk, turning his hand to be palm to palm with mine. He pulls my hand closer and holds it to his lips, pressing a gentle kiss on the back of it. The flutter in my chest becomes a thunderstorm of rolling vibration and cracking lightning. I move closer to him as he lowers my hand away, our fingers still clasped together. He widens his legs on the desk so I can slip inside them, getting as close as I can to him.

I stretch my face to his. We stay there for a moment, our noses brushing against each other, our mouths so close I can feel his hot exhale on my lips. It's a temptation we can only hold for so long. I don't even know which one of us initiates it, but soon our lips are touching. His mouth opens and my top lip slips inside. I feel his tongue run along my lip and I reach up and grab the back of his head, pulling him into a harder kiss.

We kiss, our bodies press together, Remy slides himself off the desk, grabbing me and lifting me onto it. He towers over me like a shield, a shield against all the shit we've been dragged into. Right now none of that other stuff matters it's just us. We kiss and our hands move frantically over each others bodies. I run my hands over his back feeling the strong wide muscles around his shoulder blades. His hands move over my shirt and my breath catches as his palm slides over my breast, his fingers gentle but wanting to squeeze.

We kiss, each of us wanting to devour the other with our lips and hands. All our thoughts are lost to devouring and being devoured. One minute, ten minutes, half an hour, I'm not sure how long we lose in each other's embrace before I hear the rattle of the door handle.

"Here you are," Sally says as the door swings open.

Shocked by the sudden interruption we hastily pull away from each other, our faces red from heat and embarrassment. We wipe our mouths and smooth our clothes in a neffing pointless attempt to tidy ourselves up and clear away the evidence.

"Sorry," I say, "we were just..."

Sally waves my explanation away. "I don't care about that. You kids do whatever you want – within reason – the point is we've been trying to find you. Everyone is meeting in the briefing room right now. Mackenzie and Wells have made a breakthrough."

MACKENZIE and I are standing in the briefing room as everyone gathers together. Sally is the last to enter. "Alright," she says as she sits at the far end of the table. "What have you found?"

In all the excitement following our discovery, though I'm not sure excitement is the correct word – perhaps panic, agitation or terror would be more accurate – we never actually decided who was going to explain what we've uncovered. I push my glasses up my nose. "Well," I say, "perhaps Mackenzie should explain it."

"Okay, so this is what we already know," Mackenzie says. "The Institute for the Betterment of Humanity was set up as a conduit for the Xenocrustaceans to share technological advancements with humans through instruction and training of the world's best and brightest young people. That was the official mandate. However, we've long suspected that experimentation and some form of mind control was being undertaken on the students. This has been confirmed by Remy, Wells, and Molly. Remy believes the experiments are designed to activate something within their brain structure that has been altered as a result of EV-B. We have seen the effect of this firsthand – his powerful telekinetic abilities.

"But the reason for all this was completely unknown, until now. It's all part of what they call Operation Vassal. What we've found so far paints a pretty clear picture. There's an artifact somewhere, which they call the Obelisk. The plague and the Obelisk work together, but the Obelisk is stolen – that's important, because it's what's bringing the others."

"The others?" Art asks.

"The Xenocrustaceans aren't refugees from a war," I say. "They're the other side of the war. The losing side."

"Right," Mackenzie says. "The Xenocrustaceans, at least the ones we've got here, are the losers of some sort of civil war. They're a group called something that translates as something like *the Schism*. From what we can gather, it seems like the war was over the Obelisk."

"I've seen the Obelisk," I say. "Not in person, but when I first melded with Number-One – that's the Xeno leader – I saw images of it. It's a sort of pillar carved with symbols. The Obelisk seems to be the catalyst for the Xenos' ability to communicate telepathically. It doesn't seem like the Xenos even know where the Obelisk originally came from, they evolved with it on their planet and that's why they communicate exclusively through telepathy. We don't know what started the war, but the losing faction, the Schism, stole the Obelisk and secretly fled their planet. When the remaining Xenos found out, they sent a fleet in pursuit."

"Working with a government group known as Majestic-12, Operation Vassal is how the Xenos' plan to turn the tide in this war," Mackenzie continues. "They deliberately crashed their ship on Earth and released the plague, which, as we know, had an effect on human genetics. The majority of the population seemed to be unaffected, but they weren't – they've been altered to be more receptive to the mind-control and telepathic techniques used by the Xenos.

One fifth of the population, those incompatible with the Xenos' genetic manipulation, died, while the small number of people who survived EV-B, almost entirely young people, have become like Molly, Wells, Remy and," Mackenzie looks at me, "myself. They have enhanced cognitive capabilities and varying levels of telepathic and telekinetic abilities. The Xenos refer to them as nodes."

"Nodes?" Sally says. "Like points in a network?"

"Exactly," I say. "The Xenos aren't invading. They're creating an army."

"An army of super-powered teenagers," Molly says, "just like we thought."

"Um, not quite," I say.

"See, that's the kicker," Mackenzie says. "The students of the Institute aren't the soldiers. They're the 'nodes' of a mind-control network. Under the guise of preparing for integration with humanity, Majestic-12 is going to spread the 'nodes' out around the planet. When the enemy fleet arrives, the Xenos will switch their network on. The Institute students will, with the power of the Obelisk, turn everyone into soldiers. Every single human being on the planet will fight the Xeno war."

"Neffing hell," Molly says.

Everyone else is speechless.

"Every single human fighting for the Xenos," Sally says. "Billions of people. I think I preferred it when we thought it was an invasion."

"So we need to stop the students leaving the Institute," Molly says. "If they can't spread themselves out, they can't control everyone. Let these other Crabs come and take care of our problem for us."

"The problem is, the Schism will still be able to maintain control over a large population," I say, "perhaps the entire United States. I think the only real solution, though I don't have any idea how we could actually do it, is to stop this at the source by destroying the Obelisk."

"In that case," Sally says, "I want everyone trawling through those documents. Let's see if we can't find out where this thing is."

"Plus," Mackenzie says, "we need to find out as much as we can about Majestic-12. They seem powerful, a shadow government in their own right, and there are rumors they have access to all kinds of advanced technology, including weapons, alien-human hybridization, and cloning."

"Alright," Sally says. "You –"

Just as Sally starts speaking the windows along the side of the briefing room shatter. It takes everyone a split second to realize what's happening. Several objects have smashed through the glass.

I look down and see one of the objects roll out from under the table. It seems to be moving in slow motion, turning over once, twice, three times, before coming to rest, rocking on its axis. It's a canister of some sort, matte-black – a grenade? No sooner has the thought crossed my mind than the canister explodes. There's a sudden flash of bright light and a bursting sound. The room fills with smoke, but I can hardly see anything because of the jagged, lightning-like lines of white and purple across my vision. I hear shouting, from both inside the briefing room and outside. There's so much noise, and it all blends into a confusing mess behind the ringing in my ears.

Cracking sounds and sharp hissing whistles split through the ringing. Things start thudding into the wall.

"Get down!"

I don't know who's yelling but I feel someone grab my wrist and pull at me. It's Mackenzie. She's already on the ground.

"Wells! Get down!"

Oh my god. Someone's shooting at us. They're shooting in

through the windows of the room. I see Remy get shot. He flops back, hitting the wall, his face twisted in a grimace of pain.

"Remy!" Molly screams.

Mackenzie pulls at me again. "Wells! Move!"

I look down at her. This doesn't seem real. People are shooting at us. Who –

ONE MINUTE we're listening to Wells and Mackenzie explain the Crusties' plan to turn everyone on the planet into cannon fodder for their space war, next thing there's neffing grenades flying through the windows and everything turns to chaos.

A burst of light and sound leaves the world blurred and buzzing. Shooting. Shouting. We've gone from being in a briefing to being in a war. I can hardly see. My eyes are covered with after-images of bright light but beside me I see Remy get hit. He grunts and grabs at his chest, collapsing back against the wall and sliding into a heap on the ground. Jank. I drop down beside him, trying to stay low. Through the ringing in my ears I can hear the cracks and thuds of what must be bullets hitting the wall. I have no idea what the hell is going on.

"Remy." I turn his face toward me. His eyes are closed. "Remy. Come on. Remy, please." I grab his shoulders and shake him, but his eyes won't open. Shit. Shit. Shit. I flinch and drop lower as something, a bullet I guess, whistles above my head, close enough that I feel my hair move. I pull up Remy's shirt, expecting to see blood gushing from a bullet wound, but there's none. Instead, there's something stuck in his skin. I grab it and pull it out. It's a dart with a needle protruding from the end. They're not firing bullets at us. They're firing tranquilizers. Tranq bullets, like the cops use in riots. Whoever is attacking us, the SECPOL or the Men in Black or whoever, they want us alive.

I look around through my burnt vision. Wells is still at the front of the room, just standing there like an idiot. Mackenzie is telling him to get down, but she's too late – his head snaps back, one of the tranqs lodged right in his forehead.

"Stay low and get out of the room!"

Uncle Art's voice booms through the noise. He's pulled a handgun from somewhere – I didn't even know he was carrying one – and is firing back out the window, but it seems a little like squirting a water bottle in the direction of a tsunami.

"Get out and split up!"

But that's the last thing Uncle Art says before he staggers, grabbing at his shoulder, and crumpling into a pile on the floor. Some people make a break for the door. Sally, crawling along the ground, comes toward me.

"Go, Molly. We've got to go!"

I look at Remy on the ground and shake my head. "I'm not leaving him."

"I don't know what they'll do if they catch you," Sally says.

"I'm not leaving him."

Sally stares at me for a moment. I think she's going to tell me to leave, but she just nods and continues on, grabbing at those who aren't already unconscious and making them move.

"Molly!" Jesse is lying facedown on the floor several feet away, his arms wrapped protectively over his head.

"Jesse," I say, "you need to go with the others."

Jesse looks up at me, goes to move, but drops again as something whistles overhead.

"Stay down!"

"Don't move!"

Soldiers dressed in uniforms similar to the SECPOL – though these are black, and they're wearing balaclavas, with no identifying patches on their shoulders or names on their chests – start clambering in through the blasted-out windows, kicking shards of glass out of the frames with their heavy boots. The door is kicked inward.

"On the ground! On the ground!" Soldiers bark at us. They swing their rifles around the room until no one moves.

After a few moments, two men in pressed black suits enter. They've each got the same government-issue short-back-and-sides haircut. One of them points at Wells. "Grab that one."

Two of the black-uniformed soldiers move toward Wells.

"Piss off," Mackenzie says, "you're not touching him."

As casually as you like, one of the soldiers raises his gun and fires a tranq bullet into Mackenzie's chest. She sinks into a boneless pile on the floor and the soldiers grab Wells and drag him away.

"That one too," the suit says, pointing at Remy.

"Oh, hell no," I say. Just like Mackenzie, I'm unable to keep my objection to myself. "You keep your neffing hands off him."

The soldiers approach us.

"Him too," one of the agents says, pointing at Jesse. I need to do something. If only I knew what I actually did when we escaped from the N.E.Z. I squeeze my eyes shut and concentrate, but there's nothing. I need Remy to teach me how to use these neffing stupid powers.

As the soldiers reach for Remy I try to fight them, clawing at their arms. One of them kicks me in the stomach, a sudden and unexpected strike that drives the air out of my lungs and slams me back against the wall. I gasp as I try to breathe against the pain.

"Molly!" Jesse calls as soldiers grab him. "Help me!"

I launch myself up and, dropping my shoulder, I spear-tackle the soldier holding Remy's legs. He's a lot heavier than me, so I barely manage to push him back. The other soldier drops Remy's arms, winds back his balled-up fist and lands a staggeringly hard punch on my cheek.

I feel like I sit straight up, ready to continue the fight, however futile it might be, but apparently that isn't the case. My cheek is throbbing, my head pounds, and the soldiers are gone. Remy and Jesse are both gone, too. I suddenly feel woozy and drop back. Someone catches me. It's Uncle Art.

"Woah. Take it easy Mol."

Around the room those who were shot with tranqs are stirring and starting to come to. Soldiers are standing near the doorway, but there are only four of them now – the rest have gone.

"What's going on?" I ask.

Uncle Art shakes his head. "I don't know."

"They took Remy. And Wells and Jesse."

"I know," Uncle Art says. "They've been back and taken a few more."

"What are they doing to them?"

Uncle Art doesn't answer, but it's clearly nothing good.

"How did they find us?" I say. "I thought we were safe."

Uncle Art looks at me. "Are you sure you were never injected with nanomites?"

"What?! No, I told you, they never got a chance. Remy and Wells rescued me before they injected me."

"There was no other time they did anything to you?"

"You think I led them here?"

"I didn't say that."

"That's what you're implying though, isn't it?"

"Molly," Uncle Art looks toward the soldiers and lowers his voice again. "I'm not saying you did it on purpose, but did they ever have a chance to inject you with anything?"

"No," I say. But then I stop. Oh jank. My leg. They sprayed that stuff on my leg.

"Molly," Mackenzie says as she approaches. Her eyes flash with anger. "You could have done something."

"What?"

"You know what."

"Mackenzie," Uncle Art says, "we're all upset right now. But come on, Molly couldn't have done anything."

"She knows what I mean."

"I couldn't," I say. I have no idea how she knows. Someone must have told her – probably Wells – but now isn't the time to press that. "I don't know how to control it."

"You should have been honest with us from the start. We could have helped you. You could have practiced. We're supposed to be a team here."

"Mackenzie, what are you talking about? This isn't Molly's fault." When she doesn't answer him, Uncle Art turns to me. "Molly?"

Mackenzie's right, though. I led them here and I couldn't use my powers when it mattered. This is my fault.

I wake on the floor. My head feels as though it's been caved in from the front, but when I reach up I find only a marble-sized swelling on my forehead. I suppose I expected something a little more dramatic after being shot in the head.

"It was only a tranq bullet, Wells. You'll be fine."

I know that voice. I push myself up and turn toward the source of the sound and sure enough, there she is: Charlotte. She's not in her Institute uniform anymore – if she ever was an Institute student – instead she's dressed in the same unmarked black fatigues as the soldiers who attacked us. I realize the blur of the world around me is more than just an aftereffect of the bullet to the forehead. I'm not wearing my glasses. Even wearing cracked glasses was better than no glasses at all. Standing beside Charlotte is another familiar face, this one much more menacing: Mr Thorn.

"Mr Marsden," he says. "You've had quite the adventure. Really, though, did you honestly believe you could hide from us?"

"What are you going to do to me?"

"You and I need to have a discussion."

"We do?"

"Indeed. Why don't you tell me about Margaret?"

"What?"

"Margaret," Mr Thorn says. "I believe you called her Maggie. She was your sister."

"Yes, I know who Maggie is," I say.

"Why don't you tell me what happened to her?"

"She died."

"Yes, but she died in a very specific way, didn't she?"

Heat flares in my face, put there by anger, shame, and fear. For once, though, anger rather than fear wins out. "Everyone dies in a specific way," I snap. "I'm not talking about my sister. Especially not to you."

"You don't like talking about her?" Charlotte asks.

"No," I say. "My sister died when she was six years old. Why would I possibly want to talk about that?"

Charlotte stares at me. I see her look shift from intimidation to concentration. Almost immediately I feel that same tingle, like cold water down my spine, the feeling of my body being taken over.

"You're going to answer the questions Mr Thorn asks you, Wells," Charlotte says, "or I'm going to make you gouge your own eye out."

I try to move. Unsurprisingly, I can't.

"Molly was right about you," I say.

"Oh really, and what does Molly McManus have to say about me?"

"You really are a bitch."

I feel myself lift my right hand, raising my thumb and directing it toward my left eye.

"Wells," Charlotte says in a mocking sneer, "I thought you liked me."

"Now now, Charlotte," Mr Thorn says, "I'm sure Mr

Marsden is going to cooperate of his own free will. Isn't that right, Wells?"

My hand stops. I can't lower it though. Charlotte holds me tight in the grip of her mind.

"Now, your sister," Mr Thorn continues, "we know what happened to her – she was hit by a car. But there's more to the story, isn't there?"

"No," I say. "She ran out into the street, a car hit her, her head hit the road and she died from head trauma."

I'm surprised at how easily the lie leaves my mouth. It's habit now, an automatic reaction to the subject, a lie I've been telling for so long.

"She languished in a coma for several days," Mr Thorn says. "That must have been heart-wrenching for your parents. I can't even imagine their pain."

I don't say anything.

"Imagine their heartache had they known the truth. Why don't you tell me the truth, Wells?"

"That's what happened."

My thumb presses firmly into the corner of my eye.

"How did your sister die?" Charlotte asks again.

"She was hit by a car," I say.

My thumb pushes in hard. There's a sudden immense pain and my vision, explodes with stars. I can feel the soft sphere of my eyeball compressing under the pad of my thumb. "Stop!" I call out.

"Who killed your sister?" Charlotte says, a sudden heat in her voice. "We want to *hear* you say it."

"Why?!"

There's a squelch as my thumb pushes hard and slides in beside my eye. Lancing pain fills the side of my head and a rush of warm blood floods along the side of my nose. I vomit. If I was in control of my body I'm sure I would collapse, but Charlotte holds me stationary. I try to scream, but Charlotte cuts it off.

"Who killed your sister?" Charlotte asks again.

"Me!" I scream through the pain. "I killed her! I killed my sister!"

It feels as though a hole opens beneath my feet, a rush of feeling that seems to alternate between hot and cold. I knew this was where they were heading, but that doesn't lessen the blow. It's a secret I've held locked away for four years. A secret that has gnawed at me like a cage of rats desperate to eat their way to freedom.

I pull my thumb out, or Charlotte does – I don't even know anymore. I must have control of my body again though, because I'm on the floor, grabbing at my eye and sobbing and retching.

"Just imagine if your parents knew it was you who killed your sister."

I groan, and feel at my eye. Despite the pain and the blood, it's still in its socket. I can only open it a sliver, and all I can see is a blur of dark color and a buzzing swarm of lights. I let it close.

"Who is Omega?" Mr Thorn asks.

"What?" I manage.

"Do you want us to tell your parents the truth about your sister?"

"No, please don't tell them."

"Then tell us who Omega is."

"I don't know," I say. "No one does."

"There are always things people fear more than pain, Wells. Yours is this secret. You've carried it for so long. We can torture you, but revealing the truth to your parents would break you even more, wouldn't it?"

I can't speak. My throats cracks in sobs.

"Who is Omega?" Thorn asks again.

I shake my head. "I don't know. I promise I don't know."

"Why protect him?" Charlotte says. "What has he done for you? Just think – if you hadn't had your nanomites removed they'd be working right now to repair your eye, probably saving your sight. What can Omega possibly offer you?"

"I'm telling the truth. I don't know."

"You are on the wrong side, Mr Marsden," Thorn says. "Omega and his followers believe they are going to save the world, but it is *we* who are saving the world. You think Majestic-12 is leading humanity toward endless servitude to an alien race, but in fact we were founded to avoid exactly that. Our mandate is to protect Earth from extraterrestrial threats. We've been doing that for seventy years.

"What the founding twelve started we have continued, and we do not go into this struggle without forethought. Humanity cannot stand against the Xenocrustaceans, you must realize that. A race advanced enough to travel faster than light, to stage a crash and survive, to infect the entire planet with a genetically customized plague? Humanity doesn't have the capability to overcome such a technology gap – we are the Aztecs, they are the Spanish.

"What you have learned is true, the Xenocrustaceans are preparing an army, an army of all humankind, but what you don't realize is that it is Majestic-12, what the public officially knows as the Department of Extraterrestrial Affairs, who runs the Institute. I am the head of Majestic-12 and I am working for the benefit of mankind, not the Xenos. I am uniquely positioned to ensure humanity navigates this war, and that we are better as a result. Eventually this dark chapter will pass and we will emerge into a bright future, free from the Xenocrustaceans. If, in the end, they do not leave in peace, we will take peace ourselves.

"Omega foolishly believes it is possible to stand up to the Xenocrustaceans – it is not. If we do not cooperate, they will simply take what they desire. But if we accept what they offer, then the possibility of dictating our own future still lies within our grasp. Omega poses a threat to that end. Omega poses a threat to the safety of all humanity."

"I don't know who Omega is," I say again.

I feel the same cold chill in my spine and my body stiffens. As if in response, Mr Thorn says, "No Charlotte, leave him be. I believe him." The feeling of control dissipates. "Alright, Mr Marsden. From this moment forward you work for Majestic. You will remain with Omega, but you will do your utmost to discover the identity of their leader. Do this and we will keep the truth about your sister's death hidden."

My eye throbs with a piercing pain that shoots back into my skull. I can hardly concentrate on what he's saying. "You want me to spy?"

"Yes, Wells," Charlotte snaps, "or we reveal to your parents how you killed your sister, probably kill them too, and I take your other eye, just for giggles."

I shake my head. "I can't."

"Do you think," Thorn says, his voice quiet and low, "that your parents will forgive you? That Omega would want a sister-killer in their midst anyway? You will lose everything."

I shake my head, but it's weak. No one can know the truth about Maggie. It's not fair to my parents. It really would destroy them. I don't want my friends to know either. If I play along, maybe I can tell them the truth, find a way out of this. Mackenzie or Sally or Art, they'll know what to do.

"They'll suspect something," I say.

"After this chaos I doubt that. But in the event that someone does begin to suspect a mole inside Omega, we've got this for you."

Charlotte moves to the door, opens it and says, "Bring him in." Two of the Majestic soldiers drag Jesse into the room, dropping him, still unconscious, on the floor.

"You don't know what happened," Mr Thorn says. "You were tortured. You passed out. You woke up on the floor next to Mr Hill here. It's amazing how untouched he is, isn't it?"

I stare at him, not really understanding.

"Almost like we just let him go," Charlotte adds.

And then I do understand. "He's a decoy," I say.

"Perhaps," Mr Thorn says. "That's your prerogative. Now, hold still." Mr Thorn approaches with a small syringe in his hand.

"What are you doing?"

"We need a way to communicate, Wells. Behind your right ear, in the spot already marked, I'm going to insert a small device. When it begins to buzz, that means we want to talk."

"How?"

"We will contact you. You just need to ensure you are alone and cannot be overheard."

Mr Thorn grips my head and tilts it to the left, then pushes the syringe beneath the skin behind my right ear. I feel the sting and then the pressure of him depressing the plunger.

"Done," he says. "Any moment now you'll also notice the sedative that was in the syringe."

Even as he's speaking, a sudden dizziness fills my head, a swirling fluid in my brain, and I feel the unrelenting advance of drug-induced sleep thundering toward me.

Mr Thorn's voice is the last thing I hear. "We look forward to working with you, Wells."

WE'VE BEEN in the briefing room for hours. I'm getting neffing sick of people locking me in rooms all the time. Every now and then people are brought in or taken out – still no sign of Remy, Jesse, or Wells, though. Sally was brought back maybe fifteen minutes ago, her nose broken, heavy purple bruises already forming under her eyes and her bottom lip busted open. She said they were questioning her about the identity of Omega. Doing most of the questioning with their fists, it seems.

This time when the door opens the soldiers shove Wells and Jesse into the room. Jesse spins back to the door and yells something I can't make out, then he turns, and his eyes meet mine. Relief floods through me and I smile at him. It's not a smile he returns. Instead, he turns his attention to Wells, who is buckled over at the waist. He has his hand planted over one of his eyes, and there's blood on his cheek.

Mackenzie approaches. "Let me see."

Wells shakes his head.

"Wells," Mackenzie says, gently taking hold of his wrist and lowering his hand. "Show me."

Wells gives in and lets her guide his hand away from his eye, which is ringed with purple. Streaks of blood and tears have run down his face. His eye is puffy with swelling, and horrifically red.

"She –" Wells' voice catches in his throat. "She made me do it myself."

Neffing Charlotte. It has to be. Just the thought of her forcing Wells to do that twists my stomach. Someone really needs to teach that bitch a lesson.

"It's alright," Mackenzie says. She puts her arms around Wells and he drops his head against her, his body shaking in silent sobs. "It's alright."

I move closer. I want to say something, but I don't know what. Mackenzie looks at me, and I can see the anger in her eyes. I don't know if it's because she blames me or because she wants to kill Charlotte as much as I do. Probably both. I decide not to interrupt. I just place my hand on Wells' shoulder. Jesse turns and walks away.

"Jesse, wait." I reach out and grab his arm. He turns back to me. "Are you okay? They didn't hurt you too?"

"No, I'm fine."

Greta, the other Omega who was undercover as SECPOL, is examining Wells' eye. She's a trained medic. "Look straight ahead for me Wells."

Wells does what Greta says, wincing when she pulls down his swollen eyelid and shines a small torch into his busted-up eye.

"Neffing hell, poor Wells." I turn back to Jesse. I should tell him that I'm sorry I chose to go after Remy instead of him. Instead, I ask again. "You sure you're okay?"

"I'm fine," he says, then turns away and walks to the other end of the room, where he sits against the wall.

So that conversation went well.

Greta is wrapping a bandage around Wells' head, covering his wounded eye. The soldiers let Greta go and fetch her medical kit to tend to people's injuries. Seems like a humane thing to do until you remember they're the ones who caused the neffing injuries in the first place.

Once Greta is done and Wells has been cleaned up, I approach. "Jesus, Wells," I say. "I'm sorry. What did Greta say?"

"She said we won't know the extent of the damage until the swelling goes down, and even then I really need to see an eye specialist to know whether I'll be able to see again."

"I'm sure Omega will get you the help you need."

"Yeah," he says, "if we manage to get out of here without having our memories erased."

"What happened?" I ask. "I mean, they obviously tortured you for information, but..." I glance toward Jesse. His head is lowered onto his arms, which are resting on his bent knees. I'm sure he can't hear me, but I lower my voice anyway. "What did they do to him? He won't talk."

Wells looks over at Jesse. "I don't know." He shrugs. But it's noncommittal, and Wells is about as good at hiding his emotions as a toddler.

"What?" I ask. "What is it?"

"Nothing." His cheeks, even as his face is still pale from pain and shock, flush with color.

"Wells, I know you've been through a lot, but you need to tell me what's going on."

He sighs. "He said they asked him a few questions and then knocked him out with a tranq."

"That's it?"

"Yeah."

"What's the problem then?"

"Nothing," Wells says. Then, as if after a moment of inner struggle, he says, "Just seems like everyone else is taking a beating and he walked out of there completely untouched."

"What do you mean?"

He shakes his head. "Forget it."

"No," I say, a little more forcefully this time. "What are you trying to say?"

Wells exhales heavily, glances at Jesse again and then turns back to me. "Look, they asked me what I knew about Omega, same as they're asking everyone. I couldn't tell them anything because I don't know anything. They didn't believe me, so Charlotte made me do this." He points to his bandaged eye. "I don't know." Wells looks toward Jesse for a third time. "Just doesn't seem like anyone else was left alone when they couldn't answer."

"If you're accusing Jesse of something just come out and neffing say it."

"Before they took my eye out they offered me a chance to find out what I could about Omega and report the information back to them. They wanted me to spy. I refused, and that's when Charlotte took control of me. I'm not saying Jesse said yes, but it seems like a coincidence, doesn't it?"

"Nope," I say. "No way. Jesse wouldn't do that."

"Probably not," Wells says. "Like I said, just forget it."

The door opens again and I spin around, hoping they're bringing Remy back. But it's not him. It's Thorn. He locks his eyes on me and points in my direction.

"Her now," he says to his Majestic soldiers. "It's time to talk to Miss McManus."

Ω

Mr Thorn walks in front of me without speaking. He usually drones on in his Bond villain monologue, but he doesn't even do that now. I'm sure that isn't a good thing. His soldiers lead me to a small windowless room with shelves of old rotting boxes along the walls. It stinks like a musty cupboard and is lit like the world's worst disco venue. A single light globe swings gently on a chain, throwing sliding shadows off everything.

Thorn stands to the side and watches as the soldiers push me in.

"Watch her," Thorn says as he turns. "I'll just be a moment."

When he returns, that bitch Charlotte is following him like the lap dog she is. After her comes Remy. I'm thrilled to see him, but scared, because he isn't walking under his own power. He's passed out and floating into the room – Charlotte is using her powers to bring him in. Then, following all of them, ducking its enormous flat head to make it through the doorway, is a Crab – a real-life in-the-flesh Crustie.

The thing moves like a freakish monster, a mutant sea creature. It folds and unfolds until it stands in the room looking at me. At least, I think it's looking at me. I can't tell which way its beady black eyes are pointing. Ugh. It's neffing gross. I can smell it, all slimy and wet and weird. It's covered with blue painted symbols and the only thing it wears are clear plastic boots filled with a green-tinged liquid. It lets out a clicking noise.

Remy drops to the floor in front of me.

"Hey!" I say to Charlotte. "Take it easy with him, you janking bitch."

The monster leans forward, tilting its big flat head to the side. A deep, fast series of clicks come from somewhere in its throat.

"Yeah!" I yell at it. "Bring it on, you oversized crab! You smell like asparagus piss!"

I'm flung backward. I slam into the shelves behind me, smashing the back of my head on the protruding wood before landing heavily on the ground. I push myself up, doing my best to ignore the pain.

"That all you got, Charlotte?" I say. "Disappointing."

"Alright," Mr Thorn says, "that's quite enough posturing, thank you all the same Miss McManus. Besides, your temper is ill-directed. It isn't Charlotte using her powers."

I look at the Crab.

"No," Thorn says, "not her either. Our Xeno friends possess telepathic communication, but only genetically altered humans like you, Charlotte, and *I* can use telekinesis."

I stare at Thorn. He's got powers too. Great. Just when I thought he couldn't get any worse.

"Good for you," I say as I kneel beside Remy. No one tries to stop me. "Remy, can you hear me?"

Nothing.

Remy? I try with my mind.

Still nothing.

"Despite your apparent lack of respect, Miss McManus," Thorn says, "I'd like to introduce you to Number-One." He gestures to the Crab.

"What's it doing outside the N.E.Z.?" I say. "Isn't that illegal or something?"

"No. The N.E.Z. exists for their protection, not ours. Number-One has joined us here today because of you."

"Me?"

"Yes, Miss McManus. Your raw abilities far exceed anyone we've ever seen. Number-One believes, as I do, that you would be invaluable in securing the future of both our species."

"I feel like we've already had this discussion, and I think I told you to go and get janked."

Mr Thorn looks to Charlotte. "Would you mind waking up Mr Dufort for me?"

"Of course." Charlotte holds her hand toward Remy. She makes a twisting motion with her fingers, rolling them into a fist. For a moment nothing happens, then I hear a sudden rasping wheeze. Remy suddenly sits upright, sucking in long deep breaths, as if he's been underwater for too long.

"Welcome back, Mr Dufort," Thorn says. "I trust you had a restful sleep."

"Yes, thank you Mr Thorn," Remy says, which is not the reaction I expected. "I am feeling, 'ow you say, quite refreshed."

"Excellent," Thorn says. "You see, Molly, Remy has had a change of heart. Perhaps you shall too."

"Change of heart," I scoff. "Change of neffing mind, more like. I know what you've done to him. It won't stick, though. Your brain-masher doesn't work on him."

"Admittedly, of all the students at the Institute, Remy has shown the most remarkable resilience to our techniques. In fact, we had no idea just how resistant he had become. But you see, our machines are barely an approximation of the abilities of the Xenocrustaceans and their melding. Once he had been made a little more amenable to the idea, Number-One gave him a rather deep melding – a very dangerous endeavor, but luckily it seems to have worked with just some minor loss of cognitive function. We can be assured that Remy's indoctrination will remain in place this time."

He's bluffing. God neffing damn it. I hope he's bluffing.

"Remy," Charlotte says. "Come here."

Remy moves to stand in front of Charlotte. She looks at me and smiles – a sickening smile.

"Don't you hurt him!" I yell.

She continues to stare at me, holding her serpent smile. Where did they find this bitch? I've always thought of her as Thorn's little sidekick, but suddenly I think she's worse. I can see it in her eyes. She's evil, like a lion playing with its food.

"Remy," Charlotte says. "Kiss me."

My heart pounds ice around my veins as Remy leans in. Charlotte puts her hand on his cheek then slides it around to the back of his neck, running her fingers through his hair as their lips touch. They kiss – a long, passionate kiss – my neffing kiss.

"Get off him!" I scream as I run at her. I'm going to destroy her. I'm going to tear her perfect hair out and use it to strangle her. But instead I fly back, slamming into the same set of shelves again. I drop to the floor and grab at the back of my head.

Charlotte pulls away from Remy and gasps, slapping him hard across the face. "What kind of girl do you think I am?" she says in mock outrage.

Remy's head flicks to the side under the force of the slap, but he shows no reaction at all. His face is motionless.

"Alright Charlotte," Thorn says. "You've more than made your point." He fixes his eyes on me. "Show us your abilities, Molly. Let them out again."

"I can't," I say through short breaths and clenched teeth. "I don't know how."

"Charlotte," Thorn says. "Enough playing, I think."

Charlotte nods and pulls a pistol from a holster on her thigh. "Kneel, Remy." Remy drops to his knees before her, and Charlotte presses the pistol to his forehead.

"Show us your abilities, Molly," Mr Thorn says. "What you did escaping from the Alpha Compound, how you brought down the force field. I would like to see you do that again."

"Alright," I say. "Neffing shit. Alright. Just let me try."

I close my eyes and concentrate. I don't know what I'm doing. I still have no idea how to control it.

Molly.

I hear Remy in my head. It's faint, but he's there.

Remy? What have they done to you?

Don't use your powers.

What? Don't be stupid. If it saves you –

NO!

The force of the thought almost knocks me back.

No, he repeats. *When you use your powers you become vulnerable. Thorn will get control of you. That's how he got me. Don't use your powers.*

I can't let them shoot you.

There's no reply.

Remy?

Nothing.

Remy? I keep trying, even though I know he's gone. I can't feel him anymore. At least, not *my* Remy. I can only sense this other Remy, the one they control, and he's like a blank slate. He either can't talk or has no intention of doing so.

"We're waiting," Charlotte says.

I open my eyes and shoot her the shadiest look I can muster. "I'm neffing trying, bitch." And I am. I don't care if it makes me vulnerable, I really am trying. But even as I know Remy's life hangs in the balance, I can't make anything happen.

"Remy was among our most prized students," Thorn says after a moment. "He was going to play an important role in the war to come, and the future of mankind afterwards. That is why we were trying to take you alive when you escaped. That was, until we saw what *you* were capable of. You displayed such raw power, you've made yourself our number one priority. Unfortunately for Mr Dufort here, that means we are willing to sacrifice him to secure your compliance. You have ten seconds to unleash your power again or Charlotte will shoot Remy in the head."

"You want me to use my power," I say. "Why? So that you can have some better chance at controlling me? This doesn't make any sense. If I'm so powerful I'll use my power to kill you all right now."

"Yes," Thorn says. "I can see how you may draw that conclusion, but I'm ready for you now. I have to admit, you caught me at a disadvantage previously, but I'm more than capable of countering your abilities with my own. It is you who faces the conundrum, not us. Continue to resist and we will kill Remy. Give in and accept your place in mankind's future and Remy will live. You'll even be together."

"What guarantee do I have that you won't just kill him anyway?"

"Because, despite using him as bait in this rather crude way, we would still prefer to have him maintain his place in our endeavor."

"I don't know how," I say. "I swear." I wish I didn't sound so neffing begging-for-my-life.

"Hurry up," Charlotte says before adding with a sneer, "*bitch.*"

"Ten seconds, Miss McManus," Thorn says.

"If I knew how to do it I would."

"Nine."

"Look, take me with you. I'll go back to the Institute. You can plug me into your machines or whatever you want. Just leave him alone."

They all just stare at me. The Crab clicks, its head tilting toward Thorn. Thorn nods absently. Neffing hell. They're talking to each other in their minds.

"Five seconds," Thorn says.

REMY! I scream, trying desperately to wake him up, break him free of this control. But again, there's nothing.

"Four."

The Crab gazes at me with its impossible-to-read face, its flicking antennae and beady black eyes.

"Three."

Thorn's face is cold and emotionless, almost as unreadable as the alien's.

"Two."

Charlotte sneers with evil delight.

"I don't know how!" I scream again.

"One."

"NO!"

The gun cracks. The sound fills the small space of the storage room and seems to expand until it envelops my entire world. It echoes inside my mind. Remy falls and I see it happen so slowly that it's like it's the only thing my hot and blurry eyes will ever see again. But then his body is slumped awkwardly on the floor, and there's too much blood.

A hole has opened inside me. Not just the sick hollow that fills my stomach, but something in my mind, a black hole where that sense of Remy used to be. I can't feel the link between us. The connection we shared has been severed as if we were talking on tin cans and someone took scissors to the string. He's gone. Remy's gone.

She *actually* did it.

She did it.

I shift my gaze from Remy's empty body to Charlotte, locking eyes with her. My lip quivers and my breath comes in short, sharp bursts. My muscles shake uncontrollably, and the hole inside me suddenly fills with white-hot liquid rage that pours from my broken heart. I make a sound that might be a growl or a scream, I don't know. I don't care.

I feel it inside me, that same sense of power I felt as we tried to escape the N.E.Z. Here it is again. Fuelled by hate and anger. It's going to burst, but it's too late now isn't it? It's too late to save Remy. Still, I can use it to flay the skin off Charlotte's evil-murdering-bitch face. I scream again. With that sound my power, my will, whatever it is, is released in a wave toward the Crab and Thorn and Charlotte.

This time though, instead of sending them back through the warehouse walls or blasting them into cinders like I neffing want to, it stops. The shimmering wave of energy stands like a wall between myself and the three of them. Mr Thorn holds out his hand, holding my power back. And dammit if he wasn't right – he's so strong. It's like trying to spray a hose at a brick wall. I'm never going to be able to break through. My power slides back across the floor toward me, effortlessly turned away.

I push. For a moment I manage to hold it in place, but then Thorn overpowers me again. I feel him reaching out to grab control of me, like long fingers stretching through the air toward my mind. Just like Remy said. By using my power I've opened myself up to him. It's like ice down my spine as he closes in on me.

From somewhere distant there's the electric sound of a plasma gunshot.

Thorn releases his grip on me. One of the soldiers has his plasma rifle raised, pointing it at Thorn. The barrel smokes. Thorn is stumbling. He's been shot in the shoulder. I feel his hold on me weaken, and begin to push my power outward again.

"Charlotte!" Thorn yells. She spins, but is too slow.

The soldier utters three words, "We are Omega," and fires again. His shot hits Thorn in the middle of his chest. Charlotte fires two successive shots at the soldier and he goes down, but even as he falls, so too does Thorn. And with Thorn gone, the full force of my power is freed. It bursts out like foaming white water from a ruptured dam. No, it's more powerful than that. Last time it might have been water from a dam, but this time it's like the blast wave of an explosion. I can feel it spread from the point of detonation, and that point is me – a neffing human mushroom cloud.

In front of me the Crab bends over and tucks itself into a protective ball, like one of those bugs that rolls up when you poke it with a stick. My shockwave passes over it and its shell cracks before segments begin to tear away, leaving behind white flesh, muscles and blue blood. Beneath its shell it looks horrific, like a slimy human-shaped slug, but the sight doesn't last long as it's soon torn to shreds.

As the shimmering wave spreads across Charlotte and Thorn,

I sense Charlotte trying to hold it back, but she's nowhere near strong enough – it's like a fly trying to push back a windshield. As the wave passes over them they both disintegrate. Their flesh tears off their bones, and I glimpse their skeletons for a split second before they too are turned into particles of dust and blown away on an unseen wind.

My death-wave spreads further. It moves through the warehouse, smashing doors off hinges and leveling people. Outside of this room, where I can't see, I feel it flatten people to the ground or throw them back against walls, Omega and Majestic alike. It's too powerful for me to control.

When it's over I drop to my knees. Remy's body lies on the ground, untouched by my explosion but still unmoving – just as dead as he was before. I see tiny fragments of shell, like those you might find at the beach, stuck to the wall that was behind Number-One. When I turn to where Charlotte and Mr Thorn had been, I see nothing. The only trace of them is some dark shading on the floor and some torn shreds of their boots and clothes.

I drag myself over to Remy. His eyelids are closed. Part of me wants to open them, just to see those dark eyes one last time, but I can't bring myself to because I'm terrified there'll be nothing but an empty stare. I reach out and touch his cheek. It's still warm. Kneeling, I pull the heavy weight of him up onto my legs so that his head rests against my thighs. I stroke his hair. My fingers come away bloody, but I don't care.

"Remy," I say, barely able to speak. I pull him to me, rocking and crying, then look up at the roof and scream. I scream and cry and wish they had killed me because this hurts too much. I drop my head and feel my body shake with sobs. I know I'll never be able to fix this hole inside me. I'm broken. Everything's broken.

"WHAT THE HELL WAS THAT?" Art says as he pushes himself up to a sitting position, rubbing the side of his head.

Others have started moving too, rousing from where they were splayed over the floor or pushed in a heap against the wall like leaves after a heavy rain. The briefing room is in chaos. The long table in the center of the room has been upended against one wall and shattered into several pieces. Some people are jammed between it and the wall, others impaled by fragments of wood, groaning. Others are quiet, and that's worse.

"It was Molly," I say.

Mackenzie moves beside me. I see Jesse over in the corner and try to ignore the guilt that smacks me like a hammer, but the feeling rings through me, impossibly loud. Almost as soon as Molly asked me about him I started planting suspicion. I did it without a second thought, to protect myself, to protect my parents.

"Molly's power," Mackenzie says. "The same power she used to take down the force field."

I nod. "If she's done it again that means she's in trouble."

"We're already in trouble," Mackenzie says.

"No," I say, "I think for her it's a purely emotional reaction."

Art doesn't need any more convincing than that. He moves toward the door, picking up one of the soldier's rifles. They're still out cold.

"Sally, can you –" Art turns to Sally but stops when he sees her. She's on the ground, blood matting her hair. A section of table nearby is stained with splatters of crimson. Art stares at her, takes a deep breath, and turns to Mackenzie. "Mackenzie, get any surviving soldiers restrained."

Mackenzie keeps staring at Sally's body. Her eyes are filmed with the beginning of tears.

"Mackenzie!" Art barks and Mackenzie snaps her attention to him. Art closes his eyes, obviously trying to calm himself. "We mourn later," he says. "Right now we need to take the initiative." He pulls a handful of black plastic cable ties from a pocket on the soldier's uniform and passes them to her. "Get the soldiers secured and take their weapons. I'm going to find Molly."

"I'll come with you," I say.

"And me," Jesse says. "I'm coming too."

Art looks as though he's going to object, but then he nods. "Alright, but take a rifle each. Do you know how to use a rifle, Jesse?"

"I've never used one of those," Jesse nods at the alien-based plasma rifles, "but I've shot my Grandad's rifle." He looks at me. "What about you, Wells? Can you use one?"

I pick up a fallen soldier's plasma rifle and flick the thumb switch to charge it. It hums as the bright blue light begins emanating from the vents along the body. "Yeah," I say. "I can handle it."

"Come on," Art says as he leads the way out of the room.

"How do you know how to work the enemy rifles?" Jesse asks me, keeping his voice low.

I look sideways at him. "Remy showed me when we were escaping the Institute."

He hurries ahead to catch Art and, feeling a rising unease, I follow.

Ω

The three of us move from room to room with Art on point, our rifles raised, trying to cover all possible angles, like the world's most unqualified SWAT team. The majority of rooms are empty, but we eventually come to a storage space filled with dust-covered barrels. The air is thick and heavy. Six Majestic soldiers are lying motionless on the ground. Art crouches beside one, feeling at his neck for a pulse.

"Dead," he says, whispering.

We move to the door at the end of the space. It's slightly ajar, and Art pushes it open with the end of his rifle. He moves forward cautiously, but soon lowers his rifle and hurries inside.

In the room, crouching on the floor, is Molly. She looks up as we enter. Her face is pale, her black hair stuck to her forehead with sweat, her eyes red and swollen. She's holding tight to Remy's clothes, gripping them in white-knuckled hands. She's pulled him up onto her knees. She stares at us blankly, as if it takes her a long time to realize who we are.

"They killed him," she says. "They killed him."

My rifle clatters to the floor. I might have disagreed with how he'd done it, but Remy was responsible for me finding the truth and getting me out of the Institute. I might have thought what he did was wrong, but I never thought he deserved this.

Art approaches his niece and wraps his arms around her as she begins to sob. Art doesn't speak again for a long time, just lets Molly cry. Eventually, as she begins to quiet, he asks her, "What happened? Where's Thorn?"

Molly points toward the center of the room. I'd missed it at first, I think we all did, but there are shreds of black clothing spread out on the gray concrete. A shadow on the ground trails off and fades to nothing, reminiscent of the after-images of people following the nuclear bombs that were dropped on Nagasaki and Hiroshima.

"You did that?" Art says. "You killed them?"

Molly nods.

"Who was it?" Art asks. "Thorn and who else?"

"Charlotte." I answer for her. "It was Charlotte, wasn't it?"

Molly nods. Even after everything she did, even after she made me jam my own thumb into my eye, I still feel a pang of sorrow. I wonder, not for the first time, whether the attraction I felt to her was natural or if it was all just part of the indoctrination process.

"There was a Crab here too," Molly says.

"What?" I say. "Outside of the N.E.Z.?"

"Thorn called it Number-One. It's dead too."

"We can't stay here," Art says. "They know where we are."

"It's my fault," Molly says, her voice cracking with emotion. "It's my fault they found us."

"What?" Art says. "What do you mean?"

"My leg," Molly says, little more than a whisper. "At the Institute they healed my leg with nanomites. They must have snuck some of the tracking ones in. I should have said something, but I didn't think. I wasn't injected like Remy and Wells. And now...now it's my fault they found us. It's my fault Remy's dead."

"No," Art says. "I should have insisted you were all scanned by Mackenzie. I was responsible for security. This is on me, not you. I'll call Camp. If you're being tracked we'll fix that. With Sally gone I'll have to split up the cell. We've planned for this."

Molly looks at Art. "Sally's dead?"

He nods.

Molly speaks slowly. "Was that me? How many others?"

Art shakes his head.

"How many?" Molly asks again.

"Sally. Harry." He points at one of the motionless soldiers near the door. "Gordon. Some more, probably. We don't know yet."

"No," Molly says, emotion destroying her face.

"What do we do?" Jesse says. "How do you speak to Omega?"

"We don't," Art says. "He's always contacted us."

"What then?" Jesse says. "What do we do?"

"We leave. We take the data and abandon the cell." Art fixes us both with a penetrating stare. "We run."

Ω

When we return to Mackenzie's lab we find it devastated. The wall-mounted screens are shattered, the plastic melted back against the wall by plasma rifle fire. Tiny shards of glass are scattered over the benches and floor. The computers that make up Mackenzie's precious 64-core cluster have been torn from the racking and thrown onto the concrete. It looks like someone's taken a sledgehammer to them. All Mackenzie's other equipment has been tossed around too. It's obvious their aim was to destroy the data I stole.

Sitting on her swivel chair in the center of the carnage is Mackenzie. She looks up at us as we enter.

"It's gone," she says. "We never had a chance to back it up, or get it off-site. All that data, the proof of what's happening inside the Institute, the information on the Obelisk - we've lost it all."

Art looks around. Then, letting out a howl of frustration and rage, he kicks a busted piece of electronics across the room. It tumbles end over end until it hits one of the smashed computer boxes.

"At least we've still got Wells, Molly, and Remy," Mackenzie says.

Molly lets out what must be an involuntary sound at the mention of Remy's name. She's staring ahead into an abyss of nothingness.

Mackenzie turns to her, casting her eyes over the people in the room and I see recognition dawn. "Oh no," she says, "Remy?"

Art nods. "Killed by Thorn."

"Shit," Mackenzie says. "He was going to be so valuable."

"What?" Molly says. "Valuable? He was more than valuable to your fucking cause, Mackenzie. He was a person." Her voice breaks she can't continue.

"Molly," Mackenzie says. "Sorry. I didn't mean it like that. I didn't know him like you did, I'm sorry."

Molly doesn't reply. She's lost again to that distant stare.

"We'll mourn all those we've lost," Art says, "I promise you that. But right now we have to focus on what we do from here. We've still got a mission ahead of us."

"Mission." Molly almost whispers the word. "We aren't military like you, Uncle Art. We can't just switch off our emotions and finish the job."

"I'm not saying you switch them off. No one can do that. You're grieving and you're angry. But we need to act. We need to get the job done."

"We might have lost the data but there is something else," Mackenzie says. "I always keep a little something squirreled away for a rainy day."

Mackenzie moves to a cupboard, the contents of which – electrical cables, a multimeter, a soldering iron, and other tools for working with electronics – have been rummaged through. With a shove of her palm Mackenzie reveals a false panel at the back of the cupboard. Pulling it free, she reaches behind the panel and grabs a hot pink laptop covered with stickers. She covers her hand with the sleeve of her vintage bomber jacket and sweeps a section of the desk clear of plastic and glass shards, then puts the laptop down and opens it.

"After you went to find Molly I came here hoping to salvage something. The only thing I found still useable was the cloned cell phone I'd left on the desk. They'd thrown it against the wall but it still had a notification."

She says this last part as if we should understand the significance. I certainly don't, but Art does.

"Omega," he says.

Mackenzie nods. "There's a message from him."

IT'S MY FAULT. All my fault. That's all I can think as Mackenzie opens a browser on her laptop and types some numbers into the address bar. If I'd said something about the nanomites they treated me with or if I'd said something about my powers or if I'd done *something* maybe everyone would still be alive. If I'd cared about actually learning how to use my powers instead of Remy and I just— God. Remy. Remy's gone. The thought repeats over and over in my mind. Remy's gone. Remy's gone.

After a moment an image appears on Mackenzie's screen. It's a blood red arc, almost a complete circle, with two horizontal lines extending out from the bottom – the Greek letter omega. A disembodied voice, a voice disguiser making it sound deep and buzzing, speaks over the image.

"It is with great sorrow that I address you now. After the leaps and bounds we have taken recently with the help of our new recruits, today's events are a tragedy, a direct attack the likes of which we have not previously encountered. But we are Omega. We are strong. None of us were naive enough to believe that we entered into this fight without risking casualties. Still, it is with a heavy heart that I ask you to abandon this cell. Arthur, you are in command here now. Take our new assets and lay low.

"To further complicate matters, I have been continuing to monitor the N.E.Z. and transport aircraft have been leaving the Alpha Compound at an increased rate – far more regularly than at any time in the past. The only assumption we can make is that they have begun positioning Institute students around the world to boost global mind control. Unfortunately, it seems the pieces are already being set in place.

"I have made contact with your Omega brothers and sisters in Las Vegas. They will be meeting at a safe house beneath Apollo's Bar tomorrow night. They are preparing a mission to regain intelligence about the plans of the Xenocrustaceans in order for us to make these plans public. Once they are ready for further action I will make contact again. Until then, disappear, lay low, and be safe.

"I am. You are. We are Omega."

The laptop screen returns to black and Mackenzie lowers the lid, clicking it closed.

"So that's it?" I say. "We're just going to hide?"

"Yes," Uncle Art says. "We do as Omega asks."

"I don't even know who that is," I say. "Shit, *you* don't even know who that is. Some faceless voice gives the order to roll over and hide like a frightened dog and you just do it? He even said they're getting ready to start their mind control. We can't just do nothing!"

"Omega has never steered us wrong, Molly," Uncle Art says.

"Remy is dead!" I shout, my eyes as hot as my voice. "I'm not going to let them get away with that!"

"Molly," Uncle Art starts, but I cut him off.

"No! I'm not going to let them!" I want to continue my protest but a thick lump of emotion lodges in my throat. Uncle

Art puts his arm around my shoulders and it's all I can do not to sink to the floor in a blubbering mess.

"I know you're hurting," he says, "and I know you blame yourself for this, but you have to trust me. Omega is right, we should lay low. We'll be back in this fight before you know it."

"*Your* fight," I say.

"Bullshit, Molly," Mackenzie says. "You want to fight the Crabs as much as any of us, and you know what else?"

"What?" I say, more than a little surprised by Mackenzie's change of tone.

"This was Remy's fight too."

I stare at her without saying a word.

"We do as Omega asks," Uncle Art says, "not because we're mindless drones but because we trust him. We choose to fight for the survival of mankind. We are the only ones who can."

We shouldn't be laying low. We don't need stupid files from the Institute anymore. We know what the Crusties are doing and we know how to stop them. We need to destroy the Obelisk. I don't care what some faceless Greek letter says, every moment we spend hiding from the Crusties is another moment I'm not making them pay for what they did to Remy, what they made me do to everyone else, what they did to my parents.

"You said that cell phone still works?" Uncle Art says to Mackenzie.

She nods, passing him the phone. Uncle Art taps in a number through the smashed screen, holds the phone to his ear, waits, then says just one word.

"Braveheart."

He waits a moment longer before hanging up, then holds the phone in front of him as if expecting a return call. It buzzes with the rattling chirp of Skype. He answers.

"Camp, we need a pick-up." He looks at me. "And we need

you to bring the EMP dialysis machine. You think you can get it working in the back of your van?"

Ω

I turn the clear cylinder over in my hand, looking at the gluey fluid inside. Bubbles are trapped in the gunk, like lemonade frozen in time. Supposedly the nanomites pulled from my blood are in there. It frustrates me that I can't see the little robots swimming around. It's their fault the Majestic agents found us. These tiny little machines too small to even see, are the reason Remy and so many others are dead.

I've just been unhooked from Camp's dialysis machine after spending the last hour or so hooked up to it in a cage in the back of his van. Wells, Jesse, Mackenzie, and Camp are in the back with me. Uncle Art is driving. After Uncle Art made the call to Camp, we had to wait a tense few hours for him to arrive, worried that Majestic would send more soldiers. But they never did.

"We best get rid of that then, lass."

"Huh?" I look at Camp, not really catching the words that have dragged me away from my dark thoughts.

"I said we best get rid of those nanomites, lass," Camp repeats. "That jar's got the last thing this Majestic lot can use to track us."

I look down at the cylinder in my hand again.

"Allow me," I say. I stand, grab the handle of the van's sliding door and pull it open. Air whips my hair and buffets my ears with a thumping roar as we speed down the highway.

"What are you doing back there?" Uncle Art says, turning to look into the rear of the van. "Shut the door while we're driving!"

I cock my arm back and toss the container of nanomites out over the embankment at the side of the road. It lands somewhere in the yellow-brown of the dry desert grass. I lose sight of it immediately, but still feel a sense of freedom as we roar down the road away from that neffing Crab juice. I close the van door with a slam, silencing the wild, churning wind.

"Well," Camp says, "good a way as any I suppose."

"So, where exactly are we going?" Jesse says.

"Nowhere related to Omega," Uncle Art says. "There's an old motel in Garrison, back near the border. It doesn't see much in the way of traffic. We'll stay there for now."

"Garrison," Wells says. "That sounds like a fitting place to hide."

"I don't think it's actually going to be a garrison Wells," Jesse says.

"Really?" Wells says. "I was expecting a drawbridge and moat. What a disappointment."

"Back toward Nevada?" Mackenzie asks, interrupting the bickering before it can really get started. "Garrison is only twenty minutes from Little Basin. Are you sure that's a good idea?"

"Fact is, we're on our own at the moment," Uncle Art says. "Omega has told us to avoid all contact with others in the group. Majestic won't expect us to head back in that direction, and besides, remaining in the desert, away from populated areas is probably our best bet at flying under the radar."

"Alright," Mackenzie says. "You're probably right. Hopefully they have wifi."

I look through the windshield at the orange-brown desert plains, fragments of enormous boulders the only thing breaking up the landscape.

Wells sighs. "I wouldn't get your hopes up about wifi."

"AND THE WIFI password is *visitor123*, all lowercase," the elderly man at the front desk says as he places our keys on the wooden countertop.

"Okay," I say, as Mackenzie looks at me, "I was wrong about the wifi."

We're at the Garrison Holiday Motel, though I'm not sure many people would come here on holiday – the main clientele are probably drug dealers waiting for their customers. The motel is just outside the town of Garrison, which only seems to be three houses. All twelve of the motel rooms are lined up parallel to the road on a large slab of concrete. There's no fence or trees or pool, or anything remotely decorative at all.

Art hires us a room each, assuring us Omega will cover the cost through untraceable credit card transactions. According to our cover story, Molly, Jesse, Mackenzie and I are on a school trip, a type of science camp, and Art and Camp are our teachers. Not that the man at the desk seems interested. He doesn't even question our cuts and bruises, or the bandage over my eye. He just grunts something and turns his attention back to the small television, which is showing an American football game.

"Why don't we all get some rest?" Art says.

Exhausted, everyone agrees. Lying on an actual bed seems like the most luxurious idea I've ever been presented with. Plus, I think we all need some time to process what's happened. The rooms are gloomy and basic, bare of all but the simplest necessities: a toilet, sink, and shower in the bathroom – a space so small that the door hits the ceramic toilet bowl before it can open all the way. There's a bed, a small wooden bench with one chair, a microwave and a television that's at least twenty years old on an arm extending from the corner of the room.

I flop onto the bed. I'm sure under any other circumstances I'd consider the mattress, lumpy and uneven, but right now my muscles and bones sink into it like a welcoming embrace. I'm in a daze halfway between wakefulness and sleep when a buzzing in my skull draws me back to consciousness. It takes me a few moments to realize it's coming from a spot behind my right ear. At first I think there's a mobile phone under my head, but then I remember what Mr Thorn did to me – what I agreed to do.

Wells.

The voice sounds like it's coming from behind me. I sit up and turn, but of course there's nothing behind me but the wall.

I'm speaking to you through subtle vibrations in the bones of your skull and ear. I want you to answer me only if you are alone. Are you alone?

"Yes," I say.

Good. As my voice is synthesized you will not recognize it, but I am the individual you know as Mr Thorn.

"What? That's impossible. Molly killed you."

She may have reason to believe that, but I assure you I am as much the individual you know as Mr Thorn as the one you met.

"I don't understand."

You don't need to. We are contacting you as per our agreement. You should also be aware that through this device we are able to hear everything that you hear. As an example of this, we are now aware of the gathering of Omega agents at a bar in Las Vegas. We thank you for that.

"No," I say. If they're listening all the time that changes everything. I thought I could figure a way out of this, maybe lie to Majestic and try to tell Mackenzie or Art the truth. But it's too late. I've betrayed Omega already and I didn't even know. "If you do anything in Las Vegas it will be obvious someone is spying."

What we do with the intelligence you gather is none of your concern. You have already planted suspicion against Jesse Hill, I would suggest you continue that line of misdirection.

This can't be happening.

There are two tasks we need you to work toward. First and foremost, we need you to continue your investigation into the identity of the individual known as Omega. Secondly, as you are aware, Majestic agents managed to successfully destroy the computer equipment used to decrypt the information you stole from the Institute server. We want you to ensure this was the only copy of the data in Omega's hands.

"It was," I say. "It was the only copy we had. That means Omega isn't as much of a threat, doesn't it? Can't you just leave us alone?"

Ensure this was the only copy. And Wells?

"Yes?"

Before you consider trying to remove the device from behind your ear, know that any attempt to forcefully remove it will result in an instant release of a highly refined cyanide-based poison into your bloodstream. Likewise, if we suspect you have revealed your status as a double agent to another member of Omega, vocally or otherwise, we will remotely trigger the cyanide release. In both cases you will be dead within fifteen seconds. Do we have an understanding?

I don't reply, and the silence hangs heavy with the threat. I sit on the bed for a long time, but Mr Thorn doesn't speak again. The spot behind my ear tingles with the after-effects of the vibration. My right eye burns with barely contained emotion, and the continuous pain from my ruined left eye flares up. I swallow down a vile, acidic taste.

How do I get myself out of this? If I try to remove the bug behind my ear I'm dead. If I tell anyone what I'm being forced to do I'm dead. If I don't play along I'm dead. In all cases, they'll tell my parents the truth about Maggie, and then they'll probably be dead too – if not at the hands of Majestic, that news alone will be enough to kill them. I've already cost some Omega agents their lives, but if I do what I'm told I'm sure I'll cause more death– maybe Mackenzie or Molly or Art. My friends, the only friends I have.

There's only one way out.

I open the drawer in the bench. Just as I hoped, it contains cutlery – two knives, two spoons, two forks and a teaspoon, but it's enough. I grab the knife, a butter knife with a slightly serrated edge, and hold it up, squinting to try and examine it. It doesn't look very sharp.

I swallow and press the knife to the spot behind my right ear. My hand shakes. I have to do this quickly before the last of my resolve completely abandons me. If I do this, then the mole inside Omega will be gone and my friends will be safe.

I squeeze the handle of the knife, increasing the pressure against my skin, getting ready to cut and hoping that cyanide kills painlessly. A tear runs down my cheek. If I kill myself now my friends will be safe, but what about my parents? They're the reason I agreed to this in the first place. The shake in my hand grows until the blade of the knife moves against my skin. I can't hold it still.

I open my hand and let the knife fall onto the bed covers. I drop heavily onto the edge of the bed, catching my face in my hands and sobbing. I can't do it. I'd like to believe it's because of my parents, but I know it's not. I'm not brave enough. I'm not brave enough to sacrifice myself to save my friends. I can't kill myself. I don't want to die. I hate what I'm doing, but I hate even more that I'm not brave enough to end it.

$$\Omega$$

Later, thankfully once the tears have stopped and my eyes – or at least my eye – have dried, Art comes to my room with a small box of cereal, an almost empty carton of milk and a box of painkillers.

"Here," he says, "eat this. It's not much, but we're sharing it around. I'll go out and collect some supplies tomorrow. Also, I found some pain relief for your eye."

He looks at me and his demeanor changes. There's a concerned dip in his eyebrows, a slight tilt of his head. I'm sure he knows I've been crying. He doesn't say anything, though. His mouth just turns up in the faintest of reassuring smiles, and he reaches out and takes hold of my shoulder.

"How are you holding up, buddy?" he asks.

"Alright," I lie.

"You know," he says, "I'm here if you need to talk to anyone about what's going on."

"I'm fine. Thanks for the cereal and the painkillers," I say, putting on my best attempt at a passable smile. "I'll see you in the morning."

I close the door and lean against it, exhaling heavily. Is Art really just concerned about me or does he suspect something? I don't know. I drop the cereal and milk on the counter. I don't feel like eating.

Barely five minutes later there's another knock on my door. I wish everyone would leave me alone. I don't want to talk to anyone – not now that I know Majestic is listening in on every

228 / JUSTIN WOOLLEY

conversation. It's best for everyone if I have as little contact with them as possible.

"Wells, it's me," Mackenzie says, knocking again. "Can you open the door?"

I get up off the bed, knowing I don't have any excuse not to – I obviously can't tell her the truth. When I open the door she smiles at me.

"Art sent you, didn't he?" I ask.

"He told me he was worried about you, but I was going come by anyway. I've got something for you."

"Oh really? What's that?"

"Can I come in?"

"What do you want to give me?"

Mackenzie cocks her eyebrow. I didn't mean for my voice to sound so sharp-edged. I just don't want her to give me anything Majestic would want to know about.

"Wells," she says, her tone not inviting any argument, "go and sit on the bed."

I relent, knowing it's a fine line between trying to protect her and making it obvious to Majestic that I'm trying to push the other members of Omega away.

Mackenzie enters the room and closes the door behind her. "I understand if you want to be alone. I get like that too sometimes, but trust me when I say it's not always a good idea – especially with the weight of everything that's happened. We don't have to talk about anything if you don't want, but I'm just going to hang out for a while. That alright?"

Emotion wells inside me again. Even my maimed eye tingles, like maybe it hasn't completely lost the ability to cry. If I speak I'll betray the surge of emotion I'm feeling so I just nod, my mouth pulled tight to hold everything in.

"Good," she says, "because I'd like to stay. Like I said, I've got something for you." She digs into the pocket of her bomber jacket. "I made you this."

When she pulls her hand out something drops to hang from her fingers. At first I think it's just a black strap tied into a loop, but then I see the semicircular piece of shiny black fabric sewn to it. It's an eye patch.

"I know it's a bit rough, probably a little too Captain Blackbeard maybe, but I didn't exactly have a lot to work with. I thought it might be good to replace that bandage. Besides, everyone knows eye patches make you look badass. You want to try it?"

I nod again – it's all I can manage without collapsing into a spluttering mess. Mackenzie unwraps the bandage. I shy away, not wanting her to see the disgusting wreck of my eye, but she touches my cheek and gently turns my head back toward her before slipping the elastic around my head, adjusting the patch until it covers my damaged eye.

"See," she says, "total badass. I'm going to have to start calling you Snake."

I manage a smile. "Thanks."

"You're very welcome."

"How did you make it?"

She laughs. "I'm not sure you want to know."

"What do you mean?"

"Well, the patch is cut from the cup of my bra and the elastic is from my underwear."

"What?" I say, feeling at the patch over my eye, the silky soft feel of it making me blush even harder. I go to pull it off but Mackenzie grabs my hand, laughing.

"It's fine," she says, "I washed it."

"That's not really what I was worried about. It's more the principle of the thing."

Mackenzie laughs again. "I told you I didn't have much to work with."

I push thoughts of my betrayal away as another thought strikes me. "But if you cut up your underwear to make this, then..."

Mackenzie smiles mischievously. "Then..." She leans in close to me, moves to whisper into my ear, her lips only centimeters from my skin. Butterflies rush into my stomach like a mass insect invasion. She continues in a breathy voice, "...it's lucky I remembered to bring more underwear."

I pull away and look at her and she breaks into laughter again.

"It's just too easy with you sometimes."

Ω

We've been staying at the motel for two nights when Mackenzie bangs on my door early in the morning. My room is still dark, and when I slide out the locking chain and open the door I see that the sun is only just brightening the sky in the east, spearing burnt yellow through the purple of the retreating night.

"My room," is all she says before she moves off to bang on the door beside mine, the room where Art is staying. It's strange that she's so abrupt. Something must be wrong. I look to my right. The doors to Molly's room and Camp's room are open. The two of them are emerging, obviously roused by Mackenzie in the same way. I lock eyes with Molly and she shrugs, indicating her confusion.

In a few minutes we're all in Mackenzie's room, her laptop open on the small table. We must have received a message from Omega. I was wondering how long it would take. The Las Vegas meeting of Omega agents was last night. There's a tingling behind my right ear – not a real sensation, just a psychosomatic response to the awareness that everything Omega says will be relayed straight to Majestic-12. I desperately want to tell the others that Thorn is still alive. I don't know how it's possible. The beginning of a panic attack rushes through me. My chest tightens, and my skin explodes with heat. My heart pounds. I don't have it in me to even try to control myself. I just try to keep still and quiet as my nervous system roars like a beast inside me.

"A message from Omega?" Art asks.

Mackenzie nods. "It came through during the night."

"I just need to go to the toilet," I say, looking for any excuse to get out of the room.

"It's not very long," Mackenzie says as she accesses the secure FTP server where the messages from Omega are uploaded. "You can wait."

The screen of the laptop goes black and the familiar red omega symbol appears.

"Good morning," Omega says in his altered voice. "I'm going to be brief with my message for reasons that will be apparent soon enough. You'll recall that in my last communiqué I informed you that your fellow Omega agents would be meeting at Apollo's Bar in Las Vegas last night. The following is CCTV footage from the street showing the entrance to Apollo's Bar at 0143 hours this morning."

The image of the Omega symbol cuts away to grainy black-and-white footage of a street corner alight with the glow of flashing neon and bright lights. One of the bars toward the center of the screen has a sign above the door that says "Apollo's". The street is busy with people, groups of partygoers staggering and stumbling. There's no sound accompanying the video, but it looks as though they're yelling and singing and whatever else people do in the streets of Las Vegas at night. The scene seems innocent enough, until suddenly they all turn their heads to look at something out of frame and begin to scatter. A moment later the reason for the hasty departure comes into view: two large vehicles with flashing lights on their roofs drive up come to an aggressive stop in front of Apollo's. Each is black and labeled SWAT on the side in large white letters. The back doors of both vehicles burst open and heavily armed police explode out. Only, they're not wearing anything that would identify them as police – in fact, their black fatigues, black helmets, and black balaclavas are identical to those worn by the Majestic soldiers who attacked the warehouse.

The police, or more likely Majestic soldiers posing as police, stack up in a formation at the front door of Apollo's, each with a hand on the shoulder of the man in front. One of them nods, motioning forward with a hand signal, and another swings back a large object, some kind of battering ram. It slams it into the wooden door, causing it to splinter and burst inward. The soldiers storm forward into the darkness of the entrance and out of sight.

The image on the screen cuts back to the symbol of Omega.

"As you can see," the electronic voice resumes, "forces likely belonging to the group we know as Majestic-12 stormed Apollo's Bar, the site of a gathering of Omega agents."

Omega pauses. I swallow, and the sound is so loud in my ears that I hope no one else can hear it.

"However," Omega speaks again, "there was no gathering of Omega agents at Apollo's. Inside Apollo's those soldiers would have found empty tables and dusty bottles of flat beer in a bar long closed for renovations. Apollo's Bar is not an Omega safe house, and there was never any mission being planned to recover further intelligence about Operation Vassal. That information was a plant. I've suspected Majestic have been trying to leverage a mole within Omega for some time, and now have strong reason to believe they have succeeded.

"It's important for you to understand that the only time I've ever mentioned Apollo's Bar was in my previous message to you. I'm sure I don't need to explain the implications of this.

"One of you is a traitor to our cause, a double agent working for the very organization that is orchestrating this betrayal of the human race. Although you six are our greatest strength in the fight against the Crabs, you are also carrying with you our greatest Achilles heel, someone who aims to bring about our destruction. Therefore, unless you can determine the leak and address it, you will be pruned from the tree, exiled from the group. You have one week.

"I am. You are. We are Omega."

Even before the omega symbol has completely faded from the screen I turn to look at Jesse, only to find him staring at me. His eyes meet mine and thin into a suspicious glare. My neck blooms with a hot rush – a stress rash. Nobody speaks. We eye each other with a mix of shock, concern and evaluation.

"Well," Molly eventually says, breaking the silence, "this is neffing bullshit, right?"

"I SAID this is bullshit isn't it?" I repeat. "We don't have a traitor. Omega must be wrong. Maybe his message got hacked or something."

"Impossible," Mackenzie says. "Even if someone did manage to hack into our secure server, I programmed a digital ink-bomb into it myself. If anyone opened the message I'd know."

"Maybe it's not the real Omega then," I say.

"It is," Mackenzie says. She doesn't bother explaining but I'm sure if I pushed she'd have some nerdy computer jargon for me.

"What do we do now then?"

"We find out which one of us is working for Majestic," Uncle Art says.

"Great," Jesse says, "so we're having a witch hunt?"

I look at Jesse, trying to get him to at least acknowledge me, but he doesn't. I don't think he's spoken a single word to me since the attack on the warehouse and I have no idea where we stand with each other. Sure, I know I hurt him and he feels like I chose Remy over him or whatever but after everything that's happened, after what happened to Remy, I would have thought he'd at least try and see if I'm doing okay. I neffing need him to be my best friend right now.

"Unless anyone wants to come forward and save us the trouble, I don't really see an alternative," Uncle Art says. "Anyone want to get this over with?"

"Yeah," I say, "because that's going to neffing work."

"I'd like to suggest that whoever's responsible for leaking information to Majestic quietly leaves," Mackenzie says. "Nothing will happen to you. No repercussions from us. Sometime in the next few days, if one of you suddenly disappears, then that's that. We won't try and follow."

"You're saying *you* a lot," I say to Mackenzie. "How do we know you're not the traitor?"

"Mackenzie has been with Omega since the beginning, Molly," Wells says. Even longer than your uncle. I doubt it's her."

"What about you then?" Jesse says to Wells.

"What?" Wells says. "You're the one who came out of the attack perfectly unharmed. Look what they did to me."

"Stop it. This is what they want," Mackenzie interrupts. "They want us to tear ourselves apart."

"Well they've done a neffing good job, haven't they?" I say.

As if things weren't bad enough after losing Remy and the others, now we're going to fight each other and Omega has basically abandoned us to do it. I don't much care whether I'm part of Omega's secret resistance army or not – all I care about is getting revenge for everything the Crabs have done. I can help root out the traitor and go back to taking orders from a robotic-voiced Greek symbol or I can rely on myself to do what's necessary. Since my parents died I haven't relied on anyone for anything. Why should I start now?

There's a chime from Mackenzie's computer. She looks down at it. "Turn on the TV," she says. When no one moves she almost shouts. "The TV!"

Uncle Art grabs the remote, aims it at the ancient TV in the corner of the room, and turns it on. The image on the screen shows a ship, shining silver-blue metal hovering above the skyscrapers of a city at night. It's made of the same material as the Crustie ship that started all this jank. But this one is a proper flying saucer shape, and it's bigger, a lot bigger. The ship is so large that the image doesn't capture all of it – it's like the entire sky is metal. It looms over everything, reflecting the colored neon of the city below. The text at the bottom of the screen says: Tokyo.

"Neffing jank," I say. "Not again."

The image changes. This time it's Paris. A similar ship appears on the screen, this one above the iconic Eiffel Tower.

The screen changes again. Mumbai. This one is a distant shot, the first to capture an entire ship. It takes me a moment to notice the buildings for scale. The ship hangs above of one the world's largest cities, enveloping it all in shadow.

Lagos. Chicago. Rio de Janeiro.

The footage eventually cuts to two news anchors, a man and a woman staring down the camera, visibly pale even under their make-up.

The female anchor speaks. "If you're just tuning in what you're seeing are images of what appears to be a global phenomenon. Ships unmistakably similar to that of the Xenocrustaceans have begun appearing all around the world."

The male presenter begins speaking. "At the moment we have no official comment from the Alpha Compound or the White House, but we'd like to reiterate that there is no evidence to suggest these vessels mean us any harm."

"They want the Obelisk," Mackenzie says. "The war is starting."

$$\Omega$$

"As you can see, the ship is just hovering as it has been for the last few hours, but police are advising people to return home and stay indoors until more is known about the reasons behind these new arrivals."

"I'm sorry Felicity, we're going to have to leave you." The television cuts from the reporter on the streets of Chicago back to the anchors in the studio – Carl Allen and Samantha Lamar, according to the caption. Carl is speaking, holding his finger to the earpiece in his ear. "We're receiving word that we're being patched into a transmission from the Alpha Compound." He glances off camera. "Now, is it? Okay. Yes, we're going to a live announcement direct from the Alpha Compound."

The image goes black for a moment before it is replaced by the logo for the Institute for the Betterment of Humanity. We glance at each other. I have a sudden urge to scream obscenities at the television, but I restrain myself. When the logo disappears we're looking at a podium. The seal of the US government's Department of Extraterrestrial Affairs is on the wooden lectern.

A man steps onto the podium and my breath leaves me in a sudden rush. It feels like someone has punched me in the stomach with a jumbo jet.

"What the fuck?" I say.

Right there, on the TV, is Mr Thorn. He's standing at the back of the stage, looking into the camera like I didn't disintegrate him into pink mist a couple of days ago. There's no way he can be there. I spin to look at the others, hoping they'll have some explanation, but they're all staring at me.

"You told us you killed him," Mackenzie says. I know what she's thinking. She's thinking I lied to them, and if I lied about that then maybe I'm the traitor.

"I did kill him!" I shout. "I saw him die!"

Mackenzie doesn't respond, but she doesn't take her eyes off me.

"Stop looking at me like that!" I say.

"Maybe this isn't live," Uncle Art says. "Or maybe you were just mistaken. Are you sure he was dead?"

"Yes I'm sure! He was blown to pieces. Him and Charlotte and that Crustie called Number-One."

"It's live," Mackenzie says. She's on the edge of her bed, her laptop open in front of her. "Broadcasting live on every channel and across the internet. It's a direct transmission time-stamped right now. That's him, Molly." She looks up at me. "That's Thorn."

"It's not possible!"

"Speaking of Charlotte," says Jesse.

And there she is, climbing up onto the stage and moving to stand behind the lectern, dressed in her Institute uniform.

"You are neffing kidding me," I say. "And before anyone says anything, I swear to the janking high heavens I killed the bitch too. I swear it."

After Charlotte, a Crab steps up onto the stage, moving grotesquely as its segments of shell slide over each other. It wears those clear boots over the lower sections of its legs and has the same curling blue lines over its body as Number-One. It's not Number-One, though. It's a different color, a bit paler, with maybe a smaller head.

"Good afternoon," Charlotte says, smiling at the gathered press. "My name is Charlotte Yorke. I'm speaking to you today as a representative of the students of the Institute for the Betterment of Humanity and," she gestures to the Crustie, "as spokesperson for the Xenocrustaceans here on Earth."

"You're neffing dead is what you are," I say, but Uncle Art shushes me.

"There is no doubt the arrival of the Xenocrustaceans has been the most monumental event in human history. All of us were touched by the effects of the plague, all of us have lost people, and we will never forget them. Our society was rocked to the core and it has taken many years for us to recover and recognize what a miracle it is to be able to make contact with a species from across the cosmos.

"Like a phoenix rising from the ashes, humanity, together with the Xenos, will see a world born anew, better than ever before. Over the coming years the world we live in will be fundamentally changed, but it is not a change to be feared. I assure you, this change will be for the better, to create a world free of disease and hunger and poverty, achieving a utopian existence for us all.

"I come before you today, however, to warn of forces that do not want that future for mankind. The peaceful Xenocrustaceans who crashed here on Earth were attempting to escape the persecutions of their world. Now those who mean them harm have followed them across the stars. All over the planet ships are settling above centers of human population. We have welcomed our peace-loving guests to Earth, and so these new visitors mean us harm, too.

"But we will stand with the Xenocrustaceans of Earth. We will not see them taken back to slavery and oppression and torment. As citizens of the cosmos we have a responsibility to stand against injustice wherever it may happen. Students of the Institute are already in locations around the world to lead this stand.

"Now, more than ever, human and Xeno must stay united. What you do in the coming days or weeks, or however long it takes to drive these attackers from our skies, will be remembered. We will fight together, we will win together, and when this is over we will look forward to the future, together."

The screen returns to the newsreaders in the studio.

"Well, there you have it," Carl Allen says. "A message of unity and an ominous warning about the intentions of these new Xenocrustaceans, though what –"

Uncle Art switches the television off. No one speaks for a long moment, until Wells breaks the silence.

"Holy heck."

"What are the Xenos doing?" Uncle Art says. "If they want the Obelisk, why don't they just go straight to the compound? Why do they have to attack the whole planet?"

Mackenzie taps her fingers against her lips. "Maybe they're not."

"What do you mean?" Uncle Art says.

"Maybe they're not attacking. Maybe they're searching. The ships are hovering over population centers all around the planet, but not all of them, and not even some of the biggest ones. I mean, there's no ship over London or Beijing, no ship over New York or Los Angeles. I was trying to work out why they're positioned where they are. Then I checked the distances. The ships are almost equally spaced. They're all separated by around four or five thousand miles. I don't think they're attacking, I think it's a search party. They're trying to find the Obelisk. The question is, what happens when they do?"

"WHAT THE HELL is going on with the news?" Jesse says. He's switched the television back on – part of our intermittent check on the coverage. It's a welcome break from the conversation we've been having about what we're going to do. That conversation hasn't gone anywhere in the last hour, and has primarily been an argument between Molly wanting to attack now, Art wanting to take a more cautious approach, and Mackenzie wanting to focus on ridding us of the traitor – me, but of course they don't know that.

"Seriously," Jesse says, "there's something wrong with the TV."

"What do you mean?" I say.

Jesse points at the screen. "Look for yourself."

"It's a news desk."

"Well," Jesse says, "given how intelligent everyone claims you are, you might notice that there's nobody sitting at the news desk telling us the janking news."

"Right," I say, "It's probably just a mistake or something. Maybe they cut back to the studio too early."

Jesse begins flicking through channels. There's a re-run of

Friends, a stock market update, a map of Utah and surrounds showing the weather for the next seven days, and a cooking show. He stops on another popular news channel – it too has an empty desk where there should be newsreaders.

"That *is* a bit strange," I say.

Jesse continues moving through channels. The next two show a network logo and an apology for technical difficulties. He goes back to the original news channel, which is still showing an empty desk under bright lights, as if they were in the middle of a broadcast.

Mackenzie, who's sitting on the bed propped up against the pillows, spins her laptop around, showing the screen to everyone. "This is from Melbourne," she says.

I feel a rush of concern upon hearing the name of my home city. The screen shows a video shot on a mobile phone. A Xeno ship hangs in the sky and thousands of people are walking the streets. They're all staring straight ahead with emotionless but determined faces. A man's voice narrates the video.

"Seriously, what the fuck is going on?! Everyone's just walking. They all just started walking."

There's a sound a lot like a fluxer as dark shapes flash by overhead. The image is too blurred to get a good view, but they don't look like human aircraft.

"There's something falling from the ship!" the narrator continues. "What are those things?"

The jittering video turns to focus on the Xeno ship. It's hard to see anything against the backdrop of the impossibly large vessel, but as the shaky vision zooms in I can make out fast-moving dark spots, tiny things dropping away from somewhere near the center. I count ten of them, possibly a few more. They plummet downward, and the man doing his best to film the objects zooms out to track their descent.

Each of the objects is some kind of black metal cylinder,

falling end first, like a darkly shining seed pod. As they grow nearer a faint blue glow emanates from the underside of each one. Their descent slows, but they're still falling with a high enough velocity that they land hard. Several of the pods land close to the camera. One crashes through the overhead wires for the trams and slams into the road with a crunch, plowing a divot in the tarmac. Another lands off to the side with a horrendous smash, and the camera spins to capture the pod speared through the roof of a police car. The vision turns back to the pod in the street. It hisses, and the front begins to hinge open. There's a dark shape inside, but we lose sight of it as the people in the streets charge at the pods. The footage suddenly spins wildly as the phone is knocked free, landing facedown on the road.

Mackenzie changes to another video. It's chaotic. Someone is filming from among a crowd, trying to fight against the flow of an overwhelming number of people. The image is all arms and legs and flashes of faces. The cameraperson fights their way free by climbing up onto a yellow taxi, the hood and roof popping under their feet. When they lift the camera again the view is of a street, an American street – this must be Chicago, the only city in America with a ship overhead. One of the small Xeno ships, the ones the fluxer design was obviously based on, flies in at tremendous speed and stops to hover above the throng. It fires blue plasma down onto the street, shooting in front of the crowd, almost like a warning shot, an attempt to keep them back from the pods that have landed here as well.

The pod in view of the camera is open, and a tall black figure, obviously a Xenocrustacean but completely covered in some kind of armor, is standing nearby with its hands outstretched, like it's feeling for something in a dark room. The crowd attempts to surge forward but another blast from the small Xeno fighter craft forces them back, throwing some humans into the air. Off to the side the crowd begins to part. The camera spins to show they're making way for a figure dressed in an Institute uniform. It's a dark-haired girl I don't recognize, but as she draws near the front of the crowd she lifts her arms. She pauses momentarily, then throws her arms forcefully down. The Xeno aircraft follows the arc of her movement and smashes into the street with a horrendous whine of flux engines and the crunch of rending metal. The armored Xeno spins to see the craft crash and then turns back in time to see the crowd surging at it. The video feed cuts out.

"These videos are being posted on social media," Mackenzie says. "But there's hardly any action on any social network. Not what you'd expect with what's going on. There are only a few people reporting what's happening."

"Jank," Molly says. "It's the mind control, isn't it?"

"Forget about what's happening everywhere else," Jesse says. He's standing by the glass door at the back of the motel room. "Look what's happening here." He slides the door open and walks out. The rest of us follow and then, in an almost synchronized movement, we turn our faces up.

Above us, darkening almost the entire sky and casting a huge shadow across the ground, is an enormous ship. The sky seems to boil around it, the clouds lit orange with fire as the silvery shape pushes its way down through the atmosphere. It's enormous. Something that big should make a hell of a noise, but it doesn't – it moves in almost complete silence. There's a faint rumble, like thunder in the distance, but that's all.

"It's moving in the direction of the N.E.Z.," Uncle Art says.

"They've found the Obelisk," Mackenzie says.

"So what do –" Molly begins, but stops as Camp and Art suddenly rush away.

"Uncle Art, what's wrong?" Molly says, but Camp and Art jog to the van without looking back. "Uncle Art?"

Molly glances at us in confusion. I shrug. Art and Camp jump into the van.

"Uncle Art?!" Molly repeats. "What are you doing?"

The doors close. Molly runs to the driver's side and grabs at the handle, trying to open the door, but Art has locked it from the inside. He turns to look at her but his expression is blank, creepily void of anything resembling emotion.

"Uncle Art! Where the jank are you going?!" The van rumbles to life. Molly bangs on the window with her fist. "Hey!"

Camp and Art ignore her, even as Art backs the van out of the parking space and the side mirror clips Molly, spinning her out of the way. The van stops, turns, then drives out of the car park and away down the highway.

"Hey!" Molly keeps calling as she runs after them. "Hey!" Standing on the edge of the highway she turns back to look at us, searching for answers, but we're just as confused as she is. "What's going on? Where are they going?"

It's Mackenzie that answers. "The mind control – people all over the world are acting as if they're being driven by something, it's probably that. It's got them too."

"Hello?" A voice comes from inside the room. "I think we're still broadcasting. I don't really know. I hope someone can hear me." We hurry back into the room at the sound of the desperate voice coming from the television. A young woman has appeared on the empty set in front of the news desk. She's wearing stylish black-rimmed glasses and a headset over one ear, with a microphone extending down to her mouth. She looks awkwardly into the camera. Her voice wavers as she continues. "I'm just an assistant. I've only worked here for a month but if anyone is watching, I don't know what's going on. They all just walked out: Carl and Samantha, the camera crew, the director – everyone. They just left. I think I'm the only one here.

"I've been outside and the streets are filled with people and cars all going in the same direction. There've been accidents, but no one seems to care. I saw a little boy screaming for his dad and a wife desperately grabbing her husband's arm, trying to stop him. But they just kept walking. It's like every person in the whole of Vegas is walking out of the city. I feel like I should be going with them, but I don't know why."

She's started crying, her voice speeding into a desperate cadence of terror and confusion.

"Please, if anyone can hear me, I'm in the KNV News studios in Las Vegas. My mom and dad won't answer their phone, and they live all the way up in Maine. Is this happening everywhere? Please, someone come and get me. I don't want to go back outside."

Mackenzie picks up the remote and turns off the television. She sits on the edge of her bed, opens her laptop and begins tapping away.

"What are we going to do?" Molly says from the doorway.

Mackenzie looks from Molly, to Jesse, to me. "You were right, Molly," she says. "We've got to act. But we've got to do it together. We might be all that's left of Omega. The others might be under mind control like Art and Camp. No matter what's happened until now, this is up to us. We are Omega."

Molly stares at Mackenzie for a long moment and then nods. "We are Omega," she says.

"First," Mackenzie says, "I want you to know who Omega is."

No. I want to tell her to be quiet. I want to tell her that Majestic can hear everything she's saying. Please, Mackenzie, *please* stop talking.

"What about the traitor?" I say, trying to stall her.

"That's not important anymore. We need to go now. I'll be keeping you three close. If one of you is the traitor we'll know soon enough."

"Omega said it himself, we can't do anything until we can guarantee there's no traitor among us. We've been exiled."

"Wells," Mackenzie says, "trust me. We haven't been exiled from Omega."

"What do you mean?" As I ask the question I realize I know the answer. I can feel it. The train of truth thundering down the line toward me.

"We haven't been exiled because I *am* Omega."

"No." The word is out before I even realize I've said it. "No, no, no."

"Sorry Wells, I know it's a shock, but it's true. It's me – it's always been me."

"Well, jank me," says Molly.

"No, you're just saying that, right?" My insides have torn open. Ice water pours into me, the churning, rushing water of fear and panic.

"It's true Wells," Mackenzie says. "When I began having suspicions about the Crabs, when the chaos of the world suddenly gave way to love for the aliens, I went underground and started this organization. I created the Omega moniker to draw people in and create an identity people could get behind. As time went on and I realized just how dangerous the situation was, keeping my identity secret became more imperative."

"No!" I shout it at her. "They can hear you!"

The change in her face is almost instantaneous. I can see the moment she realizes. "It's you?" she asks. It's a question but also a statement of such raw accusation that it's more painful than gouging out my own eye. A tremor rocks her voice. "Wells, what have you done?"

My vision blurs as my one good eye fills with hot tears. I wipe at it. "I can't help it, Mackenzie. I didn't do it on purpose. They put something in my ear. They hear everything I hear. They know you're Omega now. You need to run."

Molly speaks, her words like razor blades. "What did you do?"

"Molly," I say, "I'm sorry."

But she ignores my pleas and launches at me, landing on top of me and slamming my head back against the floor.

"What did you do?!" she repeats, pinning me to the floor and slapping my hands away as I try to raise them protectively. "Is it your fault? All of this?"

"Molly, stop!" Mackenzie calls.

Molly grabs one of my flailing wrists and holds it down as she punches me with her other hand. Her fist lands right on top of my eye patch, right on my damaged eye. I cry out as stinging pain shoots through my eye socket. Molly rocks back, preparing for a second strike, but Mackenzie grabs her. She wraps her arm around Molly's waist and pulls her off me even as she swings wildly and connects with my face again.

"You lying piece of shit!" Molly shouts. "We trusted you!"

I sit up, feeling at my eye and gently putting the patch back in place.

"Is Remy dead because of you?" Molly asks me, her voice cold now. "Sally? All the others?"

"No," I say. "No, it was when they attacked us. That's when they put the bug behind my ear. Majestic finding us at the warehouse is still on you."

Molly launches herself at me again, but Mackenzie is quick enough to restrain her.

"Fuck you Wells!" she cries.

"Enough," Mackenzie says. "Why didn't you just tell us, Wells?"

"They said they'd go after my parents. They said they'd tell them about what I did to my sister."

"What are you talking about?" Mackenzie says.

"I killed my sister." I take a steadying breath. No one interrupts me. "Four years ago, a few days before Christmas, my parents had to do some last-minute shopping. They left me to babysit my sister, Maggie. We were playing in the front yard, tether-ball, and I was getting annoyed because she kept hitting it the wrong way. It was such a stupid thing to argue about but we started fighting. I pushed her and she stumbled, tripped down the curb and fell onto the street. She got hit by a car and died. I never told anyone the truth. That's what Thorn threatened me with. He was going to tell my parents that I killed her. It would be the final straw, it would break them." Another realization hits me. "They said if I told anyone the bug would release cyanide and I'd be dead in seconds."

Mackenzie stares at me with a look of such contempt that I wish the cyanide would hurry up. I think I'd rather die than live with Mackenzie looking at me like that. I'd rather die than live with knowing how she must feel about me now. A buzzing comes from behind my ear and Thorn speaks to me through reverberations in my bones.

Thank you Wells. Your mission for us is complete.

"No!" I shout, shocking those around me with my sudden outburst. "No. Please. Leave her alone."

We will leave your parents alone, Wells. That was the deal. What we do with Omega is none of your concern.

I look at Mackenzie. "Please, Mackenzie. Please run. They're going to come for you."

Mackenzie fixes her gaze on mine. Something is missing from her eyes. A glow of happiness, a glint of friendship. I never noticed it when it was there, but I notice the absence of it now.

"I'm not running from them, Wells."

And Wells, we'll leave you happy in the knowledge that there is no cyanide in the bug inside your head.

I drop to the floor as if my body is liquid. I grab my head in my hands.

"We need to act now," Mackenzie says. "Let's go."

Everyone moves toward the door. I move to get up, but

Mackenzie turns to face me. "Not you, Wells. You don't leave this room."

She says it with such finality that I'm gobsmacked into silence. They leave, closing the door behind them. There's silence for a moment and then I hear glass breaking. I move to the window, pull the lace curtain aside and see Mackenzie, Jesse and Molly climbing into a faded red car parked in front of another of the motel's rooms. Mackenzie is in the driver's seat. She's leaning forward, fiddling under the steering wheel. Eventually the engine rumbles to life and the tires crunch over the gravel as the car drives away, leaving me feeling more alone than I ever have in my life.

We're caught in a wave of vehicles heading for Little Basin. Cars are flooding down both lanes in the same direction, and those that are big enough are ignoring the road altogether and driving straight across the desert. Jesse sits in the back, loading ammunition for the rifles we, I guess *acquired* is a good word, from an empty hunting and fishing shop we passed on the highway. I can't believe Mackenzie knew how to hotwire a car. She also taught Jesse how to load the clips, so the guns are ready to use. That's pretty badass. Then again, she is Omega. I can't believe it.

I watch Mackenzie as she drives down a long, straight section of Highway 50. The car's engine screams in a high-pitched whine as she keeps her foot flat to the floor, trying to keep up with the other vehicles, all of them rushing toward Little Basin and the Crustie ship in the sky.

Mackenzie and I may have had our differences, but I'm glad to be with her now. Remy was right: sometimes we need other people. I'd expected to have a slightly bigger crew behind us when we finally started fighting the Crusties, but the three of us are all that's left. We are Omega. I thought Wells was with us too, but obviously not. Thinking of him makes me angry. So. Neffing. Angry. I don't care if he was protecting his parents. What about protecting us?

Ahead, a group of maybe twenty people – men, women, and children – are walking down the highway, seemingly oblivious to the fact that it's jammed with cars veering around them.

"What the hell are they doing?" I say.

Mackenzie plants her hand on the horn. None of them move. They don't even flinch. Mackenzie slows to a crawl behind them. No one else slows, though, they just swerve around them, coming way too close to hitting us. Mackenzie pulls onto the shoulder and drives around the small crowd of people. None of them look at us as we pass. I roll down my window.

"Hey!" I call. "Get off the road!"

No response.

"It's no use," I say as I roll up the window, "the mind control has them locked up. Pull over up here, Mackenzie. Maybe I can get through to them."

"No," Mackenzie says, glancing up and down from her cell-phone. Is she texting while driving? Now, of all times? "We get to Little Basin as quickly as we can."

"Molly's right," Jesse says. "Someone's going to hit them. They're going to get killed."

"No," Mackenzie says.

"I just think we should –"

"No," Mackenzie cuts Jesse off again.

"I thought things were a bit more democratic than that," Jesse says. "We are Omega, remember. *We*. It's all of us."

"Don't misunderstand me," Mackenzie says. "We'll work together. But don't mistake me for the loveable, whimsical computer geek you thought I was. I'm not some goofy girl – I'm the one who brought Omega together. I'm the one who funds this operation and I'm the one whose orders every Omega agent across the globe has been following for the past three years. Just because you've found out I'm Omega don't think I'm not still giving the orders around here because, as Molly would say, I neffing am."

Jesse sits back in his seat, silent. I catch Mackenzie's eye fight the urge to clap. I'm sorry Jesse was on the receiving end, but it's good to see her let the bad bitch out for once. I knew she had it in her.

After about half an hour we hit the outskirts of Little Basin. Everywhere, people are walking like preprogrammed robots, and the road ahead is jammed with cars. It's chaos. With the crunch of shattering plastic, a black pick-up ahead of us crashes into an old Volkswagen that was trying to veer around the traffic that has begun to move slowly as cars and trucks back up trying to get through town. The pick-up doesn't even stop, it just pushes the smaller car along. Eventually the VW hits the back of another pick-up, jolts free and continues on, half its bodywork dragging on the road.

Mackenzie slows as she threads between small groups of people, which eventually join together to form a large mob walking down Main Street, headed in the direction of the N.E.Z. Mackenzie turns down side streets to avoid the main group. The crowd here is smaller, but it still takes us a long time to weave our way through town.

Once we reach the other side of Little Basin, Mackenzie drives along the back road that leads to the N.E.Z. As we drop down over the hills she slows to a stop. There are thousands of vehicles around the fence to the Exclusion Zone. Some have been abandoned as their passengers left to join the enormous crowd gathering near the main gate. Other vehicles are driving across the dirt, trying to get as close as they can. Those already at the gate are just standing there, as if they're waiting for something.

The impossibly large shape of the Xeno ship hovers in the air over the Alpha Compound.

"What are they doing?" Jesse asks. "Waiting for the Xenos to attack?"

"I don't know, but I'm not going to get us through that crowd," Mackenzie says.

"What is that?" I say, leaning forward to get a better look.

Above us, coming from the bottom of the Crab ship, are what I can only guess are Xeno attack ships. They're not very large – each is maybe the size of a small plane – but they move insanely fast and come swirling down from the mothership in a spiral, black with glowing blue on the bottom, like a swarm of giant fireflies.

The ships peel off to arc around in a circle surrounding the N.E.Z. Before I can say it looks like they're about to neffing attack, there's a sound like angry thunder as blue fire erupts from every one of the hundred or more Crab aircraft. They all fire inward, toward the force field. As the blue-white plasma hits the force field it erupts in the same blue lightning as when I struck it with my fist, only about a billion times brighter. I hold my forearm across my eyes to shield it from the light. When I look again I see that the force field is still there, shimmering in blue.

"They didn't get through," Jesse says. "All that and they didn't get through."

I stare at the scene in front of us. A hundred alien attack ships unable to break through the force field. Uncle Art was right when he said it was impenetrable. Except it isn't, is it? Because I got through. I just have no idea how.

The aircraft begin moving again. They spiral around the force field and break off into smaller formations, then begin shooting at it again. This time they fire in succession, each of the smaller formations hitting the same point as they pass. They must be trying to concentrate their fire on one spot to see if they can breach it that way. The barrage continues for a minute or more, the bright flares pounding into the force field and lighting up the dome. Eventually the planes fall silent and spiral up again, disappearing into the mothership, the force field still as solid as a rock.

"They can't get in," I say. I almost laugh. "All this way across the stars and the neffing door is locked."

"The problem is we don't know what's going on in the rest of the world while they fail to breach the force field here," Mackenzie says. "The longer they're delayed from getting the Obelisk, the longer the whole planet's at risk."

"Well then, Mackenzie," Jesse says eventually, "you're in charge. What exactly is the plan?"

"Molly, how confident are you about using your powers?" Mackenzie asks. "You're our secret weapon here, our only real chance at this. We're going to need you to take down the force field. You up for that?"

"I can do it," I say.

"Your uncle wouldn't like me forcing you onto the front line," Mackenzie says. "But I don't see any alternative. You might well be the only person on the planet who can penetrate their defenses."

"Look, there are alien ships in the sky and the entire population of the planet is walking around like mind-controlled zombies. There's nothing you or Uncle Art or anyone can do to keep us safe. We're the only ones who know what needs to be done, and I'm the only one who can get us inside. Besides, Uncle Art always told me I needed to take some responsibility for my actions."

Mackenzie nods. "Alright, they want the Obelisk. That should be our target. We incapacitate the Alpha Compound, find the Obelisk and let them take it. Then they leave."

"Or we just destroy it," I say. "You said they need that Obelisk thing to make their mind control work, so why don't we just blow it up? Get rid of the neffing thing altogether and free everyone."

"Wells said that, when he melded with Number-One, it seemed like the Obelisk was some kind of religious artefact," Mackenzie says. "We don't know how the Xenos, new or old, would react to us destroying it. It might just make things worse."

"Why does it matter what Wells said?" Jesse asks. "How are we supposed to trust him?"

"Jesse's right," I say. "Let's just forget Wells. He's a traitor. Whether it started before or after the attack on the warehouse makes no difference to me. He neffing betrayed us. And who's to say these new Crabs aren't just going to do the same thing as the other ones? Maybe it's all part of another plan. Maybe they're going to take the Obelisk up to their ship and use it to conquer the planet. Seems like a lot of effort for a whole fleet of ships to travel across space just to get a totem pole back."

"Our primary aim is to let the Xeno fleet take back the Obelisk and hopefully leave in peace," Mackenzie says. "I'll concede there's a chance they'll react in an unpredictable way, but I believe what we learned about the Xeno war is true. These new Xenos are only holding Earth hostage because they want the Obelisk."

"Okay," I say. "You're the boss. Back up. We'll get in where Jesse already knocked down the fence."

Mackenzie starts the car again, shifts into reverse and heads back down the hill. We drive along Dry Springs Road, following the line of the fence. I'm not going to argue anymore, but I'm not ruling out destroying the Obelisk. If Mackenzie wants to use me as a weapon, I get to decide what I'm aimed at. This is my chance to get the revenge I've been craving for six years. This is my chance to make the Crusties pay for Mum, Dad, Remy, and for every single person on the planet who died because of them. As much as I respect Mackenzie, this thing is bigger than any of us.

I LIE on the bed in Mackenzie's motel room staring up at the oddly stained roof, where water must have soaked into the plasterboard years ago. There's an emptiness inside me – I just want to lie here for the rest of eternity. The people who had become my closest friends hate me. They've abandoned me here like the traitor I am. Thinking about how Mackenzie must feel sends waves of nausea through me.

Even my parents, the ones I thought I was doing this for, are probably controlled by the Schism and fighting a battle against their will, just like Art and Camp and billions of others. No wonder Majestic was so happy to leave my parents alone. They knew it was only a matter of time until they'd be trudging along mindlessly with the masses.

At least, I hope they're mindless. I hope they're not aware of what's happening to them. I've felt what it's like to be controlled, to be a prisoner inside your own body. In a fraction of a moment the physical form you've existed in your whole life becomes a shell, betraying you, acting on the whims of another. Billions upon billions of people all around the globe are experiencing that right now, confused, terrified, alone.

I sit up on the bed. I can't abide that. I *won't*. I can't just lie here in self-pity, not when I know how that feels. It's like a sudden weight on me. The world is falling and I'm Atlas – a nerdy Atlas, trying to hold up the world with arms that have never once lifted weights, unless you count extra-large cans of energy drink.

Even as I resolve to do something, a mobile phone begins vibrating on the bedside table. It's one of the phones Mackenzie brought with her from the warehouse. It rotates slightly on its own axis with each buzz, like a creature with life of its own. It vibrates twice and then falls silent. On the screen a notification pops up: 1 new message.

My first instinct is to ignore it. It's not my phone, after all. But after second glance I pick it up. It's a message from Mackenzie.

Daksec, my laptop is in the bathroom drawer. Find out how Thorn and Charlotte have pulled off this Lazarus trick and help us out. This isn't for the lolz. This is hacktivism. Redeem yourself, ok? Aunt M

A tsunami of emotion washes over me, a fresh surge of my harbored guilt, but there's also a sudden happiness, or perhaps it's hope.

Climbing off the bed I walk to the drawer in the bench beneath the microwave. Just as the one in my room did, this drawer contains a sparse collection of cutlery, the same spoons, forks, and knives. There's also a small paring knife with a red plastic handle, the type with a slightly curved blade, for peeling fruit and vegetables.

I grab the knife and head into the small, dimly lit bathroom, a yellow gloom permeating through the murky skylight overhead. I flip the switch and the white fluorescent light blinks on. I look in the mirror, turning my head to the right and pulling my ear forward to see the small, pimple-sized protrusion where the bug sits beneath my skin.

I take a deep breath and hold it as I press the blade of the knife to my skin. This time, knowing the threat of cyanide was just a mind game, it's only the pain I have to fear. I clench my teeth, take a few more steadying breaths, then cut.

I grunt as I feel the first visceral bite of the blade. My hand shakes, not from fear this time, but from trying to resist the urge to pull the knife away. I white-knuckle the plastic handle and push harder, feeling the blade cut deeper into the thin flesh, the pointed end of the knife tracing a line along the bone. I open my mouth and the clenched grunt turns into a cry as I refuse to let myself stop.

Warm blood runs down my neck, forming a crimson pool at my collar and soaking into my shirt. With a final shuddering effort I slice through far enough to open the lump containing the Majestic bug. I drop the knife in relief, and it clatters into the sink, splattering red droplets over the curve of the ceramic bowl.

I turn my head and squeeze the lump, like I'm trying to pop a pimple or push out a splinter. It only takes a moment. I see a small black circular object appear through the cut skin. It drops into the sink, blood sticking it to the side of the bowl. It's no bigger than half a centimeter in diameter and covered with the ordered silver criss-crossings of a circuit board, blood pooled between the tiny ridges. I turn on the tap and let the blast of water wash it away.

Pulling a long streamer of toilet paper off the roll and pressing it against my wound, I open the top drawer and see Mackenzie's pink laptop resting in the otherwise empty space.

The lid is adorned with an array of stickers promoting computer games, shoe brands, science-fiction television shows, flowers. It's almost as if this object is a microcosm of her personality.

I settle on the bed, prop myself up with pillows and get to work. Mackenzie has organized the files we decrypted into two folders, *read* and *unread*. I open the *unread* folder and start reading. I skim over a lot of the documents – those containing information we already know or things that aren't relevant, or that refer to medical tests or experiments too complicated to try and understand right now.

I read for ten, maybe fifteen minutes before I find something, a briefing about the Obelisk. Unfortunately it doesn't tell us the location of the Obelisk itself, but it does say that, as well as being essential to the Schism's ability to control the minds of everyone on the planet, it's actually essential to Xeno life. Without the Obelisk, the Xenos lose their ability to meld with each other. On their planet, being cut off from the Obelisk is the harshest punishment that can be inflicted, something they call "the silence." No wonder a fleet has arrived to retrieve it.

Further reading reveals little more, other than confirmation that both Mr Thorn and Charlotte are members of Majestic-12. There's nothing that provides any insight into how they could mysteriously reappear after Molly blasted them into atomic dust.

So, when the data turns up nothing I have to look elsewhere. I head onto the dark web, the domain of hackers, drug dealers, and the black market. The dark web isn't a nice place, but it's the only place I'll find information that hackers or whistleblowers have released. Back before I was sent to juvie, I read a lot of information about the Xenos on the dark web that was never released to the public.

Using a Tor browser I navigate to a password-protected, unindexed web forum, an information-sharing collective called *The*

Treehouse of Horrors – a hub for sharing information about the Xenos. I start searching until I find a post by XenoLeaks, the hacker that Mackenzie and myself have been getting Xeno information from for years. The last of his posts was only three days ago, a thread titled, "The Truth about MJ-12."

I click on it and the first thing that loads is a scanned image of an old black-and-white photo. It shows twelve men standing around in three-piece suits or starched military uniforms adorned with brass stars and rows of ribbons. Many of them are smoking and holding glasses of what I imagine is whisky. The clothing suggests the photo dates back to mid-last century, and the caption confirms this: "Taken at the alleged first gathering of Majestic-12. November, 1952."

One of the men in the photo is circled. Despite the differences in clothing, and a moustache he no longer wears, he is unmistakable. It's Thorn, and it doesn't look like he's aged a day. Several of the men in the photo are named: Dr Lloyd Berkener, Dr Vannevar Bush, General Robert Montague, James Forrestal and others. However, it seems that the circled individual, the one we know as Mr Thorn, was as much a mystery then as he is now.

The first part of the post covers history that I'm familiar with. Majestic-12 was formed in 1952 by order of President Truman as a secret government task force mandated with investigating claims of extraterrestrial intelligence, eliminating possible threats, and acquiring technology beneficial to the United States.

The post goes on to explain the role MJ-12 members played in the cover-up of the alien crash in Roswell, New Mexico, as well as other UFO encounters, and describes their involvement in the US space program. It goes on to explain that all traces of the organization had disappeared by the 1980s.

XenoLeaks says that information about the organization reemerged in the wake of the Xenocrustacean crash, an event that they were never going to be able to brush under the carpet. He believes that the long-held rumor is true: MJ-12 no longer consists of only twelve members, at least not in the way you would imagine. He believes the crash at Roswell in 1947 was a Xenocrustacean vessel, some sort of scout ship. From the wreckage, MJ-12 acquired technology that enabled full organism cloning decades before the world had ever heard of Dolly the sheep.

Majestic-12 is not Majestic-12 anymore, XenoLeaks writes. *I don't know how many members there are now, but this unknown man* – he's referring to Thorn – *is one of them, cloned continuously over the years.*

"Clones," I say to myself. "This just keeps getting better, doesn't it?"

Maybe Molly really did kill Thorn, and the one we saw on television was what, some kind of cloned replacement? That probably means Charlotte is a cloned member of Majestic, too. There's got to be something else XenoLeaks knows that could help. Contacting him is a long shot, I know, but maybe he's an EV-B survivor too, someone impervious to Xeno mind control.

I click on his name am redirected to a profile page containing, unsurprisingly, no personal details. There's an option to begin a direct message chat, and a small green circle indicates that XenoLeaks is online right now. About time some luck came my way. I suppose, if XenoLeaks is anything like me and Mackenzie, it's no surprise he'd head straight to a computer at a time like this.

I open a chat window as a guest user, changing my login name to something a little more familiar than Guest108748, and start typing.

Daksec: Hello? Are you there?

. . .

I stare at the screen, and with each passing beat my heart sinks a little lower in my chest. This is Plan B, and I don't have a Plan C.

Just as I'm about to start racking my brain for another idea, a line appears below mine.

XenoLeaks is typing...

Holy heck. I grip the sides of the laptop and sit up in anticipation.

XenoLeaks: I'm here.
   Daksec: Oh, thank god. I've read your post.
   XenoLeaks: Are you the real Daksec?
   Daksec: Yes. I need your help.
   XenoLeaks: I don't talk to just anyone.

I should have expected such a cautious response but surely he's noticed that everyone in the world is walking toward their death right now?

Daksec: Aunt M sent me.

Another long wait with no reply.

Daksec: Are you there?
   Daksec: ?
   Daksec: ???????

. . .

Then I think again.

Daksec: I am. You are.
    Daksec: We Are Omega.

XenoLeaks is typing...

XenoLeaks: We Are Omega.
    XenoLeaks: What do you need?
    Daksec: You've seen what's happening?
    XenoLeaks: Of course.
    Daksec: We know how to stop it, but we need help. What do you know about the Obelisk?
    XenoLeaks: Nothing.
    Daksec: Nothing?
    XenoLeaks: No.
    Daksec: But you've heard of it?
    XenoLeaks: Rumours.
    Daksec: That's what these new Xenos want. So you don't know where it is?
    XenoLeaks: No. Most of the information I have is about MJ-12.
    Daksec: Is there anything you haven't posted yet? Anything that might help?
    XenoLeaks: Yes, but it's unconfirmed. I haven't had a chance to cross-check it for reliability. It's from one of my primary sources, though.
    Daksec: Right now anything might help. What is it?

XenoLeaks: *Information about another Majestic clone. Apparently they use Xeno tech to rapidly create fully-aged human clones. They use it for the Majestic members, but a while before the arrival of the new Xeno fleet, a source within Alpha Compound – who I can no longer contact – claims they've made a new clone, but it's not a Majestic member.*

Daksec: *A new clone?*

XenoLeaks: *They said it's never happened like that before. They sent me this.*

[XenoLeaks has uploaded an image: new clone.jpg]

I click on the filename and an image pops open on the screen. Holy heck.

It's a photograph, a close-up of a face submerged in some kind of murky orange liquid behind the slightly reflective gleam of clear glass. The face looks odd, and it takes me a second to pinpoint exactly why – it's hairless. The top of the head is completely round and smooth and, disturbingly, it has no eyebrows. But even in this state, and submerged in goo, the face is still recognizable.

It's Jesse.

I grab Mackenzie's phone and try calling the number her message came from, but it rings out and, unsurprisingly for the queen of hackers, there's no voicemail. I make a sound of frustration before typing a message and sending it to her.

Mackenzie. Thorn and Charlotte are both clones. The Jesse that's with you is a clone too. Probably switched during the attack on headquarters. Get away from him.

. . .

I snap a photo of the image on the laptop screen and send that too, not wanting to seem like I'm throwing around unwarranted accusations again. I hit send and then wait, staring at the screen, my leg bouncing, my fingers tapping a hectic rhythm on the quilt. I clamber off the bed and pace the room, staring at the screen the whole time. Nothing comes back, there's no reply from Mackenzie.

I shove the phone in my pocket, snap the laptop closed and grab it, and make my way out into the bright sun. There's a single white car parked near the small demountable reception building, the only vehicle that hasn't been steered toward Little Basin. I hurry over and try the handle, but it's locked. I know it belongs to the crotchety old man who runs the motel, so I head into the empty reception.

I search the cluttered desk, pushing aside an antique carbon-paper credit card swiper, a keyboard filled with food crumbs, and numerous coffee-ringed papers. When I don't find anything I open the top drawer and see a set of keys tossed on top of an amorphous mash of paperclips, pen lids, staples, post-it notes and other office supplies. I grab the keys and return to the vehicle.

I unlock the door, toss Mackenzie's laptop on the passenger seat, and climb in. When I turn the key in the ignition the car barks loudly, makes a grinding sound, and lunges forward. Clutch, I forgot the clutch. I adjust the seat so I can better reach the pedals and then depress the clutch. This time when I turn the key the engine fires to life.

I exhale. I've driven before. We did driver education while I was in juvie, but that was in a smaller car, with an instructor sitting beside me the whole time. Plus, the controls were on the other side of the vehicle, and I had two eyes and glasses back then.

I move the gearstick into what I hope is reverse, let the clutch out slowly as I ease my foot onto the accelerator, and back out of the car space. I breathe, shove the stick into first gear, and...stall. I stall twice before I finally get moving. It doesn't help that my anxious legs are bouncing on the pedals. I manage to get going though, and I drive off, joining the throng of cars headed for Little Basin.

As we stand outside the fence Jesse left mangled and torn open, Mackenzie turns to look at us. She holds a rifle, as does Jesse. I thought Mackenzie would look weird with a rifle but I have to admit it doesn't seem unnatural at all. She holds it like she knows what she's doing. She's probably ex-Special Forces, too, or the President's daughter or something.

"Where's your rifle, Molly?" she asks.

"I don't want one," I say. "This is my weapon, right?" I tap the side of my head.

"Molly," Mackenzie says, "I trust you, but just in case your power doesn't work, I think you should bring that last rifle."

I can tell from the way she's looking at me that there's no changing her mind, so I return to the car. When I reach in to grab the last of the loaded rifles I hear the unmistakable buzz of a phone vibrating. It's coming from the plastic console between the two front seats.

I lean over and grab the phone, looking at the caller ID on the screen. It says "Phone 2 – Left for Wells." Mackenzie must have given Wells one of her phones. I stare at the phone, letting it vibrate in my hand, then glance back toward the others.

Mackenzie is pointing in the direction of the Alpha Compound while Jesse listens intently. I look back at the phone and consider calling out to Mackenzie, asking if she wants me to answer it. But what could Wells possibly want? Probably just ringing to neffing apologize again. I toss the phone onto the driver's seat and close the door. Wells can try to make up with Mackenzie some other time. Mackenzie can call him back later if she wants. Right now we're a little busy trying to save the neffing human race.

I join the others and we walk through the opening in the fence, stepping over razor wire that has buried itself in the dirt, like a dangerous thorny plant. If you told me when I was escaping from the N.E.Z. that I'd soon be walking back in voluntarily I would have said you were neffing crazy.

"Alright," Mackenzie says, "I doubt they're keeping the Obelisk on the ship. The compound extends deep underground, and the lower levels are highly restricted, so that makes them the most likely location."

"So I take down the force field, knock all the SECPOL in the entire compound on their asses, we drive in, find the Obelisk and end this before millions or maybe billions of people die fighting aliens. *Easy*." I take a breath, steadying myself.

"How far in is the force field?" Jesse asks.

I pick up a palm-sized rock and throw it toward the force field. About twenty feet away it collides, sending ripples and sparkles of blue out in a pattern, as if I threw it into a pond.

Mackenzie turns to me. "This is your chance to see if you can control your powers."

I've been acting uber confident up until this point, but like Mackenzie says, it's time to put my money where my mouth is. I close my eyes, breathe in and out, and listen for Remy. He tells me I can do this. He tells me that, just like when I shared my pain with him, this isn't about what's happening around me, it's about what's happening inside me.

I think of the force field splitting apart like before. I can feel the power filling me up, but it's not driven by anger or fear this time. It's just like Remy said, I fill up the dam of my mind and get ready to let it out. I seek out the wall in front of me, looking for the link between myself and it. This time I don't feel like an atom bomb about to explode, I feel like a scalpel, a precision instrument, much more controlled. I can do this. I open my eyes and just as I'm about to burst the dam wall I see Jesse lift his rifle. He points it at me.

"I can't let you do this, Molly," Jesse says. "That force field is the only thing stopping the Xenos above us from deploying their forces against the compound. You bring the force field down and they'll take the Obelisk for themselves."

I turn to look at him. "That's the neffing point, Jesse," I say. "What –" My words fade as understanding dawns. "Are you for real?"

Jesse shrugs. "That depends on what you mean. Am I really pointing my rifle at you? Yes. Am I betraying you? That's a matter of perspective."

"Perspective?!"

"Yes. I've never been on your side, so it's not possible for me to betray you, is it?"

"There's only one of you, Jesse," Mackenzie says, pointing her rifle at him. "You so much as flinch and you'll die. Molly, can you hold him with your mind?"

I nod.

"No," Jesse says.

"Oh yes I can," I say. "All those years of friendship and you go and do this. Why? Because I told you I don't love you? Neffing hell."

"You don't seem to understand. That wasn't me. And even if you can control your abilities, you won't be able to hold me with your mind because I'm not alone." He glances in the direction of the force field, and with a shimmer like the clearing of heat haze, a squad of SECPOL led by Thorn and a Crustie appear, standing beside black jeeps.

"Oh, for jank's sake," I say. "Invisibility now? When's this shit going to end?" I don't know whether to laugh or cry at the futility. Every time I think we're getting somewhere, either someone betrays us or the stinking Crabs reveal yet another trick.

"The clouding of perception is easy once you get the hang of it," Charlotte says as she moves to the front of the group. "A shame you never got the chance to learn. I'm sure Remy might have taught you but, you know, he can't now."

I let out a primal sound, unable to even shape my anger into anything resembling actual neffing words.

"Drop your weapons," Thorn says.

Mackenzie and I hesitate for only a fraction of a second before complying. Clicking sounds come from the Crab standing beside Thorn. It has the same swirling blue lines over its body as the one I blasted into non-existence. It's the one from the TV.

"How are you even here?" I say to Thorn. "I neffing killed you." I look at Charlotte. "Both of you."

"No," Thorn says. "You killed a different version of me, and of Charlotte. In the strictest sense of the word, I've never met you, but I have memories of meeting you – several times in fact. This body may be new but we are a continuous being. The necessary cellular and genetic components are harvested regularly, and used with a partly pre-constructed body when a replacement is required."

"Shit," Mackenzie says. "You're a clone. I'd heard rumors of cloning developed from Xeno technology, but they were never confirmed."

"Enough talk," says Thorn. "You have lost. Remy is dead, Wells was spying for us, and Jesse here is also a clone, not your friend. Molly, your uncle has joined us and soon your leader here will be interrogated to the very edges of human endurance. There is no hope for you."

"If this is a clone then where's the real Jesse?"

"He was replaced during the attack on the warehouse," Thorn says.

"Where is he?" I say. "Is he alive?"

"Why would we leave him alive?" Thorn says. "That makes no strategic sense. We put a bullet in his head as soon as the cloning was successful."

Anger fills me yet again, and I force my power out toward him. Clone or not, I want to eviscerate this Mr Thorn just like I did the other one. But as soon as I release my power I know it's a mistake. Thorn stops the push of my will, then, having left myself vulnerable, he's able to grab me with his mind. I feel a shiver run down my spine and I can't move. In my peripheral vision I see that Mackenzie's frozen too.

"Excellent," Thorn says, a sneer of satisfaction in his voice. I can't believe how neffing stupid I am. I let my stupid anger get the better of me yet again, and this time it could mean the end of us – and the end of humanity.

Mr Thorn, still on the other side of the force field, moves to stand in front of Mackenzie.

"And here we have the infamous Omega, one Mackenzie Hooper. Slated to come to the Institute yourself, Miss Hooper, weren't you? But then you vanished. We knew you played a role in Omega, of course, but we never suspected you were the head of the organization. Perhaps we should have, though. In hindsight, it's easy to see it had to be someone resistant to the virus.

"I want to make clear my respect for you, Mackenzie. Willing to stand up for humanity when you thought it was doomed. It's not, of course, but it still takes great gumption to seek out those few people resistant to control and stand up for what you believe in. As I've said to Miss McManus before, we have the same aim, you and I: the preservation of humanity."

"Look around, Thorn," Mackenzie says – apparently he's left us the ability to speak. "The entire population of Earth are unwilling participants in a war. That doesn't seem like the preservation of humanity to me."

"Temporary measures, Miss Hooper. Believe me, nobody wants this, but the arrival of this new Xeno fleet is a threat to both our survival and the survival of our friends and benefactors."

"They stole the Obelisk," Mackenzie says. "The Schism. Your friends are the bad guys in all this."

"The politics of another world are of no concern to me," Thorn says. "I only want what is best for this one." He claps his hands. "Now, it seems our new visitors have detected the location of the Obelisk. Right now this force field is the only thing stopping them. You can see why we can't have you disrupting it, Miss McManus. Bring them in."

The squad of SECPOL move forward. One activates a device on his belt so they can pass through the force field. Another calls for a fluxer. They grab us and carry us through to the other side like we're neffing statues.

"It's good you've arrived early enough to play your part," Mr Thorn says. "I know my predecessor was very disappointed at having let you slip away."

"Our part is to end this," Mackenzie says. "That's our role. To stop you."

"I'm afraid I'm speaking to Miss McManus here," Thorn says, shooting Mackenzie a look of absolute contempt. "You have no role in this anymore, *Omega*."

With a *whomp whomp whomp* sound that takes me back to our ill-fated escape, a fluxer flies in low and fast over the ground and lands nearby. The SECPOL lift me and Mackenzie like we're neffing luggage and carry us up the ramp and into the back of the fluxer, dropping us roughly into the seats and strapping us in. I can see Jesse, or clone-Jesse anyway, through the opening as the ramp begins closing. I watch him standing there. He watches me. I don't care if he's a clone. There's some emotion on his face. There's some of my Jesse there. There has to be.

I KNOW the car can go faster than this, but right now the main limit on speed is my desire to not die before I arrive at the N.E.Z. Most of the vehicles on the road behave in a predictable way, but every now and then one of them does something crazy, with no concern for the other people on the road, including me.

The behavior of the mind-controlled masses is strange like that. Everyone is trying to do the same thing, they're all headed for the same place, but there still seems to be some amount of individual decision-making going on. Even with the Xenos using the "nodes" from the Institute to amplify their powers I don't think they're managing to control the billions of people around the planet in the way Remy or Charlotte controlled me. It seems more like the Xenos send out a kind of message – an urge to act that people can't help but obey.

Once I reach Little Basin – easy enough to find when the entire mind-controlled population is going there – the traffic grinds to a halt as it tries to squeeze its way down the main street. Everyone seems to be taking the most direct route to their destination. It's as though they're all iron filings, being drawn toward a magnet along lines of force.

I drive away from the main group, heading in what I think is the direction of the N.E.Z. My intuition proves correct; the road rises up over the hills and turns to gravel as it winds back down toward the fence of the Nevada Exclusion Zone. As I crest the hills I see the front gate, where masses of mind-controlled people have gathered. They're just standing there, waiting, as if they're gathering an army.

There's a rumble from the sky. At first I think it's distant thunder, or maybe the arrival of more Xenos, but I soon realize it's the whining roar of fighter jets. At least thirty or forty jets fly low overhead with a screaming reverberation that seems to rattle the car around me. The formation flies directly toward the hovering Xeno ship.

A swarm of smaller ships, Xeno fighter craft, drop from the bottom of the enormous ship and fly toward the fighter jets. The Xeno craft are faster and more maneuverable than the jets, darting sideways, rolling over, rising and falling in an impossible insect-like dance. They close the distance quickly and engage the jets about halfway between me and the ship. The fighters launch a barrage of missiles at the smaller Xeno craft, which streak across the sky, leaving trails of white. Some of them find targets, but most don't, and no sooner have the humans launched their missiles than the Xeno fighters let loose with fire of their own, streams of blue-white plasma that send burning fighter jets plum-meting to the ground like falling fireworks. Those that aren't hit turn sharply to attack again, but it's obvious they stand little chance.

The mind-controlled military are trying to attack the ship, but the Xenos wipe them out with very few losses of their own. Once the last of the human fighter jets is sent spiraling toward the ground, the Xeno craft all swarm back up into the ship. That gives me pause. This Xeno ship can't attack the compound directly because of the force field, but the gathering army of mind-controlled humans at the gate is outside the force field. They could easily kill every single person there, but they don't. They only seem to fight when they need to defend themselves. They want the Obelisk back, but I don't think they want to hurt us to get it.

I turn away from the gate and drive as fast as I can over the loose shale, hoping this is the road we escaped along in Jesse's truck. I follow the road away from the gate, searching ahead for the break in the fence – I'm sure that's where they'd try to get back in. As I crest a rise I see it, the hole in the fence, as well as the car they left the motel in. There's no sign of them though. God. I'm too late.

What I do see as I draw closer are two SECPOL officers, standing at the fence, obviously left to guard the breach. I'm driving too fast to react before they notice me, and I'm almost on them as they rush toward the road, raising their plasma rifles and yelling something I can't hear. I don't know what to do, so I stamp on the accelerator as hard as I can and turn off the road, bumping down over the rough tufts of desert grass. The car's engine roars and the distance between us is closing fast. I hear a plasma shot and the windscreen beside me bursts inward, half-melted, half-shattered. I duck down below the dash.

Plasma fire hits the front of the car. I hazard a look through the shattered windscreen. The officers are still standing in my path, firing at the car. I hit the brakes, but the wheels lock on the sandy ground and I plow into them. One slams face-first into the bonnet with a sickening thud and rolls up over the windscreen. The other almost manages to leap out of the way, but the front clips his legs, sending him spinning off to the side.

I keep my foot planted on the brake but the car still plows into the side of the car Mackenzie hotwired. I'm thrown forward, then snapped back into place by the seatbelt, and my vision explodes with white as the airbag instantly inflates around me, cushioning my impact. As soon as I recover, I start flailing at the airbag.

I see blood smeared across the windscreen, and the only thing that stops me from vomiting is the knowledge that another soldier is still out there. I unclip the buckle of my seat belt and open the door. It crunches and groans against bent bodywork, only opening a fraction of the way, but I fight my way out and look behind me. I can see the soldier I first hit, lying still and broken on the grass. The second one, the one who suffered only a glancing blow, is groaning on the ground. He looks up, sees me, and begins crawling toward his rifle, which has landed a short distance away. I hobble over, my legs feeling like jelly, shaking beneath me. I'm not hurt, just in shock, I think, and I manage to reach the gun before the SECPOL does.

I grab the rifle and aim at the soldier on the ground. He starts crawling toward me again.

"Stop," I say, my voice quavering.

But the SECPOL doesn't stop. His face is emotionless. He just keeps pulling himself along the dirt toward me.

"I said stop."

He's not going to respond to me though, and he's not going to stop. He's being controlled by someone else. I press the switch on the side of the rifle, the one Remy showed me, just near the trigger. The rifle hums and the slots in the barrel slowly light up with increasing brightness. I slip my finger inside the trigger-guard, feeling the concave surface of the trigger against my fingertip.

"Just stop," I say. "What are you going to do? You can't even stand."

I look around. There's no one in sight, just me and the SECPOL pulling himself along the ground, getting closer and closer to the end of my rifle. I tuck the rifle into my shoulder and use my thumb to click the small circular switch from "safe" to "fire", then hesitate. I don't want to do this. I think about the

Xenos up there, not wanting to hurt us, only fighting to defend themselves. I don't want to hurt anyone either, but just like them, I need to defend myself. I aim the rifle at the crawling man and squeeze. The rifle kicks slightly and releases that same electrical discharge. The shot of plasma hits the SEPCOL on the left shoulder, just near the side of his neck. He stops moving and his face drops into the dirt.

Holy heck. Holy heck, holy heck, holy heck. I killed somebody. Two people, if the one who splattered against the front of the car is dead too. I'm always going to be that person now. A killer. I drop the rifle, or at least it falls from my hands. He wasn't even in control of his actions. He probably has kids.

I turn and stumble back toward the car. I have to keep moving. I have to keep going. I can't think about it. What I need to think about now is how to get through the force field. How can I get in and find Molly and Mackenzie? If they're even alive still.

I reach into the car and grab Mackenzie's laptop. Art said the SECPOL used a transponder code to phase through the force field. That transponder must be communicating with a computer system somewhere, and wherever there's a computer system with external comms there's an opportunity to be hacked.

A transponder like that would probably operate on shortwave radio. I sit cross-legged on the ground and open Mackenzie's laptop. I scan through her applications and spot what I was certain she'd have installed: a radio-communications app. As I boot it up I see that she has the hardware for radio comms, too. I'd expect nothing less from every hacker's wise aunt.

When I search for signals across the entire shortwave frequency range I find a number of them, though only four are encrypted. Of those four, three are constantly active with traffic on the channels. The other, low-level encrypted, is mostly silent, with just the occasional ping. That must be the one. I roll my shoulders back, crack my fingers and start coding.

It takes me all of about fifteen minutes to break the encryption on the radio traffic, building on some of Mackenzie's existing algorithms. Then I bash together a program to record data transmissions across the channel, isolating the call and response codes. I sit and wait. I've seen fluxers flying around inside the N.E.Z. since I've been here, most of them well inside the domed force field, but there seem to be a few zipping around the outside, too, either patrolling or moving personnel. I need one of them to activate their transponder and fly through the force field in order to record the code.

After almost ten minutes, somewhere out of sight across the N.E.Z., a SECPOL must set off their transponder because the radio signal suddenly flares with a series of unintelligible beeps. I might not be able to decipher the sounds, but the computer can. My program has already read the transponder code for the force field and recreated it, ready for transmission. So that's step one done. I should be able to get past the force field now. I just hope I'm not too late.

I snap the laptop closed and clamber to my feet, tucking the computer under my arm as I make my way through the hole in the fence. I wonder how long it will be until someone starts wondering what's happened to the two officers out here? I push the thought out of my head – if I start thinking about what I've done it will completely unravel me. I make my way across the desert grass, trying to judge the spot where the force field might be. Apparently I don't judge it very well, because I slam right into it, sending blue streaks spreading out across the force field. I'll blame it on being one-eyed and not having glasses.

I open the laptop. I hope this works – the battery is running low, so this might be my only shot. I load the recorded transponder code in and then click to send it. Nothing seems to happen. I reach my hand out tentatively, but I don't feel anything. A slight glow surrounds my hand as it slips through the force field. I keep walking slowly forward until I'm one hundred percent sure I'm on the other side of the force field. It worked. I'm back inside the Nevada Exclusion Zone.

Oh, holy heck. I'm back inside the Nevada Exclusion Zone.

I look in the direction of the Alpha Compound. It's two or so kilometers away, tucked in behind the hills. I start walking. How I'm supposed to stay hidden and what I'm going to do when I get there, I have absolutely no idea.

I OPEN my eyes feeling as though I'm waking up, but not from being asleep. Last thing I remember I was being carried into a fluxer by the SECPOL, and then, with a kind of jerk, like the skipping of one of those old CDs my parents had in the garage, I'm here. Just another neffing mind trick, I suppose. I remember Remy saying how he lost time in the Institute. I have absolutely no idea how much time I've lost. It could be hours. Neffing days, even.

I pull against the restraints pinning my arms and legs in place. I'm relieved I can move my body, but neffing furious that I'm once again a prisoner of the SECPOL, or Majestic, or the Xenos, or whoever is actually in charge of this joint.

I'm in a chair like the one in the Infirmary, angled back with the same straps holding me in place. It might even be the same chair, but the room is different. It's not the medical facility with the army of machines staring me down. This is a cold space, a concrete box that seems to have been recently fitted out. There are still machines scattered around, but they lie on the floor or are haphazardly positioned on wheeled tables, with tubes and cords curling away over the floor like snakes in a pit.

"Miss McManus." I turn my head in the direction of the voice, not that I need to see who is speaking. I'm familiar enough with that sniveling sound. "You caused a large amount of damage to the Infirmary last time you were here, or at least Mr Dufort did. Such extensive damage to our facility, all in order to free you. Such a prize you are. Such a —"

"Oh shut up," I say. "Give it a neffing rest."

"Right then," Mr Thorn says, "we shall dispense with conversation, shall we?"

I push at him with my mind, hoping to toss him across the room like the scrunched-up piece of trash he is, but I instantly feel a push back, an increasing pressure that eventually forces me back in the chair.

"Please cease attempting to overpower me," Thorn says. "I guarantee you cannot succeed. The Xenocrustaceans have phenomenal psychic ability, but cannot extend that ability to the physical world around them. With the right tweaks, humans are able to engage in such telekinesis, but their brains are not structured for maximum efficiency. In order to achieve true power, you need to be a hybrid of both, a combination of human and Xeno."

"Let me guess," I say. "That's you. A goddamn freak."

"You say freak Miss McManus, but we at Majestic believe hybridization is the next step in evolution."

I roll my eyes. "So not only are you a back-up clone, you're a traitor to two races? How does that make you feel?"

Thorn's eyes thin. "You know nothing, Molly McManus."

"You say you're half-human, half-Xeno, and yet you're betraying both."

"That's enough."

"Double traitor."

"Silence!" Thorn roars, the veins in his neck bulging, his eyes flaring. His wide eyes, long arms and legs, thin body, all his odd features and proportions suddenly make sense, now that I know the truth about him.

"You've met Number-Two," Thorn says, recovering his composure and indicating the Crab that enters my field of vision off to his right. It stares at me with its disgusting sideways-jawed beady-eyed face. "Number-Two has replaced his mother in the role of commanding the forces of the Schism. You met his mother. She was known as Number-One."

"The warehouse."

Thorn nods. "Yes. Perhaps you could apologize for murdering her."

"Maybe," I say, turning to look at the Crustie, "he could apologize for murdering my mother, and my father, oh and a whole lot of other people too."

An inhuman clicking sound comes from somewhere behind that face. The sound and smell of the creature. The unnatural shape of it. It's all disgusting.

"I can't understand you," I say, "I don't speak throat-clearing."

I feel the creature tugging at the thread that links us and then the world disappears, sucked off into the distance until I'm standing in misty black emptiness. Number-Two walks through the mist toward me.

Can you understand me now, human? I have studied your language and though I do not have the correct anatomy to make the sounds that comprise your unsophisticated communication, I can recreate it here, in our melding.

What do you want?

You think yourself clever, but you are not. Your intelligence is a thing to be marveled at, if only for its valiant attempt to be anything more than animal. The simple structures of your mind, so easily manipulated and replicated, are a thing for study.

Number-Two stops before me in the misty darkness.

You talk a big game, I reply. *But like Thorn just said, you can't do shit to me other than talk, and even that is only because of the Obelisk. Without it you are nothing more than we are – probably less. I killed your mom, remember, and I did that using only my simple brain.*

You are an outlier, Molly McManus. You are an interesting case to study. While we make the rest of your species fight to protect us from the heretics who have come to defile our Obelisk, the necessary components of your body will be harvested and studied to determine how to generate such power in the rest of your kind. Then the heretics will be utterly destroyed.

I stare at the creature. *These new Xenos that have arrived, they don't like you much, do they?* I say this, *think* this, if only to try and stall. I don't know what I'm neffing stalling for. Nobody's coming to my rescue, but every instinct is telling me to delay my death for as long as possible.

The Xeno throws his arms up in exasperation. I've never seen a Xeno display an emotional outburst before, at least not in such a human way. *They are heretics. They have forsaken the sanctity of the Obelisk. They believe they have the right to play divine, to create more Obelisks to ensure none are confronted by the silence, no matter how far they travel, but there can be only one.*

Oh, neffing hell. This is a religious thing? You morons are destroying the population of our planet because you worship a big pillar, and you actually think you're more advanced than us? Sounds a lot like some dumb shit humans would do.

It is not religion as you understand it. Our species exists linked with the Obelisk. We had no choice but to protect it from the heretics who would desecrate it and risk its destruction.

And you decided to use or planet and our species to fight this war for you. We don't have any part in this. Did you even consider how this would affect us? Did you consider the ethics of forcing another race to unwillingly fight?

The Xeno tilts its head. Somehow, even with its ugly, featureless face, I can tell that it's smiling. *Do humans consider the horse when it is unwillingly used to work a field? It is the way of things. The strong appropriate the weak.*

And we're the weak?

Is that not obvious?

If you're so powerful, why do you need us to stop you getting your butt kicked by the rest of your race? Seems like you're the weak ones here. Weak in fighting. Weak in morals. Weak in –

ENOUGH.

The force that strikes me is so powerful it throws me out of the misty forever and back into the real world. Well, well, somebody has a temper too. The air suddenly smells like the ashes of an extinguished fire mixed with old sweaty gym socks – the smell of Xenocrustacean anger leaking out of Number-Two. Thorn walks to the door, opens it and calls out to someone, "Come in and sedate her."

Two white coats come in and inject something into my arm. Within seconds I feel spacey, distant, ready to vanish into the abyss of drug-induced sleep.

Thorn pauses for a moment. I feel a gentle push from his mind, testing to see if I can use my own abilities, but with whatever they've given me soaking into my brain I can barely concentrate. He and Number-Two turn and leave. As I'm drifting away I see the white coats leave, too. Everybody is abandoning me in the concrete box. Even as my eyelids droop closed and I know there's little hope, I can't help but smile. Because Thorn and Number-Two just showed me their weakness.

I know, because it's the same as mine.

They get angry.

I STAY low as I crest the last rise before the Alpha Compound. There's another fence between myself and the compound, higher and more intimidating than the one at the edge of the N.E.Z. I'm almost certain this is as far as I'm going to get, until I see hundreds of vacant-faced people walking single-file into the compound through a heavily guarded security checkpoint. I have no idea why they're being taken inside, but I know an opportunity when I see it.

I fight every single instinct and force myself to stand up tall, walking slowly, eyes forward, trying to mimic the vacant expression on the faces of the mind-controlled. I wander over, coming from a slightly different direction, although no one seems to notice, and join the line as they march in through the security checkpoint. I feel like I'm in that scene in *The Wizard of Oz* where Scarecrow, the Tin Man and the Cowardly Lion dress up as members of the Wicked Witch's army and sneak into the castle to rescue Dorothy. Except I'm the Cowardly Lion, and I'm doing it alone.

I walk between an older lady in a sundress and a young man in dirty, sun-faded laborer's clothes, concentrating on keeping my face emotionless and steadying my breathing as I pass the SECPOL. My heart's rhythm increases to the point where I'm convinced that's what will give me away. But I walk through without getting a second glance.

The destination of the mob soon becomes clear. We walk into the Alpha Compound, passing through the third fence in much the same way, and form a line heading down the length of the runway. The SECPOL are like farmers directing sheep through wooden runs to be sheared or, perhaps more accurately, directing them onto trucks destined for the abattoir.

Midway down the tarmac are two long racks set up in parallel, each one extending for a hundred meters or so, all loaded with plasma rifles. As the crowd files past SECPOL, soldiers work frantically to hand rifles to everyone who passes. The mind-controlled masses take the weapons, prime them with a continuous cacophony of hums, and then hold them vertically against their right shoulder before marching on down the runway and peeling off in different directions at the end. It's like well-practiced choreography, but of course none of these people have even held a plasma rifle before.

I take the rifle I'm handed – once again anxiously preparing myself for recognition that doesn't come. I prime the rifle, just as those around me do, seeing its blue-white glow and feeling it hum in my grasp. The majority of the crowd move off to encircle the compound in a kind of defensive perimeter. A smaller number, around fifty, are entering the circular Institute building. I move in quick steps, continuing to keep my gaze forward, to join the group headed inside. I have no doubt Molly and Mackenzie are in there somewhere.

My mind is screaming at me that going back into the Institute is a bad idea, the worst, but I push the thoughts back. We walk along the road, pass through the open blast door, the orange light pulsating at the top, then continue down into the tunnel I first entered in the jeep with Charlotte. The sound of our rhythmic marching echoes up and down the empty tunnel as we head underground. We continue past the main entrance to the Institute. The blast door that was sealed when I first arrived now stands open, retracted into the roof above. Behind it, the tunnel continues down into the lower levels.

I follow the group into the deepest levels of the Institute, like the underground part of some dwarven mountain lair. The entire time I march, I'm working out exactly what my plan is going to be. When Remy, Molly and I escaped from the Institute that was unplanned, too, and I could barely handle the thought. Now, though, I don't have a choice. I've got to find Molly so she can stop all this. I'm just going to have to take a leaf out of her book and improvise.

As I march with the group of mind-controlled humans I know we can't have much further to go. Once we reach our destination, probably the Obelisk, my opportunity will be lost. I'm going to have to sneak away. Each time we reach the bottom of a ramp it turns one hundred and eighty degrees and continues its descent. At each of these corners I notice that the gray concrete wall houses an alcove, a small opening with a door that must access some kind of service tunnel. I don't expect the door to be unlocked, but every second level has a vent above the doorway, and I figure that might be worth a try. If nothing else, the small recess is shadowy enough that I can use it to hide.

I make my way to the outside of the group, pushing through the crowd as casually as possible to position myself close to the wall. As we round the next corner I sidestep and dash into the alcove. My heart pounds as I plant my back against the door, where the shadows are the darkest. I expect an alarm to sound and every single mind-controlled person to turn and lock eyes on me, but it doesn't happen. They continue on in a steady flow until I'm left alone.

I wait in the shadows until I feel like my muscles are going to twitch out of my skin. Eventually I convince myself it's safe, and I turn to look up at the vent above me. I can't see how it's secured in place. It doesn't look like it's screwed in. Maybe if I can hoist myself up I'll be able to pull it free.

I stop as I hear the thunk of a heavy lock and the door in front of me opens with the groan of barely used hinges. I stumble back. The barrel of a plasma rifle appears first, followed by a SECPOL officer, then another. After the two of them comes a familiar face: it's Jesse, standing with a rifle pointing at me.

"Put your rifle on the ground," he says.

I don't have much of a choice. I do as he says.

"That's better," he says. "Hello, Wells."

"Jesse," I say. "Is it Jesse? Or do you have some clone name?"

He smiles. "Jesse is fine. We have the same name."

"Right," I say, looking to the SECPOL standing either side of him. "Not the same friends, though."

"Did you honestly think you could sneak into the Institute without being noticed? There are surveillance cameras everywhere, and they're constantly running biometric face recognition."

"And you're the welcoming party, are you? Just you and two SECPOL – to be honest, I'm a little bit offended by that."

"Molly was the real threat," Jesse says, "and she's been dealt with. Thorn and the others have more pressing concerns than a one-eyed half-blind weak little traitor. It won't take any more than us to handle you, Wells."

"You've got a lot of audacity calling me a traitor, Jesse."

"I'm no traitor. I've always been loyal to Majestic."

"Because you're not real."

"I'm as much a human as you are." The clone's voice is loaded with emotion. Clearly, dealing with the truth of his existence is troubling. "I have all of Jesse's memories, if only to help me blend in. I can't say I have the same motivations, though."

"Face it, you were created. You were created purely to be a plant inside Omega. I don't know if I was the contingency for your failure or the other way around, but either way, your mission is complete now. Your usefulness to Majestic has ended. You're just a nobody again."

Jesse storms forward and shoves the barrel of his rifle up under my chin. His eyes are alight with flame. My heart pounds against my ribs, as if planning to try and escape by itself if I don't get out of this situation soon. I tell myself I know what I'm doing.

"You don't have to be a nobody though," I say, feeling my Adam's apple press against the slightly warm barrel of the weapon as I swallow. "We never thought you were."

"You did," he growls. "You always did. Just like the others. You all thought I was worthless, but here, with Majestic, I'm part of something."

"Is that how they're controlling you? Trying to make it seem like they actually care about you, and telling you we thought you were worthless? Nobody thought you were worthless, Jesse. I don't have powers either, remember. We were all just doing what we could. You know it was Thorn who told me to cast suspicion on you? He didn't tell you that, did he?" He doesn't answer, but the change in his eyes tells me all I need to know. "You might not be the Jesse I knew, but you claim to have his memories. I'm sure you've been indoctrinated, made to believe that what Majestic is doing is right, but I bet even beneath that you still feel the same way about Molly, don't you?"

"Molly McManus is a threat to the future of humanity, but if she is controlled she could be its greatest weapon. I believe Omega is a terrorist organization that should be eradicated. I believe you are a criminal hacker and a disappointment to the Institute for the Betterment of Humanity."

"Do you want to know what I believe?" I ask.

"What?"

"I believe that you love Molly McManus and you've always been there for her. I believe those feelings are strong enough to shake the foundation of whatever indoctrination they've put you through."

"You think love conquers all?" Jesse asks. "I didn't think you would go in for such garbage, Wells. I thought you were more logical than that. You're here to destroy the Obelisk."

"No," I say. "We just want to let the rest of the Xenos take back what rightfully belongs on their planet. That's how we keep humanity safe, not by fighting a war."

"Grab him," Jesse says to the SECPOL. They do as they're ordered, grasping me tightly by the arms. "I'm taking you to Thorn."

"They're going to kill Molly," I say as the SECPOL shove me back out onto the ramp. "They won't risk trying to control her again. She's too dangerous."

"They're not going to kill her," Jesse says. "If they were going to kill her they would have done it at the fence."

He's cracking, I can see it. My suspicion was right. No matter how they've manipulated him, how much they've tried to indoctrinate him, he's still Jesse. They needed him to fit seamlessly into the real Jesse's place, so they couldn't turn him into a complete robot, they had to maintain his personality, at least to some extent. I might not have got along with him very well, but I know he would do anything for Molly, and that runs deeper than anything Majestic might have done.

"Listen to me Jesse," I say. "Jesse Hill wouldn't let Molly McManus die."

"I'm not Jesse Hill," he says, gesturing for the SECPOL to move me along. They shove me forward, Jesse walking along behind us.

I twist my head to look back at him. "But you *can* be. You remember going to school every day with Molly. You remember helping us escape and joining Omega – all for Molly. You remember how you feel about your best friend."

He doesn't respond.

"You're not one of them Jesse, you're one of us. I am. You are." I stumble as the SECPOL pull me roughly along. "We are Omega, Jesse."

The rifle fires, two quick shots, and the SECPOL are thrown forward, releasing their grip on me. They land on their faces, smoke curling up from the blackened holes in their backs. More innocent dead. I don't look at them. Instead, I try to focus on what's at stake.

Jesse squeezes his eyes closed, as if there's still some internal battle raging inside him. When he opens his eyes he bends to collect one of the SECPOL's rifles and passes it to me. "Follow me."

Ω

Jesse leads me back through the door in the alcove. Just as I suspected, it's some kind of service tunnel, two or three meters wide. The floor is steel grating, and I can feel cold air circling around us. Above and below are more levels of the same steel grating. We're in a thin space encircling the central cylinder of the Institute, between the main structure and the outer wall that's holding back the tons of dirt and rock that must surround us. The walls are full of twisting electrical wires, thick pipes and small white signs indicating the directions to the vital systems of the Institute. It's like a peek behind the curtain of the shiny facility. Jesse moves ahead, following the gentle curve of the tunnel, his boots clanking on the steel floor, until he reaches a ladder and begins climbing down.

"There's an access door near where they're holding Molly and Mackenzie, but as soon as we exit they'll spot us on camera," Jesse says.

"And how long will we have until the SECPOL arrive?"

Jesse looks at me but doesn't answer.

"That bad?" I say.

He shrugs. "Thirty seconds, maybe a minute."

"And Molly and Mackenzie are being kept in separate rooms?"

He nods. "We'll only have time to save one."

I already knew it would be more important to save Molly than Mackenzie, but I still feel a sudden rush of feeling – not quite anger, more a powerful vexation at the inevitability of the decision. "You don't need you to convince me," I say. "I know we need to get Molly out first."

I follow Jesse down two more levels until we drop off a ladder onto solid concrete instead of another walkway of steel grating. This must be the bottom, the very lowest level of the Institute. I'm not entirely sure how far underground we are but it must be at least ten stories. I follow Jesse to another access door.

"Out here and to the right. The first door is the temporary infirmary where they're keeping Molly. We'll need to move fast. I have no idea who's going to be in there."

"Are you willing to shoot one of them if you need to?" I ask.

"Of course," Jesse says. "Are you?"

I nod. "When we get her out we head straight back here, alright? We'll try to lose them in the tunnels and give Molly a chance to do whatever she needs to do."

"The Obelisk is down here too," Jesse says. "It's in a central chamber. The entrance is on the opposite side, so we should be able to use the tunnels to get around there too."

I grab the handle of the door. "On three?"

Jesse nods.

"One, two, *three.*"

I open the door. Jesse moves through and begins to sprint down the corridor. I follow him to where he's stopped in front of an unmarked door. He tries to open it, but of course it's locked. He steps back, levels his plasma rifle at the door and begins to fire. Plasma burst after plasma burst hit the electronic lock until it's nothing but runs of melted metal. He squares up and kicks the door with his foot. It shudders. He kicks again and it bursts open.

Inside, the room is mostly bare concrete. There's a smattering of medical equipment, but the most notable thing is the chair in the center of the space. Molly is in it, held in place with restraints. She's not moving.

"Shit," Jesse says. He hurries over and crouches to check that she's breathing. I follow close behind. "I think she's unconscious. Help me with these straps." He starts unclasping the stiff metal cuffs around her wrists.

"They clearly want her alive," I say, "but they can't risk her being awake. I'm surprised they've left her unattended, though."

"We didn't leave her unattended."

We spin to see Charlotte in the doorway. In one hand she's holding a mug of something, presumably tea, and in the other she's holding her phone. She takes a sip from her mug. A SECPOL officer enters the room after her. Almost at precisely the same moment Jesse and I raise our rifles. The SECPOL doesn't hesitate in doing the same.

"I have to admit I'm surprised to see you here, Wells," Charlotte says. "Thorn and Number-Two were convinced we needed to bring in a force to guard the Obelisk, even though you were the only one left out there. I didn't think you'd be brave enough to try something like this, especially after you betrayed these people in the first place. It's nice to see you giving it a red-hot go, though. Unfortunately, all you've done is put yourself in a situation where you'll get killed. A little like how you put Margaret in a situation where she got killed."

I feel the familiar build of shame and guilt and fear.

"Give it up, Wells. Give it up and maybe you can live through this," Charlotte says. "It would be good if your parents got to keep at least one child."

My eye grows hot. It stings under my eye patch. Pain burns inside and out. I shake my head. "No," I say. "You don't get to use that against me anymore. It's not going to control me anymore."

Charlotte smirks. "Oh, but I can control you, can't I?"

I feel a cold tingle down my spine. No. No, no, no, not again.

"There are two of us with rifles and only one of you," Jesse says. "Let us take Molly out of here."

"I can't do that Jesse, you know that," Charlotte says. "Besides, do you think we'd let a barely controlled clone like you wander around without a failsafe?"

I try to move, but I can't.

Jesse's eyes thin and his brow crinkles into concerned lines. "What do you mean?"

"That threat Mr Thorn made to you, Wells," Charlotte says. "The threat of a cyanide kill switch? Even though we didn't have time to implant you with one, it wasn't just something he made up to scare you. It is something we've done before."

"What are you talking about?" Jesse says. He turns to me. "What's she talking about, Wells? What does she mean?"

Charlotte takes another sip of her tea and presses her thumb against the screen of her phone. Jesse, his eyes alight with terror, looks from Charlotte to me and then back again. He lurches, his breath catching in his throat with a sudden gasp, and his rifle drops to the floor. A gurgling sound escapes his mouth. It's guttural and hollow and seems to be coming from somewhere deep inside him. He clutches desperately at his throat, and I suddenly realize he can't breathe.

I want to scream, but I can't. Charlotte has paralyzed me yet again.

Jesse stumbles. He grabs at my arm, but his grip is so weak that his hand slips away and he drops to his knees. A bubbling white-yellow foam forces its way out of his mouth and runs down his chin. Jesse's throat pulsates. More choking sounds fight their way out through the foam at his mouth, which has turned pink with the tinge of blood. He drops forward onto his face and lands motionless on the floor.

"See, it's a shame we didn't have a chance to get one of those installed in you, Wells. It would have made things a lot easier. You don't think we've got enough to worry about right now?" Charlotte looks from Jesse's body up to me. "Yes, Wells? You look like you want to say something."

"You murdered him!" I shout, suddenly able to speak again, but still unable to move. "Just like that. You're a monster."

"I didn't really murder anyone. Jesse Hill was already dead. That was..." Charlotte makes a vague gesture toward the body on the ground. "A nobody. I don't think you can murder a nobody?"

"You're a clone," I say.

Charlotte scrunches her mouth as if considering. "It's all a muddle when it comes to me, Wells. I haven't existed in my original form for forty years. It's hard to say exactly *what* I am at this point."

"Dead." Molly pushes herself awkwardly out of the chair. Her voice is airy and floaty. "That's what you are."

Charlotte's face changes from playfulness to panic. Her eyebrows lift, her eyes widen, and she spins to the SECPOL beside her. "More sedative, now!"

I try to stop myself as I turn to point my rifle at Molly. "Molly!" I fight it. I clench my teeth. I won't be used like this anymore. "You...can't...control...me!" I push desperately back against the great force of Charlotte's power. I'm not going to be blackmailed with Maggie's death anymore, and I'm not going to shoot Molly.

Charlotte looks at me as she struggles to impose her will. Her face collapses rapidly from panic through fear to anger. She turns to the SECPOL. "Shoot them!"

But she's too late.

Molly, despite appearing to be barely conscious, closes her eyes in determination. When her eyes fly open Charlotte and the SECPOL fly too – backwards. The SECPOL, still clutching his rifle, is lifted into the air, straight through the still-open door and into the corridor beyond. I see him hit the far wall, his head snapping back and leaving a splatter of red against the white paint. Charlotte hits the edge of the doorframe at an angle and slumps to the floor, trailing tea through the air. She lands on her back, half in and half out of the room. Groaning, she rolls onto her stomach and begins to push herself back up. The sensation of coldness down my spine vanishes. I look at Molly, but she's dropped back down into the chair.

"Molly," I say, "Charlotte's still moving over here."

Molly moans in response, tries to push herself up again, but drops heavily. Charlotte, gathering herself, stands and turns to face me.

"Oh Wells, I thought we were friends, you and I. I thought –"

A thin trail of white smoke rises in twisting curls from the barrel of the plasma rifle in my hands. It's shaking. I'm shaking. Charlotte slides down the doorframe. The front of her chest is scorched from the super-heated bolt of plasma, her clothes disintegrated and the flesh seared and burned away. I swallow as she finally drops in a heap. I turn away, averting my eyes.

"She...deserved it, Wells." I turn to Molly. She's trying to sit up again.

I hurry over to her, kneeling down to lever the clasps free from around her ankles.

"We can't kill that bitch enough times," she says.

When I've managed to free her feet I grab her by the fore-arms and help her up. She's unsteady, and I have to grab her awkwardly around the waist to stop her falling.

"I'm okay," she says. "Just give me a minute."

"We don't really have a minute. Can you incapacitate the compound, take the force field down?"

Molly scrunches her face before shaking her head. "I can't. Not yet. I can't focus."

"Alright," I say. "Let's just get you out of here."

I lift Molly's arm and drape it across my shoulder, taking most of her weight. We head for the door but she stops me as we pass the body of Jesse's clone. She stares down at the body, his open eyes, his mouth and shirt stained by the pink foam that escaped his mouth.

"It wasn't him," I say.

She nods. "I know. He's a clone. But I never got to mourn for the real Jesse."

Molly lowers herself toward him. I try to stop her. "I'm sorry Molly, I really am, but we have to go."

"Just one goodbye, Wells. That's all."

I relent and take her weight as she kneels beside him. She gently runs her fingers down his face to close his eyes and then kisses him on the side of the forehead.

"Alright," she says, "let's go."

I help her up again. As we exit the room and turn toward the door to the service tunnels we are confronted by six armed SECPOL. I try to raise my plasma rifle, but it's awkward to lift while I'm supporting Molly.

"I can do it," Molly says.

She tosses her arm sideways in the general direction of the SECPOL, in a motion that almost topples us both off-balance. She's obviously not strong enough to blast them into non-existence, but the six SECPOL officers are still thrown violently into the wall, their heads slamming against the hard concrete. They collapse into a muddled pile of rifles and dark blue uniforms. Not all of them are knocked unconscious by the blow, but even those who aren't lie groaning in the pile of bodies, struggling to gather themselves.

"Come on," I say, feeling Molly's weight grow heavier against me. If we can get into the service tunnels we'll be safe – well, not exactly safe, but at least we'll be away from the ever-present eye of surveillance cameras. Maybe we'll even have a chance to get to the Obelisk and end this. I'm not under any illusions, though. If whatever they drugged Molly with doesn't wear off soon I'll just be prolonging our inevitable capture. I need her to get her full powers back – sometime in the next few minutes would be great.

"Stop," I say to Wells as he leads me further along the dark corridor of pipes and cables. My head is spinning more wildly with every step, a wicked fireworks display is exploding across my vision, and my mouth is suddenly watering with pre-vomit saliva. "Wells, I've got to stop."

"We can't, Molly. All the way around to the other side. That's what Jesse said. That's where the Obelisk will be."

"I'm going to throw up."

Wells still doesn't stop.

"Please, Wells."

He slows, sighing. "Alright."

We stop and he lifts my arm from his shoulder. I slip down to sit on the ground, resting my head against the wall. The wall opposite seems to be pulsating, the unpainted concrete moving like a wave. I close my eyes to block out the sight before I bring up what little I have in my stomach.

"Do you feel any clearer?" Wells says.

Whatever Thorn's goons drugged me with is playing havoc with my powers. It's like when you've got the flu and your head is all foggy. I can't find that reservoir of strength that Remy taught me to tap into. I can manage small things, like throwing Charlotte or those SECPOL soldiers around, but anything more than that feels like trying to lift a truck.

"You'll know when I feel like I can do something because I'll neffing well do it, Wells," I say. "I'm not waiting for some dramatic moment for the hell of it."

"Sorry," Wells says. "It's just, we're in the thick of it now. I don't know if we're going to make it out of here. What do we do if you can't use your powers?"

Wells is pacing, talking to the air around him as much as to me. He's growing increasingly anxious. I know my outburst wasn't justified – it's not his fault, he's come here to save me. Shit, after everything that's happened, here he is.

"I'm sorry, Wells," I say. "We're just so close and I can't neffing do anything."

"Do you think your powers are going to come back? My entire plan was to find you – everything after that kind of relies on you saving the day."

"Jeez, no pressure."

Wells stares at me with his one good eye. This ordeal has changed him. His hair is a tangled mop of curls, and with his black eye patch and the rifle held across his body he looks like an action hero. He might still act like a nervous wreck, and he's skinnier than any action hero I've ever seen but, like I said, he's here. He made it into the Institute and rescued me, and that takes balls.

"Listen Wells, what you did, betraying us all like that, I know you justified it to yourself because of your sister, but that was a dick move. A real dick move."

"Don't you think I know that?"

"But," I say, holding up my hand to cut off his fiery reaction, "you coming for me, that means a lot. I mean, a one-man mission to infiltrate the compound and find me – that was stupid, but it's awesome stupid. If you hadn't made it in here we wouldn't stand a chance. We might still be screwed, but at least we're a little less screwed. Maybe we can end this after all."

"If we do get a chance to end this, you should know that the Xenos above haven't attacked anyone. They've had plenty of time to destroy the gathering humans, but all they've done is defend themselves. I think Mackenzie is right – they just want to take the Obelisk and go."

"So we're just going to believe these new Crabs are the nice Crabs?" I say. "Do I need to remind you we've been fed that cookie before?"

"I know, but the Obelisk is important to them. It's important to both sides. That's what caused this war in the first place. The Obelisk is what allows the Xenos to meld with each other. Without it, they can't communicate. On their planet, being cut off from the Obelisk is the worst possible punishment, a fate worse than death. They call it the silence. The Schism stole the Obelisk and fled, leaving the entire population of their planet in the silence. It's like the entire population of Earth suddenly being left deaf and mute – maybe worse."

"What could be worse than that?" I say. "Oh, I know, killing one fifth of the planet. That's pretty bad, too."

"That was the Schism. It wasn't these Xenos that did that."

"The Crabs are all the same to me," I say. "If I get a chance to destroy the Obelisk I'm going to do it."

"I just want us to do the right thing."

"Don't worry," I say, "I intend to do the right thing – the right thing for humanity. What about Mackenzie? Do you know where she is?"

He shakes his head. "No."

I climb to my feet. My head still feels like it's going to float off my neck, but at least the lights have stopped exploding across my eyes and the spinning has slowed to a lazy tipping. I put my hand on Wells' arm. "We'll find her. Now, let's keep moving. They must know where we're headed."

"They do," Wells says. "I saw the people who are meant to stop us. There's a lot of them."

"Okay, well, let's not keep them waiting."

We continue walking around the curving tunnel until we reach an access door, the same as the one on the opposite side. Wells unlocks it, opens it a fraction and peers out.

"There's no one there," Wells says, surprised.

"That's a good thing, Wells."

"Well, yes, I was just expecting them to be waiting for us."

We exit the service tunnel into the white-walled corridor. It's as bland as the others – nothing on the walls or floors to indicate there's anything of interest down here at all. Ahead of us is a set of double doors made of the same opaque glass used everywhere in this place. There are no handles, but there is a complicated series of panels off to the side.

"Coded entry, retinal scanner, handprint, the works," Wells says. "This must be it. Do you think you can get it open?"

"Yep," I say, taking a step back and steadying my breath.

"Wait," Wells interrupts just as I'm about to blow the door inward. "Are you ready?"

I look at him and nod. The truth is, I have no neffing idea. I feel better. I feel like the cloudy wall that surrounded my mind has drifted away. I feel like I'm going to be able to let fly with my full strength. I also know I've probably only got one shot at this.

"Are you sure?" Wells asks again.

"Yes, Wells."

"Like, one hundred percent positive?"

"Just let me open it."

Wells nods, and I push out against the door. It begins to bow. Cracks start crawling across the surface, splitting into smaller and smaller branches until it shatters, bursting inward in thousands of shards that fall to the ground with a tinkling sound. When he sees what's beyond the door, Wells does something I've never heard before. He swears.

"Fuck."

Past the door is a cavernous space. It must take up most of the lowest levels of the Institute – it's at least three stories high and as large across as a football field. In the center of the space is a slab of concrete, like an altar, and on top of that, rising forty or fifty feet high, is an orange-brown pillar. It's square for most of the way up, but tapers to a pyramid at the top. The surface is covered with carved symbols. Some are swirling flows, others are made up of straight or jagged lines, like its covered with a bunch of different languages.

Around the outside of the Obelisk, standing on raised platforms, are students of the Institute. At least a hundred of them, each one facing the Obelisk with their eyes closed. A rhythmic sound fills the space, a hum like a kind of chant, or weird praying. In fact, that's what this place looks like: a cathedral.

Beneath the low humming there's a deep, almost inaudible sound; more a feeling than sound, a rumbling in my chest. I can feel all these students connected to the Obelisk, using it to boost the threads joining them to the "nodes" around the world. This is the center of the mind-control.

The problem is, guarding the Obelisk and facing us, all with their rifles raised, are row after row of mind-controlled people. My first instinct is to run, but I hold my ground and reach inside my well of power, whispering an apology to all these innocent people. But as I prepare to flatten them I feel him. Thorn. He's standing on the raised base of the Obelisk watching us. Even from here I can see the smirk on his face. As soon as I let loose my power, he's going to grab my mind, and this time he won't let go.

"Come on!" I grab Wells' arm and pull him back through the door and into the corridor.

"Wait! What?" he stammers as I pull him out of the way just as plasma erupts through the doorway and slams against the wall, the super-heated bursts leaving blackened scorches and gouges in the concrete.

"Holy heck!"

"Fuck was better, Wells!"

We stumble into a run as continuous bolts of plasma turn the doorframe into superheated rubble. Dust fills the air, and we hold our hands up protectively as chunks of concrete fly around us.

We make it down the corridor away from the carnage. I stop and turn back. Surprisingly, no one is following us.

"What was that?" Wells asks me, panting slightly. "Why didn't you do something?!"

"I can't."

"I asked you if you were ready!"

"No, it's not that. It's Thorn, he's in there. I can't use my powers around him."

"Oh good," Wells says, tossing his arms up in exasperation. "Excellent. Great. Now what?"

I don't say anything.

"Well?"

"I'm thinking, dammit!"

"This was a bad idea. I knew this was a bad idea."

An ominous sound echoes up the tunnel toward us. Foot-steps. It's Thorn, walking with unhurried motions, his gaze fixed on us. Wells just stares at him.

"This is not the time to have a freeze reflex, Wells." I grab his arm. "Let's go!"

To my surprise, he pulls his arm free. "You go," he says as he raises the rifle at Thorn. "I'll cover you."

Jank me. He's not frozen in fear, he's being brave. I feel a rush of admiration for him, but I still grab his arm again. Thorn stops.

"Give it up, Miss McManus, Mr Marsden. You cannot win."

"Come on, Wells, don't be stupid. You can't –"

Wells' arm is ripped free of my grip but it's not him pulling it this time. His whole body is thrown tumbling upwards. He rises into the air, slams face first into the roof, and then drops. But he never hits the ground – he's brought to a sudden stop about halfway down. His legs bend down and his neck whips back, like he's a stick being snapped over someone's knee. Thorn releases him. Wells drops to the floor and doesn't move.

"Wells! Dammit, Thorn, you didn't have to do that!"

"He would have shot me," Thorn says. "You would not hesitate to throw me around if you had the chance. There is nothing that makes your cause more noble than mine, nothing to suggest I should treat you any differently to the way you would treat me."

I stare at Thorn. If I make a move he'll pounce, lock up my mind, and that will be the end of it, both for me and for the slim chance that I can keep humanity from being dragged into this war. I need a way out. If he can grab my mind when I use my powers, maybe I can do the same to him.

"The difference is, you deserve it, you're a traitor to both your races. Who were you originally?"

"I am more than I ever was," Thorn says.

"Except you're a clone," I say.

"For all intents and purposes, I am the Mr Thorn you have met previously."

"Except you're not. You're more like a restored backup."

"I am the culmination of more than seventy years' work in hybridization, and I hold all those years of knowledge and experience."

"Backup."

"I am not a backup."

"Back. Up."

"That's enough!" He calms himself as the anger fades from

his voice, if not from his eyes. "I can see what you are trying to do, Miss McManus. It will not work. You will not bait me."

"Okay. Tell me though, do you lose anything when you're restored like the backup you are? How do you know you're still the same?"

"You have no control of your mind Molly. You can never overpower me."

"I overpowered Charlotte easily enough," I say. I see his face tighten, my words visibly hitting a nerve. "Oh, I see. Was she your little girlfriend, you old creep? Well, your little girlfriend is dead. Again. And if all this is destroyed, there'll be no bringing her back, will there?"

Thorn snarls. "You will not speak about her in this way."

I realize it then. I should have seen it before, the resemblance was there. "Well, neffing jank me. She's your daughter, isn't she?" I almost laugh. "Well shit, sorry to say your daughter's dead. Is she your daughter the old-fashioned way, or did they just rip some cells out of you and cook her in a vat? Is she...sorry...*was* she half a Crab, too? You better hope you've got her backed up somewhere."

Thorn stalks toward me. His nostrils flare. Come on, you piece of shit, use your mind against me. But he doesn't fall for it. He lets out his anger another way. He moves faster than I thought he could and grabs me by the throat, slamming me back into the wall. He's strong. Maybe that's the Crustie part of him.

Behind me, splayed out on the ground, Wells moans. "Molly," he mumbles, his voice cracking.

"It's okay, Wells," I manage. "I've got him right where I want him."

"Molly, I can't feel my legs!"

"Hang in there, buddy," I croak out.

Thorn squeezes harder, his fingers digging in around my throat and cutting off my airway. I can't breathe.

"Molly!"

Through the stars creeping into the edges of my vision I look back to see Wells pawing his hand toward his rifle. It's just within reach. He stretches out, immense pain obvious across his face, and grabs it. He lifts it, turns it awkwardly and points it at Thorn. Thorn looks over to see the rifle aimed at him.

Go on. Do it. Do it now.

The rifle drops to the side, but Wells fumbles it back up again. My vision darkens. My lungs are screaming for air.

Thorn looks from Wells, to me, and then back again. Wells slips his finger into the trigger guard.

Go on. Go on.

Wells' face goes slack, his finger stopping before he can pull the trigger. I sense Thorn reaching out along the thread that joins him to Wells. But this reach is not two-way, like with Remy and me. This is less like telephone cans and more like a net stretching from Thorn and wrapping itself around Wells. I've never tried to control someone the way Thorn or Charlotte or even Remy could. But I suddenly see how it's done. I see the way Thorn grips Wells' mind and then slips inside, putting him on like clothes.

This is my chance and I take it, stretching out my own will, cracking the dam open just enough to try and grab Thorn. I immediately sense resistance. I push harder, and Thorn pushes back. He glares at me, and I let the dam wall inside me burst. Thorn stumbles back under the force of my mind and drops me. I land on my knees, sucking in air in painful gasps.

Thorn pushes at me with his mind and I start pushing back. We're locked in a stalemate, equal and opposite forces pushing at each other. But we're not equal, are we? He's holding Wells even while doing this, and still the weight of his power is crushing down on me. I feel a tingle down my spine as he wraps me in his spider webs. I try to do the same, stretching my own web at him, but I can't grab him while fighting to keep him from doing the same to me.

I can sense him gripping Wells' mind harder, taking control of his nerves and muscles. I start to panic. I should have realized he would be too strong. I have no experience in telekinetic mind battles. What the jank was I thinking?

Thorn forces Wells to point his rifle at me. I reach out and try to control Wells too, trying to push his rifle back toward Thorn. Poor Wells, it must feel like a madhouse in there, his muscles fighting against each other.

With my focus on Wells, I feel the protective shell I've built around myself starting to waver. The pain in my throat is making it hard to split my focus. That's it, though. I think of how Thorn, the old Thorn, held me back so easily in the warehouse until he was shot by that undercover Omega agent. That sudden loss of concentration allowed me to get the upper hand.

Wells, I send my thoughts to him. *Can you hear me?*

Molly? Yes, I can hear you. Are you melding with me? What the heck is going on?

Shhh. Listen. I can't hold him much longer. I'm going to let you shoot me.

You're going to do what?!

He's trying to make you shoot me and I'm going to let him.

Why?

Just listen. I'm going to try and direct your aim to the outside of my left arm. I want you to fight to do the same. Just a glancing blow would be nice, because I would like to survive this neffing shit if I can.

Molly, I don't –

We're doing it before I change my mind.

I push Wells' aim toward the spot I want him to hit, and I can feel him doing the same. I clench my jaw. My body is shaking, trembling as if I'm holding a jackhammer. I let out a shout and release Wells' finger.

The blue-white plasma strikes me a glancing blow on the outside of my left arm, just below the shoulder. The bulk of it continues on to hit the wall further down the tunnel, but even the minimal hit I took is enough to drop me. I scream. It's the most painful thing I've ever felt. It burns like goddamn hellfire. The instant it hits me my flesh burns, blisters, and sizzles away right down through the muscle to the bone. My head rolls on the ground as I scream. I don't look at my arm, though. I can't bear to. I know that despite my agony I have to act.

Thorn seizes control of my body, holding me in place, thinking he's won. I remember the lesson Remy taught me: all living things are connected. I grab hold of the thread that connects me to Thorn. I know I won't be able to brute force my way through his defenses, but I don't have to. I just have to do what Remy taught me – what we did that night in the warehouse.

I dump all of my pain onto our connection: the pain of my incinerated arm, the pain of my crushed throat, even the pain of losing those I love. I unload everything I have. It hits him all at once and he reels back, screaming. I reach into Wells and take his pain, too. I feel it momentarily pass through me, the tearing of his eye, the nerve-shattered pain of a broken back, the death of his sister, and I pound that into Thorn as well. He stumbles against the wall, his power suddenly retreating back inside him. I strike.

I reach out and grab Thorn, slipping my grasp around him like a vice. I could kill him right now, I know it. And he knows it too. I sense his fear – I can smell it.

I think about Remy, how he regretted killing those SECPOL during the escape from the Institute. I've killed people now too, aliens, clones, and accidentally killed others using my powers. I don't think I've fully processed that yet. Maybe I never will. I think about what Remy said about there always being a choice. I look at Thorn, cowering in pain and fear. Would Remy show him mercy now? After everything that's happened, would he choose to spare his life?

I lift Thorn into the air and send him sideways, slamming his head into the concrete wall, not hard enough to kill him, but hard enough to be satisfying. Hard enough to knock him out.

"Molly, what are you going to do?"

"I'm going to destroy the Obelisk."

"Molly, remember what I said. The Xenos just want it back. They're not here for us. You destroy that Obelisk and you're punishing all the innocent Xenos who have done nothing. You'll be destroying an entire species."

I think again of all those I've lost – Mum, Dad, Jesse, Remy – and all those the planet has lost. Ever since the plague I've dreamt of having this opportunity, a chance to wipe out the Crabs in a storm of vengeance.

"Look what they've done to us, Wells. Look what they've put you through! Your eye, your back, forcing you to turn on us!"

"It wasn't the Xenos up there who did that, Molly. It was those down here, those and the people working with them."

"Like him," I say, nodding to Thorn. "He's part of it, maybe worse than any of them. Why shouldn't I kill him?"

"He's no threat, Molly. Once the Obelisk is gone no one will have these sorts of powers anymore. They don't work without the Obelisk. Drop the force field – let the others come and take the Obelisk."

"Don't you want me to punish him?"

"Yes." Wells' single eye glazes in the white light of the tunnel as it fills with tears. "Yes, but I don't want you to become like them. I don't want you to destroy an entire race to accomplish your aim."

"Oh, neffing jank, Wells," I say. "So I take the force field down and what? We just hope these Xenos don't grab the Obelisk and do the same neffing thing as their cousins here?"

"Right."

"We could be making a choice that leads to the end of humanity," I say.

"Or we could be proving why we're even worth saving."

I sigh and drop Thorn to the ground. "You're coming with me then, Mr Glass-Half-Full."

"How exactly –" he starts, but I've already lifted him with my mind and started floating him toward me.

We return to the door of the Obelisk chamber. I know that as soon as we appear, a tide of plasma will come toward us.

"Ready?" I ask.

Wells nods. I reach out to feel all those people in the room beyond. I clear my mind and take hold of them, fifty strings spreading out like a web before me.

"Okay."

We turn into the doorway, or what's left of it. With a single thought, the crowd guarding the Obelisk part like the Red Sea, revealing the full height of the Obelisk before us. The students around the outside stir, but they don't move, all of them still connected to the impossibly complex task of maintaining control over the rest of the planet.

"I'm going to take down the force field," I say to Wells. "Do you think that will be enough?"

He nods.

I close my eyes and feel for the force field. I bombard it with everything I have. What happens is the very definition of an anti-climax, at least down here. Up above us, over the entire compound I feel the force field buckle and disintegrate, but down here there is nothing but silence. Nothing happens.

I collapse to my knees on the concrete floor, and Wells drops. I just manage to catch him and lower him gently to the ground.

But then, exhausted, I have to let everything go. With a feeling like the jabs of ten thousand hot knives, the pain in my arm returns. Wells howls at the same time, and I know his pain has come back too.

Several Institute students have dropped their connection with the Obelisk and turned their attention to us. The people guarding the Obelisk turn to face us again, raising their rifles.

"Molly?" Wells says through his teeth, gritted against his pain. It's both a warning and a question. I try to force my will out again but I can't, I'm too tired. My eyes blur and every fiber of my body, every organ and cell screams for sleep.

"I'm sorry, Wells. I can't hold them back."

The mindless mass with their plasma rifles close in around us while the Institute students close in on my mind. Just as I tell myself that at least I died to save others, an enormous rumbling comes from above. Even buried this far underground, the world seems to shake. Dust falls from the roof in swirling sheets, followed by fist-sized pieces of concrete as cracks begin forming and snaking their way through the roof, splitting wider as they go, each of them racing toward a focal point at the center but stopping short of joining together and bringing the roof down on us. The rumbling stops.

A series of crunching thumps hit the roof above, sending more pieces of concrete hurtling to the ground. Most of the students around the Obelisk remain unmoved. Those who have already broken free of their trance have suddenly pulled their attention away from me. The humans down here have done the same, turning their rifles upward.

Glowing circles begin appearing all over the roof, rings that turn from gray to black to orange and then yellow-white. Concrete begins to drip away like lava, falling as super-heated rain. Some of the drops land on the people below and they are instantly smashed to the ground, seared by heavy molten rock.

Most disconcerting of all is that under the mind control there are no screams, just soundless crumples and thuds. Inside, they must be in agony. One by one, the concrete center of each ring drops away, revealing nine or ten cylindrical pods of black metal falling through the newly created holes. They're same pods we saw on the videos from around the world. All around the base of the pods are blue-flaming plasma torches that are flickering out now that they've burned their way through the concrete.

As soon as they land, the mind-controlled people turn their rifles toward the pods and open fire. Plasma flies in all directions – it's like that time Chuck Jordan accidentally set off an entire box of skyrockets on the fourth of July last year. The plasma strikes the pods and leaves scuffs of gray, and slight burn marks, but other than that it doesn't seem to damage them at all.

With a series of hisses the pods begin to open, a section on each one sliding up to reveal the interior. Inside each pod is a Crab, dressed in black armor like another layer of shell on top of the one they've already got. It makes them look even larger and more imposing than they normally do. The plasma shots continue to fly, striking them and causing them to stumble, but the plasma sparks off their armor in the same way as it does off the pods.

The Crabs move out in slow methodical steps, each of them raising their arms, on top of which are barrels glowing with the same white-blue as a plasma rifle. These neffing Iron-Man-armored Crab super soldiers open fire on the students all around the Obelisk. Some of the armored Crusties take enough hits from the humans that they are knocked back into their pods or collapse to the ground, smoke rising from their armor. Wells was right, though – even as this is going on, the Crabs never once shoot at the innocent humans. They concentrate all their fire on the students that are mind-controlling the world. They are innocent too, tricked into coming to the Institute just like Remy and Wells were, but the Crusties shoot them in order to end this. The sight makes me sick to my stomach.

With the deaths of the students, the shooting slows. It's replaced by growing confusion and hysteria. The people in here are free, just as people all around the world will be. But how can you expect people to react after an experience like the one they've had? Some people drop to their knees and sob, others stand motionless, simply looking around in awe at the carnage that has unfolded. Others scream or run, while some laugh and embrace. The place becomes a chaotic mix of raw human emotion.

Despite my exhaustion, I reach out to speak into the minds of everyone here. I broadcast out thoughts like an emergency warning signal.

Please stay calm. You need to get out of here. Go back the way you came, up the ramps to the surface.

A few individuals react straight away. Most don't.

I said get the hell out of here!

This booming declaration finally gets most of them moving, and soon everyone is rushing out the door. After several minutes they're all gone except for me, Wells and the black-armored Crusties who came cannonballing in from above. One of the hulking black Crabs moves toward me and Wells. It reaches up and presses something at the side of its helmet, and the helmet retracts back in a series of sliding plates to reveal the Crab's head. It looks just the same as the others who came to Earth.

It seems to be evaluating me, but it doesn't speak, it doesn't meld with me. In fact, I don't think it could communicate with me even if it tried. I can feel all the strings between these Crusties. Now that they are back under the influence of the Obelisk they are able to meld with each other again, but what is passing between them is completely alien. The Crustie before me doesn't speak, and yet I know it's thanking us.

It returns to the others of its kind. They walk as a group toward the Obelisk and kneel before it. Each of them retracts their helmet in the same way as that first one, and they press their wide flat heads to the ground, bowing in respect to this object they travelled across the stars to recover.

They rise, and each of them retrieves a large cylindrical object from their pods. They attach them in a ring around the base of the Obelisk, each one hissing as it seals itself to the pillar. After a moment the objects begin to emanate the *whomp-whomp* sound of a fluxer. The Crabs attach more of the small engines until the Obelisk floats, then they guide it out of the large chamber.

After they're gone and we're left alone, I turn to look at Wells, who is lying beside me. "Well, how the jank are we supposed to get out of here?"

MY BACK IS BROKEN. That much is obvious from my inability to move anything below my waist, but surprisingly, it isn't anywhere near as excruciating as I thought a broken back would be. Don't misunderstand me, it hurts, it's just not as bad as the ripping pain of gouging out my own eye. That's if I remain perfectly still, at least. If I try to move, nerve pain tears through me like an electric shock.

We've been left alone, just Molly and myself in the empty space that was the epicenter of the Schism's mind-control. And so we wait, unable to do anything else. Sections of the roof fall intermittently to the ground.

"You should go," I say. "Get yourself out. You can probably make it if you try."

Molly looks at me. "I'm not leaving you." I see her glance toward the door. I know what she's thinking.

"You want to go back, don't you?" I say. "Find Thorn and finish him off?"

Molly doesn't answer, but I can tell that I'm right.

"You've already beaten him," I say. "Without the Obelisk he has no power anymore. You don't need to prove anything."

"I know," Molly says.

And, in a sight that surprises me more than it probably should, Molly's face cracks. She squeezes her eyes closed and begins to cry, deep, body-shaking sobs. To me she's always seemed the strongest of us, stronger than Art or even Mackenzie. When things were at their worst she just seemed to grow angrier. I recognize now, in what probably should have been obvious, that it was just her way of coping.

"Are you alright?"

She nods, even as tears continue to run down her cheeks, angling away from her face and back into her hair as she lies on her back. "I'm sorry Wells. Once again, you're the one who's come off worst. I don't even know why I'm crying."

"It's okay," I say, because it really is. "There's catharsis in just letting it all out. You should have done this a long time ago."

"You psychoanalyzing me now?" she says.

"If anyone here knows about managing mental health it's me."

She laughs. "I really hope your parents are alright, Wells."

"Thanks. I'm sure yours would be proud of what you did here today."

She nods, her mouth tight, clearly struggling to control her emotions.

"You know what, though," I say. "I'm sure your uncle is proud of you, too, and he'll tell you that when we see him."

"Oh god Wells," she stammers as her emotions overpower her. "Fuck." She may be crying again, but this time at least she's smiling as well.

After a while people do come to rescue us, six of them, but they're dressed in the dark blue uniform of the SECPOL, a uniform that's so synonymous with our enemy that Molly's reaction is exactly as you'd expect.

"What the neffing hell do you janking goons want?"

The group parts and lets one more person through. It's Art.

"You did it, Molly. You actually did it," Art says, smiling. "The Xenos carried the Obelisk out and have been collected by a smaller ship. They're taking it away. All over the world, the ships are leaving. It's utter chaos, but at least everyone is free." He moves quickly to his niece and wraps his arms around her gently, being careful not to hurt her damaged arm.

"Told you so," I say.

Molly laughs through her sobs as she buries her face in her uncle's embrace. Eventually, she pulls away. "I saw stretchers in the infirmary," she says. "You'll need two."

After a while – more time that I have to lie staring at the roof, awaiting its imminent collapse – the soldiers return with the stretchers. They're reluctant to move me with a spinal injury, but I tell them it's a little late for that and they gently lift me and slide the stretcher underneath. They carry us out of the chamber and toward the winding ramp up to the surface. The Institute has been destroyed, but in an extremely careful and deliberate way. The center of the building has been annihilated, leaving a neatly cut crater all the way down to the Obelisk chamber. Everything around the outside is relatively undamaged – including the ramp curling back up to the surface. I don't think it will remain undamaged for long, though. Eventually the supporting structure will collapse, and the Institute along with it.

"Wait," I say to the soldiers. "There's another room we need to check."

I lead them around to the door next to where Molly was being held, the room Charlotte must have come from. The destruction has fried the electrical system that was powering the electronic locks, and failsafe locks have engaged. The soldiers kick and shoulder the door for a while, but with no luck.

"S'no good," one of them says. "It's not opening. What's in there anyway?"

"Not what, who," I say.

"Go and get some plasma rifles," Molly says.

"This place isn't safe," the soldier in charge says. "We need to keep moving. We don't take orders from you anyway."

"Go and get some plasma rifles and get this neffing door open," Molly says, "or I'll make you do it. You've already felt what it's like to have someone else pulling your strings – I'm sure you don't want to go through that again."

"Do what she says," Art interjects.

The soldier stares at her on the stretcher.

"Just put us down and hurry," Molly says. "We'll be fine until you get back."

When the soldiers have jogged away to find some weapons I look over at Molly. We're laid out next to each other like patients in a hospital. "You know your powers won't work now that the Obelisk's gone?"

"I know," she says. "But they don't know that."

The soldiers return, carrying a plasma rifle each.

"If there's anyone inside, stand back from the door!"

They open fire. The door takes a surprising number of shots before it eventually falls inward off frayed and melted hinges. They enter, and from inside I hear one of them call out.

"We're going to need another stretcher."

"About time you did something useful," Mackenzie says as she's carried out.

"Mackenzie," I say, "I'm so sorry. I –"

"Shut up," Mackenzie says. "Jank."

Mackenzie, battered and bruised from torture, still manages to crack a smile.

The SECPOL soldiers, with Art hurrying them along the whole way, carry us out of the Institute. Around us, everything is a chaotic mess of people trying to come to terms with the events of the last few hours. The entire world has been rocked to its foundations again, and now, without the controlling influence of the Xenos, I wonder how it's going to respond.

An enormous rumbling fills the air. The sounds of destruction emanating from the center of the compound are like a concentrated earthquake as the Institute collapses in on itself. Great plumes of gray dust and brown dirt billow up into the sky. The sound continues for a long time, and even as it begins to dissipate there are moments of sudden crunches as pieces of the building give up their defiant stand and drop. And then the Institute for the Betterment of Humanity is gone.

Above us, not quite soundless but much calmer than the launch of a human spacecraft, which is all explosive power, roaring flames and jarring vibration, the Xeno ship moves upward, rising through the scattered cloud and growing smaller until it's a shining dot in the blue Nevada sky, and then it's gone.

"I wonder what happens now," Molly says, staring up at the sky. "Now that humanity's alone again."

"The future," Mackenzie answers. "The way it was supposed to be."

"Does anyone have a phone?" I ask. "I want to ring my parents. I need to make sure they're okay." I pause. "And I need to tell them something."

"So that's it?" Molly says. "That's actually the end of this?"

"I think so," Mackenzie says. "After all, we are Omega. We are the end."

DAYS AFTER LOSING THE OBELISK, the Xenocrustacean known as Number-Two surveys the rows of tanks. Each of the fifty or more cylindrical glass tubes glows softly with the luminous orange fluid inside. Here, in this concrete bunker a mile beneath the dry Nevada dirt, lies the future of his race on the planet humans call Earth.

The Xenocrustaceans decided to keep this facility secret even from those supposed human allies, and now that the tunnel providing access to the bunker has collapsed, damaged during the devastation caused by the rogue human group called Omega, Number-Two and his colleagues are able to work uninterrupted.

And work Number-Two must, if only to distract himself from the horrifying emptiness, the loneliness, the abyss left after the removal of the Obelisk. Number-Two sees his surviving siblings across the room working on seeding the tanks, but he cannot feel them. They must be experiencing the same terror at the unthinkable horror of being alone, individual entities unable to feel the constant melding with those around them. He only hopes that each of them will be strong enough to stave off the insanity that can the great silence can bring long enough to rebuild and take revenge on those who followed them across the stars and stole back the Obelisk. This battle hasn't ended yet.

Without the stem cell-grown pre-prepared human frames, the maturation process in these tanks will be slow, but at least it has begun. Number-Two moves to stand before one of the tanks. Floating inside, visible through the slightly murky haze of the biological soup, is a human embryo, curled around itself, tiny and alone. As alone in the vast tank as he himself feels without access to the minds of his kin.

Number-Two looks across the room at the shard of brown-red stone on the central table. Though it goes against their most fundamental tenants, they will use this shard of the Obelisk to unlock its power and rebuild a pillar of their own.

This human in the tank may be an embryo now, but it will grow. The DNA used to seed this subject was already genetically activated prior to their acquiring it. Now that they have it, in this environment, Number-Two will ensure the subject is controlled. Indoctrination will begin when its life begins – there will be no uncontrolled variables to interfere. They will use their own Obelisk to control it and to unlock its immense power. And when the embryo is grown and ready to be pulled, wet and dripping, from the tank, Number-Two will name it after the human from which it was seeded.

He will name this creature Molly.

<<<<>>>>

THANK YOU!

This part of a book is usually reserved for acknowledgements where the author thanks everybody who contributed to the production of the book - or everyone who had to put up with the author during the writing of a book which is often a much more demanding task.

In this book I want to do something a little different and acknowledge you. Thank you very picking up and (assuming you haven't jumped straight to the back for some reason) finishing We Are Omega. Writing a book is a solo endeavour, but story, that's something we do together. A novel doesn't serve its purpose until it is read - it's a little like the tree falling in the woods with no one being around to hear it - does a story exist until it is read? I might not know you, we might never meet, but we've taken the journey of Molly and Wells together. Straight from my head to yours and I hope you enjoyed the ride. The idea that people out in the world are reading my stories and being entertained by them still fills me with absolute joy.

If you did enjoy We Are Omega it would be so great if you could leave a review on Goodreads or the retailer where you purchased the book. Leaving a review to help other readers find the book is the best thing you can do to help an author and their work.

You can keep up to date with my news and new releases by signing up to my newsletter here: https://www.subscribepage.com/justinwoolley I often use this to reveal covers and news first and give books away cheap or for free to my most loyal readers.

Once again thank you! And, if we never meet in person, I hope you'll join me in the pages of another of my books soon.

Justin

Justin Woolley has been writing stories since he could first scrawl with a crayon. When he was six years old he wrote his first book, a 300 word pirate epic in unreadable handwriting called 'The Ghost Ship'. He promptly declared that he was now an author and didn't need to go to school. Despite being informed that this was, in fact, not the case, he continued to make things up and write them down.

Today Justin is the author of the Australian set dystopian trilogy *The Territory Series* consisting of the novels *A Town Called Dust, A City Called Smoke* and *A World of Ash*. He has recently released his fourth book, a young adult science fiction thriller, *We Are Omega*.

Justin lives in Hobart, Australia with his wife and two sons. In his other life he's been an engineer, a teacher and at one stage even a magician. His handwriting has not improved.

Follow and reach out to Justin on social media at the following places, he enjoys hearing from readers and finding out about other excellent authors and books he should be reading:

 facebook.com/woolleysworld

twitter.com/Woollz

instagram.com/woolleysworld

A Town Called Dust
A City Called Smoke
A World of Ash

www.ingramcontent.com/pod-product-compliance
Lightning Source LLC
Chambersburg PA
CBHW021402110726
47901CB00008B/2028